The Laboratory Insider

KELLY LIBATIQUE

The Laboratory Insider

ISBN: 978-1-7375552-3-0

www.KLVoice.com

"Responsibility finds a way.
Irresponsibility makes excuses."
-Gene Bedley

Chapter 1

"Hello, Jimmy," came the soothing voice through the tiny speaker. It was still seductive like before, though this time it held a taunting smirk.

He sat back and looked at the near empty tumbler that had been full of Johnnie Walker Black Label about ten minutes ago. Gyrating his wrist, he gently swirled the ice cubes around.

"No, *hello darling* for me?" this time with a touch of mockery.

He drained the glass in one final gulp. Although she was subtly trying to sneer at him, the voice didn't sound all that happy, those hints of satisfaction from a job well done. Perhaps a part of her just might be feeling a little guilty. Good.

"What do you want," he grumbled.

The tone turned cold and calculated. "Get something to write on. I have instructions for you."

"Sure, *darling*. Hang on." He pulled out a notepad and pen from a desk drawer.

She laid out directions. He scribbled.

"You won't let me down, will you, Jimmy?"

"Go to hell, *lǜ chá biǎo*."

He hung up. Hopefully, he'd never hear her voice again.

***

Jim Mueller felt his pulse quickening as he made the left turn onto the street that led to the security checkpoint. The road appeared narrower this morning, the trees in the small island dividing the lanes more noticeable. And for the first time since he could remember, he glanced, one by one, at all five security cameras pointed in his direction, documenting the make, model, license plate, as well as the face behind the windshield, of every car that approached the two guardhouses. He'd seen the video surveillance footage and it captured everything in remarkable detail.

Do nothing out of the ordinary. Just another Tuesday morning, right? Take the left lane, the usual one. Or was it the right … quick breath. *No, it was the left.*

There were three cars ahead as he slowly got in line. He watched the vehicle at the front as the guard stepped out of his little shack and took the Homeland Security Presidential Directive 12, better known as an HSPD-12 ID badge, from the driver. He stared at it for a moment, then stared at the driver, before handing it back with a nod and wave. The car moved forward, causing the line to lazily advance.

Jim's eyes went back and forth between the two security posts. The guards at each gatehouse were dressed to intimidate. In full military style camouflage, complete with body armor around their chests bearing pouches filled with stun grenades and extra magazines, they looked prepared for war. Strapped to their sides, at straight-arm reach against a thigh, was what appeared to be maybe Glock 19 pistols with high-capacity magazines. Jim wasn't terribly familiar with firearms, but knew enough to be dangerous, as the saying goes. Additionally, there was a third watchperson standing off to the side keeping a wary eye on both guardhouses with what appeared to be a fully automatic AR-15 style rifle slung around his neck and shoulder. Jim heard they only hired former military or cops for these guard positions, made sense.

Was it sexism no one ever saw female guards? More likely, it was the nature of the job – these guys had to stand out there in the blazing heat of the summer and freezing cold of the winter. Not that California had the extremes many other states did, still though, it wouldn't be fun buttoned, zipped, and strapped up in all that gear which probably caused spinal and other musculoskeletal problems after standing in it every day for a few years.

He looked down and glanced at his own HSPD-12 badge, held securely in the rigid plastic holder attached to his lanyard. With index finger and thumb, he rubbed the soft straps that draped around his neck. In years prior, lanyards had been constructed of woven or leather cords and designed to be durable. Today, most were made of light cotton and came with a breakaway quick release in the back in case the thing got caught in moving machinery and strangled the person wearing it, a fate that had befallen an unlucky few in years past.

He'd never really looked at the writing on the straps, but now as he waited, glanced at the embroidered letters. "SECURITY DIVISION," it said in all caps, followed by "INTEGRITY, HONESTY, EXCELLENCE." Jim himself wasn't any security person by trade, experience, or formal education. In fact, he often wondered how he'd gotten the role of technical writer and trainer for the laboratory's physical security system. It had a been a good gig though and paid nicely, enough to blow even more money on things he shouldn't. No complaints.

Except from Vaneesa, the soon to be ex-wife.

The car in front moved and everyone pulled forward. Only one car ahead of him now. He glanced in his rearview mirror and saw about five other cars now behind. With a practiced pull of a finger, he slid his badge out of the holder. Rules were such that the guard had to physically take the card and examine it, front and back. They took their job seriously. There were occasional attempts to access the facility with counterfeit badges, as well, guards were periodically tested with actors bearing phony credentials.

Jim looked at his badge, a plastic object the size of a credit card, and wondered how easy it would be to fake something like this. The HSPD-12 ID card, also known as a Personal Identity Verification, or "PIV" card, was a type of ID used by federal employees and contractors, in this case, for a well-known Department of Energy research facility. At the top left, under the words "United States Government," was a picture of himself he hated even more than the insipid image gracing his driver's license. Next to the picture and above the DOE symbol, was a month and year indicating when the card would expire, and the pain in the ass renewal process would need to start about forty-five days prior to that. Below the picture was his full name, MUELLER, JAMES W., and below that an embedded gold-colored microchip no thicker than the card itself.

Between the microchip and magnetic strip on the back, the information contained in the badge included Personally Identifiable Information, known as P.I.I., such as the badge holder's name, date of birth, employee number, and biometric data, in his case, a right thumbprint and the hand geometry biometrics of his right hand. There was talk that soon eye retina scans would be included. For now though, access to most "Q-only" areas of the facility required users to insert this badge into a reader and enter their personal PIN. Some more high-sensitive areas also required users to place their thumb against the small glass rectangle of the scanner to be identified. Really high-security areas might even require a hand scan; Jim occasionally accessed a workspace like this – the Helios lab.

Jim stared at the "Q" printed to the upper right of the microchip. It had taken a little over a year to acquire this letter, the civilian equivalent of a military Top Secret clearance. One couldn't just apply to get such a clearance – it was requested for you at a managerial level and then approved at a director's level. If the right people decided you needed it for your job, the close to $6,000 investigative process was initiated by the Office of Personnel Management in New Mexico.

He thought about a conversation he had during the first month of his employment with Kirk Willis, a coworker who took photos and video for the lab. Jim had noticed an "L" on Kirk's badge rather than a Q. Jim had never seen one, so he asked about it.

"Oh, an L is cheaper than a Q," Kirk had told him. "Saves my group some money."

"Why's that?"

"They only go back seven years on your history and the overall investigation is less extensive."

"Is it still top secret?" Jim asked.

"It's halfway there. An L means I can access confidential and some restricted information, but not at certain higher sensitive levels."

Jim shook his head, there was so much to learn around this place. Because he was in the Security Division, he'd gotten a Q, and for that they go back at least ten years on a person's history. If anything suspicious was found, they'd go back even further. He'd been through a full background and criminal check, several drug tests, and in addition to calling former employers, they had even sent agents out to speak face to face with his neighbors to see what kind of reputation he had. Did he burn American flags? Did he talk about clandestine excursions to places like North Korea or Syria? Did he ever reveal a desire to renounce his citizenship or allude to planning or partaking in some plot to overthrow the United States government?

His financial life had also been scrutinized; people who owed lots of money or who otherwise were in financial dire straits were susceptible to bribes.

"You don't gamble, do you Mr. Mueller?" Jim had been asked by his Personnel Security Program interviewer.

"No," he lied. In fact, he enjoyed occasionally playing Blackjack in Vegas or Reno. "But I always wished I learned how to play poker."

The agent gave him an odd look, then shrugged and continued.

Jim laughed at the thought that his investigation had been boring for whoever all had been involved. He had very few social media accounts, but they'd been probed as well for either statements or behaviors that would raise flags. Conduct that put a person on the radar included flaunting an adulterous affair, regularly getting drunk, excessive gambling, or admitting to engaging in prostitution or illegal drug use. Men with such habits were vulnerable to blackmail. After all, with a Q-Clearance, one had access to Top Secret Restricted Data, Formerly Restricted Data, and National Security Information, among others. All these things were written or spoken of in acronyms that had taken Jim months to get used to: TSRD, FRD, NSI, and so on; the government loved acronyms. There were numerous cheat sheets devoted to page after page of acronyms and what they stood for, kindly listed in alphabetical order.

"A Q-Clearance doesn't mean you're entitled to go wherever you want and look at whatever you want. There's still the old *need-to-know* rule in full effect," he was told by a counterintelligence officer at his clearance briefing. Meaning, access to whatever information needed to be necessary for a person to conduct his or her official duties.

The rule included anyone else one deemed necessary to share info with.

But despite all the rules and threats that accompanied the breaking of those rules, things were shockingly lax. In fact, the general public would be appalled if they knew how easy it was to gain access to and share sensitive information. The reason? It was a system with an astonishing reliance on trust. For the most part, it all added up to little more than a complex and expensive honor system. You can install all the barriers you want, spend money until there's nothing left to spend, but at the end of the day, if the people in charge of those barriers couldn't be trusted, it all was for naught.

The car in front moved forward. Jim swallowed hard. With heart fluttering, he released the brake and let the engine glide him into place while rolling the window down. He'd seen this guard many times before, who's brass nametag pinned smartly to his camouflage shirt read, "Pardes, Enrique."

Jim held out his card between fingertips, his picture facing forward. "Officer Pardes," he said, with a pleasant but not exaggerated smile.

Business as usual.

Officer Pardes peered at him then took the card, glancing at the front, then turning it around to look at the magnetic strip and long barcode on the back. Looking Jim in the eye again, he paused for a moment longer than usual, his eyes slightly narrowing, causing Jim's heart to give two huge thumps that resonated in his head. Jim could only stare back, wondering if his eyes were betraying him. But then Pardes returned the card and nodded him through.

The guards were trained to be friendly enough not to scare people, but at the same time remain serious and distant. Even if you knew the guard personally, knew his wife's and dog's name, he still wouldn't be chummy with you. Say you accidentally left your badge at home but tried to convince a guard to let you through anyway. "Come on, Enrique, it's me!" Not a chance, not if the guard was doing his job. The assumption is that you may have just been fired and were trying to get inside to do something you shouldn't. Disgruntled employees have caused colossal damage to regular private sector companies; it was unimaginable what they could do here.

Actually, it *was* imaginable, because Jim had given a lot of thought as to what he planned to do today.

As he moved forward, the guard with the AR watched as he drove by. Jim nodded, but the guard only stoically stared back.

Feeling relief, but trying not to show it, Jim turned onto the main road, conscious about not exceeding the twenty-five mile per hour speed limit inside the facility.

Chapter 2

Three months earlier …

In the People's Republic of China, in the heart of Beijing, deep within the bowels of the Ministry of State Security, one of the most covert intelligence agencies in the world, Liang Huang hovered over a report displayed on one of several fifty-four-inch flat screen monitors.

Officially in the Sixth Bureau: Counterintelligence, it was an honor and privilege to serve in the Chinese government's largest and most active foreign intelligence agency. The MSS was also involved in domestic security, but the international matters were what made the work exciting.

He glanced at the monitor of a machine booting up and saw the MSS' mission in big bold font displayed across the top, which was "… to ensure the security of the state through effective measures against enemy agents, spies, and counter-revolutionary activities designed to sabotage or overthrow China's socialist system." This reminder was showcased everywhere in the building in both print and digital form.

That was all true, but Huang's mission was a bit more unspoken.

"What exactly do you do for work?" Alix, Huang's ex-girlfriend had asked. He couldn't say he discreetly gathered foreign intelligence from targets in various countries overseas to see how it could be used to give China more leverage on the world scene. So instead, he'd answered that he was a "data entry specialist" for China Southern Airlines. It felt stupid and weak, but she'd believed him.

There were two ways China acquired foreign intelligence. First, it had inanimate spies installed all over the place. Some were actively at work, others were hibernating, awaiting their turn. Everyone heard about China secretly adding tiny microchips to server motherboards, potentially affecting companies like Apple and Amazon. Of course, everything was "debunked," and nothing was proven. Please. Any knowledgeable person could pick a dozen places malicious firmware could be hidden on a board, and many more components large enough to house implants.

But what the public wasn't told, and what only some in the American federal agencies knew, was that parts and components from China to modify and upgrade some of America's key energy and telecommunications infrastructure for more than a decade were in place and did, in fact, have many hidden surprises. Only relatively recently did all this come to light. America's Congress was approving millions trying to find and eliminate these things, fearing China was either listening in on everyone's phone conversations, or could flip a switch at any moment and turn off the United

States' power grids. It wouldn't be that simple, but it was fun to watch the Americans scramble.

But Huang had nothing to do with any of that. He was part of the living, breathing bodies constantly at work implementing new ideas. As he sat reading, he reflected, as he often did, that he was glad he wasn't one of the hundreds of globally dispersed agents always at work operating under non-official cover in Canada, Eastern and Western Europe, Japan, and the United States. They were bankers, translators, journalists, businesspeople, teachers, and many other occupations. The difference between Huang and all of them was that he got to do it all from computers in one place.

"What fires are you putting out today?" a female voice asked from the doorway. It startled Huang for a moment since most of his time down here was spent alone.

He glanced up to see Fung Lin, one of the management's administrators. Although he didn't know for sure, she was probably in her mid to late forties. Today she wore a black suit jacket and a tight gray knee-length skirt. She'd been flirting with him for over a year, making it clear he had an open invitation to be her boy toy whenever he wished. She was still fairly attractive and kept in shape, and was now giving him that mischievous look, but he just never had the desire to get that close to her.

"Which one?" Huang asked, managing a small smile. He'd worked for three years in counterintelligence and political security in the Intelligence Bureau of the Joint Staff, the MSS' military counterpart, but found a new passion when it was discovered he had a knack for piecing disjointed information together in ways that sometimes even advanced artificial intelligence could not.

Lin leaned against the doorway. "It would be too dull to spend all day gathering and analyzing information from other people's phone call and email records," she said, hinting she knew more about his work than she was supposed to. But Huang actually had a more specialized gig, which felt more like a game to him, and there were probably less than five individuals in the building who knew the full extent of it.

"It's kind of fun," Huang said, leaning back. "Seeing what people do on the internet. Hundreds of millions of users meeting and debating; it's a treasure-trove of info directly about, or indirectly referred to, individuals."

"That's spying," Lin said with mock disgust, her mouth curling in a subtle smirk.

"Name a country that doesn't spy," Huang said. "When people write blogs, add their friends, and make posts on social media or chat groups, they're doing free work for intelligence agencies. That information can be used strategically."

Lin rested her head against the doorway, communicating she was in no hurry to leave, her eyes resting on Huang's diplomas that hung from the wall. "Nauru," she said.

"Huh?"

"Little raised coral island country in the southwestern Pacific Ocean, a few thousand occupants. I doubt they spy on anyone."

"Oh," Huang said, shrugging. "They wouldn't know what to do with the information."

"Well, I would still be bored."

Huang didn't mention that he mainly looked at data collected under the radar from social apps used by people around the world who hadn't a clue what was happening. Not only was it fun, his brain had an uncanny ability to marry patterns and behaviors in ways the Chinese government considered valuable.

They want to pay me to do this? he'd asked himself several times.

He gave a quick glance at his diplomas as well. He was proud that he'd been a rising star in China's "socialist democracy" since he graduated top of his class at the prestigious Tsinghua University, also in Beijing, with a Master's in Computer Science and Technology accompanied by a minor in Foreign Languages and Literatures. Fluent in both Mandarin and Cantonese, he could also read and speak English at about a college sophomore level. But his foreign language forte was Russian, which he could now read and write more like a college post-graduate.

He'd especially gone after pa-Russki after developing a love for, well, okay, a *fetish* for hot, Russian *dévuška*. Their Caucasian Eastern European contrast to the black-haired females of Han descent he was accustomed to drove him mad.

But it had almost cost him, dearly.

Last year, after months of an intensive and secretive online search and much correspondence with half a dozen young women, he'd begun plans for a trip to make contact.

Despite taking every precaution to be stealthy, and doing nothing on work systems or devices, someone had been watching and collecting data – ironically similar to what he routinely did to others around the world. One fine day as he strolled through the long corridor several stories below ground to his secret intelligence-gathering cubby, he was met by two stern-faced individuals in dark suits who turned him around and escorted him back to the elevators.

The head director sat casually smoking a Dunhill cigarette, regarding the nervous but serene young analyst.

"Come now," the director had said. "We can't let our most valued servant of the people go and do something rash like engage with a foreign national, now can we? Be sensible, we can provide an unlimited number of safer alternative sources to get your cravings satisfied." And they had. "You're very fortunate we stopped you before you did anything … unwise."

Play along and get rewarded; play stupid and everything is taken away. An effective system. Still though, that damned forbidden fruit was most persuasive, perhaps more so because it was now *officially* forbidden.

Huang promised not to even think of doing such a foolish thing again and resumed his duties.

Huang suddenly thought of a way to get rid of Fung Lin. "Hey," he said, thumbing over his shoulder. "You see that camera on the desk? Stare at it for a moment and think of something that makes you angry. I'm running a test on some software enhancements."

Lin's eyes got wide for a moment. "No, thank you," she said, turning. *"Dasvidaniya,"* she said, with decent pronunciation, the Russian word for goodbye.

"Okay, *doh vstrey-cheh!"* he replied, smiling cheerfully. Lin turned and looked at him. "See you later," he said, waving. Lin winked and started down the hallway.

Huang laughed. He'd played a role in improving the technology that perfected China's capacity to monitor its massive population, mainly via social media, and more recently, facial analysis software. In America and other democracies, there were laws guaranteeing the privacy of its citizens. Of course, those laws were broken all the time, but at least one could make a stink of it when some company or agency was caught. You might even become a world-famous martyr like Edward Snowden.

But there were no such laws in China. Whatever anyone did anymore, any purchase made, every event on one's calendar, every meeting, every location travelled to, was all monitored and recorded.

If you were foolish enough to think you could gather information to hurt the government, discuss a corrupt politician, or organize a protest online, forget it. Both humans and artificial intelligence will be watching. Public posts and even live chatting were censored automatically when key words or phrases were entered, like "Tibet," "Dalai Lama," "Tiananmen Square," or references to certain religious groups.

And in recent years, there was a "social credit score" the government now kept, where citizens were categorized by their behaviors both online and off. This, everyone is told, was to look for "risky" behavior signs that could lead to negative consequences. Tallies were kept on a person's hobbies, interaction with friends, shopping habits and lifestyle. A person's purchasing history was now a compilation that translated into financial creditworthiness. If your score dropped below a threshold, you were barred from social privileges like buying certain goods, renting cars without a big deposit, working certain jobs, and travelling. If it kept falling, you could eventually be arrested and interrogated, or hauled away to a "reeducation camp."

Huang often thought about the activities – or lack of activities – that took points from one's social score and tried to think if he ever did any of them. Perhaps you didn't pay a utility bill on time; perhaps your doctor warned that you were drinking excessively, but you continue anyway; perhaps you have a bad habit of coming to work late. Such things were now tracked.

As these thoughts swirled through his mind, Huang stared at the words and numbers in the Hei font style, the Chinese equivalent of Sans-serif, that blanketed his screen.

A smile formed on his lips. He'd made a selection for a subject of interest to start zeroing in on, a small fish that could possibly help catch a bigger one.

Men everywhere could be persuaded by the same desires, couldn't they?

Chapter 3

Jim Mueller adjusted his reading glasses and sighed as he reread for the hundredth time a system manager's guide he'd created for Helios. It outlined how a pool of server hosts documented and organized sensitive entry points engaged around the laboratory.

Over the last almost two years, he'd become quite knowledgeable about the access control and intrusion detection system that electronically guarded the site twenty-four-seven, 365 days a year. Helios was a big system and it'd taken Jim several months to get his head wrapped around everything.

The phone rang. "Hello."

"Jim," said the familiar voice of Francis Lane, the associate director of his group. "How are things?"

"Couldn't be dandier," Jim replied. He liked Francis. Not a micromanager, she empowered her employees and always kept an open-door policy.

"Good. One of our new hires, Jennifer Nelson, is on her way over. I need you to give her an intro to the lab and what our group does."

"Am I already that important?"

"You're who's available."

"I'll take that as a compliment."

"It was. Have a good day, Jim."

Five minutes later, there was a knock on his doorframe. Jim stood to see a Black woman in her late thirties, professionally dressed and with a pleasant but somewhat shy smile.

"Hi," she said, stepping forward. "I'm Jennifer."

Jim held out his hand and they shook. "Jim, nice to meet you. Welcome aboard. Let's go for a ride."

There were thirty or so golf cart type vehicles that were shared around the site. Jim referred to them as "moon rovers" due to their odd shape and round plastic windows that enclosed the passengers. In the winter it made for a nice shield against the wind and rain, but it was a bit hot and cramped in the summer. Fortunately, it was a crisp and cool fall day.

Jim spoke like a tour guide as they slowly made their way around the lab's narrow streets. "So this place is basically a one and a half square-mile multi-building facility, laid out somewhat similar to a college campus. It's divided into what's referred to as 'low side' and 'high side' areas. Like over there, behind those tall fences with the barbed wire on top," he said, pointing down one of the side streets. "That's a high-side area."

"What do they do in there?"

"Three-D printing, like weapons parts. Also, four-D live cell bioprinting for body parts and organs."

"Are you kidding?"

"Welcome to the lab."

"I take it you can't go in high sides, right?" Jennifer asked.

"You can if you have a Q clearance, but you'll not able to get into most rooms once inside, unless you work there." He gestured around. "So each area is assigned a number representing an access list you have to be on to gain entry. The 'higher' the area, the more security needed and the more credentials you need to get through. To access the really high sensitive areas, you need to be on the right access lists, have the right clearance, and the correct attributes."

"Attributes?"

"For example, are you a US citizen? Do you have only an L instead of a Q? Are you in good standing in the Human Reliability Program, aka 'HRP?'"

"Will I get an L or a Q?" Jennifer asked.

"If you do any work for the security division, probably a Q. But you can ask Francis. Will you be working on Helios?"

"I was told I may be helping," Jennifer said. "What's that?"

"The system that guards this place and let's only authorized people into different areas." He stopped by one of the main gate entrances on the other side of the campus. "There are a hundred and eighty two remote access terminals on this site with small touchscreens, a slot to insert a security badge card, and a fingerprint reader. They're all connected to Helios. These mini kiosks control the physical portals – doors, security booths, or turnstiles – the first line of defense within the main perimeter. Out there," he said pointing toward the main entrance, "is Area Zero. Public access. Anyone walking, biking, or driving in from a zero side is assumed guilty until proven innocent and has to show their badge to the guard to get through. Contractors carry a different badge. Employees have one like mine," he said holding his up so Jennifer could see. "And new employees like yourself have that temporary badge that doesn't have a letter or chip."

"Helios looks at everyone's badge?"

"When you use one of the kiosks, yes."

"What if I accidently leave my badge at home?"

"Well, you couldn't just show the guard your driver's license, you'd have to go to the badging office and get a temporary one. They'd go through the rounds to ensure your identity and verify your PIN, then give you a paper badge with green ink that begins turning red when exposed to light. Temp badges have a date on it of course, but those are easy to miss. So by the next day, the red ink would advise any guard paying any bit of attention that you should have reacquired your regular badge by then."

"What if I lose it altogether?"

"In that case, or worse, it got stolen in a smash and grab because you left it dangling from your rearview mirror, you'd have to pay a visit to the Locks and Ciphers group who'd make you sit through their hell, fire and brimstone lectures about precaution and vigilance while they code a new badge for you."

Jennifer laughed.

"They'll also write you up. It's not happened to me, fortunately. What's worse is if your whole lanyard is lost or stolen because of your identification card for the TESA locks. You don't have one yet." He held his up for Jennifer to see.

"Those heavy-duty looking stainless-steel boxes with a badge slot and mechanical number pad on the doors?" Jennifer asked.

"Yep. The TESA system is separate from Helios and guards access not only to the buildings, but to offices and other areas like the mail and copy room. If your site identification card is lost or stolen, it's assumed it may be used for malicious purposes, so all TESA locks have to be reset and everyone who had access to the same building or buildings you did would need to have their site identification card recoded."

"Wow," Jennifer said.

"This place isn't for everyone." Jim pulled over to stop again next to the main cafeteria. "The way to envision how the physical security works around here, is to imagine yourself in the shoes of a wannabe intruder. An elaborate physical infrastructure of gates, barbed wire, and controlled entry awaits anyone from the outside, and although it appears impossible, some daring people have gotten through the initial gatehouse with faked or stolen credentials."

"Really?"

"Oh yes. But just getting into the general protected area isn't enough. You still have to know where to go in this small city that makes up this thirteen-billion dollar a year facility.

And even if you knew the building, you'd still need to get by the TESA locks. If your goal was a classified area, there are even more locked doors, safes, and vault-type rooms."

"They don't make it easy."

"They gotta justify all those tax dollars. And the assumption is that ultimately, anyone could either inadvertently or very deliberately compromise national security for any number of reasons. But despite all these security measures, which hangs on the false belief that action equals effect, it's really only effective against outsiders. *Insider* threats are a whole different story."

"Has that been a problem here?"

"Yes, but other labs have had it worse."

"So this system you write training for, it's called Helios?"

"Named so after the all-seeing god and personification of the sun in Greek mythology."

"Clever. How does it work?"

"Well, it does more than just control access, it also detects intrusion." Jim looked around, gesturing again. "All over the lab are thousands of hardwired sensors physically attached to Helios which knows the real-time state of every single sensor. Balanced magnetic door switches, for example. Configurable alarms, so that if, say, a door to a sensitive area was held open too long, the system would assume it'd been deliberately propped open which triggers an alarm and an armed response. There are also tamper switches to detect if the small doors like electric boxes have been opened."

"That's a lot of wires."

Jim started moving the rover again. "You bet. At sites where there's a PIDAS, there are also infrared sensors watching for heat signatures of bodies. The big lab out in New Mexico is like that."

"What's a *pie-duh-s?*"

"Perimeter Intrusion Detection and Assessment System – a multi-fence border like what you see surrounding high security prisons. Those typically have weight sensors buried in the ground between the outer and inner fences that trigger alarms when anything over a hundred pounds is detected. There's also a plethora of motion detectors and cameras. Enormous databases keep raw video, recorded nonstop, and any date and window of time can be played back at the click of a mouse."

"How does Helios organize all this? Sorry for all the questions."

"I'm actually impressed with your questions. That's how I learn. So … sensors are compartmentalized into alarm sectors. An alarm sector could be one room, several adjacent rooms, a building floor, or an entire building. Each sector is controlled by a remote processor. Firewall rules stipulate that it listens only to commands from the unique identifiers of the sensors connected to it. Everything else is ignored. Would-be hackers that wanted to deactivate sensors would need to know specific IP addresses and variables to fool it."

"I'm starting to feel a bit overwhelmed."

"No worries, I've got explainer videos that go over bite-sized parts of this stuff."

"So what about these remote processors?"

"There's one right there," Jim said, stopping near a small fence surrounding a small parking lot and warehouse looking building. "That object that looks like two boxes vertically connected by a pipe. Each processor has its own solid-state drive and if the main Helios system was destroyed by fire, explosion, or flood, each one, along with a ten-hour battery backup in case the power went out as well, could continue to independently guard its assigned sectors. Now, you're probably wondering where the alarms go."

"It hadn't crossed my mind yet, but it was going to, I promise." Jennifer grinned.

Jim chuckled. "All alarms are sent to one of two console operators always on duty in a classified, underground high-tech basement."

"You've seen it?"

"Yes. I got the nickel tour last year. To get there, you go through an unmarked, inconspicuous door on the side of a small, unremarkable building. We passed it back there," Jim said, thumbing over his shoulder. "Below ground, a dimly lit area where a minimum of two console operators always sit behind a large desk, each with an identical array of monitors, displaying video feeds, various monitoring systems, and an AutoCAD three-D diagram of the entire facility that includes every gate, street, building, floor, room, door and window."

"Why a minimum of two operators?"

"Because the assumption is that one may have an unexpected health or other emergency and become disengaged. Also, as alarms and issues come in, operators divvy ownership and tasks."

"And you train on this entire system?"

"I oversee training personnel on its function and use, yes. There are actually a handful of technical writers that help document hardware and software upgrades, and it looks like you may be one."

"Are there other DOE laboratories that use Helios?"

"Yes. To date, five other labs around the country, and each system fully air gapped, completely self-contained, and nearly impossible to hack from the outside."

"So when there's problems, the developers here have to travel to help troubleshoot those systems?"

"That's how it used to be. Travelling all the time. But recently, they made it possible to remote into another Helios site via a highly secured encrypted two-layer VPN tunnel. This way, an engineer in California can look at a problem a system in Texas was having, but that's only done when absolutely necessary." Jim turned to Jennifer. "I'll let you in on a secret."

Jennifer's eyes got wide for a moment.

Jim laughed. "It's okay. The Department of Defense, specifically the Air Force, picked up on Helios three years ago and has been beta testing on at least two of their bases, one in Colorado, and another in Florida."

"Did you help train on those?"

"No, they have their own testers and trainers. It's all been quite a learning experience. But every system has weaknesses. One of the many functions Helios performs is tracking patterns. It knows, via a classifier algorithm, what most people typically do every day. Similar to how cybersecurity keeps track of what computer systems users normally log into. Likewise, Helios knows what doors and buildings personnel normally frequent. When patterns are broken under certain qualifying criteria, anomaly alarms are issued."

"I guess that makes sense."

"Yeah, but it's how those alarms are produced that's the problem. They come up in the form of reports – agonizingly boring regurgitations of old school text-driven information on a screen, printable if desired, that someone is supposed to peruse every day."

"Does someone?"

Jim shook his head. "Not a chance. Unless there's an incident. Some of the old timers who were working in the '80s and '90s when life and work was much slower did. But a new generation that's decided everything can and should be automated is running the show now and don't follow all the old protocols."

"You could email alerts."

"Yeah, you could start sending mails or even texts. But what happens when you flash a sign every day?"

"It gets ignored," Jennifer said, sitting back.

"Yeah, the brain is amazing that way. Well, back to the salt mines," Jim said, turning the moon rover around in an intersection. "Welcome again to the laboratory."

Chapter 4

The young, sharply dressed man adjusted his dark sunglasses and looked around. Everything appeared normal. The mid-morning traffic in downtown Brentwood had been light when he'd driven in and parked several minutes ago.

Using special tools and acquired skills, he'd removed the battery from his mobile phone an hour or so ago and placed the parts in the glove box. The adhesive that glued the back cover for water resistance was long gone, but what the hell, he didn't make calls in the shower.

Protecting the phone from water was the excuse consumers were given for why batteries could no longer be removed from mobile phones. Ridiculous. The government told phone manufacturers to create the illusion batteries could never be removed so that phones were continuously broadcasting a signal, even when they appeared powered off. Most people didn't know, but the many public Wi-Fi's scattered about made triangulating a mobile phone quick and easy, with precision accuracy.

Looking in the rearview mirror and down the sidewalk, he smiled to himself as he stared at the yellow sign with the words "Hung and Fat Mart" in thick, bold letters. The name of the multi-family business was originally "Hung-Fat Market," but a couple years ago he'd convinced his Uncle Wong-fat that it would be funnier to Americans as it was now. He tried to explain but it never quite resonated because "Fat" in Chinese is pronounced "F-ah" or "F-uh" depending on the dialect. Nonetheless, the advice was taken, and the name was changed.

Inside the store, the aroma of sizzling sunflower oil, vinegar, garlic, ginger, and soy met his nose pleasantly. The place had started as a convenience store for some of the more uniquely Asian grocery items such as all manner of ramen noodles, sweet chili sauces and tea, huge bags of rice, unusual fruits and vegetables, quail eggs, fresh herbs, and of course, several varieties of pocky. But it had evolved into a small eatery as well, with a sectioned off area in the back with small tables where one could enjoy freshly cooked Chinese and Vietnamese dishes. It was a popular quick lunch stop for workers in the downtown area.

He made his way down the seafood aisle looking at the whole tilapia, catfish, striped bass, and various sizes of squid resting on beds of ice. He paused for a moment at the two large bubbling aquariums filled with live lobsters. When he was younger, he used to stare in both awe and pity at the poor doomed creatures with their claws secured by thick rubber bands, crawling over each other in a futile attempt to find an escape.

Walking into the seating area, he nodded at a young second cousin of his who was wiping a table. He found an area in the back of the room and settled down while taking a laptop computer out of his bag.

Months ago, the nephew convinced his uncle to set up a free public Wi-Fi to attract more customers. He also suggested security cameras, clearly visible both inside and outside. At first, his uncle didn't want to because of the cost. "Don't worry, I will help pay for it," he told his uncle. He then fronted the initial T1 broadband setup costs.

His cousin brought over a freshly brewed cup of oolong tea. Producing an envelope with $150 in cash, the nephew handed it to his cousin. "Please give this to Uncle."

The cousin nodded and took the envelope containing the monthly expenses for the Wi-Fi and cameras. Payments were always in cash, never through an app, never through a wire transfer, never through a credit or debit card. Just another traceless transaction.

"Don't tell anyone I pay for this," he'd told his uncle, gazing for a moment at the scar that ran down the left side of his uncle's face.

He knew his uncle would never say a word, even under interrogation, if it ever came to that. Years ago, when Uncle Wong-fat was a younger man himself, he'd come to America to escape a government who suspected him of being a dissident, which in fact, he had been.

In 1989, Uncle Wong-fat witnessed firsthand the Tiananmen Square protests and massacre. He hated his government after that and used to openly talk about it at his small eatery off the famous Wangfujing Street in Beijing.

His business had done well selling bean juice, steamed rice, pea cakes, and mutton soup, and he enjoyed a steady stream of regular customers. His place was even featured in tourist guides.

When he spoke his opinion, he talked quietly to groups of individuals he thought he knew. But not all his customers were friends.

One afternoon when he was closing shop, a large SUV drove up and five men in dark suits quickly entered his small establishment. Startled, he dropped a tray of plates he'd been holding which crashed to the ground. One of the men casually picked up a large, sharp piece of broken porcelain while two others took Uncle Wong-fat by the arms and seated him roughly into a nearby chair.

The man with the piece of plate pulled a chair close, sat down, then leaned back and crossed his legs while casually pulling a package of cigarettes out of his coat pocket. He slowly lit the cigarette, looking steadily at Uncle Wong-fat while inhaling, then blowing a large cloud of smoke in the air.

"We hear you don't like how our president is handling the rebels of our glorious socialist democracy republic," the man finally said.

Immediately, Uncle Wong-fat's heart sank. He'd been somewhat careful but realized then he hadn't been careful enough. He should have known better, the scared looks on nearby faces, the darting eyes, the people close to him casting glances at strange faces watching and listening.

The man took another pull on his cigarette. "What should we do with you, Wong-fat?" he asked, tapping the flat edge of the porcelain shard on his leg.

The way China dealt with its citizens they considered dissidents was swift and brutal. They'd all heard the stories. Sometimes, as a person was trying to speak to the press, particularly a foreign press, snatch and grab teams watching from nearby vehicles would leap out, seize the person, and physically haul him or her away.

To threaten and intimidate, family members of suspected dissidents would sometimes be placed under house arrest, preventing them from traveling and publicly protesting. A step up from that was to trap a person in their residence, preventing one from going out to get food and supplies, then detain and interrogate anyone who came to visit.

They also used tactics similar to the American mob by showing one pictures of their children going to school or their spouse or parents in the local market. These photos came with the threat that these loved ones may disappear, or worse, die a lavish death should their rebellious behavior continue. At the very least, they'll take down any social media a person has; while social media was only in its birth in 1989, it was common practice today.

If any of that fails to stop a person, their door will be kicked in at some random point and one will be dragged away, possibly never to be seen again. In some cases, the official reason given for the disappearance is that a person did something "crazy" and had to be locked up in a psychiatric hospital, a gentler term for a reeducation camp, where a combination of physical and psychological torture was employed to turn your thoughts around and make you a good citizen. If you still refused to cooperate, you were probably euthanized and if healthy, your lungs, heart, liver, and kidneys would be harvested and sold on the black market.

Uncle Wong-fat stared back at the man, not to challenge, but with more frightened resignation. After all, they could have shot him dead, or pulled him outside and set his shop on fire, or be driving him away to "disappear" him. If he cooperated, he might get lucky. He decided to play along and beg forgiveness. He felt large drops of sweat forming on his forehead.

"I did not mean what I said. I was just venting to a few friends, exaggerating my feelings. I feel shame now. I believe President Shangkun is doing a supreme job in keeping our republic safe." He lowered his chin, like a scolded child.

The man laughed so hard while exhaling smoke, it made him cough a couple times. He waved a hand while recovering his voice. "You're a good performer, and you're also full of shit."

Uncle Wong-fat started to say, "Please, I —"

"Shut up!" the man snarled, dropping the cigarette to the floor and stepping on it with a shiny, expensive looking shoe. He stood and leaned in closely.

Uncle Wong-fat pressed himself back into the chair but wasn't able to go far.

The man got right into his face. "We're just hear to give you a quick reminder to keep your defiant opinions to yourself." He looked around. "You've got a nice establishment here. You attract tourists to our great city. We wouldn't want you to be missed." His right hand flashed up and pressed the point of the broken plate piece on Uncle Wong-fat's temple, then quickly slashed in a downward motion.

Uncle Wong-fat screamed and tried to grab his face, but his arms were still held tight. He felt hot blood ooze from the wound and start to trickle down his chin and neck.

The man stood straight while tossing the porcelain shard aside. He then nodded at the other two men who were standing by watching. At once, they quickly strode further into the small eatery and began throwing any breakable objects they saw and turning over tables.

Uncle Wong-fat closed his eyes and listened to the shattering glass, the wood and bamboo snapping, the big crash of what he knew was the glass on his prized refrigerated bakery display case being smashed. After a couple minutes, they returned.

Uncle Wong-fat felt his arms released and opened his eyes to see the five men walking out and back to their car. Without another glance at him, the car doors shut, and the vehicle sped away with a small squeal of tires.

The young nephew thought about that story every time he visited his family's small market. His uncle had gotten lucky that day, it could have been worse. How wonderful it was to now live in a country where things like that didn't happen all the time. At least not yet.

He also cursed himself for a mistake he'd made several years ago when he was younger, a bit more zealous, and less careful. When Proton Mail emerged in 2013, it seemed like the answer. End to end zero-access encryption, "self-destructing messages," and more. He'd been using the service to communicate with a friend of the family who was a protest leader in Hong Kong.

One day, his contact, unaware that email subject lines were not encrypted, used the nephew's real name, Jin Chou, when sending pictures and video of police brutality against the "rioters." The nephew would also find out that IP addresses were logged in case anyone wanted to investigate a crime. He quickly took the email account down and didn't think much of it at the time, but later realized a clever individual with the right tools could now go back in time and link his alias to his real name.

Although he never saw evidence he'd been compromised, he began keeping a very low profile. He made sure his real name showed up almost nowhere. He had his alias name and address delisted from the White Pages and every online site that contained personal contact information. He changed his phone service and mobile phone to yet a different name. He had no social media, never gave out his location or talked about employment, and never texted anyone. He never did anything anymore without extreme precaution. The only other loose end was that when he'd first started his current job, he used his original alias which coworkers now knew him by, so it was too late to change that.

The Wi-Fi he'd set up for the Hung and Fat Mart was special. At each table was a four by six plastic sign holder with neatly printed instructions on both sides. It advertised the Mart's free online service that one could access by going to a website URL.

This website displayed a terms of service agreement and provided a field to enter one's mobile phone number. After clicking the Agree button, three input fields would appear: a login and password field prefilled with a randomly generated username and sixteen-character password, and a third field to enter an access code that was sent via text to the user's mobile phone. A warning note at the bottom said this username and password was good for one hour and then it would be reset.

Users then logged into a VPN with top-of-the-line security complete with 256-bit AES, DNS/IPv6 leak protection, a kill switch, and split tunneling. At this point all traffic between endpoints and one of the many randomly used VPN servers was encrypted. This setup was mainly to discourage "man in the middle" aka "the evil twin" attacks, whereby someone sets up a phone network connection and secretly relays communications between two parties while stealing information. But it was also to protect the data packets he sent from this location from prying digital eyes that could be anywhere.

The nephew however, only needed to enter a thirty-two-digit password, a phrase he knew could never be cracked, into the mobile phone number field and that took him to an even more encrypted network hidden behind the public one.

And this was only the beginning. The laptop he used was never purchased as a complete unit, rather, it was pieced together with parts from different vendors. Spoofing tools on it always hid the machine's IP address, as well, changed the MAC address. To ensure even more privacy, he swapped the network adapter out every couple months so that the actual MAC address was never the same for too long.

But that still wasn't enough. From a small, zippered pocket on his bag, he produced a USB thumb drive and inserted it into the side of the laptop. He hit the power button and waited. When the *Press F10 to boot from external device* message displayed, he pressed it and selected the USB drive.

In the next couple minutes, his laptop's operating system was temporarily transformed from a common Windows one to Linux Tails. In this mode, no information was ever kept on the local hard drive; the laptop would now only utilize RAM to store session information so that no digital footprint would be left anywhere on the machine. Using the Tor browser and network, he could now go wherever he needed to with as much privacy as possible. It wasn't one hundred percent foolproof, nothing was. But it was the best he could do for now.

He prepared his thoughts, logged into his dark web blog site, then began writing.

The Chinese Communist Party, also known as the CCP, the largest secret society in the world who rules a predatory autocratic regime, continues its anti-human rights campaign in the so-called "meritocracy." Its economy, based on "guanxin" or having the right connections involving gifts, bribes, exemptions, and preferential treatment, is catching up to it.

We have it from credible sources that two more bloggers who dared to expose some of the CCP's latest crimes, have been confirmed to have disappeared in the last two months.

Caihong Hé was on a two-week road trip just last week travelling northwest to Xinjiang to meet with a United Kingdom news outlet when her car was run off the road shortly before turning on to Highway 216. She was reportedly going there to gather more intel on a recent number of Uyghurs and other minorities who have been kidnapped and sent to extermination camps for heart, kidney, and liver harvesting. Witnesses say three men dressed in tactical gear pulled her from her vehicle, threw her into a truck and she has not been seen or heard of since. Her picture is below. If you have any information on her whereabouts, please contact us.

Wei Jiǎ, who many American Chinese have nicknamed "Wei To Go!" for a couple years now, was disappeared last Friday. His home was raided after he posted a particularly damning report providing evidence of how one of the members of the Politburo Standing Committee had funneled up to $120 million U.S. dollars into offshore tax havens in Panama, Switzerland, and the Caribbean Islands through members of his immediate family. All the money was from bribes acquired during the big Shenyang Urban Rail Transit Expansion in which countless properties were seized and anyone who voiced concerns about safety or the environment were silenced.

The blog post went on to discuss many details and included ways readers could anonymously send leaks, whistleblowing information, and the process to officially disavow the CCP. After rereading it three times and making adjustments and corrections, it was posted through a network of anonymous supporters. The blog, which was reposted and mirrored on multiple platforms, had an estimated eighteen million views each week, some on the dark web, others anonymously on various social media platforms, and it acquired more readers as it was moved along.

The nephew shut down his laptop and put everything away. Taking a long sip from his tea, he thought about all the ways he was potentially putting himself and his family in danger with what he was doing. Even here in America, thugs were sent across the ocean to harass and intimidate, or worse, dissidents of the CCP.

For the time being though, he would continue to take his chances. Some risks were worth taking.

Chapter 5

It was a typical Tuesday. Jim Mueller wanted to take a walk, but it was too hot outside. He glanced out the window to the garden again and watched a small grey fox lurking around, probably hunting for rodents.

A small beep indicated a new work mail had come in. It was from Shane Wells.

Yo, JM, it read. *Got a new LTO backup system we're beta testing right now. Gonna need some documentation. Release in 12 days.*

Jim shrugged his lips. He had no idea what an LTO system was. He hit reply. *Np. Lemme know when I should stop by the workshop,* then hit Send.

Jim always liked Shane. Shane was a natural stark blond, a bit overweight and not very healthy, but a brilliant software and database engineer. He was one of just a handful of individuals who knew Helios inside and out better than anyone else in the world. He was also very friendly, which unfortunately was a more rare than common trait among people of his technical caliber. A couple years ago he'd been shipped up from a weapons assembly laboratory in Texas and had bemoaned at the time that he wasn't compensated for moving expenses as he'd been promised.

Shane's one weakness was that he didn't know how to explain complex technical stuff to the average end user. His brain functioned at levels too high for most; what was obvious to him was often confusing to others. But that's where Jim Mueller came in.

In a typical scenario, Jim would sit with Shane with a digital sound recorder and sometimes have a program running that recorded a screencast, while Shane demoed some new software or hardware release. Jim would then take the information and turn it into easy-to-follow descriptions and instructions. Shane complimented Jim on several occasions, saying, "I don't know how you turn all that info dump into training material." It always made Jim's day to hear things like that.

Jim gazed back out the window to the makeshift employee garden and smiled as he thought of a comment a coworker's ten-year old once made during the laboratory's biennial family visit day. "This place would be perfect in a zombie apocalypse!" the boy had said. And that was probably true. With two huge fences surrounding it, it was already protected. It had a bunch of armed guards, lots of vehicles, two cafeterias with full kitchens, its own gas station, a firehouse with two firetrucks, and a small hospital. And with this garden, food was even being grown in it. It was a little self-contained city in and of itself.

The garden, located in an area between some utility buildings and spread out alongside a section of one of the perimeter fences, had expanded over the years and had over eighty plots. Employees grew tomatoes, green beans, peas, carrots, cucumbers, squash, and a number of other things. Jim had walked over there a couple times, opened the little latch gate, and strolled through. It was actually quite relaxing to walk the narrow dirt paths between the plots.

But for two reasons, Jim would never eat anything that grew in that garden. The first was that the laboratory had faced decades of accusations that facility operations contaminated the soil and groundwater with hazardous chemicals and radioactive wastes. Occasionally, it was still a topic of contentious debate.

In years past, the entire site was actually farmland. But on December 7, 1941, Japan launched a naval attack on Pearl Harbor, lighting the fuse of fear of an air attack on San Francisco or the Oakland area. With the increase in air traffic along the West Coast, the U.S. Navy began looking at other possible locations for a training field. So one fine day in November of 1942, a group of men pulled up in a couple Chevrolet BG Master DeLuxe's and Ford pickup trucks, hopped out, and told the farmer the United States government needed the land for the war effort, and it was no longer his. Thank you for your service to your country.

From there, the seized roughly two square miles was converted into a flight training base and aircraft assembly and repair hub. This kind of work required the abundant use of paint, solvents, and degreasers, among other things. And rules were lax back then. Used oil and old fuel were routinely dumped around the perimeter, which, back then, was just miles of barren fields, not the encroaching housing tracts and strip malls you see today. Who knows how much of that stuff had stayed in the ground.

Then, maybe fifteen years later, the Atomic Energy Commission formally took over and promptly turned it into a weapons design and physics research laboratory. A few years after that, it went to the U.S. Department of Energy.

Efforts to clean up years of producing waste included the excavation and removal of thousands of cubic yards of contaminated soil during which the government provided alternative water supplies to local residents.

Today, one can see blue pipes with yellow labels emerging from the ground all over the site, more than a hundred of them used to monitor contamination – groundwater extraction and injection wells and soil vapor extraction wells. At the top of these pipes is a round hinge lid with a padlock. Jim had been taking a morning walk one day and noticed there was no lock on one of these pipe lids. Looking around, he opened it and saw a thin cable that went down into the ground. He tugged at it and could have pulled it up but decided not to.

All this was why he'd never eat anything that had been cultivated in the soil around this place. He was surprised the tomatoes weren't glowing a fluorescent green or something.

Another beep. Shane returned the mail.

Tomorrow at 10?

Sure, see you there, Jim typed.

He sat back and looked at his cell phone on the desk. It beckoned, or something did, so he picked it up and thumbed on the screen. A cute *twinkle* sound effect alerted him there was a new message on his relatively new favorite app, Lù Chá. He opened to find the image of another fresh young beauty with jet-black hair looking at him with a smile so seductive it made his heart flutter. It was impossible to tell anymore if images like this were of real people who'd been digitally redone or something that was 100% computer fabricated. No matter, it looked good.

Pronounced "loo-cha," he'd read the words translated as *Green Tea* in Mandarin Chinese. Maybe he should study some Mandarin. Used by more than a billion people worldwide, it was the second most spoken language in the world, Hindi being the first. Besides, maybe he'd hook up with one of these dark-haired temptresses someday.

He smirked bitterly. There were plenty of wonderful women of all stripes out there, only none of them were attracted to him. Not anymore anyway.

He glanced at his ring finger. He'd been relieved when the ghost ring finally faded away several months after taking it off, a thing that now symbolized more pain than anything else.

Jim's wife, soon to be ex, a smart and angry attorney named Vaneesa, with the ironic maiden name of Loveless, specialized in the areas of employment and labor law, representing both private and public sector employers. But her practice included defending suits alleging wrongful termination, harassment, discrimination, retaliation, unfair labor practices, fraud, and various other employment-related claims.

Armed with evidence she'd acquired about various women Jim had been in contact with online, some of whom had numbers associated with escort services, she would know exactly what to do to milk the separation to the hilt. Despite the fact that she averaged a higher income stream, she would ream him good, and often reminded him of that fun fact. She'd made him miserable in a, well, *loveless* marriage, now she was promising to make him more miserable financially.

To be fair, the broken matrimony wasn't all Vaneesa's fault, but with her hard-headed cantankerous personality and cold manipulation control tactics, it had been difficult to be faithful to her. Thankfully, his job, a lifeline now, paid very decently, and was something he couldn't take for granted.

He looked at his phone again. The app's default icon of bright red lips in a puckering kiss flashed. He clicked it and saw there was a new message.

Hey there Jimmy, it read. *Saw your profile. Just saying hi, nice to meet you. :) Maybe we could learn a little about each other? Check me out and let me know. –Iris*

Interesting. Many of the messages he got were clearly from massage parlors or other services that fronted illicit activity. They always started with stuff like, *hey handsome*, *hi sexy*, or *I love American guys!* Plus, they almost always included the hugs and kisses *XOXO* or something at the end. And when they sent nude photos or things like that, he just deleted it. When he was in his twenties and thirties, sure, but not now. He was done with all that.

Considering the profile he had, under the name "Jimmy C.," there were only two types that wrote that sort of cheesy B.S., and none of them legit. It used to be fun, to indulge in the fantasy. But too many ugly things had happened as a result of playing with such illusions. It now produced bitter feelings.

He clicked on the Account menu, and then, My Profile. Up came a selfie he'd taken not more than six months ago. It showed him for what he was – an already tired forty-one-year-old with bags forming under his eyes. His hair though, a distinct salt and pepper, was still thick and could be styled to suit. The thin goatee was a bit darker, more like the dark brown of his youth, but the grays were becoming more predominant. His face was thin and his spent eyes, a dull, garden variety brown, looked back through plain black, horn-rimmed glasses. He actually wasn't too bad, all things considered. He kept reasonably trim, though the battle with weight was getting worse by the day. A few years of drinking too much had definitely added mileage to the somewhat weary look he now bore most of the time, but it hadn't ruined him. Not yet.

He'd thought about faking his profile like so many do by posting an image of a man ten years younger and twice as good looking. Maybe imply there was an extra zero on his income stream and net worth. But all that did was disappoint anyone you actually ended up connecting with in person. That is, if he was going to bother to do that sort of thing anymore. Is that what he thought would come of this kittenish app? Shouldn't he be on a real dating site where members were supposedly screened, everything was legit, and there were people actually looking for a meaningful relationship?

Then why did he stay on this app? Because he had to admit to himself, he wasn't really looking for love, he was still looking for a fantasy. Love was too scary. A big part of him was still the lonely soul who didn't enjoy his youth very much and still craved the excitement he believed he'd mostly missed out on. He had no illusions as to why – creative and introspective, he never much enjoyed being social or had a lot of friends. He always thought human interaction was too phony to appreciate. And yet here he was, gravitating toward connections that were clearly disingenuous.

He shook his head. He was either a masochist or just plain nuts.

He went back to the message. *Hey there* … it started. That wasn't even all that flirtatious sounding. To boot, the avatar attached to the message was a generic vector image of an Asian girl that was more cartoonish than real. It depicted a woman who was above average in looks, not by a whole lot, but with a pleasant smile. It was somewhat attractive, with large, inviting eyes, but not intended to be sexy so much as just friendly. He found himself attracted to the simplicity of it right away for a lot of reasons.

Okay, he thought. I'll bite. He hit reply and typed, *Hello*. He almost typed, *how are you?* But everyone asks that when they can't think of anything else. Pausing, he considered adding more details about himself and asking some questions. He'd read that women tend to respond more if you used her name and showed curiosity during introductions. But she had reached out to him first.

He added, *Tell me a little about yourself.* He wouldn't even take the time to read her bio and ask about interests or hobbies or things like what her favorite restaurant or music is. Not yet. Let her hit the ball back over the net, see if she's serious.

He pressed the Send button. If there was never another message from "Iris," he wouldn't care.

Chapter 6

Zhang Zhan was finishing up her last pedicure for the day. Her American friends knew her as "Iris."

Working at Katherine's Nails in San Francisco had been a good job for the last couple years, where all her coworkers were Chinese except one who was Vietnamese. Although she'd become quite skilled as a manicurist and pedicurist, she was ready to move on. Her goal was to become a translator and linguist. She'd studied hard and got good grades in her dual-language immersion courses at San Francisco State University and was looking forward to graduating.

A relatively new immigrant from the southeastern coast of China, she was already a native Fukienese and Mandarin speaker. Her English had excelled rapidly in the last five years, and she'd worked relentlessly to speak without an accent, recording herself and listening back, getting feedback from her American friends.

On a dare to start dating, she recently posted a profile on the Lù Chá app. At first, she thought it was a sleazy platform, but "Green Tea" sounded innocent enough, and she saw a few profiles of people who appeared genuine.

"You need to meet someone special, a nice American man who likes Chinese girls," her friends told her.

"I don't want to post my picture or anything," she protested.

"You don't have to, just use an avatar."

So she'd gone for it. She posted a simple profile with very little personal information and an avatar that sort of resembled her. She wasn't what most would describe as beautiful, but then she wasn't bad either. There was someone for her. She began the process of carefully and casually reaching out to profiles that interested her.

She was immediately turned off by most of the replies she'd gotten. They all said the same thing in one way or the other, along the lines of, *show me your real picture, are you hot?* and, *what do you really look like?*

So it was obvious what most were after on this site. If this continued, she'd delete her profile and try something else.

But recently, she'd ran into a guy named "Jimmy." She was immediately attracted to his simple profile picture which showed a man in maybe his late thirties or early forties with hair starting to grey. It was a closeup of his face, unassuming and unpretentious. He also looked intelligent. She didn't want some young guy who wasn't established and still looking for himself, not to mention just prowling for quick flings. She wanted a mature man who was in a real career and already comfortable in his own skin. Someone who knew what he wanted. Jimmy had that look, so she'd reached out and he'd replied with a simple, *tell me about yourself.* She liked that.

She sat in her car in the parking lot outside of Katherine's Nails and logged into the Lừ Chá app while thinking about what she was going to say.

But immediately upon logging in, she was met with an ominous message that said, "YOUR ACCOUNT HAS BEEN SUSPENDED. This account was permanently revoked by an administrator for a violation of our platform's policy involving the use of a counterfeit profile and explicit content."

What? That didn't make sense. She'd used her real first name, at least her American name, and lots of users on the app used an avatar instead of a real image. And explicit content? She'd never done anything like that.

Fine. Forget this stupid Lừ Chá app. She'd find another more legitimate dating site.

***

Jim strolled down the hallway to the main kitchen where a coworker had set up a makeshift convenience store more than fifteen years ago. Restocked every two or three weeks, it contained a variety of sodas, chips, candy bars, and even frozen burritos. Payment for snacks was a small metal cash box that sat on the mini refrigerator. It made sense that an honor system like this could actually work in an atmosphere where integrity and staying within the lines was drilled so thoroughly into everyone's heads.

Jennifer Nelson popped her head out of a doorway as Jim approached. "Good morning," she said.

"Morning. How's your first week going?"

"I feel like I'm locked out of everything except the bathroom," she said, smiling.

"Yeah, that's normal. In another few days they'll have your card encoded to the doors you need to access."

"Can I bother you to show me where the mail room is? I'm still like a mouse in a maze around here."

"No problem, follow me."

They started down the hall.

Jim began talking. "This building is more of a giant mobile modular structure. It has forty-three offices, a classroom that can fit about thirty-five, a conference room that can comfortably seat fifteen, a kitchen and break room, and two smaller kitchenettes with a sink and microwave oven. It's officially a Common Access area that many trainees access and nothing classified is ever done in here."

"The doors still have those TESA locks."

"Oh yeah, all buildings around here do, except the cafeterias. But on this one they're unlocked between 6:00 a.m. and 6:00 p.m. Outside those hours, you need to be on the access list and use your badge."

"How come you haven't been moved to the Helios building?"

"Good question. I'm still here because they lack office space there. But honestly, I like it here – always ample parking, the environment not as tense as in the restricted buildings. Besides, we've got a nice view of the garden."

"Well, you do. I'm on the other side and my view is a big fence."

"Yeah, sorry about that."

"So there's no classified computers here?"

"No. All the computers here are hooked to the regular employee internal network, separate from the classified. It's forbidden to ever bring classified material in – printed or digital storage. In fact, this building is often referred to as 'The Cooler,' because part of one of the hallways is occupied by new hires like yourself, or contractors who are temporarily housed here while their L or Q is being processed. Until you've got a clearance, it's considered a full-blown security breach to so much as lay eyes on anything sensitive."

"Oh please."

"They're very serious about that. Well, here we are," he said, stopping at a doorway. He inserted his badge into the lock and opened the mailroom door.

Jim watched as Jennifer looked around at the mail slots, trying not to let his eyes wander impolitely up and down her figure. He said, "You know, when I first came on board with the laboratory, I assumed there were just two types of material – classified and unclassified. But that isn't quite true, technically speaking. There's all kinds of layers."

"Is Helios classified?"

"Most of it's considered to be highly sensitive. And in some cases, when vulnerabilities or malfunctions are discovered, it's full-blown classified."

"Sounds fascinating."

"Kind of is in the beginning, then it gets old. First off, everything in Helios is what's called Official Use Only by default, made clear by the big OUO letters on the top and bottom of everything both in print and digital form. But occasionally, I see other types of material."

"Like what?" Jennifer asked as she came back out of the mail room.

Jim paused, wondering how much he should divulge. As a trainer for Helios, he had access to a certain internal directory where developers and engineers stored much of their material. These directories were on a secure network and housed in a highly guarded server farm somewhere in Kansas City, smack dab in the middle of the country because laboratories from coast to coast utilized it. Access to this internal repository required the collaborative approval of managers, associate directors, then two different network security individuals, one in California and one in Kansas. All activity within the system was recorded. But the weakness was, once that digital portal was punched open, it could be accessed from any computer imaged with the laboratory's VPN software by someone with the right credentials. That meant the people who had the rights to post things in those directories had to be trusted.

But people make mistakes.

They started back toward Jennifer's office. "The variety of classification categories could make a person dizzy and it's often unclear how the rules around them differ," Jim continued, dodging her question. "OUO is considered sensitive enough to be used only when necessary to perform the job. It's never emailed outside the secure network, never emailed internally without encryption, and if it has to be temporarily put on media like a portable drive, only an encrypted one like an *Ironkey*, is acceptable."

"I don't have one of those."

"I'll ask Francis to have one of the IT guys assign you one."

"What if someone posted something OUO on social media," Jennifer asked with a smile. "Hey everyone, look what I'm working on!"

"If someone was ever crazy enough to do that, they'd suffer consequences like having their clearance revoked, getting blacklisted from ever having another clearance job, paying a fine, and even possibly facing jail time, depending on the level of infraction and damage caused. You should have heard all this in new employee orientation."

"Mine is tomorrow, all day."

"Ah, okay. Well, above OUO comes various levels – Restricted Data, National Security Information, Critical Nuclear Weapon Design Information, and so on. It almost makes no sense to have all these distinctions since it comes with the same restrictions."

"I guess that explains all the military looking guards around here. There's so many."

"There used to be more. This lab is a Sigma 1 site, which means personnel here work on the theory of operation or complete design of thermonuclear fission weapons or their unique components. But there are four other sites around the country Helios also protects that are Sigma 2. They also work with the high explosive system *and* nuclear initiation system. In other words, they have the combined materials and know-how to construct fully functional nuclear weapons."

"I have to say wow again."

They found Jennifer's office and stood by the door. "To a new hire like yourself, the main difference between Sigma 1 and 2 is the security presence. Here, you're met by one or two armed guards at the front entrance. Around the campus, you see security vehicles making their rounds, but nothing more than what one might describe as 'extra security.' But at a Sigma 2 site, there are four guards per car who surround each one entering and examine the entire vehicle as your badge is getting checked. Once inside, there are guards everywhere, like in a military base camp, and fences with ominous signs that proclaim, 'Use of Deadly Force Authorized.' A Humvee with an M2 Browning 50-caliber machine gun mounted on the back randomly roves around the site all day."

"You've seen this?"

"Yep. I travelled to a Sigma 2 site in Tennessee to perform some Helios training. It was fascinating as a visitor, but it'd be tedious to deal with it every day. The concrete barriers and walls, the high fences with barbed wire, the grim-faced guards eyeballing you. And I was told stories. Several years ago, a Helios technician from here had been working on a remote processor that managed three alarm sectors. After installing a software update, he impulsively rebooted the hard drive without telling security what he was doing. This took down close to thirty sensors causing the alarm console to light up like a fancy slot machine. Within minutes, a helicopter was flying over and about fourteen guards with automatic rifles were converging on the area as fast as wheels and human legs could transport them. The poor tech peed his pants, raised his arms, and slumped to the ground while babbling apologies. Due to a clean record, and because no damage was done, he got off with a stern warning."

"Oh my god, that must have been terrible."

"Lesson learned. Like I said, this place isn't for everyone."

Chapter 7

Li Ming Tan smiled as she read the login instructions. Iris, huh. Pretty name and a pretty flower, although she preferred the Lotus.

She killed a little time by doing some quick research. Gleaned from the Greek word iris – "ee-r-ee-s" – it meant "rainbow." In ancient mythology, Iris was the goddess of the rainbow, who rode it like a multicolored bridge from heaven to earth. What mind altering drugs did people take to imagine such things? But she did like the symbol of power and majesty the goddess represented.

When Li Ming was a little girl, she'd dreamed of becoming someone of high prominence, an esteemed leader and world-changer. She'd even entertained the idea of being a famous actress but knew she didn't have the looks or connections for that.

Instead, she'd led a career of secrecy and with it came a cost most were unwilling to pay. Even at home, there was always a target on her back. She constantly had to maintain solid tradecraft and stay off the radar. And especially when on travel, she was often surrounded by those who would either kill her at every opportunity or capture and interrogate her. Instead of long paid vacations, she found herself working all the time. She had her "cover jobs," where she was posing as a businesswoman, interpreter, or attaché. But when doing so, she was always looking for that person who possessed knowledge the government would want, the stuff not conveyed through public or political channels. Her life had been one of mainly gathering human intelligence – finding, assessing, and cultivating potential sources of information. As such, she became an expert in feigning interest in whatever the target was interested in.

The process was simple, but could be taxing mentally, especially after the initial stage of cultivating, because then came the recruiting. As a female, she had occasionally been obligated to become a temporary lover or just a pleasure servant. She laughed at the thought that most people believed her job was about assassinating or sneaking into offices to break into the wall safe hidden behind the painting. In reality, she was more a salesperson, an expert in manipulating and exploiting vulnerabilities.

Hardly the life of her childhood dreams. But that was okay, it was her duty. Perhaps after her rebirth.

She clicked the URL to open the login page and entered the name and password she'd been given from MSS Counterintelligence.

***

Jim sat in his office reflecting on some of the things he'd told Jennifer Nelson. Employment at the lab had been an interesting experience to say the least. He'd already been in demand, employment wise, because of his bachelor's and master's. But after acquiring a top secret clearance, things went to a whole new level. Suddenly he was getting hit up by recruiters all the time, but many of these messages were quite random. One asked if he'd consider being a dimensional inspector for an aerospace company. Another asked if he wanted to be an instrumentation and controls engineer for a nuclear architecture company. Huh? Were these legitimate offers or spies from Russia or Iran?

But with a security clearance also came responsibility and a trust. When Jim had been briefed as part of his Q-clearance, it had been drilled into him that going forward, his life was under potential scrutiny. The things he did online, the places he went, the activities he engaged in. He didn't think much of it because he was just another cog in the wheel, no one of power and authority. Still though, it did make one think.

And today he was thinking about an ordinary, unremarkable Wednesday morning a few months ago when he'd first run into a category of Helios-related material that made him nervous. It was called "UCNI."

U, C, N, I, huh ... Now what? Am I gonna get in trouble for looking at this?

The next day when Jim was in the Helios lab, he saw Dirk Reynolds, a QA engineer for Helios updates. Dirk was at the mock alarm console testing a new video playback feature.

"Hey Dirk, what's, U, C, N, I?" Jim asked.

"Oh, that's *uh-k-nee*," Dirk said. "Another level of pain in the ass classification." He picked up a coffee cup and went back to his testing.

"What does it mean?"

"It means more pain in the ass rules and restrictions."

"I mean the letters, the acronym."

"Oh, uh, unclassified controlled nuclear information." Dirk laughed. "Whatever the hell that means. Probably just having to piss in a few more cups if you work with it."

Jim decided not to ask any more questions, although Dirk wouldn't have cared one way or the other. Dirk's priority anymore seemed to be getting the workday over with so he could indulge in his favorite activity – downing chilled bottled Guinness.

Dirk turned and looked at Jim. "Why do you ask?"

"Oh, I dunno," Jim said, casually shrugging. "I saw the term somewhere on … *something* around here."

Dirk watched him for a moment. "Best you keep your nose clean, unless you need to know." He raised his eyebrows. "Know what I mean?"

Jim feigned a small chuckle. "Right."

The UCNI material Jim had viewed was the schematics for a new high-security double-door booth. It almost startled him when he first came upon it. There were no warnings, nothing to indicate anything was out of the ordinary. Just the letters "UCNI" in red, eighteen-point bold Verdana font at the top and bottom of each page. It wasn't so much the material itself, which he figured was covered with a

Q-Clearance. It was where he'd found it – in that repository in Kansas City that DOE employees across the country used, including Helios developers and engineers in California. Jim occasionally prowled it for information when looking for material for training projects. He didn't want to get asked, *did you need to know about this?*

Later, he did a little research. UCNI, by its official definition, is "a category for identifying, controlling and limiting the dissemination of unclassified information on the physical protection of special nuclear material, vital equipment and facilities." UCNI subject areas included safeguards and security for high explosives in nuclear weapons, nuclear nonproliferation, uranium and plutonium laser isotope, and radiological emergency response. So it made sense that the booths that acted as gatekeepers for this stuff would be in this classification. It was noted though that "most UCNI subject areas" overlap with classified subject areas, so perhaps it shouldn't have been posted in this repository.

He drummed his fingers on his desk and then decided to pick up the phone and call someone he trusted – Shane Wells.

"Shane, what's goin' on?" Jim asked.

"When I know, you'll be the first to know."

"You mean the second."

"You gettin' technical with me, Mueller?"

"Nah. Listen, I was wondering if I was going to have to put together any training material on these security booths."

"What security booths?"

"Well, er, uh, I ran into some material in the Helios hardware folders. I was just curious."

There was a pause on the other end. "You must be talking about the upgrades in Nevada. And New Mexico, I think. But not here. They're only used at certain sites," said Shane.

"I didn't know there were different kinds."

"There's several flavors. Not really my department, but Pete and Gerard can tell you all about them. They've been building one for testing."

"Oh, okay. It made me curious. I saw the letters U, C, N, I on the docs."

"Uh-k-knee, makes sense. If you have to use one to get into places where there's research or work involving fuel or parts in reactors, or uranium or plutonium. You know, the stuff in fission weapons that goes boom-boom."

"So these booths aren't like the one we go through from the parking lot to the Helios building area then."

"Oh no, not even close. That booth is bare bones by comparison. Just a Q and PIN is all you need. These ones sniff you and weight you and probe you."

Jim thought about how intimidating it was the first time he went through one. To enter, all one needed to do was press a large button next to the door and wait for the metallic *thunk* as the internal lock disengaged. From there, one could turn the handle and pull open the heavy door. Once inside, nothing would happen until the low side door shut and automatically locked. At this point, you were effectively trapped.

The interior of the booth was maybe the size of a typical elevator, if it were elongated, though not as tall, and a claustrophobia sufferer would not fare well. No more than five individuals were allowed into the booth at a time. The idea was that if you were up to no good and didn't have the credentials to get to the high side, an alarm was sent, and security would be dispatched. You'd have no choice but to stand there and wait.

"It always freaks me out a little when I'm in one. Like what if I get stuck," Jim said.

"They have emergency contingencies," Shane said. "If there was a fire or whatever and your badge wouldn't let you out, there's a release button that unlocks the low side door. That would also trigger an alarm and you'd be met by an armed response. Even if you got away before the guns arrived, multiple cameras inside and out would have recorded you. For non-emergencies, there's also a telephone that when picked up, acts as a bat phone directly to the security console."

"These things look like vaults."

"Oh yeah," Shane said. "Solid steel framed structure, the doors thick glass, impervious to the initial blows from sledgehammers and bullets. This way, no one can break in, or out, without a lot of time and effort, and a guard or whoever can always see who was inside."

Jim had never thought about the design of these booths. Never had a reason to. He was just grateful when the high side door unlocked and let him out of the glass and steel enclosure. But now he'd seen the schematics of one, and a highly sophisticated one at that. As expected, there were a lot of parts to the thing. The metal frames were packed with wires and circuit boards, and the doors were triple fortified. The diagrams were highly detailed and displayed each wire and circuit, described their voltage inputs and outputs, and the sequence of events that made things work. A multi-page encyclopedia of graphical representation with text descriptions told the whole story.

Jim said, "I'm always amazed at the lengths to which the government will go to fight the innate tendencies of human beings to be dishonest or even deadly for either personal gain or ideology."

"Ha ha, spoken like a trainer. Like I said, talk to Pete or Gerard if you wanna know more."

"Will do. Thanks, Shane."

It was daunting to think of how many people around the world were paid to protect others and their assets or information from evil – from security guards to police officers, to FBI and CIA agents, to NSA personnel, cybersecurity experts, Department of Justice personnel, and jail and prison workers, not to mention all the branches of the military.

That was okay though, it made for good employment.

His cell phone beckoned again. Jim picked it up and glanced at the new message icon from the Lù Chá app. Opening the message, he was somewhat pleased to see that it was from Iris.

Hello Jimmy, thank you for replying. Sorry I'm not sharing my real image online. I'm not very comfortable with that. Hope you understand. Maybe privately sometime. Anyway, I was just listening to one of my favorite '80s songs list and thought of you. I'm not sure why. You remind me of someone from that era. LOL. Anyway, just saying hi back. Nice to meet you. :)–Iris

Jim actually laughed out loud. In high school someone once told him he *kinda* looked like Jon Bon Jovi. The comment didn't strike him all that much at the time since he wasn't a big fan. He liked a couple of their tunes like "Wanted Dead or Alive," and enjoyed tinkering with it on the guitar, but otherwise didn't own any of their albums. But it did make him pause. Was Iris an '80s girl? That meant she was aging, like him. It wasn't fair to women, but he'd half expected and fully *hoped* she was younger, given that her avatar depicted a woman in her 30's maybe.

He was still intrigued though. The tone of the note, again, wasn't really flirtatious, just friendly. It didn't expect a response or ask a bunch of questions. It just kind of gently threw the ball back into his court, like we're just talking here. And for some reason he both liked and respected her for not posting a real picture of herself online. Women did need to be more careful, after all. Besides, if she'd posted a picture of some drop-dead gorgeous model, he'd not believe it was her anyway. Hopefully she wasn't drop-dead *ugly* though, that'd be letdown.

What was also appealing was she apparently liked his kind of music – classic rock – unless by '80s she meant Madonna or Cyndi Lauper. Maybe she was his age, or even a bit older, but perhaps it was time to invest himself in a more mature individual.

He hit reply and prepared a message. This time he might mention his musical taste and the fact that he was a trainer by profession. He wouldn't say what he trained or where, just that he was an expert in the art of making learning engaging.

Chapter 8

Jim checked his watch as he stood inside the booth – 9:50 a.m. Perfect timing. Shane was sometimes a couple minutes early. He exited the high-side door and made his way toward the Helios building, an older, three-story structure that had been layered repeatedly with new coats of paint over the years.

The lanyard around his neck bobbed and swayed as he walked. Adorned with his HSPD-12 badge, site identification card, hard token and MyPass key, it had enough weight to bounce a little when walking quickly. Regulations required that the badge always be out and visible between one's neck and waistline so guards could easily see it.

As soon as he entered the Helios building, he was met with the annoying sound of hissing, rushing air from the end of the main hallway. The continuous sound emitted from a device about the size of a shoebox attached to the electrical conduit pipes and cable sleeve-covered ceiling at the end of the hallway next to the entrance of the Helios lab.

"What's that thing for?" Jim had asked one day to Pete, one of the security engineers.

"It stifles unwanted eavesdropping," Pete said. "Detecting a hidden recording device that doesn't broadcast is nearly impossible because they don't transmit a signal for radio frequency sniffers to find. But a white noise generator is remarkably effective against microphone-based snooping with digital recorders, RF transmitters, or someone with a shotgun microphone out in the parking lot."

"It runs all day?" Jim asked.

"All day and all night, all year around. And you know why the Helios lab is a self-contained structure with no windows, right?"

"Enlighten me."

"Laser microphones. They can turn a window or any other smooth surfaced object inside an enclosure into a giant ear drum. Responds to the pressure waves and vibrations created by noises in the room. Effective up to 1,200 feet. A receiver in the laser device converts these vibrations into audio signals with surprisingly clear sound."

"The learning fun never ends around here," Jim said.

Jim slid his badge out of the lanyard holder as he approached the remote terminal mounted to the wall next to the Helios lab door. Next to the terminal was a hand geometry unit, known in the security world as an "HGU." The lab was a highly secure room, an alarm sector all its own. Outside normal hours and during weekends, unless special arrangements were made with security, the place was in secure mode, and no one was supposed to be there – all sensors would send alarms.

It had taken a climb up an approval chain to get on the access list. He then had to sit down with one of the security engineers to have both his right thumbprint and hand scanned into the system.

Inserting the badge, chip first, into the slot of the terminal, the machine beeped and displayed the digital number pad on the six-by-six monochrome touchscreen with an "ENTER YOUR PIN" challenge. He tapped in his eight-digit PIN and waited. The number pad disappeared and was replaced by a framed note telling him to press his right thumb on the small rectangular scanner. A green glow briefly appeared under his thumb and a "Welcome!" text flashed. This always amused him. What would it say if you weren't supposed to be trying to get into the room, *wait here for arresting officers?*

Now for the HGU. Hand geometry units also had a number pad and screen, though the screen was smaller, maybe two by five inches. There was no badge slot, but below the number pad was a flat steel plate with a dotted line in the shape of a right hand with small, round pegs positioned at the base of the joints where the finger webbing went.

Jim placed his hand on the plate, palm down, and slid it forward, letting the five pegs spread his fingers apart and guide his hand into the proper position. The pegs sensed when a hand was there, and the device began scanning. The thing always creeped Jim out a bit. The idea was that the shape of human hands have unique characteristics, and the machine recognizes you after measuring your hand's shape, surface area, bone and flesh thickness, length and width of each finger, and distances between joints and knuckles. After several seconds, the thing beeped and the small screen asked for his PIN, which he entered again.

He waited, while thinking about the fact that he was one of the few on site not in the Human Reliability Program, but still had access to this lab. The reason was because he didn't actually touch the source code or the hardware for Helios, he only wrote about it. Just as well. People with HRP status had to take more drug tests – "P-tests" as they were called – mental and medical evaluations, another even more comprehensive background, reputation and financial check, *and* undergo a polygraph every couple years.

No, thanks.

After a moment, he heard the lock on the Helios lab door disengage and he entered. Stepping in, he paused and made sure the door shut and locked again. He didn't want armed guards rushing in asking who left it open.

He entered the first of three large connecting rooms. The first was where the software engineers hung out when fixing a problem or playing with a new release. Large monitors and desktop computers graced the tables that ran along the walls. Above them, multiple security cameras mounted around the ceiling documented every angle of the room.

He saw the wide back and dark hair of Ricardo Martinez, one of the Helios software engineers, as he hunched over a screen.

"Que paso, Ricardo?" Jim said as he strolled by.

"Hey, what's up?" Ricardo replied, barely glancing up. Ricardo spoke with a noticeable Costa Rican accent and usually appreciated his colleagues attempting to speak his native tongue. But he was busy.

Jim continued into the next room where one wall was covered by mounted Helios remote terminals of every shape and variety that had been built since the first version in the mid '80s. It had gone through quite a lot of changes, getting slicker and a little smaller every several years, the number pad evolving from mechanical to touchscreen.

On the other side were test remote processors – the two large steel boxes connected vertically by a thick pipe. The upper box contained the electronics, the lower, the battery backup system.

Jim knew quite a bit about remote processors, but it was always interesting to look inside one and see its guts. He opened the top panel. A small, glowing blue light at the top indicated that everything had power. He looked at the main motherboard mounted to the back of the box, the daughterboard, and several others that had various tasks.

"Oh hey, Jim," a voice said behind him.

Jim turned to see Lewis Van Asten, an old timer with the lab who'd been around long enough to have contributed to the evolution of many Helios components. He admired Lewis and wondered if he'd still be working at that age.

"Hi Lewis. I've always admired the engineering of these things."

Lewis stood staring for a moment, then nodded. "They've come a long way. In the eighties and nineties, they weren't fast enough to be the self-contained mini-Helios systems they are today. Solid state drives were the game changer."

"I thought solid state drives came out in like ninety-one."

"They did. Then it took us eight years to redesign, test and certify."

Jim laughed. That was typical. "Are they still limited to seventy-five total sensors?"

Lewis looked at Jim. "Limited? It used to only be thirty-five."

"What changed?"

"We made room for an additional board. Now we've got a full seventy-five regulated lines hard-wired to any kind of sensor."

Jim nodded and listened even though he already knew most of this. Voltage levels, regulated by resistors, change if a line is damaged or tampered with. This, in turn, changes the digital value of the line. The voltage levels which determined these conditions – open, closed, shorted out, line cut, deactivated, and so on – are classified, and any condition other than "Okay" sends an alarm.

"Amazing stuff." Jim looked at his watch. "Well good seeing you, Lewis. Take care."

Continuing to the third and largest space of the Helios lab, he entered the mock alarm console room. He glanced at the back of the room where they configured HGUs and thumbprint scanners and looked at the very realistic silicone hands on sticks they used for testing.

Shane Wells sat at one of the consoles. He was a few years younger than Jim and never dressed in anything but jeans and a t-shirt. On cold days he wore a sweatshirt hoodie.

"How's it going?" he asked, looking up and seeing Jim.

"Still vertical with blood pressure, and a tad more jaded than last year. How you doin'?"

"Can't complain – like anyone's listening anyway."

"People listen to you, Shane. Even Kay listens to you. You wanna see a schmuck get ignored, watch me try making suggestions at your next developers meeting."

Shane laughed. "You're not supposed to give suggestions to developers. You know how we are. Try giving your doctor advice on how to treat you."

"Right," Jim said, pulling up a chair and rolling next to Shane. "So what's this LTO back up thingamajig?"

"Is that an official training term?"

"Absolutely."

"We're dumping the hard drive system. All data backups are going to tape."

"As in magnetic tape?"

"Mm-hmm."

"At every Helios site, even here?"

"Yup."

"Kind of archaic technology, isn't it?"

"It's the way to go. Especially now that they're in cost-cutting mode."

"So the old classic solutions are still relevant."

"More than ever. Tape may seem outdated, but it's still a great solution. Affordable, high capacity, better than disk drives and file servers. Capacity isn't even an issue. A one terabyte portable hard drive is almost ten times more expensive than a tape cartridge with the same capacity. Plus, tape cartridges don't require power or cooling."

"You sound like a salesman."

"I've had to be. At the quarterly two months ago, I was met with the usual fierce resistance to change."

"Are tapes more secure than digital?"

"As long as the tape is in offline storage. Most will keep 'em in a safe or vault room. Not vulnerable to hacking and cyberattacks. Data is separated from the read/write ops, which creates the air gap. Of course, all Helios systems are air gapped anyway, just saying."

"No data storage in the cloud?"

Shane just glanced at him with raised and furrowed eyebrows.

"Right."

"The one disadvantage is that to restore an entire system would take several hours," Shane continued. "But that's a small price to pay when you consider the benefits."

"How long will they keep the tapes around?"

Shane shrugged. "Five years. Ten years. Whatever they want."

"Then destroy them?"

"Of course."

"How are tapes with classified info destroyed?"

Shane looked up in thought while unwrapping a Hershey's Kiss he'd grabbed from somewhere off his desk. "I think for magnetic tape media, the DOE requires either degaussing or pulverizing. Also works with hard drives." He plopped the chocolate in his mouth.

"What's degaussing?"

"You ask a lot of questions."

"I haven't survived this long in the tech writing and training world by not being curious."

"You expose the media to a strong magnetic field to disrupt the recorded magnet domains. Wipes everything out. The field is generated with either a big magnet or an electromagnetic coil. Why?"

"You never know. I may need to train someone how to dispose of classified material."

"Nah, they already know how to do that. Trust me."

In the next hour, Shane walked Jim through how both the hardware and software was going to be distributed to the different sites. Jim's task was to write up the training guide on how to set up and plug everything in, then configure the LTO software for the site's many options. The software was very comprehensive and one had full control over what to backup, when and how often. He already had some nice ideas about diagrams and pictures he was going to use.

Kay Allison walked in just as they were finishing up. Kay managed the software engineers and had a reputation for putting out fires with on-the-fly hero coding. It was rumored she was the one who really pulled the strings in the Helios program and that her "supervisor" was more just a go-between for the laboratory and the DOE liaison in Washington. It was also rumored she made more money than anyone else in the program, even her alleged boss.

Kay was tall and slender, close to five foot, eleven inches, and today had her dirty blonde hair pulled back in a ponytail. Jim guessed she was in her late thirties and marveled at how well she kept herself in shape. Her daily ritual was brisk walking at least thirty minutes around the site no matter the weather, and she probably had enough knowledge on healthy eating to be a professional nutritionist. She was a bit stern and humorless most of the time though which made her relationships with colleagues no-nonsense and business-only. Jim appreciated that but wouldn't want to hang out with her outside of work.

"Shane," she said. "I found the missing indexes causing the events server slowdown the other day."

"Do tell," Shane replied.

"Nothing to tell. It's fixed. I'd asked you to look into it, but now I'm telling you don't bother."

"Aye aye, Captain," Shane said.

She looked at Jim. "James."

From the very beginning when he'd come onboard, she'd called him James. For almost a year while he was waiting for his clearance investigation, he had to be escorted into the Helios building by another cleared individual and be watched the entire time.

Being escorted was a pain, especially for the person doing the escorting. The day before the visit, an email no one paid any attention to had to be sent to all the building's residents announcing that non-cleared individuals were going to be around. It had to list who they were, and during what window of time they'd be in the building. And on the day of the visit, at least two hours prior, you had to put signs out in the hallway in big letters that said the same information. Escortees had to be met in person by their escort at the front gate to the restricted area, never left alone for the entire visit, and when finished, walked back to the gate to make sure they exited.

The first time Jim had been escorted into the Helios building and met Kay, she just stared at him suspiciously for a moment, then looked at the name on his badge. She'd called him James ever since.

"Kay," Jim said back, nodding. He hadn't seen her in several weeks but knew not to bother with pleasantries.

"You free next month?" she asked.

"Define *free*," Jim said, not attempting humor. The word always reminded him of Janis Joplin crooning out the words to the song "Bobby McGee" – *Freedom's just another word for nothin' left to lose …*

"Free to travel."

"Uhm, maybe. Why?" Jim disliked travel anymore. It was somewhat exciting a few years ago, but more an inconvenience now. Especially when traveling for work, due to all the paperwork and approvals, reimbursement and so on.

Kay frowned; she preferred a quick and definite yes or no to questions. "One of our beta sites is experiencing some issues. They asked who the best person would be to document what happened and how they're troubleshooting."

"And you threw my name out? I'm flattered."

"I threw your name out because you're the training lead," Kay said without blinking.

Shane smirked.

Jim glanced at Shane for a second. "Okay, where?"

"Nevada."

Shane turned and looked at Jim with raised eyebrows.

Jim asked, "Where in Nevada, not Vegas?"

Kay folded her arms. "If you agree to go, you'll be filled in as you go along. I'll need an answer soon."

"Say yes," Shane whispered loudly, with sarcastic secrecy.

Jim considered everything going on right now, which wasn't a whole lot. Besides the usual humdrum and daily grind, his schedule was pretty open at the moment.

"I guess I can," he finally said. "For how long?"

"Just a couple days. So, yes?"

He glanced at Shane again. "Sure."

Kay nodded, then turned and strolled out.

"I'll be filled in as I go along?" Jim said to Shane. "What is this, a *Mission Impossible* movie?"

"Close." Shane picked up another chocolate, this time a mini candy bar and turned to face Jim. "Are you ready to hear something cool?"

"Depends. Knowledge can be a terrible burden."

"Sure, but this is fun knowledge." He glanced around the room even though they knew they were alone.

Jim laughed. "Okay, you've got my attention."

"You know the Air Force has been looking at Helios, right?"

"Yeah, I'd heard. Couple different sites, or bases, or whatever they are."

"You ever hear of Groom Lake?"

For years, Jim held a fascination with the possibility of alien life and government coverups and knew some of the conspiracy theories. While he wasn't a fanatic, he'd watched his share of documentaries and immediately made the connection. "Sure, known to the world as the mysterious area fifty-one."

"Area what?" Shane said with a wink.

"Come on," Jim said. "Lincoln County, Nellis Air Force Base. The CIA officially acknowledged its existence in two-thousand thirteen. Didn't give any details of course, just said it was an air force base for developing new combat aircraft, like stealth bombers and spy planes. People have known about it since the fifties. UFO buffs were actually disappointed they didn't mention the flying saucers or alien bodies recovered at Roswell."

Shane was staring, chewing his chocolate. "Dang, you even know the county."

Jim shrugged. "I read things. You ever hear of Rachel, Nevada? Tiny trailer park town just north of area fifty-one. UFO seekers hang out there part of the year. Residents have been seeing strange flying objects for years."

"You believe all that?" Shane asked.

"The alien stuff? I don't have any concrete beliefs one way or the other. All I know is that sightings of unusual aircraft isn't proof of aliens."

"Okay, well, here's something that's real. Don't mention this to anyone. And don't tell Kay I told you. Something may fall through and you don't go."

Jim shook his head. "Are you about to tell me that Helios is being tested at area fifty-one?"

"Yep." Shane leaned in closer and lowered his voice. "There's a small testing stage in a section called 'S-thirty-eight,' an auxiliary facility adjacent to Papoose Lake. A fence with a turnstile portal was set up around two old storage warehouses and then Helios was installed to guard it. All sensors – cameras, motion, heat, weight, everything."

"Did you help set it up?" Jim asked.

Shane shook his head sadly. "No. I just prepped some of the hardware. Gerard and Mike did though. They wanted specialists. I'm more of an all-purpose guy. Besides, Kay wanted me to stay here to work through an SQL ORM problem we had going on. I was pissed. They told me all about it though."

Gerard Murray was an employee of a DOE laboratory in New Mexico but spent fifty percent of his time in California as a security design engineer for Helios. Mike Foster, a former Navy guy who had worked on weapons systems for nuclear submarines, was the resident database guru.

"For months they've been testing how good Helios is by trying to break it," Shane continued.

"And they broke it."

Shane paused then shrugged. "Not really, but they found something, yes."

Jim's mind reeled. A trip out there would actually be exciting. More exciting than anything he'd done in a long time. Besides, he hadn't been to Vegas in a couple years and the last time all he did was blow money on blackjack and an expensive hooker.

"Why would they want to send me?"

"Kay just said. They want an end user's trainer perspective."

"What did they find?"

Shane pursed his lips. "Can't go into that. Not yet."

"Shane …"

Shane laughed. "Just tell Kay you'll do it. Be an experience of a lifetime. They'll probably send Gerard with you."

Jim gathered up his notes and stood to leave. "Okay, thanks, Shane."

Shane smiled and grabbed another mini candy bar.

Chapter 9

Jim read the reply from Iris a second time.

A technical trainer? Interesting career. You must be good at putting information together and then transferring the knowledge. When I was younger, I thought about becoming a teacher, but the only thing I would even consider teaching is college. I couldn't deal with high school kids who didn't want to be there. LOL. But teaching college means getting a PhD :(I knew I would never have enough patience for that! But one thing I found out I was good at was graphic arts and design. I've won some contests. In fact, I designed my own avatar here. (Sorry, not bragging!) Recently, a book publisher hired me. They're doing a book about government coverups and wanted this really cool desert-looking scene with a flying saucer crash in the distance. I'm guessing New Mexico, right? I've had a ton of fun with it. I love that stuff. Tell me more about your training. What kind of subjects do you train?–Iris

Wow … She spoke his language on several different levels. He often used the term "knowledge transfer" when describing his work to others. In years prior, he'd also turned down teaching high school jobs for the exact same reason she described – he was only interested in adult learning. *And* she was intrigued with alien stuff? This was exciting him. It was starting to feel like too much excitement in one week. Should he be suspicious? His luck was never this good.

He began writing. He'd tell her something about his training but wouldn't go into a lot of detail or divulge where he worked yet. His employers wouldn't appreciate that.

Shortly after replying to Iris, Jim found himself staring out the window when a knock on his partially opened door startled him. Danny Weng, one of the lab's facility and equipment guys was standing in the doorway with a big grin. Weng was part of a group called UAD – Utilization and Destruction.

Everyone liked Danny. He wasn't quite thirty yet and still had the energy of a teenager, always smiling, always friendly. He typically donned a nice pair of dress slacks and a colorful dress shirt which always looked good on his trim and toned body. Today the shirt was a shiny purple.

"Danny, ni hao?" Jim said, fumbling the words.

Danny laughed. "Fine. I was in the neighborhood."

"You're spying on us again, Sir."

"You'd be surprised how many people put sensitive stuff in the regular garbage or the paper recycle bin that's clearly labeled: 'No sensitive material.'"

"I suppose. But even in this building?"

"Yep. That's why we keep our eyes, and ears, on everything."

"What a job."

"It's fun. Especially when we get to destroy classified equipment. We got all kinds of toys – pulverizes, incinerators, P-seven shredders –"

"Degaussers?"

"Yes! You ever used one of those?"

"No, but I've heard about them. What's a P-seven shredder?"

Danny leaned against the doorframe. "High security document shredding." He held out a hand and started tapping his fingers. "Stuff we shred around here like documents, maps, blueprints – in other words, 'flexible media' – even those older diskettes. For those we use shredding levels P-three through P-seven grading."

"I should be taking notes. I may have to train on this stuff someday."

"Our group already has comprehensive training."

"Oh okay, please continue."

"P-one shredding leaves paper strips a half inch wide, and P-two, a quarter inch wide; neither are acceptable here. Non-sensitive material starts at P-three, which leaves strips no wider than two millimeters. But for classified material, it's always P-seven, which not only creates strips no wider than one millimeter, but also adds cross-cut fragments no taller than five millimeters, making reconstructing data almost impossible."

"I just learned sum'm new. I can see why it's fun – destroying things all day."

"Not every day. It's actually kind of a pain in terms of process. Emails back and forth to the OSSIO, coordinating the removal with the Classified Admin Specialist and ISSO. That can take a couple weeks. But once that's done and everything's been certified, it needs to go to us within twenty-four hours, or you start the process all over. Happens all the time."

"Why?"

"Because things get tampered with. Once that safety orange 'DESTROY' sticker is on the computer or hard drive or whatever, it cannot be touched. If it's left for a few days somewhere, it's assumed someone messed with it, stole a drive out of it, copied something off it, whatever. That's why things need to be destroyed as soon as practical."

"So you gather them up and take them to the shredder."

"Well, we take them to a vault type room over in two thirty-eight. From there, material is carted to its final destination – paper to the shredders, electronic equipment like desktop chassis, laptops, solid state drives, external drives, et cetera, to the parking lot across from the old press room. In that big industrial white tent you've seen. The two EPA-compliant incinerators we have can destroy not only paper, but plastic and wood. But logistics and cost are an issue, so we shred whenever possible."

"That's quite an operation."

"Yeah, with a lot of rules, especially for hard drives. Once removed, they must be protected from anyone unauthorized or it's a data breach. The serial number of each drive is always recorded, and information linking the drive to the originating machine and user is logged. After going bye-bye, a certificate of destruction is issued with those numbers and info which the OISSO has to sign."

"So out there in that parking lot, you guys spend a lot of time disassembling machines to get at the data storing devices."

"You got it. And never alone. The policy is at least two people and a witness, like the system security officer. So no one pulls any hanky-panky. But we usually have three. Maybe you could come work for us some day."

"I'll think about it."

Just then, Jim's phone, resting on the desk in plain view beeped and vibrated. The Lǜ Chá app appeared, changing his phone's screen into a bright, fluorescent pink with a cute, winking girl in the middle.

Danny looked at it and smirked. Embarrassed, Jim swiped the phone off his desk and put it in his pocket.

Danny's smile vanished. "Sorry. I thought it said '*lǜ chá biǎo.*' I thought it was a joke."

Jim noticed that Danny pronounced the words with the subtleties of a native speaker. "I didn't know you spoke Chinese. It's actually just called *Lǜ Chá.*"

"I'm an ABC, but I spoke Mandarin at home growing up. I still speak it to my uncle and grandparents. I know some Cantonese from friends and family in Hong Kong."

"ABC?"

"American Born Chinese."

"Oh, right. So what's … *loo-cha-bee-oh?*"

Danny's smile returned. "*Lǜ chá biǎo* means, green tea bitch."

"Really?"

"Chinese slang. A girl who acts innocent and charming, but is actually a manipulative, calculating slut. The phrase was originally for actresses or models who hang around celebrities or politicians for personal gain, but it's made its way from high society to the workplace and schools, like a girl who pretends to be your friend but backstabs behind your back. With the apps' name and that girl I saw on the screen, it made me think that's what it was." He held up his hands. "Sorry, I'm not trying to pry or anything. I'll get going."

"No worries, Danny." Still embarrassed, Jim felt the need to explain himself a little. "It's kind of a dating app. The wife and I are on the brink, any time now. Just trying to get out, have some fun…"

Danny grinned. "Hey, you don't need my permission. Have fun. But be careful with those Chinese apps, they spy on you."

"Kinda like you do, right?"

Danny laughed, turned, and strolled out.

Jim stared at his phone. "Green tea bitch, huh," he muttered to himself. Opening his computer browser, he went to the lab's safe web site, a function that bypassed the institution's secure network. The lab encouraged employees to utilize this platform when doing legitimate things like banking or sending a quick email to family and friends.

Whoa to the idiot though who ever used it for gambling sites, running a side business, or surfing porn.

Opening his email, he entered the address of a buddy of his he had a beer with now and then.

Hey Gary, he typed. *I learned something interesting today from Danny Weng, a co-worker. Do you know what a "Green Tea Bitch" is in Chinese? Lol ...*

***

Hi Jimmy. Hope all is great, the note from Iris read. *Thanks for telling me a little more about yourself. I am gearing up to take a little trip to meet up with a girlfriend. Take some needed time off. I hope you get to do the same. After I get back, I'll shoot you a note and tell you about it. Any travel plans yourself?—Iris*

He loved the simplicity of this girl. Everything about her was appealing and he'd not even seen her real face. But since she designed her own avatar, it probably looked somewhat like her. He hoped, anyway.

He hit reply and typed, *I just so happen to be going to Las Vegas next week. Not just for fun. I'm actually going on business, but why not have some fun while I'm there? :) We can talk more when we both get back. Perhaps a quick phone chat? Take care, safe travels. – JC*

A reply came back within the hour.

Jimmy, you're not going to believe this. I'm going to Vegas too! Wow. Hey, I have an idea, if you feel like it. When was the last time you were on a blind date? I know it's taking a chance with me. But I promise not to disappoint ... too much? 8-P LOL. Let me know. We can meet at one of the big hotels, grab a drink. – Iris

Jim sat back grinning and shaking his head. Wow, wow, and wow. Every time it was more wow. It was almost too good. And what a coincidence. He excitedly hit reply and told her more about his upcoming trip.

Absolutely, he'd love to have a blind date.

Chapter 10

Deep under the bustling city of Beijing, Liang Huang let his gaze go back and forth between three different data reports he'd massaged into something organized. He mused to himself that while he never formally studied psychology, he'd become somewhat of a behavioral analyst in recent years.

He yawned; he'd been staring at this stuff nonstop for hours and knew a break was in order. Feeling his thoughts swimming, he paused, leaned back, and tried to perform some of the "mindfulness" exercises he'd learned about.

Closing his eyes, he tried to focus all attention to what was going on in his body and mind at the present moment. His thoughts immediately drifted to Polina, an indescribably beautiful Russian woman he'd had some recent covert correspondence with. Her glowing hazel eyes on a heart-shaped face looked right into him. And what was color of her hair, very light brown? Very dirty blonde? What a shame if that wasn't her real picture.

Oh wait, he wasn't supposed to let his mind drift. Back to here and now. But what was here and now? Just these reports. Did he accomplish all the to-do's from yesterday? No … stay here, today, now. Feel your heartbeat. Breathe deep, in and out. Listen to the hum of the computer cooling fans. Feel the fabric of the chairs.

Huang opened his eyes and laughed. What a stupid waste of time. Back to honing in on the subject's psychological attributes and what he'd learned so far.

His phone rang. "Huang."

"Mr. Huang," a voice said. "Would you be so kind as to come up to the seventh floor. There's someone who wishes to talk to you."

It wasn't a request. It never was. Huang's mind whirled. Was he in trouble? "Uh yes. You mean now?"

"Yes, now," the voice said with a touch of impatience.

Five minutes later, Huang was ushered into an office and introduced to a middle-aged woman called Doctor Shang. She looked Huang up and down with a round, pudgy face that expressed impassive curiosity. Her graying hair was cut short, almost in a man's style.

Huang gave a small bow and sat.

"Mr. Huang, I am a behavioral psychologist from the Psychological Society."

Huang immediately felt red flags. The Chinese Psychological Society was a non-profit academic organization. For her to be here meant she was more likely from the State Council which regulated the Minority Health Disparities Research and Education Act, among other government policies. He needed to be careful.

"We're in the process of evaluating worker's performance as well as creative and independent thinking," Shang continued.

It's always in the guise of something positive, Huang thought to himself.

After a pause, Dr. Shang said, "I understand you've become quite knowledgeable in human personality attributes."

"I suppose that's become one of my de facto specialties," said Huang. "But not the way most think of it."

"Please elaborate."

"Well, most generalize the concept, reducing it to 'quiet and reserved' versus 'loud and outgoing,' but there's so much more."

"Such as?"

You're asking me? Maybe he could impress his superiors with this. He sat back. "At a deeper level, it's distinguishing biopsychosocial characteristics, which include traits related to general mood and worldview, as well as values, goals, and motivations."

"And you use this as part of your work?"

"Absolutely. Almost all interaction with the digital world, whether social media or not, reveals something about an individual's personality. Traits, as you know, are the more consistent ways of thinking, behaving, and feeling across different situations. Values are things most important to a person. With this data, one can make predictions about a person."

"And do you find your predictions to be accurate?"

"Well, some are obvious. For example, people who love their occupation will inevitably make more money than their counterparts who dislike or find no meaning in what they do. But some are not. For example, the top five professions where there are both higher rates of and longer lasting marriages are clergy, directors and educators of religious activities, firefighters, dentists, and architectural and engineering managers."

"How do you feel about that?"

Huang paused. He was definitely being tested. "I don't really think anything of it. It's just data to me."

Dr. Shang raised her eyebrows and then looked down and jotted some notes. "Please, continue."

Huang folded his hands. "Patterns of traits and values can be measured. People can generally be categorized by their openness, introversion versus extraversion, conscientiousness, agreeableness, and emotional stability. Once this is translated to numbers, you can identify values that are universally recognized – altruism, taking pleasure in life, achieving success and so on. Values are always closely tied to self-perception, personal goals, and behavioral patterns. As such, values can also make reasonably accurate predictions about a person's life, including their physical and mental health, longevity, quality of relationships, and antisocial behavior." Huang paused, then said, "These predictions can be used to manipulate conduct for the advancement of the land of our ancestors."

Dr. Shang looked up, sensing Huang's phoniness, a knowing smile on her lips. "And where is all this data acquired?"

Huang chided himself while he took a deep breath. "Every time people interact online, digital fingerprints are left behind revealing traces of personality. With every website visited, every email sent, blog post written or replied to, these traces can be recorded. Images, videos, or comments that a person casually 'likes' or 'dislikes' can add up to attitudes and beliefs."

"Example."

"Well, forty percent of 'tweets' contain an image, from which themes and patterns emerge that can determine a person's social, political, and religious beliefs. Of course, I'm talking about the Western world; we have wisely blocked this app."

Dr. Shang smiled, then nodded for him to continue.

"Like so many puzzle pieces, this data can be put together to see a bigger picture about a single life or a group of lives. Data is collected everywhere now. Digital book readers document the speed at which a person reads. Phone apps record driving habits, patterns, and locations, whether driving or just walking by a cell tower. Before mobile phones, manufacturers installed chips in cars that documented every location that car has been, but that information had to be manually downloaded. Today the data is in real time."

Huang started to mention something but stopped himself knowing the good doctor would see his disdain for it. It was an experiment recently started in Beijing. Bus drivers are being told to wear electronic bracelets that track their emotions, blood pressure, exercise, and sleep patterns. As the drivers go about their routines, the smart wristbands measure biometrics in real time to detect anxiety, sickness, and overall fitness. The claim is that this will "improve safety." If successful, however, it will be used on other types of workers, and eventually on everyone.

He continued. "Even if someone online posts with as much anonymity as they can, trying to mask who they really are, social media profiles can be used to accurately predict a person's age, real gender versus gender identity, political orientation, physical and mental stability, financial health, conflicts among friends and or family, demographics, and a person's overall emotional consistency." He stopped and waited but Dr. Shang only silently jotted on her notepad.

"Tell me more about these digital fingerprints," she finally said.

"In essence, it shows who a person is, from their most public persona right down to the most private moments. It's the epitome of what Sigmund Freud called 'Free Association,' like one big worldwide therapy session without anyone aware they're being studied."

Dr. Shang smiled in a way to suggest she was impressed with Huang.

Huang thought of something else he could talk about but didn't want to. It was what social media was doing particularly to young people around the world, at least with those that had access. While some youth find meaningful relationships online, many more are distracted by it, having their sleep disrupted, and exposing them to bullies, harassment, rumor spreading, and unrealistic views of other people's lives. This was causing an uptick in depression and anxiety, amplified when prevented from going online at all. And on platforms where the focus is sharing one's image and opinions, there are many who fall into narcissistic behaviors. But the Chinese government loved the fact that youth were attracted to it – it made keeping tabs on them easier.

Adults were different. Most spend far less time online and think of it in more practical terms. Sure, some use it to exaggerate their achievements and socioeconomic status, but most engage to either maintain what they consider to be genuine friendships, seek employment, promote a business, and of course, online shopping, which says a lot about a person in and of itself. Another large percentage were there to seek illegal or immoral activities.

"Tell me about this person of interest, this American, that you are looking at now," Dr. Shang said, eyeing him carefully.

The doctor had obviously been briefed. Huang gathered his thoughts. "This particular person doesn't have a lot of social media. He isn't on many of the usual places including the very popular BitBok, which has become a goldmine of data on American social and economic life. But this person has tried a couple of BitBok's spinoff apps. Like most, he probably has no idea they're tied to each other."

"If he doesn't have much social media, why did you pick him?"

"Because he has weaknesses that can be exploited. Breaking him down wasn't difficult. If he were a criminal, he'd be what the American FBI calls 'organized,' meaning, everything he does is premeditated and carefully planned. This person is stable, but definitely has some antisocial characteristics. He isn't insane, which as you know is not considered a medical diagnosis. He knows right from wrong, or perceived right and wrong, but makes 'wrong' choices anyway. He appears to show little remorse for things he's done repeatedly, like frequently binge drink, hire escorts, cheat a little on his taxes, and lie to others about who he really is online."

"I see," Dr. Shang said, nodding and taking notes.

"He can't be underestimated though," Huang continued. "Historically, these types are above average in intelligence and this individual has an advanced college degree. He comes from a stable home with educated and employed parents. Organized criminals also tend to be above average in attractiveness, though not necessarily what others might describe as beautiful or sexy. They tend to be married or at least living with a domestic partner, and this subject is married but now appears to be seeking another partner anyway. And not just a fling this time, but an actual lover. They tend to be steadily employed, skilled in several areas, orderly and able to scheme while others around them remain unaware. They also have some degree of social grace, and may even be charming, though this subject doesn't appear to be. He strikes me as someone who could possibly be social and gregarious if he put out the effort but chooses not to." Huang paused and suddenly realized he felt like he was describing himself in many ways. He looked up to see Dr. Shang watching him.

He quickly continued. "Target subjects like this, if criminal, go to great lengths to cover their tracks and are often forensically savvy – they understand investigation methods. But beyond occasionally using an alias or false image, this subject has viewed and posted many things under his real name. Doesn't matter, since it all traces back to the same mobile phone and laptop IP addresses, MAC addresses and corresponding locations."

Although there were many tools for analyzing online behavior, Huang preferred good old-fashioned human intelligence-gathering. Hard data gained from searching online for links and connections, which make handy references. Eventually, with enough due diligence, you'll achieve the objective. This is how the American CIA tracked down Osama Bin Laden. But he didn't want to get into all that.

He continued. "Social networking sites always provide the most valuable information, unless the subject is a loner who doesn't communicate much. This subject is almost that. He doesn't participate in on-line discussion groups dedicated to political or ideological causes. He doesn't befriend any known criminals or terrorists on anyone's watchlist. This guy appears to be somewhat careful, but not the way a paranoid person would be." Huang smiled. "He thinks he can get by with aliases or just his first name, and browsers that don't track usage. To boot, none of his communications are even encrypted."

"Okay," Dr. Shang said. "So what have you learned so far?"

Huang shrugged. "For starters, although the subject had married a Caucasian, he loves Asian girls. A quick trip down his browser history and emails and forum posts reveals someone with not only a fascination, but a fetish for what Americans call the 'Asian persuasion.'"

Dr. Shang snorted in disgust.

Huang continued. "And this started before his current marriage. Years of bouncing back and forth online between hardcore pornography to dating sites to mail order bride sites, shows clearly what piques his interest. But recent activity suggests he's slowed down as he's gotten older. Now his interests vary, and sometimes he seeks out women of all ethnicities, but eighty-three percent of his time is still focused on women from Asian backgrounds."

"Give me some examples of his behavior."

"Under different aliases, the subject had made comments like 'She's hot!' or 'Where can I find this girl?' and 'Damn, what a MILF.' Each time it was for an Asian woman, typically Chinese or Korean, under the age of thirty. But more recently, another pattern has emerged. He began saying things like, 'Too sexy – she'd never go for me,' and 'If only there was such thing as real love.' So it appears he's starting to lose confidence or self-esteem, or always had the problem. As well, he's growing weary of the fantasy of having some beautiful Asian model be attracted to him."

Dr. Shang looked hard at Huang and said, "Many men have this fantasy, don't they?" She had a knowing glint in her eye that made Huang uncomfortable.

He warily continued. "Under his real name, his life is rather dull and innocuous. He listens to a lot of music in the Western 'classic rock' genre from the '80s and watches 'fail' videos, bits from older television comedies, likes whisky, with a preference for Johnnie Walker Black Label, and the most amusing, a mild preoccupation with alien encounters and government conspiracies. The waters are already being tested with some of this information."

Dr. Shang chuckled. "Aliens ..." she said, writing notes.

"Recently, under his alias, the subject made brief contact with someone on one of BitBok's spinoff apps. But I quickly took control of that situation so we can now communicate directly with him."

Dr. Shang looked up. "You seem to be going to a lot of effort to exploit some run of the mill American government worker."

"Well, yes, but he has top secret clearance and possibly access to valuable secrets that might be useful. What is more crucial though is his ties to another person of great interest to the CCP."

"And who might that be?"

Huang hesitated. This smelled like another test. "I would need to talk to my superiors before I said anything about that," he finally said.

Dr. Shang's smile dropped and she stared at him for a moment. Then she stood and said, "Thank you, that will be all."

The door opened and someone gestured for Huang to leave. He was escorted back to the elevator. Back in his workspace, he sat for a moment trying to understand what just happened. No time to speculate – his work was being thoroughly scrutinized and he had to move quickly. Grabbing his phone, he dialed the five-digit extension to the MSS' Foreign Infiltration Office, although it wasn't officially called that.

"Yes?" a curt female voice asked.

"I need to put in a request for a bait and switch team, time urgent." Huang said.

"How many operatives?" the voice asked.

Huang thought for a moment. A seasoned female operative was already engaged with the subject and ready to travel. "Two. One female and one photo-video expert, gender not relevant."

"Will the age bracket be critical?"

"Yes, for the female. She needs to be underaged."

"Location?"

"Las Vegas, Nevada."

Chapter 11

The work week flew by with appalling speed and Jim Mueller found himself tapping the steering wheel as he drove to Oakland International Airport to catch a Southwest flight. He was singing, "It feels so good, feelin' good again ..." to Robert Earl Keen's famous song. He wasn't a Country fan, but Keen had written a couple he liked.

The fact was, it had been a long time since he'd felt this elated. How good could his luck be? He was getting paid to travel to an extremely unique and hopefully very interesting place, *and* meet a woman he was excited to see. Sure, nothing at all may come of this chance encounter with Iris, if that was even her name. But what better place to have it than Vegas? Plenty of other things to do if that didn't work out.

He turned the radio on to his favorite classic rock station and drove the rest of the way to the tunes of the Steve Miller Band, Tom Petty, and Pink Floyd. In high school, like so many kids, Jim had gone through the wannabe rock star stage. He played guitar mostly but had taught himself a little bass and drums as well. He'd hooked up with some decent enough musicians but saw right away how powerful personality and ego conflicts could be and marveled at the longevity of famous groups that had been around for decades. For a place to practice, they had rotated garages of band member's homes, at least where their parents put up with the noise. It seemed to be going along okay and they'd even come up with a couple original songs. But by the third year of college, the original lead guitarist had quit, the rest were making plans to go their separate ways, and the dream fizzled.

Jim was trying to imagine what he was going to see in Nevada. Everyone has seen that famous photo of Area 51 someone had taken with a telephoto lens from a nearby hill showing the rows of white-colored buildings in the far distance, the image a bit blurry and obscured from the waves of rising heat. As well, the satellite picture that shows the huge runways adjacent to those buildings. But that was back when people could get a little closer. Since then, they had pushed the surrounding viewing places back further so that now, Tikaboo Peak was the closest one could legally get. And it's not much of a view, twenty-six miles away.

Jim was glad his interest in alien conspiracies wasn't enough to drive him to make such excursions. The two-hour drive from Vegas to Tikaboo wouldn't be so bad, but then one needed a four-wheel drive for a rough twenty-five-mile climb, then a steep, long and hot hike to the peak with as much water as one could carry, and very powerful binoculars. So he'd read. Ten years ago, maybe, not now.

After the almost hour of waiting in line, getting checked and x-rayed by security and having his luggage searched, Jim found himself in a plastic seat at Terminal 2 eating a breakfast sandwich and a small orange juice that had cost fifteen dollars.

Gerard Murray strode up and sat down next to Jim. "Mornin'," he said.

Jim hardly knew Gerard but had liked what few encounters they'd had. The man was big, easily six-two, 250, but not because of being overweight. He had a stout, stocky build, like one who had played football in prior years.

Gerard once referred to himself as a "Leprecano" because his father was Irish and his mother was Mexican. The blend gave him a unique appearance, a chiseled face with a smooth beige skin tone and dark eyes, a look that probably would have worked well in Hollywood. With his cropped hair and medium length beard, it wouldn't surprise Jim to learn the man had been a Navy Seal or something. Jim himself was some blend of English, Irish and German, which gave him a distinct, garden variety white-boy look.

"Morning," Jim replied cheerfully.

Gerard could make light conversation, but for the most part was a bit aloof. No one took that as arrogance or standoffishness though. When he wanted to connect, he was very upfront and friendly, before reverting to his quiet, concentrating-on-something self. He went about his daily work thoughtfully and diligently, always minding his own business. Kay Allison loved him.

Jim decided to attempt a little conversation. "How many times you been out there?" he asked.

Gerard was peeling the lid off a coffee he'd just picked up. He took a careful sip and grimaced. "This stuff is crap. Glad we get reimbursed." He took another sip then set it down. "Nevada? Four times. This'll be my fifth."

"Why so many times, the Helios area fifty-one testing?"

Gerard smiled and glanced around. "You need to speak a little louder. The people three terminals down didn't quite hear you."

"Right," Jim said, feeling foolish. He took a long pull on his orange juice.

"You brought your badge, right?" Gerard asked. "Without it, you're not going anywhere near this place."

"Yep, in my luggage."

Gerard picked up his coffee. "You oughta carry it on your person in case something happens to your bag. You can buy new underwear, but the badge will be harder to replace."

Jim tipped his small rolling suitcase flat on the ground and unzipped it. "Why do we need the badge anyway? Where we're going isn't even DOE, is it?"

"Not our final destination, no. But first, we're going to go through a DOE facility."

"Where they did all the nuclear bomb testing in the fifties?"

"That's the one. First above ground then under 'til ninety-six when Clinton stopped it. You can see all the craters from the blasts."

"Why go through there?" Jim asked while slipping his badge lanyard over his head.

"Well, first off, to talk some of the Helios users at the *MAF*."

"*Mauf?*"

"M, A, F. Mechanism Assembly Facility. Maybe you've seen pictures of it from a distance on the official website. Looks like a long, narrow concrete prison in the middle of the desert, but there's elevators that take you a thousand feet underground. The idea is, if someone down there ever accidentally, or deliberately, sets off a nuke, most of the blast will stay underground."

"Makes sense. Anyone I know, the Helios people?"

Gerard blew on his coffee, sending a small cloud of steam out of the cup. "Doubt it. They've seen all your training stuff though. The system manager is a gal named Carol Rollinson. She's okay, needs a lot of handholding though. Drives the problem-fixers like Shane nuts. She's not been nice to this new gal out there named Suzanne. Been protective about her job, doesn't like to delegate or train others. I may as well stop by and see how they're getting along. Since we'll be in town."

"Will we get to go into the assembly facility?"

"Sure. I'll get us a tour. Just remember, no electronics of any kind allowed in, not even a car key. They've got those lockers up top."

"Nice."

Gerard took a long sip, draining half the cup in one shot. "Helios watches the MAF inside and out. I helped design the alarm sectors. Besides all the sensors, it manages the booths in and out, and knows every worker's average weight on a typical day. So if, one day, a worker stepped into one and weighed twenty-five pounds heavier than normal, an alarm would be sent and that worker is stuck 'til guards let 'im out and search 'im. It also watches for radioactive materials passing through."

Jim almost mentioned running into the schematics of one of those booths online but didn't want to get anyone in trouble. Heck, maybe it was Gerard who had posted it.

"I didn't know Helios was out there," Jim said.

"You're not supposed to. It's been in testing for three years, but the entire perimeter was finally certified just a couple months ago. Now it's official."

"Why is it faster to get to area fifty-one going through where the MAF is?"

"It's not really, depending on where you're going. You know where the official main gates are to area fifty-one, right? The famous mailbox and the back gate?"

"I've read about it, but never been." Jim's curiosity was thoroughly piqued. "You've been there?"

Gerard paused and closed his eyes in thought while taking another gulp of coffee. "You go up I-fifteen north for maybe twenty-five miles, then exit sixty-four for US-ninety-three north, the Great Basin highway. Somewhere up there you go left and head out into the desert. Looks like you're going nowhere for like eighty or ninety miles. You'll pass through Alamo and Ash Springs. Gas up there if you have to. Eventually you run into a fork in the road, go left and you'll end up on state highway three seventy-five, aka, the 'Extraterrestrial Highway.'"

"I've seen pictures of the sign."

"Yeah, everyone takes a pic at that sign. Just up the ET, you'll see the Alien Research Center – supposed to be a museum, but it's really a trinket shop. Pick up your 'I Love Greys' t-shirt there. Finally, you'll run into the famous black mailbox, which I've heard someone painted white. The unmarked road just past the mailbox goes down to the official front gate, which is only a big sign that says keep out. Keep going and you'll run into the 'A'Le'Inn,' a restaurant-bar-gift shop, home of the 'World Famous Alien Burger.'" He used his fingers as quotes. "The dirt road to the back gate veers off highway three seventy-five; it's the only road. The back gate is more interesting because there is an actual gate on a dirt road in the middle of a field with a few cameras and a guard shack. Otherwise no fence. You can see guards watching you."

"So you could just drive around the gate then."

"If you're in the mood to get arrested and charged with trespassing. Not to mention an ungodly fee to have your car towed back to Vegas. They're authorized to use deadly force by the way, if they think you're capable of being deadly yourself. But most people they deal with are stupid kids and UFO nuts."

"So what route are we taking?"

"From north Vegas, the same as everyone else, up ninety-five. In Indian Springs we're gonna pass by Creech Air Force Base, America's drone hub. The main runway is parallel to the freeway and entrance gate. Interesting sight. You'll notice the whole place is surrounded by a cable-enforced fence built to stop cars or trucks from crashing through. The drones are huge. Imagine something the size of a Learjet. They fly all around the globe on randomized routes and varying patterns and often low between mountains so they're hard to track."

"Wow. Jeremy's gonna love this."

"Jeremy?"

"My brother, two years older."

Gerard shrugged. "Didn't know you had a brother."

"Yeah, he looks a lot like me, but better looking. He wanted to be a pilot when he was kid. Never panned out. Can I take pics of the drones without having a Hellfire shot at me?"

Gerard chuckled. "People take pics all the time from the freeway or fence. I doubt we're gonna stop though. What's he do?"

"Jeremy? He's a pastor of a small congregation up near Redding."

"A pastor. Really."

"Why?"

"My mother wanted me to be a priest. No way."

"I hear you. Dealing with people all day. You gotta love people to have that job." *And not be a wretched, pleasure-seeking sinner like me*, Jim thought to himself.

"Anyway," Gerard continued. "After that there's not much, some Joshua trees and an Indian reservation. If you're into cigars, you can get 'em cheap there. After that, because we're the privileged DOE employees we are, we're gonna turn off a road toward a little place called Mercury. It's not open to the public."

"I'd never have guessed there's a town way out there."

"Technically a village. You'll find it interesting the first time you see it. Then it's just another hot, boring place. There's a big cafeteria that's pretty nice though. They serve a helluva grilled Southwest chicken sandwich."

Jim stuffed the last of the breakfast sandwich in his mouth and washed it down with the last of the orange juice.

"What am I gonna see there?"

"You ask a lot of questions."

"I hear that occasionally."

Gerard drained the rest of the coffee down. "Mercury itself isn't large, but the rest of the test site is huge. After getting through main gate, you'll see all manner of both standard looking military and research equipment as well as weird and different stuff – giant tents, containers, bridge-length sized roles of cable, odd-shaped vehicles, roving radar trucks, and so on. Keep going northwest and it's another forty-minute drive to the MAF. To get in there you need to get through another set of gates and guards and be HRP."

"A gate within a gate. Dang. I'm not HRP though."

"I know. I'll be your escort. After we visit, there's this dirt road nearby I'll take you on. All around on both sides are dozens of craters from all the testing back in the days. It looks like you're driving across part of the moon or something. Kinda resembles a giant slab of Swiss cheese on satellite images. You can also see parts of when they did the above ground testing, like structures to simulate houses and office buildings to see how they'd handle the blasts. There's a slightly disturbing part too where they marked off areas to place cows and other animals at different proximities to the explosions to see at what point living things could survive. We're gonna go past this spot on a hill where you can still see the benches where the generals and others used to sit and watch the testing. You'll be tempted to take pictures, but don't."

"I won't. Even if I did, I'd not sell 'em to the tabloids."

Gerard smirked. "You'd be better off selling them to China."

"Why's that?"

"Giving or selling secrets to America's enemies is slightly better than sharing them with the media because at least the enemy won't tell the general public."

Jim shook his head. "That's crazy."

Gerard continued. "Anyway, at the end of this road is a huge crater where they lit up a one hundred and four-kiloton bomb in sixty-two. The hole is freakin' huge – six hundred feet deep and over a thousand feet across. Displaced 11,000,000 tons of earth. It's kinda eerie to think humans can engineer that kind of power from stuff they pull out of the ground."

"It's not radioactive?"

"It still is, especially if you went down inside the crater. There's a chart there that tells you how much radiation you're exposed to and how it's decreased over the years to where it's safe enough now. If you keep following the little road north of this big-ass crater, you'll end up at an unofficial southern entrance to area fifty-one."

"No one's gonna shoot at us, right?"

Gerard shook his head. "There'll be people expecting us. Believe me, I wouldn't make the attempt otherwise."

"I'm surprised they'd let us in through the backdoor."

"They do it for selfish reasons, less security hassles. The Helios beta test setup is actually much closer and kinda on the way if we go via this route than if we went around through the official front gate. This way, we won't see any of the actual site you've seen in photos, which is still way north."

"Oh, disappointing. I wanted to see the runways and hangers."

Gerard laughed. "If you worked there, you'd fly in at night so you can't see much. Small, unmarked airbus that takes off from Harry Reid every evening. When you're on site, guards escort you back and forth to just where you need to go, and don't even think about taking a stroll around the place. If you think need-to-know is bad where we work … You might work there for years and have no idea what's going on in the floor above you."

"Well that last part sounds familiar. But at least we can take a lunch walk where we work."

"Yeah. Just remember, you'll be in DOD territory. Their pissing ground, their rules."

"Can you tell me what the issue was they found, or is that classified?"

"We shouldn't talk about it here, but I can give you a quick overview. The nice thing is that it's not Helios' fault." Gerard leaned in and lowered his voice. "You know that touchless badge reader on the inside of the door to the Helios lab? Not the main door, the side door next to the test console."

"I think so, yeah. Just wave your card over it and it reads it and unlocks the door."

"Right. Well, lab's policy is that we don't put those on the outside of sensitive places. Only to exit from the inside. This way, Helios knows who's still in the room and who's already left."

"Makes sense. No PIN or anything required."

"Right. And say you're in a vault type room and supposed to be out by a certain time, but Helios thinks you're still there because you piggybacked with someone else leaving. It'll send an alarm."

"Console operators must go nuts seeing all those flashing icons on the map."

"Yeah. But the real problem is there's people who know how to clone cards with them. That split second when the card's info is passed wirelessly to the reader. We only use the high frequency readers because unlike the low, they provide cryptography when transmitting the card's ID to the reader. It used to be only the low frequency was cloneable, but now the high is as well. And you had to have the cloner close by. But someone over there figured out how to do it remotely with some laser-based scanner, like two hundred feet away or something."

"Serious?"

"Yeah, and through walls. They've got smart people out there. So they've had Kay and someone else working on a way to encrypt the transmission back to the reader."

"Why don't they just do like us and only put them on the inside of sensitive places?"

"They probably do, I dunno. But they still want this fixed regardless. They've been using the low frequency ones out there for years, figuring no one could get that far in, in the first place. But they're in upgrade mode now – newer, better security and all that. So they're demanding a solution before moving forward. But it looks like we'll have one soon."

"Otherwise Helios has been working fine?"

"Like a champ, from what I understand."

"This is gonna be fun to write about."

Gerard laughed.

"Shane was laughing at me about the alien conspiracy stuff out there," Jim said.

Gerard looked down in thought, as if considering if he should say something, and then finally did. "You knew my dad was a prof at AIT, the high-tech school in Athlone?"

"I don't even know where Athlone is."

"Dead center of Ireland on the River Shannon. Anyway, he was a chemist and helped NASA solve the problem they had with the space shuttle's solid fuel. The ammonium perchlorate was oxidizing the aluminum too quickly once it reached about ninety thousand feet. They don't jettison the booster rockets until about a hundred and forty something thousand."

Jim just stared stupidly.

"Well, he got around and knew people. One of them was a retired NASA engineer who volunteered to go out to area fifty-one and look at a 'propulsion system' they were trying to reverse engineer. This was before it was even called area fifty-one and you couldn't find the place on official maps of Nevada. Totally credible guy. Nothing to gain by lying. Think about it. If scientists are trying to reverse engineer something, you gotta wonder where *on earth* it originated. They flew him in one evening and he was taken into some highly secured facility, thoroughly searched and screened, and led way underground to a nuclear bomb proof bunker. He looked this thing up and down for about a half hour in bewilderment, as everyone stood around in silence. Finally, he said, 'This isn't from around here, is it?' Immediately, they ushered him out, drove him back to Vegas to the airport, and he never heard from them again. I think they just used him to verify that in his opinion, human technology wasn't responsible for whatever the hell it was. Probably did that to a handful of scientists."

"Wow. You think it's true?"

Gerard shrugged. "Like I said, he had nothing to gain. Never tried to publicize or sell his story. Never told any other stories."

"They won't arrest me if I ask to see the flying saucers Bob Lazar worked on, will they?"

"You're free to ask whatever you want, but you won't get any straight answers."

Chapter 12

The ninety-minute flight went by fast because Jim's thoughts were running wild. He didn't sit next to Gerard as they'd made their own reservations. Just as well, he sensed Gerard had talked about as much as he wanted for now. They weren't staying at the same hotel either. The plan was that Gerard was going to pick Jim up at 6:00 a.m. tomorrow morning, they'd grab breakfast, then begin the drive north out of Vegas.

As the plane soared above the clouds, he thought of the conversation he was going to have with Jeremy. Jim's relationship with his brother had had its ups and downs. As a child, the family attended church here and there, but not regularly. By the time Jim was fourteen, he was already a bit of a loose cannon, while Jeremy was the straight shooter and compliant one. By the time Jim was seventeen, and after hearing more than once that the porn and pot he occasionally enjoyed was going to send him to Hell, he knew he didn't like church and began avoiding it. In his mind, church was just another gathering of people – that meant people games, people politics, people power plays, and tight members-only social cliques. It also meant scorn and judgement. Sure, there were many that were genuine, but Jim always felt like he had to wade through a lot of mud to get to those individuals.

Jeremy, on the other hand, was always right at home in church. And it wasn't because he was some gregarious socialite. Both brothers had inherited their mother's quiet, introspective, and rather phlegmatic personality. In fact, Jim had always wished he'd been different, more comfortable around people in general. He'd watch as Jeremy chatted easily with small groups around him and wonder why it came naturally to his sibling while it was such a struggle for him.

Jim did end up going back to church a few years later to celebrate Jeremy getting officially ordained. Jim had enjoyed himself in the beginning – the stories and music were nice. Then he listened to several speakers, one annoyingly taking the opportunity for a brief swipe at gay people, and another doling out the usual stuff about how people walk away from their faith only because they want to engage in decadent behavior. Such people, of course, ruined their lives and ended up miserable. This bothered Jim and he almost wanted to walk out. He wasn't gay, but always thought homosexuals should be left alone. And no one ever talked about how there are plenty who leave church, not to go crazy and "sin" at every opportunity, but because they genuinely didn't see evidence of what was being preached.

Sure, Jim had had his share of fooling around, but at least he wasn't a hypocrite. There were more than a few infamous stories. He didn't start a church and preach for years only to admit having a gay sex affair with a male prostitute or get caught in a motel room with a hooker. And how many flushed their faith down the toilet when all the post-mortem dirt regarding sexual misconduct and abuse came out about one of the most admired apologists ever? The list goes on.

Jim had gone home that day realizing that while he had held a dislike for all religious believers of all stripes for a long time, it had more or less simmered down to a mild indifference. This was good because he liked Jeremy as a person and wanted to maintain a relationship with him.

"So you blame God because of the sinful choices of people?" Jeremy asked one day when they were having the conversation.

Jim: "No, I don't blame or hate something I'm not sure is there. But yeah, I do hate hypocrites."

Jeremy: "Well, we're talking about two different issues. But to the second one, I strive to still love the person, no matter what their choices."

Jim: "So God, assuming he's there, hates the sin, but still loves the sinner?"

Jeremy: "It's a tough concept to get philosophical about. Sin doesn't exist on its own; it has no moral attribute apart from the person who commits it. We're all morally culpable for our choices. So when God is judging sin, he's judging the person who made the choice, not the sin itself."

Jim: "You keep talking about choice. A liar or a shoplifter knows they're doing something wrong. But what about a gay person who says, I'm not doing anything wrong, I'm just being who I am? Didn't they discover a 'homosexual gene,' as well as an 'alcoholism gene.' And a 'warrior gene,' which makes people unusually aggressive?"

Jeremy: "Blaming genes is a convenient way of absolving one of personal responsibility. A lot of that stuff though is the environment a child grows up in. A child sees a parent deal with stress by drinking, so they learn the behavior. And even if there's some truth to that, genes don't control a person like a programmed robot. You may have a propensity for temper tantrums, for example, but that doesn't mean you deliberately give in until you're angry enough to kill someone."

These conversations never did go much beyond an agreement to disagree and with Jeremy saying that you either believe there is a God you will face someday, or you don't. Jim didn't know what he really believed.

While Jim thought Jeremy was nuts to devote his life to faith and ministry, a part of him admired his brother for finding what was clearly his calling. As for Jim, it was pretty obvious that in recent years, certain choices had brought pain into his life. He knew he drank too much. He knew he lusted and ultimately, that became the catalyst for the first time he cheated on Vaneesa.

Sitting on the bed in a hotel room in North Las Vegas, he hit the autodial for Jeremy's number. It rang three times and was picked up.

"Hello?"

"Jeremy!"

"Jimmy? My word. How are you?"

"Oh, not bad. Hey, you'll never guess where I am."

"Well let's see, I don't hear anything in the background. You're right, I won't guess."

"Vegas."

He heard Jeremy chuckle in a way that had an *uh oh* attached to it. "Judging by your excitement, you didn't win a big jackpot, did you?"

"I might have. We'll see. Got a hot date."

"Well, I'm happy for you, but I'd be happier if you got officially divorced before doing things like this."

"I know, I know …"

"What's her name and where did you meet?"

"Oh, uh … Iris. Don't wanna go too much into it until I know something may work out."

"Understood. I will pray for you and Iris. But I'm also praying for you and Vaneesa."

"Don't bother with Vaneesa."

"Jimmy …" Jeremy sighed. "Alright. So why are you in Las Vegas? Not just for this hot date."

One of the qualities he liked about Jeremy was that he respected boundaries. "No. You ever hear of Creech Airforce Base?"

"Vaguely. Where they remote control the drones around the world? Is that near Las Vegas?"

"About seventy miles north of Vegas. I'm gonna see it tomorrow. Or drive by it anyway. I'll try to get some pictures for you."

"That's kind, Jimmy, thanks. I thought you didn't like travel anymore."

"I don't. But this is an opportunity of a lifetime. That's why I'm in such a great mood."

"Why is the laboratory sending you to Creech Airforce Base?"

"Well they're not sending me there. I'm just going by there. My real destination is classified."

"Oh there you go again with that mysterious top secret talk."

"It's important work."

"I'm sure it is, or you wouldn't be doing it. We're proud of you."

"We? I'm sure *they're* proud of *you*. Not so sure about me."

"Jimmy … I used to envy you growing up. Did you know that?"

"Me? Why?"

"Because you're smart. And a brilliant artist. And determined. You put your head to something and go for it and become great at it. I bumbled around for a long time. But finally I gave up searching on my own and turned to a higher power."

"The highest power I've ever heard of is nuclear power. In fact, I'm gonna see some of what it's done soon." At first, Jim meant the comment humorously, but then realized he believed it.

"Nuclear power comes from uranium, right?" Jeremy asked. "Who created that, and who gave humans the ability to engineer it?"

"Well, okay." Jim didn't want to argue with someone for whom God was the fill-in answer to every unanswered gap.

"Jimmy, I'm not preaching to you. I'm glad you called. It's good to hear from you."

"I haven't felt this excited in a while."

"Why's that?"

"Oh, I dunno. Been in a humdrum with Vaneesa. You know. This is new. Different."

"Sure."

"At least I've got a job doing what I'm good at – writing and training. I'd like to say it's my life's pursuit. But I'm not so sure."

"Do you have peace about what you're doing?"

"Usually, yeah."

"Well, that's the telltale sign that you're not where you should be. If there's that feeling in your gut. I don't suppose you pray about your situation?"

"Uhm, well, it's been some time."

"I understand."

"When were you ordained anyway?"

"Oh goodness, going on fifteen years now."

"And you really think that's your calling?"

"If I'm reading between the lines, you mean could I have done something … *more* with my life?"

"No, no, I didn't mean that."

Jeremy chuckled. "It's okay. I wanted to fly jet fighter planes when I was a kid, you knew that. But what I am doing now gives me peace and joy, so I'd say yes. If I'd gone with my plans and didn't find that peace, would it still have been *more?* What I am doing now is the highest calling I could have taken."

"You really believe that?"

"We live in a broken world, Jimmy. I've been called to stand in the gap. I'm seeing an entire young generation running around getting high, committing crimes and having sex with whoever they want and thinking these things have no impact on real life. But all behavior has consequences. A whole segment of the population without any feelings of shame for what they do to themselves and others. Is this our country's future? Do you think hatred and evil will go unpunished? I try to teach the truth because nothing is sacred anymore. I couldn't think of any other work more fulfilling."

"I hear you, Jeremy."

"Sorry, that's the preacher in me rearing its head."

"It's okay."

There was a long pause, then Jeremy said, "Since you brought up the subject of calling … one of things that's broken my heart over the years is seeing you unhappy and dissatisfied. Not with your work, but with yourself."

"What makes you think I'm unhappy?"

"You've told me. The drinking. The fooling around. The self-medication. I'm not judging you. I've had my share of struggles. I just worry for you sometimes."

"Why?"

"You've been successful, so you've found security in temporary earthly things. But many don't realize how big a role we all play in our own destruction – our money, lifestyle, the things we covet and value. How many years does it take to build up a good life of moral choices and right living, and how quickly that same life can be torn down and destroyed?"

Jim had to agree with that last statement, but he remained silent.

"I've also seen you get angry at someone or something and not let go. That can be dangerous. We need to look to our heavenly father for guidance and how to forgive."

"I don't like Christian terminology."

"Why?"

"The word 'Father.' Bugs me. Reminds me that dad preferred you."

"That's not true Jimmy. Dad loves you."

"He loves me because I'm his biological offspring. From your mother you get unconditional love. But from your father you get approval. He never approved of me."

"You did break a lot of rules. For a while I was seriously worried you'd end up getting involved with Raimondo."

"Oh no, no. I was crazy, but not that crazy."

"Crazy isn't the word. You were just misguided. Searching for yourself. In many ways you still are. There's a reason why we were protected from most of that."

Jim said, "You know what really bugs me about faith? This thought that there's a reason for everything."

"I'm not sure there is, but God can *make* a reason out of everything."

"I don't know if I buy that. I mean, every time someone survives a natural disaster or a shooting, they'll say they survived for a purpose. Then I think, so what you're saying is that your life is more important than the person who died that day? That God didn't have a reason important enough to save them."

"Jimmy, God is sovereign. He sees the big picture. He might let someone pass on so they could get ushered to heaven and save another's life because their soul still needs salvation."

"Okay. Sorry, that's the cynic in *me* rearing its head."

Jeremy chuckled. "Can I pray for you, Jimmy?"

"Sure, Jeremy." Jim didn't feel like closing his eyes but for whatever reason did as Jeremy began.

"Dear Lord, I pray for my awesome brother Jimmy. Protect him and give him a wonderful and productive trip. Remind him of his blessings and all the things he can be grateful for. Restore his marriage if that's your will, or help him move on peacefully. Knock at the door of his heart and draw him near to you. In Jesus' name, amen."

"Thanks, Jeremy," Jim said. Then he thought, *I'm not ready to draw near yet.*

"Of course. And thank you for calling. Lemme know how it all turns out with Iris, and whatever else you're allowed to disclose."

"Will do."

Jim ended the call and sat in thought. He found it hard to believe Jeremy had envied him. He actually liked his brother despite the man's crazy devotion to faith. But then again, what was more crazy, God or alien conspiracies?

And then there was Raimondo. Wow. He hadn't thought of his estranged cousin in years. Not a blood cousin, but one via marriage. His father's brother, Uncle Donnie, had married into a family that just so happened to have ties to one of the original five families that ran New York back in the day. Aunt Alma, everyone called her, maiden name of Bellini. He wasn't sure which of the famous La Cosa Nostra families but had heard the name Colombo tossed around a couple times.

Raimondo was the son of one of Aunt Alma's three brothers. They mostly saw just pictures of that side of the family and only met a few times at Christmas, Thanksgiving and a couple birthdays and weddings. But they got to know each other, and Jim always liked Raimondo's confident persona and ability to make lots of acquaintances.

But he and Jeremy had been warned by their father to stay away from that side of the family's "business."

"What business?" they'd asked. Dad wouldn't give details.

"Just be careful," they were told.

When Jim was seventeen, Raimondo pulled up one day in a brand new, shiny, yellow Dodge Charger.

"Just in the neighborhood and sayin' hi," he told Jim's mom when she warily answered the door. "Is Jimmy or Jeremy around?"

Jim remembered staring in awe at his cousin. The young man had transformed from a relatively typical high schooler to a slicked-up mob movie character – the leather jacket, the expensive dress shirt with the top buttons undone revealing a set of gold chains, the shiny shoes, the greased back hair.

"Hey. I'm going to a party. Wanna come along? Meet some of my friends," he said.

Jim had been excited, Jeremy reluctant, but they both went. Raimondo drove them to a big house on the other side of town. The street and driveway were filled with pricey sports cars. When the door opened, Jeremy almost refused to enter. They were hit with loud music, a diverse cloud of smoke, scantily dressed women, and everyone had a cigarette and alcoholic drink. Jim, of course, happily marched right in.

Twenty minutes later, after getting offered vodka and cocaine, and after a very inebriated girl started grabbing at his crotch, Jeremy walked over, tapped Jim on the shoulder, and said he was leaving.

"How you getting home?"

"I'll figure it out."

"Okay."

Several hours later, Jim remembered leaning over the kitchen sink trying to puke. The combination of tequila and pot he'd been readily consuming had turned his equilibrium so upside down, he couldn't distinguish the floor from the ceiling.

Raimondo stumbled over at some point with a tall, gorgeous redhead on his arm wearing skin-tight ripped jean shorts and a gray, sleeveless mock neck.

"This is Terry," he said.

Jim said hi, but Terry only rolled her head backward, laughed for a moment, then appeared to pass out on Raimondo's shoulder.

"I think I gotta take her to the hospital," Raimondo said. He looked around; they were alone in the kitchen. Don't worry, he'd be back to drive Jim home.

Raimondo half carried the girl out the back door near the kitchen.

The rest was a blur, until sometime later, the cops showed up. They asked if a girl had left this house at some point and who she was with. They gave a perfect description of the redhead Jim had seen with Raimondo. By then everyone was so drunk and high, the cops could hardly get a straight answer from anyone. Some vaguely remembered the girl but didn't recall her leaving.

A little while later, Jim was passed out on the couch when a slap on the shoulder startled him awake. A pale-faced and frightened Raimondo stood over him.

"Come on, let's go."

On the drive back, Raimondo told Jim that the girl had overdosed and died in his car.

"Are you sure she's dead?"

"She threw up all over herself and stopped breathin'," Raimondo said. "I think she snorted junk, three or four bags worth. Can you believe that, puttin' all that pure horse up yer nose?"

Jim didn't ask but figured Raimondo had supplied the smack.

"What did you do?"

"I left her on the sidewalk a block down from the emergency room. Listen, Jimmy. The cops are going to come askin' questions. I need you to do me a favor."

They pulled up in front of Jim's house. Raimondo turned to Jim, a scared and pleading look in his eyes.

"Don't tell them you saw me take the girl, okay? Tell 'em you don't know nothin'. I need you do to this for me. We're family right? You do this for me and I'll never forget. I'll owe you for life. Will you do it, Jimmy?"

Jim said yes, a heavy feeling in his gut.

A couple days later, two police detectives did show up. They spent an hour questioning both Jim and Jeremy about the party. Jeremy proudly told them he'd left early and never saw the girl. They believed him.

Jim, on the other hand, was questioned more closely.

"Are you sure you never saw this girl?" they asked several times, showing him a beautiful smiling photo of a pretty redhead who by then had been identified as a Terry Anderson, age sixteen.

No, Jim didn't remember anything.

"You sure?"

"Yeah, I'm sure. I was passed out most of the time."

The cops didn't appear entirely convinced, but eventually gave up and left.

Wow. Jim hadn't thought of that whole incident in years. He'd never told anyone, not even Jeremy. It took a while but at some point, he at last succeeded in absolving himself of any guilt. Yes, he lied, but he never did a single thing to anyone.

Last he heard, his cousin was known as on the street as Raimondo "Rocket Man" Bellini and ran a deli front business in San Francisco.

He was afraid to know what the Rocket Man nickname meant.

Chapter 13

Air Canada flight 8927 approached Harry Reid International Airport in Paradise, Nevada at 10:05 a.m. local time. Per the captain, the normally thirteen-hour flight from Beijing had been reduced by almost twenty-five minutes thanks to some unexpected tailwind.

Li Ming Tan and Rong Chiang sat inconspicuously in the middle cabin, economy class, separated by both aisle and five rows of seats. Never once since entering the Beijing Capital International Airport the evening before, did they so much as acknowledge the other's presence. Just two more anonymous strangers on a plane.

Li Ming was relieved when they'd finally touched down. She'd been sandwiched the whole time between two businessmen – an older American, and a pudgy, overweight Chinese man who breathed heavily and stank of body odor from under his tight-fitting sport coat. Both men wore wedding rings and thankfully, the American read books and minded his own business throughout the flight. But the fat man was another story. For the first hour, he repeatedly tried in vain to strike up conversation, before Li Ming's cold attitude finally made him give up. He continued though to periodically ask random questions and take every opportunity to let his eyes wander up and down her body when he thought she wasn't looking.

Rong was much luckier. He not only had a window view, but the middle seat in his row was unoccupied.

Li Ming was dressed conservatively in a black businesswoman's knee length skirt suit with a cream single breasted tweed jacket. She was attractive enough, but not excessively so. She mused how men rate a woman's sex appeal with numbers. On a scale of one to ten, she was once told she was between a six and seven, which was perfect for this job. A lot of jobs called for a woman like her, someone who could blend in more. Ultra-sexy/beautiful women had their place but drew too much attention for most covert ops.

She spent most of the flight studying the psychological profile of her subject but had managed to doze for about ninety minutes somewhere high above the North Pacific Ocean.

As they began their descend and approach, Li Ming breathed a sigh of relief. The last time she'd flown to this location, the airport had been called McCarran International Airport. Li Ming smiled to herself. Back in 2014, Harry Reid, then a Nevada state senator, was said to be spearheading a landgrab with his son so that the government could profit from the construction of a Chinese owned solar company. The real reason, everyone was told, was an endangered tortoise being threatened by grazing cattle. A heavily armed standoff between the government's Bureau of Land Management and some American ranger named Bundy ensued and captured the attention of the world. No one will ever know for sure what the truth was, and the conspiracies will continue. The Chinese company never did build the solar farm, and even if they had, it would have been many miles away from the rancher's cows. The Chinese themselves had sat back and laughed at the whole thing. Once again, the American government became its own worst enemy with their mismanagement of the situation. The discord between citizens of the United States and their leaders will only continue to worsen until it implodes. That will be a glorious day.

As the plane slowly taxied to Terminal 3, the fat man next to Li Ming snorted as he awoke from the last of a dozen catnaps throughout the flight. He smelled even worse. He yawed, and other than a final glance at her legs, looked out the window and thankfully said nothing as the plane came to a stop.

Li Ming and Rong casually made their way through the terminal to the car rental area, Li Ming to Hertz, Rong to Enterprise, their reservations thirty minutes apart. Both rented modest, mid-sized sedans.

After dining alone at separate restaurants, they converged an hour apart at a discreet four-star hotel along the outskirts of Paradise and checked into different rooms at different times and under different names with current Nevada state Real IDs.

At 9:00 a.m. tomorrow morning, they would meet in Rong's room and be introduced to the third and most crucial participant of the operation.

***

Liang Huang put his fingers together and then stretched them by extending his arms palms out. It had been a long few days, but everything was coming together. He prepared a brief for his superiors.

Everything is going according to plan, he typed. *Mainland operatives in place. Third party en route.*

Just the quick facts; that's all they ever wanted.

Huang sat back and smiled. He appreciated the fact that he'd long risen past that point to where his superiors no longer felt the need to micromanage him. They understood it would be a waste of time. Huang's hours were all over the place anyway, sometimes starting at 4:00 a.m. and sometimes not ending until 2:00 a.m. But the real reason they didn't was because he produced real, tangible results. So much so that he was able to make certain decisions on his own now without approval.

But better than all that, Huang loved his job. He hated the word "hacker" though, preferring "operative" instead. Hackers, after all, were everywhere now. In the '80s, they were a mysterious bunch, lurking in the shadows with the stereotypical sweatshirt hoodie in a dark room before a glowing screen. Or so people thought. But today, they could literally be anyone. With so many ways to access the internet and so many tools out there, it could be the kid next door getting into your router, or the middle-aged woman next to you in the coffee shop hijacking everyone's public Wi-Fi connection. It was a full-time job now for many, overloading systems with denial-of-service attacks, setting up botnets, or creating clever phishing mails to steal passwords or introduce malware.

Operatives, on the other hand, were an elite group. They specialized in things most people did not nor could not if they wanted to. They didn't do things for fun or fame, they did everything for a real purpose. And they took more risks.

The MSS wanted independent, self-driven people who didn't fit into any typical pigeonhole. Huang was definitely all that, and more. He didn't mind long hours alone, something many wouldn't handle well. In fact, he had gone days, even weeks at a time with hardly a single word in person to anyone.

His work wasn't dangerous or glamorous like some double-oh seven who shot bad guys, flew helicopters, and wooed beautiful women. In fact, much of what he did was lonely and mundane. He just pushed buttons, made analysis, then recommended actions.

What he wasn't warned about though was the burden a person can carry if someone else is captured, imprisoned, or tortured because you did your job poorly.

One of the mistakes of many in the intelligence community is they have no fear of getting caught, nor fear of the agents they assign to tasks getting caught, because of the unwise assumption they are smarter than the people trying to catch them.

Early in his career, when Huang was being mentored by a group of established digital operatives, he was involved in a case where they had two undercover operators worming their way into one of Israel's nuclear fuel production plants. It had taken all of three years to recruit them, and everything seemed to be going well. But Huang had seen a pattern no one else did. One of the agents, Adam "Atom" Cohen, had shown behavioral signs of either uncertainty or even possibly acting as a double agent for both China and Israel. Huang wanted to voice his opinion, but his mentor was personal friends with this agent and had nothing but good things to say about him. So Huang kept silent. Eventually, Mossad agents set up a sting and busted "Atom" who promptly turned and gave up the second agent. This second agent then quickly disappeared and was never heard from again.

Lesson learned, no matter how good or smart you are, you've no protection against other agents in any of the intelligence services.

*****

The girl stood before them, her hands in front of her nervously, fingers intertwined. Her handler, a skinny man with a stern and pock-marked face, stood behind her with one hand on her shoulder. Above a narrow mouth that appeared to have a permanent scowl, flat nose, and protruding cheekbones, he stared down at the girl with cold and cruel eyes.

"What is your name?" Li Ming asked.

"Chimeg," the girl said softly, barely looking up.

"You're from Mongolia?" Li Ming had read the file on the girl and her family and already knew but wanted to hear her speak.

"Yes."

"Speak louder."

"*Yes*."

"How old are you?"

"Fourteen."

Her English was almost without an accent, but that wasn't important. What was vital was that the girl be clearly underaged in appearance. With her hair done right and some makeup, maybe some photoshopping, she could look twelve.

Rong casually watched from a chair on the other side of the room while smoking a cigarette. In front of him on a small table were several cameras including a compact video camera.

Li Ming looked at the girl. Almost four days ago, Chimeg had begun the journey that would land her here in what Americans appropriately called "Sin City." An Air France plane inbound from China had landed at Mexico City International Airport. Waiting for the flight was a large, black SUV owned by a Chinese businessman who'd been heavily involved in drug trafficking and money laundering in Mexico City since 2007. Without security so much as giving it a second glance, the SUV had driven all the way through the airport to the tarmac where the plane deboarded.

An innocuous looking father and daughter exited the plane and were met by men who ushered them into the vehicle.

From there, the car made the long twelve-hour drive north to a safehouse in Nuevo Laredo, stopping only once for a quick restroom and snack break. At the house, the girl was locked in one of the small bedrooms.

The next evening as the sun was setting, an oil tanker truck pulled up to the safehouse. The man and girl were taken beneath the truck's tank trailer where a steel plate had been removed from the bottom, revealing a rectangular hole. A small ladder was placed in the opening allowing the two to climb up inside. The small steel enclosure was low, allowing the majority of the tank's upper portion to be filled with oil or fuel, should by slim chance it was inspected from the manhole on top. There was a blanket to rest on and a small battery powered lantern. They were given a couple bottles of water and some bread, then sealed inside. As the truck bounced along, they could hear the heavy sloshing of liquid above their heads through the thin steel.

At around midnight, the truck, which had current Texas state registration and permits, crossed the border into Laredo, Texas, an international boundary where more than 20,000 trucks pass through every day, many of them at night. The paperwork was briefly examined at a checkpoint, the vehicle itself was hardly glanced at.

From Laredo, the truck made the three-hour ride to the first major city closest to the US-Mexico border, San Antonio, a key smuggling hub sitting at the crossroads of Interstate 35. Conveniently centralized, smugglers can go in any direction from there, including north all the way to Canada.

The plate under the tank trailer was unriveted and the man and girl were transferred to a sliver Mercedes-Benz SUV with dark tinted windows. The vehicle, driven by two Chinese men who never spoke a word, headed west, and began the eighteen-hour drive, stopping twice at cheap motels to eat and rest.

Li Ming looked Chimeg over. The girl was beautiful, with long flowing hair, not black in color, but a rich deep brown. Parted down the middle, she'd braided it on both sides, giving her an almost Native American look. Her skin was light toned with an olive tinge. Her eyes were large and bright and held a deep black, slightly stained with an almost midnight blue color that was so dark, one could hardly make out her pupils. Although her body language displayed some of the timid, reserved, and shy traits many men were attracted to in Asian women, the child had a fierceness to her as well, a fighter's spirit.

Li Ming watched the girl and resisted a swelling of pity she felt. After this was over, it would probably be decided it was too much trouble and expense to get the girl back to China. She would spend the rest of her short life as a forced prostitute or laboring in a Chinese-owned factory over here.

In recent years, China had become home to a thriving sex trade and human trafficking hub. Women and children were routinely moved in for forced labor and prostitution from all over Africa and Europe, even the United States. Growing up privileged, an only child in the home of a member of the National People's Congress, Li Ming had been lucky to escape all that.

Chimeg's father had disappeared to the Czech Republic in search of work several years ago and they never heard from him again. Desperate, her mother became one of the countless undocumented migrants to China, lured by a false promise of work, only to be trafficked and used under threat. Many victims came from rural provinces with low income and high unemployment, easily deceived because of a lack of education, and were sent to provinces with more money because the demand is greater and resources are available to pay.

Decades of China's one-child policy and the cultural preference for male children resulted in a disproportionally high number of males. This led to several growing problems. Brothels were now a huge business and millions of women from the Philippines, Mongolia and North Korea who came to China in search of work, found themselves coerced into prostitution.

Another big problem of the gender gap was girls forced into marriage. Male children inherit the family name and are tasked with caring for aging parents. Thus, many unborn girls are aborted, and many that survive are "accidentally" dropped down wells or abandoned at orphanages. Males in communities with a shortage of females and pressured to marry, resort to purchasing brides kidnapped from neighboring countries, some still adolescents. Because Chinese men pay good money for foreign brides, the demand to kidnap women and girls had risen substantially in recent years. Many "brides" are treated like breeding dogs, kept locked up and raped repeatedly until they become pregnant. A small percentage of these women are allowed to return home if they leave their child behind. If they cannot bear children, they are considered useless and put into slave labor or disposed of.

But there could be no pity for Chimeg. There was a duty to the land of our ancestors, a higher cause.

Li Ming stared hard at the girl. "I'm going to prepare you for an important job. You will do exactly what we tell you."

Chimeg stared back, then suddenly blurted out, "Boovoo saa, gechii!"

The man standing behind swung her around, raised an arm high and smashed the right side of the girl's face with a backhand so hard she tumbled to the ground with a yelp.

Li Ming stood. "Stop! We don't want her damaged."

Rong, still seated and calming exhaling a cloud of smoke said, "It might be good for the cameras. We can add an element of abuse to the story."

Li Ming had to agree, but also fought mixed feelings as she watched the girl whimper and cry on the floor. But as quickly as the feelings came, they were dismissed. There were things at stake so much bigger than one little Mongolian girl. The self-righteousness and arrogant America, with its imperialistic foreign policy and world's policeman attitude, who downplays China's accomplishments, thwarts their international influence, and violates their national sovereignty needed to be punished. She was proud to play a small role in that. Besides, matters of the heart must always submit to matters of the state.

Chimeg's handler reached down, grabbed her forearm, and yanked her to her feet. Li Ming took a step forward and stared down stonily as the girl sniffed and looked up.

"Do you ever want to see your mother again?"

The girl nodded.

"Take your clothes off and go to the shower."

Chapter 14

Jim sat in one of the several spacious lounges at The Cosmopolitan. The dimly lit space offered no end of things to look at in every direction. His choice of attire for the evening was tan chinos and a black, lightweight polyester blazer over a light-blue dress shirt.

He glanced at his phone for the fifth time. 6:10 p.m. They'd agreed to meet here "around six."

Fidgeting slightly, he tried desperately to fight off nervousness. He hated this feeling, especially at his age now. It was the same one he had when he was a teenager and trying to get up the nerve to ask a girl out.

He took a sip from a tumbler the bartender had filled with Johnnie Walker a few minutes ago and looked around at the décor again. They spared no expense in these places, but there was a reason for that. People like him came to Vegas from all over the world and eagerly handed over their hard-earned money in exchange for a little cheap entertainment and the adrenaline rush of a possible win. Well, some of the entertainment was good; ten years ago, he saw Penn and Teller at The Rio, and it was actually quite impressive.

The walkways in this lounge looked like little roads, complete with a dashed divider line and miniature art deco "signposts" along the routes. Approachable from all directions, at the center where the "roads" met, was a dazzling bar. Held up by thick columns of what looked like semitransparent glass etched with modern art tree figures, was a huge, round neon-lit ceiling, almost as if a spacecraft was hovering over it. The outside of the circular structure glowed a cool dark blue and inside were curving geometric shapes, like a bunch of crop circles, with borders that glowed various colors, enhanced by the shadowy atmosphere. Soft rock music gently played from unseen speakers, the kind many called "smooth jazz," just loud enough so that one could either listen to it or the sounds of the surrounding casino. He could seriously hang out here were it not for the additional noise.

Every couple minutes, the *ding-ding-ding-ding* of some slot machine could be heard, along with random laughter or a yell of excitement. Jim thought the constant crowd murmur, plastic chips clicking and clacking, and electronic beeps and jingles would drive him nuts if he worked at a place like this. Then again, the brain has an amazing way of tuning out anything it doesn't want to hear.

It reminded him of an interesting experience from grade school. He was sitting on his bed one evening reading and preparing for a state capital test. On the wall was a cuckoo clock his parents had given him a couple Christmases ago. The little pendulum beneath what looked like a miniature model of an old European church in gothic style architecture, tick-tock-ed loudly as it swung back and forth. But on this evening, after a while of intense studying, he looked up and was startled to see the clock's arm swinging away but making no sound. It was a little eerie at first. He shook his head and stared at it until the sound slowly returned and he could hear it as normal.

All at once Jim was yanked out of his reverie by the presence of someone who had walked up and was standing next to his lounge seat. He turned to see an Asian woman watching him with an amused smile on her face.

"Jimmy?" she asked.

Jim nodded.

"I'm Iris. Nice to meet you."

"Oh, right," Jim said, setting his drink down and clumsily standing. "Call me Jim."

Iris laughed, but not in a mocking way, more one of shared humor. "Are you okay? You looked like you were in deep thought."

Jim smiled with embarrassment. "I was. Sorry. Nice to meet you." He reached out to shake and watched as she shifted her drink to her left hand.

"I already got my favorite poison," she said, raising her glass a little.

Jim took her hand firmly but gently. Her palm was cold and damp from the tumbler, but the back of her hand was warm. "So did I. Please," he said gesturing at the loveseat across from a small drink table.

He quickly looked her up and down as she settled in. Amazingly, while she didn't really resemble her Lù Chá avatar, she was almost exactly as he'd imagined. Her eyes and other features told him she was Chinese. Her face and body were what could best be described as pretty, better than average. Not really slender, but not overweight. More importantly, she had a genuine smile – not phony or forced. Plus, she was dressed fairly conservatively, at least compared to the cocktail waitresses sauntering about in their slinky little outfits. Her charcoal gray short-sleeved wrap dress hung somewhat loosely on her frame and stopped just above the knees. Her skin was smooth and very fair, not quite white, but tinted with something. It was impossible to tell her age. Was she really in her forties? She spoke with no accent; maybe she was an "ABC" like Danny Weng. So far, he liked everything he saw.

Iris crossed one leg over the other, looked at Jim staring, then shyly glanced around, smiling.

Jim caught himself. "Sorry, you had me at a disadvantage until now. You'd seen my face, but I'm seeing yours for the first time."

She beamed a smile and held up her hands, palms out. "Well, here I am. You can't be too careful."

"I understand. It is indeed very nice to meet you," Jim said sincerely.

She picked up her drink. "So, what brings you to Vegas?"

Jim already felt himself relaxing a bit. "A combination of work and pleasure," he said, also picking up his drink.

"Lucky you. What company sends people to Las Vegas?"

Jim thought for a moment. Oh, what the hell. "I'm a government guy. Department of Energy."

Iris's eyes got wide for a moment. "Really? How interesting. And intriguing."

"Intriguing?"

"Sure. Out here in the Nevada desert and all. Sounds mysterious. You told me you're a technical trainer. It's okay if you can't talk about it."

Jim chuckled. "It's not a big deal. But yeah, I can't really tell you much. Let's just say that if you wanted to protect some place from thieves or saboteurs or whoever and had some money to spend, I might have some insight on how to go about doing that."

"Wow. Sounds exciting."

"Some of it's interesting. Not sure I'd say exciting. But if I gave you any details, some men in black would show up and take us away." He said this deadpan and looked hard at her.

Iris's smile faded and she stared in exaggerated disbelief, eyebrows raised.

Jim held up his hands. "I'm joking."

Iris smiled again. "I loved that movie."

"What movie?" Jim asked, taking a pull on his drink.

"*Men in Black*. Not just because it was funny. I think there's some truth to it."

Jim was genuinely surprised. "Really?"

"Yes. It's a huge, expanding universe. Kind of arrogant of us to think we're completely alone."

"I agree."

She smiled at him for a moment, then said, "The universe has been around for so long, it's likely it's seen many civilizations come and go and we're just passing through."

"Maybe. I find the subject interesting, but I'm not entirely sure what I actually believe."

"Sure." She quickly shrugged it off and looked around. "This place is nice."

Jim glanced around as well. "Yeah, I can't remember being here before. I mean, I've been to a few around here in Vegas. But I'm digging the ambience and the music."

"Maybe they have some *tasty* snacks we could try," she said, licking her lips and taking a sip from her tumbler.

"So what," Jim said, looking up.

"Excuse me?"

"The name of this tune. It sounds like a Miles Davis classic called 'So What' that they revamped with a modern spin."

"Oh, I hadn't noticed. You're a music buff."

"I wanted to be a musician when I was younger. Played a lot of guitar."

"You gave up the dream?"

"Well, I grew up and out of the dream, I guess." He took a long pull on his drink, feeling it start to relax his mind and body. "Probably a good thing. I've heard like only five percent of musicians earn enough money on music alone to make a living. My dad told me to be practical, do something that had more of a chance of success. The truth is he never thought I was good enough."

Iris was watching him, then smiled sadly. "My parents used to criticize me. My mom told me I was fat and could never get married. So I've struggled with weight and appearance. But I've done okay."

"She called you fat?"

"I was never really *fat*, fat. But my sister was always skinny, so I was compared. She was the one who always cooperated with my parents. I was the one who made them regret having children." She laughed to communicate this wasn't some deep emotional scar that had plagued her adult life.

"I'm sorry to hear. That sounds uncannily familiar. Your mom was wrong though – you look fantastic to me."

Iris smiled shyly and looked down.

Jim chided himself – too early for comments like that yet. "So ... what do you do?"

"I design clothing ... for trans women." She looked Jim solidly in the eye. "Which is what I am."

Jim's smile began to drop.

Iris laughed. "Now *I'm* joking. Lighten up."

Jim waved a hand. "No ... no, it's okay. I wouldn't have judged you ..."

"I'm trying to get you to laugh. I read, critique, and edit books for college curriculum."

"No." Jim sat back. "You read for a living?"

"Yes. And edit. Make corrections and suggestions. Why?"

"That's like someone saying I eat comfort food for a living. That's fantastic."

"I like it. Get to learn a lot."

Jim took a drink and watched her. "But does it ruin pleasure reading?"

"How would it do that?"

"Oh I don't know. You start a good novel then think, ah, this is too much like work."

Iris laughed. "No. I read nonfiction, stuff about philosophy and science and medicine."

"For what college?"

"Fudan University."

"Where's that?"

"China. Shanghai."

"Really. So you're traveling over here?"

"I work mostly here. When I travel, I travel *there*. There's a lot of students in China that want to learn English. I look at books in preproduction they'll be using that are written in English."

"Wow. So you're fluent in Chinese?"

"Not really. I can understand a lot, but don't really speak it. I got the job because I have an understanding of both American and Chinese culture. I know how things should be worded so that the *knowledge transfer* happens in the most effective way." She drained the last of her drink.

Jim smiled. "You want another?" he asked, tipping his tumbler empty as well.

"That'd be great."

Jim motioned a waitress over. "So what's your poison?"

"Johnnie Walker. Black label of course. Never red – that's the cheap stuff," Iris said with a grin.

This was almost too much. "I'll have the same," he said to the petite sandy blonde server who looked like she served drinks only when she wasn't stripping and pole dancing.

He then turned quite deliberately to avoid glancing at the server's cute rear end bulging from under a very short skirt as she walked away. He took a deep breath. "So you're a graphics designer too?"

"Oh that's my side gig. I do that for fun. Once in a while I might get paid for a job."

"Nice. You mentioned '80s music. What's your favorite?"

Iris recrossed her legs. "Oh I like a lot of things. I used to drive my parents nuts by listening to Joan Jett. I think they were sorry they were raising me in America."

"Joan Jett was huge. Pat Benatar, Lita Ford. I think though my favorite female rocker from that era was Ann Wilson from Heart. In terms of overall talent."

Iris looked up thoughtfully. "I might agree with that."

Jim laughed. "Well, at least you didn't drive your parents crazy trying to be a rock star. You have any other siblings besides your skinny sister?"

"No, she's it. She became a lawyer and works in San Francisco for the DA's office. Makes a lot of money." Iris sighed. "And she's *still* skinny. What about you? Siblings?"

"I have an older brother named Jeremy. We're so much alike he could be my twin. Though he's a tad taller and better looking. In fact, I was talking to him earlier. He's uh ... he's a good guy." Jim stopped his thoughts there. He didn't want to mention any more about that right now. No gut-spilling or saying anything negative about himself or his family on a first meeting. He wanted to do this right. He really felt relaxed around Iris, and it was a pleasant feeling.

In the past, he'd tried so hard to impress women by hiding relevant info, embellishing things about himself, or saying just about anything to appear more genuine. But all that ever did was bite him in the end when the truth came out. And no matter what Iris said about herself, her accomplishments, talents, travels, whatever, he wasn't going to one up her with stories of his own. He liked her too much already to want to play those games.

Iris watched Jim as the waitress came back and set down two fresh tumblers filled with amber-colored liquid.

Jim held his glass up. "Here's to blind dates in Vegas!"

"Half-blind for me," Iris grinned.

They clinked glasses.

***

Liang Huang smiled to himself. Things had been on the up and up lately and he felt good. His latest round of efforts was going to tie up a big loose end that had been a thorn in the top brass's side for several years. He'd even put in for a small vacation, ostensibly to visit his parents down in the Pinglu District. But really, he was hoping to see about a girl.

Now that things were in motion for the prey they were about to catch, plans for the bigger grab were under way.

Huang loved media access control addresses, better known as MAC addresses, the unique ID assigned to every network adapter for every internet connected device in the world. For years, BitBok had been collecting and categorizing MAC addresses, bypassing protections on both Android and iOS systems designed specifically to mitigate such collection. Over the last several years, it had amassed millions of addresses, each being digitally shelved away according to the user's location, time spent online, ethnicity, religious and political affiliations, purchasing habits, news sites watched, pornography viewed if any, illegal activity, et cetera.

Collecting MAC addresses was a powerful identification tool because the address never changed unless the adapter was physically swapped out. This allows significant profiling of an individual user and their habits. Most users around the world were completely unaware, and even if they did find out, there was no opportunity to opt-out of the function. Given the recent rise in the Western world's paranoia about privacy, many users would be appalled at the amount of data collected.

Additional addons came with the BitBok installation, apps that take data packets about to be sent off, and apply an unusual encryption type, above and beyond the standard protection afforded by SSL/TLS, which only provides encryption between individual users and service providers. Huang had proudly helped develop a process that encrypts communication directly between the users of a system on top of that. The reason was simple. Encrypted data being sent from apps in the United States to Beijing wouldn't appear on Google's or Apple's sniffer radars and no one would have any idea that data with associated MAC addresses was being sent overseas.

Out of sight, out of mind.

But all that aside, there was a MAC address of interest that was never used on BitBok or any of the affiliated apps. Interestingly, it was an address that changed several times a year as well, feigning multiple users. But certain patterns told Huang it was only one individual. Whoever this was, was extraordinarily precautious, and he or she should be. The attention on this one had risen to the ranks of higher-ups who now demanded action.

One of the many tools in Huang's arsenal was a special search engine that crawled and indexed web content while continuously scanning text for similarities against a growing database of existing content. It looked for both exact matches as well as utilized an algorithm "fingerprinting" process to find non-exact matches among paraphrased or altered texts.

Using these methods, Huang was now certain he'd identified a total of seven MAC addresses that belonged to one very wanted dissident. It would be proven once this person was caught, and Huang would once again be rewarded for his efforts.

His personal phone vibrated. A new message from Polina. His heart thumped with excitement.

Chapter 15

Jim looked down at the ice cubes in his tumbler and couldn't remember if this was his fourth or fifth drink. It didn't matter. He couldn't remember when he'd had this much fun and felt so relaxed. He looked up to see Iris watching him with a curious smile, almost as if she were studying him. His thoughts were starting to swirl.

"I don't know what I'd do if I were a real gambler," he said. "I'd probably lose everything."

"How do you mean?" Iris asked.

"I don't know. I'm just not that great at controlling my impulses when it comes to taking certain chances."

"What kind of chances?"

"Oh, you know, not just things that could cost me money, but also my health and safety." *Oops ... careful.* He tipped his tumbler and felt the cold ice against his upper lip. No way was he going to accidentally spill about some of his sleazier escapades, particularly ones he'd done in this town.

Iris watched but kept her drink in her lap. She had ordered the same number of drinks, only hers had been discreetly poured out incrementally with quick, stealthy moves into a decorative bamboo pot on the floor next to her loveseat. The only drink she'd actually consumed was the one she'd had when they first met, which had been unsweetened tea.

"I knew this guy, a gambler, semi-pro," Jim was saying. "He loved to go to Reno and play blackjack. Knew and practiced every card counting trick ever made. And they even caught him a couple times. There was this one place, the Riverboat I think. He'd been kicked out about a year before. We go in there and settle down and start playing, and about twenty minutes into it the pit boss gets a call. Next thing you know my friend was told to get the hell out. In a very stern manner. 'You were warned to never come back,' blah blah. I got scared. I thought some big dudes were gonna come over and start kickin' our ass or something. Pull us into the back room. I'm telling you, that facial recognition software they got. Always watching from the eyes in the sky." He turned and raised his glass at a nearby dark tinted dome on the ceiling.

Iris kept her eyes steadily on Jim, gauging his level of intoxication.

"I almost got robbed there once," Jim said.

"At the Riverboat?"

"No, Reno. On my way in. Want another?" he asked, raising his tumbler.

"Sure, why not?" Iris said with a beaming smile.

Jim flagged down a server. He then leaned back and looked up while he thought. He hadn't rehashed this story in a while. "I was on I-80 going west toward downtown. It was early in the morning and there were only a couple cars on the road." He paused while the waitress took the tumblers and walked away. "I saw this car on the side of the road and a woman flagging me down. She looked kinda down and out and all. Kinda white-trash-ish. So I pulled over and she said her vehicle broke down and she lived close-by. Could you help? Sure, no problem. I'll give you a ride. As we walked to my car, she said she felt faint and put her head on my shoulder. Something made me nervous and I looked around. And sure enough, some dude with a knife is sneaking up behind us."

"What did you do?" Iris asked, wide-eyed with concern.

"I yelled hey! and shoved the woman away. She yells, 'you asshole!' while I took off running. The dude with the knife yelled at me to stop but I kept running, leaped in my car and took off. Lucky for me I'd left the keys in the ignition."

"That sounds scary."

The waitress returned with two more drinks and set them down.

"It was." Jim grabbed his glass and took a big drink. "She set me up. Played off my desire to help someone. That really pisses me off. Next time I see someone on the side of the road I'm just gonna leave 'em there."

He paused and waited for Iris to tell him something along the lines of how he shouldn't let the evil actions of a few deter him from doing good. That's what almost everyone said when he told that story, especially women. But Iris said nothing, only watched him. What could she be thinking? Perhaps he'd had too much to drink and was babbling or something.

"But with your training in security, you knew what to do, right?" she said smiling, raising her drink to her lips.

Jim waved it off. "I'm not a cop or a guard. Never was in the military. I just work on some security systems. Physical security, not cyber. That's a different group."

Iris glanced around. "I'll bet they've got lots of security here."

"Oh for sure, but nothing like where I work. Where I work, it'd be like breaking into a military base."

"Wow. Tell me more."

Jim chuckled. The thought that he fascinated this woman was causing a surge of elation he'd not felt in a long time. It was also turning him on. She looked at him with big, sincere eyes, eyes that had seen her mother and probably a few men look upon her with judgement. Eyes that saw her parents prefer her sister over her. He already felt a bonding with her over some shared commonalities.

"They do top secret stuff where I work," he said after a moment. "I don't work directly on the secret stuff, but I help protect it."

"How do you help do that?"

The room was starting to look surreal. The lights, the sounds, the flashy visuals. Lines on the walls and ceiling that were supposed to be straight were started to look curved and wavy.

"I write the training and documentation on it," Jim said, trying not to slur. "It's a big system with sensors watching everything. Every gate, every door, every window, and every open space really. It's top secret." He felt like a grade school boy bragging about the rocket ship his dad was working on in the garage.

"How would someone get into a place like that if they were up to no good?" Iris asked innocently, with eyes that said, *I'm very intrigued.*

Jim leaned forward. "You'd need someone from the *inside*. Someone who'd let you in. Show you how those crazy booths work."

"Booths?"

Jim sat up and tried to listen to himself talk to make sure he wasn't sounding stupid. "These booths where you walk in one side then out the other to a high security area. Inside they sniff you out – see if you gotta gun or bomb on you. Then you need the right credentials to get out on the other side and if you don't, scary dudes with guns come to get you."

"Wow. And I thought *my* job was interesting."

Jim laughed, then leaned in and lowered his voice. "I've seen the design of these booths. The ins and outs. Each one costs like a quarter-mil to make and install."

Iris stared at him intensely, a mischievous look in her eyes. "Sexy."

"Sexy?"

"Yes, imagine if you were sitting here telling me about your accounting job at the bank."

Jim laughed a little too hard, almost spilling his drink.

Iris paused and casually waited until he was done laughing. "Tell me more," she cooed.

"More about what?"

"Those booths and the security where you work."

"It's kind of boring work, to tell you the truth. I mean, it was kinda interesting at first, seeing what goes into protecting all those labs across the country. They've spent a fortune. Well, *we*, the taxpayers have spent a fortune."

A thought suddenly hit Jim and he sat back, his goofy grin fading. "You know, I really shouldn't be talking about all this out here. My coworker might walk by and bust me."

Iris gave him a pleasant smile then quickly stood. She went around the small table and sat close to Jim. Putting her hand on his thigh, she said, "Remember I told you about those college books I read?"

"Sure, yeah," Jim said, feeling the heat rising in his neck.

"I brought a couple with me. Gives me something to do during downtime." She gave his thigh an ever so slight squeeze. "Wanna come up to my room and have a look?" She paused, brought the drink up to her lips and gave him a wicked grin with her eyes. "You could give me some ... *fresh* ideas." She gave his leg another teasing squeeze, a little harder.

Jim took a pull on his drink and let his eyes quickly wander up and down the pretty Asian lady sitting next to him. Had she pulled her skirt up ever so slightly to reveal a little more of her legs? Oh, and he hadn't looked at her shoes yet. She was wearing black slingback sandals with a thick block heel; classy but not overkill, just like everything else about her. He liked her the first five minutes they'd met, and now after a few drinks, he really liked her. But wait ... did she just invite him to her room? Gerard's not going to believe this. Why did he think of Gerard just now? Oh yeah, he needed to be up early to meet him. Better remind himself to set the alarm clock.

"I'd *looove* to see them," he heard himself say.

Iris stood and Jim clumsily followed, his glasses sliding halfway down his nose. As she slid her arm into his, he noticed she was only an inch or two shorter, tall for an Asian woman. She cocked her head and motioned with her eyebrows in a, *shall we?* gesture.

Jim grinned and could only think for the hundredth time how unbelievable his fortune was. They meandered through the flashy, noisy maze and he stared numbly at the blackjack and roulette tables, his face flushed and hot. As they walked toward the elevator, they passed a row of slot machines.

Iris stopped him with a tug of her arm. "Wait," she said. "Let's spin one for good luck." She pulled a couple tokens from her purse and held them up. "Will you do us the honors?"

Jim smiled and held out his hand. Iris reached over, took his drink, and nodded with her head to follow her to a large machine that displayed a "Good Luck!" sign surrounded by flashing graphics of four-leaf clovers and eggs cracked open to reveal a double yoke.

As Jim stood gawking at the machine, looking for where to insert the coins, he didn't notice Iris set his drink on the machine next to him, twist open a capsule, pour white crystals into it, and give it a quick stir with her finger.

Jim pulled the big lever and stared stupidly at the rotating pictures of random objects until one by one, clicking and clacking away, they stopped spinning. The melancholy digital tune that resembled the *wah-wah-wah-wah* fail sound effect told them there would be no jackpot this time.

Jim turned, grinned at Iris, spread his hands wide and shrugged. She grinned back and handed him his drink. She then looked him in the eye and touched her glass to her lips. He followed and took a long, slow drink, already imagining what was going to happen soon on the bed upstairs.

They made their way to the elevators, and as Jim stumbled into one, Iris turned him around, then ran her finger across his lips. He opened his mouth just a hair and let her push the tip of her finger in just far enough to touch his tongue. As she did this, she slowly brought her drink to her lips again and tipped it back, as if taking a big, long gulp. She then pulled her finger back and watched him do the same with his drink, almost emptying it.

Jim felt his pulse rising in anticipation. This whole trip had been dreamlike, now it was beyond description. He was really going to get his hands on this sweet lady.

The elevator doors opened and Iris again took his arm and led him down the hall. As they passed a decorative table with a mirror above it, he didn't notice as she poured most of her drink out in the flower vase that rested on it.

They came upon a door and she stopped, stepped back, looked him in the eyes again and tipped her drink full up as if gulping the rest of it down. She nodded at him and he did the same, taking two swallows, and appearing not to taste the last few drops of the eighty-proof liquid.

He stared at Iris's ample butt as she inserted the key into the door lock. She then stepped aside and ushered him in first, a big seductive smile on her face. They entered the suite and he felt her gently lead him forward with a push on his back. The lights were turned down and the ghostly atmosphere played with his eyes. The walls in the room waved slightly and shapes appeared dimly in and out of his vision from the wallpaper and pictures.

After a few steps, he felt Iris step beside him and push him backward into another room until the crooks of his knees hit what felt like the edge of a bed. He sat heavily, feeling the mattress sag and bounce slightly.

Iris then stood before him in the dark room. She had a curious expression on her face, her chin down, her eyes riveted on his. It wasn't a look of pleasure, but rather one of … he couldn't tell. Had he displeased her? What had he said or done?

Jim looked around the swirling dark bedroom and felt a red flag go off in his gut. A strange feeling was hitting him intensely. He'd had his share of booze over the years and this didn't feel right. He looked back at the woman in front of him. She looked hard at him, her arms crossed, and her eyes narrowed.

"Izzz your name, rrreally Irisss?" he heard himself ask. His tongue and jaw muscles felt like mud.

She smirked, then he heard her say, "No, Jimmy. It's not." Her voice echoed slightly, as if there were comet trails attached to each word.

Blackness began to close in as his muscles lost control. His limbs became heavy and dropped and he felt himself start to fall forward. He felt the woman put her hands on his shoulders and push him back. The room spun for a moment as he toppled on the bed.

The last thing he remembered seeing was a ceiling fan with a round, glowing light in the center. It created an eerie shadowed circle around it on the otherwise unlit upper interior surface.

The blades weren't turning … why weren't they turning?

Chapter 16

Something woke Jim up. Had there been a noise?

He blinked and tried opening his mouth, but his lips felt sealed shut. Prying his mouth open, he realized his tongue and throat were sticky dry. He also felt terrible, like that rising sickly feeling before having to vomit. He lay still, trying to breathe deep and find his bearings. As awareness grew clearer out of the haze, he felt a throbbing pain start to well up in his head.

Finally able to open his eyes and focus, he recognized the first thing he saw – the four-bladed ceiling fan. He remembered wondering why it hadn't been spinning, and it still wasn't. But the light in the center was now off.

He slowly turned his head sideways and didn't recognize where he was. He turned the other way and still didn't see anything familiar. The furniture looked different, the wallpaper and décor were different.

Where was he? Where were his glasses?

He craned his head up and looked forward. The flat screen television on the dresser table was powered off. A small vase with a white rose rested next to the television.

He put his head back down. In the next couple minutes, his thoughts and consciousness slowly returned, like an ocean tide gradually refilling a bay that had been emptied the night before.

Breathe slow. Concentrate. He was in Las Vegas. He'd flown in with Gerard yesterday. He wasn't in his room. What time was it?

He turned to the nightstand to his left and saw the red digital display on the small clock. 2:10 p.m.

Two in the afternoon? The next day? What?

Feeling a slight breeze from the air conditioner, he all at once realized he was naked. Wincing as he used out of shape core muscles to pull himself up on his elbows, he looked down on his nude body and around the bed. The blanket and sheets had been pulled back. The room was dim but not dark and had a different feel now that sunlight was seeping in from the cracks around the curtains.

Feeling the pulsating pain in his head worsening by the moment, he turned sideways, slid his legs off the bed and slowly sat up. The action made him feel woozy and he stayed on the edge for a moment, trying to keep steady. He looked around again trying desperately to understand where he was.

What happened?

Iris.

Iris had brought him up to this room last night. He was still at the Cosmopolitan. It was two in the afternoon the next day and he was still here.

He put his face in his hands. "Oh my god …" he mumbled to himself.

Did I get robbed?

He pushed himself slowly up to a standing position and immediately felt so light-headed, sat heavily back down, fearing he was going to pass out. His muscles felt weak, and a small panic began to set in. His breathing felt shallow and his chest tight, like a belt was wrapped around his torso. His heart was beating in strange rhythms and his skin suddenly felt cold.

He dropped his head and closed his eyes. After about five more minutes of catching his breath, the urge to urinate made him struggle to his feet again. The room toppled back and forth as he steadied himself. Slowly looking around, he saw what had to be the doorway to the bathroom.

But first, some light. He looked toward the wall at the drawn curtains. Putting one foot carefully in front of the other, he eased his way across the floor, feeling with his toes to avoid kicking anything or tripping.

The long, thick window curtains hung from ceiling to floor and felt heavy, but he managed to pull them open a couple feet, squinting from the bright light that flooded in. He turned around and looked at the room again. Except for the bed, the place looked unused and empty. No suitcases, no one's personal possessions.

Wait … was that his clothes on the chair on the other side of the room? He staggered around the bed, almost losing his balance along the way. Everything looked like it was there – his pants, underwear, shirt, and blazer were all draped over the back and arm rests. Even his socks and shoes were on the floor under the chair. His glasses, wallet, and cell phone sat in the middle of the chair seat as if they'd been arranged side by side on display. The only thing missing was his car rental keys which he'd left back in his own hotel room.

Hold on, what was that? He fumbled his glasses on and leaned down trying to get his eyes to focus. An additional mobile phone was there along with his stuff. It was smaller than his smartphone, but thicker. He picked it up and stared at it. It was an older flip phone of a kind he'd not seen since the late '90s or early 2000s. It was plain black, no brand name. After turning it over a couple times, he flipped it open and squinted at the small pale-green monochrome screen with black text and the push button number pad below. In his blurry vision and swimming thoughts, he didn't want to try to figure this out right now.

Setting the mysterious phone down, he picked up his own phone and hit the power button. The screen immediately lit up – it had not been powered off and there were three voice messages.

Oh boy ...

Opening his wallet, he found the same $120 that was there the night before. So he hadn't been robbed. What happened then? Did he really drink that much? Never had booze made him feel this lousy.

Stumbling toward the bathroom, he stood before the toilet and noticed his urine was darker than normal. This startled him and after finishing, he leaned into the mirror and took a close look at himself. His pupils were pinpoint small and looked strange.

"You *bitch*. You drugged me," he said to his reflection.

A sudden thought frightened him, and he turned around to examine his lower back in the mirror. He'd heard horror stories of people in Vegas getting sedated and waking up to find a kidney surgically removed to be sold on the organ black market. There were no marks on his back though. Besides a nasty headache, there were no other noticeable pains in or on his body.

A terrible, fearful sensation was rising up inside him. Feeling a punch in the gut, he leaned over the sink and dry heaved several times. The pain was intense, and the booming ache in his skull became so fierce he groaned and felt like passing out. A couple minutes later, he stumbled out of the bathroom, grabbed his clothes, and began putting them back on, almost falling over trying to get his legs into the pants.

Still in his socks, he sat and hit the voicemail button on his phone.

The first message was from Gerard. "Jim, where are you? It's six-fifteen and I'm in the lobby waiting. Call me back."

The second message was also from Gerard. "Jim, it's a quarter to seven. I had the front desk call your room and no answer. This isn't good, man. I'm going to start heading up. Call me when you get to Mercury and I'll meet you at the main entrance if I can."

The third message was from Kay Allison. "James, this is Kay. Gerard told me he can't find you. What's going on? If we don't hear back, we'll have to send someone to look for you. Hope everything is okay."

Holy shit … Jim remembered being told a long time ago that DOE laboratories had a policy for personnel that went missing while on business travel; they actually sent security officers to search for them. He had no plausible excuse. He was going to lose his job over this.

After grabbing a water bottle out of the mini refrigerator, he searched for aspirin or some other pain killer anywhere around the room and bathroom and found none. He then sat back down and chugged about half the bottle down while looking for Gerard's number. What was he going to say? He'd have to explain why he never showed this morning. It had to be believable. "Sorry, I got drunk" wasn't going to cut it.

He'd tell a partial truth. There was no other way. After all, stuff like this happened in Vegas all the time, didn't it?

Heart racing, he dialed Gerard's number – it went to voicemail. "Gerard, it's Jim." His voice sounded ragged, and a little shaky. "I'm so sorry man. I, I, oh man, okay. Look, I got robbed last night. I got drugged and robbed by this woman. I'm not joking. I'm sorry. I'll try to make it up there shortly."

He started to stand too quickly, causing the room to spin like a giant roulette wheel around him. He sat heavily back down. What was he thinking? No way he could drive. He'd better make another call. Finding Kay's number in the received calls list, he dialed and waited; it also went to voicemail. He took off his glasses and rubbed his eyes as he spoke. "Kay, it's Jim. Uh, James. Mueller. Listen, I'm okay.

Call off the cavalry. I'll explain everything. I got robbed last night. But I'm okay. I'm going to try to meet up with Gerard. I'll, oh god, I … I don't know. Sorry. Bye."

Dammit, he was babbling. And his head was pounding. He gulped down the rest of the water, tossed the bottle in the small garbage bucket near the desk and took one last look around the room. He saw nothing familiar or of interest.

What did you do to me, Iris …

After pocketing his possessions and the flip phone, he stumbled to the door, opened it, and saw that it was room 312. Okay, third floor. Elevators.

Shuffling awkwardly down the hallway and using the wall to brace himself, he found the elevators and made his way to the lobby. The dim, flashy, dreamlike atmosphere of last night was gone and replaced with a brightly lit and dismal scene. There was no laughter or shouting, no positive energy in the air. A few red-eyed, expressionless people sat at slot machines, many with ashtrays and half-full beer bottles or tumblers. The air reeked of stale cigarette smoke. One or two weary looking servers roamed slowly about looking no happier than the hungover people putting the last of their money into the machines.

Somehow Jim navigated the maze of tables, dizzying carpet designs and blinking lights, and found the exit, all the while trying to think of how he got here last night. He took a couple deep breaths and looked around, squinting in the bright afternoon light. His vision jerked and warbled as he steadied himself.

A taxi. He'd taken a taxi.

A YELLOW CAB with a sign on top advertising some sushi restaurant was a few feet down from the main entrance. He walked as steadily as he could toward it, nodded at the driver, then eased into the backseat.

The driver looked at Jim through the rearview mirror. Where was he staying? Uhm, oh yeah. "Hampton, Craig road," he told the driver, who watched him for a moment before turning on the engine.

As the cab pulled away, Jim's personal phone beeped with a new email message. Opening the mail, he rubbed his eyes and tried to remove the blurriness. When his vision cleared enough to see the contents, he screamed so loud and in such a horrified way, the driver screeched to a stop in the middle of the road and turned around.

Jim looked up, white faced and shaking. "Just keep driving, please," he managed to squeak as tears welled up in his eyes.

Chapter 17

Jim Mueller sat in the upholstered swivel chair in his hotel room staring at his phone. As soon as he'd stumbled in more than an hour ago, he'd sat down and cried, or sobbed rather. He couldn't remember crying that hard since he was a child. Never in his life had he felt like the rug had been pulled so devastatingly out from under him. As he cried, he was imagining how he was going to deal with what was obviously a blackmail situation. Otherwise, he'd be in handcuffs right now.

How much were they going to ask for? But why him? He wasn't wealthy. He made enough to drive a decent but not flashy car, pay the mortgage, and keep himself fed and insured. But otherwise, he didn't have that much in the bank. Would he have to sell his house to pay off these people who worked with "Iris," or whatever the hell her real name was?

He went through the pictures he'd been sent for the third time and tried to convince himself it was all just a bad dream. The images came with no message, no warning, nothing – everything that needed to be communicated was already there.

The first photo was a side view of him lying naked on the bed. His eyes were closed, but in the context, his expression conveyed pleasure. And straddled on top of him was a naked girl who looked no older than a tween. The girl's hair had been braided into pigtails on each side making her look even younger. Her face was turned to the camera and her deep, dark eyes pierced with a look that held a combination of disgust, anger, and fear.

He moved to the next photo. This one was from the front of the bed, showing Jim's feet and the girl's back as she mounted him. But she had her head craned to the right and was looking back toward the camera, revealing a large bruise to the side of her face. The wound looked painful and real, not a makeup job, with deep purple splotches surrounded by an angry red. It looked very much as if a man's fist had struck her.

The next photo was a closeup of the girl licking his left nipple. His hand had been propped up and placed over the nape of her neck as if he were holding her there. This time her eyes were closed in a kind of grimace, as if what she was doing repulsed her too much to look. The image brought out even more painful details to the injury and welt on her adolescent face. The kid looked Asian but not Chinese; he couldn't tell.

Oh, what did it matter? What did anything matter? His life was over.

There were several more photos, some closeups of him. One with his mouth open, as if he were groaning in pleasure. Another that may have been manipulated to look like he was smiling. Another made to look as if he were holding the girl's head near his crotch.

Unable to continue, he set the phone down. He wanted to cry more but felt too spent.

A minute or two later, his phone started ringing. He looked at the screen. The area code and number appeared to be from the lab. He didn't feel like talking to anyone yet. He sat watching, letting it go to voicemail.

A couple minutes later, the voicemail symbol appeared in the upper left. Warily, he hit the speed dial for voicemail, then entered his passcode. He heard an older man's voice.

"This message is for James Mueller. Mr. Mueller, my name is Sergeant Ronald McClelland with the laboratory's security and crime investigation section. We received a report that you were the victim of a robbery while on travel assignment. I need you to return my call as soon as possible to discuss this. We need to know if anything belonging to the lab was taken, like your HSPD-12 badge, and especially equipment such as your mobile phone, laptop, or any printed documents. And if you haven't already, I need you to contact the Las Vegas Police Department and file a report. Give them a full description of the individual or individuals you believe were involved while events are still fresh in your memory. I will need the number of that police report. I expect to hear from you soon."

Jim hit the nine on his phone to save the message. He was indeed going to have to go to the police. No one would believe his story if he didn't. Surely they'd want to know if he'd exchanged any messages with the perpetrator. What would he do if they asked to see his phone? He'd have to lie and say it had been a chance encounter. Whatever he made up, he'd better be consistent.

The fear and self-pity he'd been feeling was all at once replaced by a violent rage. What did he do to deserve this? Sure, he hadn't lived a clean life like Jeremy, but he wasn't evil. He didn't hurt children or rob old ladies. All the past hurts in his life, the people he'd never forgiven or let go of, even back to high school, sprang up inside him like a shower of sparks.

He stood and started pacing back and forth, cursing and kicking furniture and throwing small objects across the room. He cursed the woman who called herself Iris. He cursed the Lừ Chá app and resolved right then and there to delete all messages and uninstall it and anything else remotely suspicious. He cursed his impulsiveness to binge drink, his propensity to lust, and the loneliness and insecurity that drove him to these behaviors. He cursed Las Vegas. He cursed gambling. He cursed Johnnie Walker. He cursed the twisted degenerates who would hurt a little girl and force her to do that. Finally, he cursed Vaneesa, his soon to be ex-wife, who was getting ready to be the next in line to beat him up.

He should have been stillborn; his parents would have been happier with just Jeremy anyway.

After several minutes of this, he sat back down, drained and defeated. He felt winded and dizzy and realized whatever Iris slipped him last night was still in his system. The headache still throbbed but he'd been so distracted he'd almost forgotten about it.

He picked up his phone again and was about to dial Gerard but then stopped. He decided to send a text message instead. *Gerard, Jim. I'm not going to be able to make it. Sorry. I have to deal with the police and file a report and all that. Have a good trip. Wish I was there.*

Wish I was there ... that sounded cheesy.

Fortunately, he wouldn't have to deal with Kay – she'd already offloaded the situation to security and crime investigation. Boy was he going to be the talk of the town upon returning, that is if they didn't revoke his clearance and he still had a job.

He looked at his suitcase on the floor next to the bathroom. He'd gone through it earlier and his laptop was still there. They, whoever they were, hadn't stolen anything. They could have, it wouldn't have been difficult as his hotel room key with the Hampton Inn logo had been in his wallet. They hadn't stolen what little money he had either. It looked like no one had been in this room. What did they want from him?

He needed to get moving. So what was the plan now, besides wait for his blackmailers to contact him on that flip phone? A feeling of serious anxiety was filling his whole body. It reminded him of when he was a kid and saw *The Exorcist* – he'd been so terrified, he couldn't sleep for a couple nights. That kind of cold dread was eating at him now.

Stay calm, keep your head screwed on.

Okay, first, he couldn't think with this headache. He would go to the small hotel store and buy pain killers, lots of pain killers. Then he was going to try to eat a little something before he got sick. Then he was going to contact the Las Vegas police department. He needed to be careful though. Should he give an actual description of Iris or make up something else? These people held all the cards and could utterly ruin him. Even Jeremy wouldn't believe him if he saw those pictures. Hell, these people may just destroy his life anyway no matter what he did. But maybe, just maybe, they'd have mercy if he cooperated and didn't give the cops anything to go on.

If though, after all this was over, they went ahead and released those pictures anyway, he'd probably just kill himself. Perhaps he'd try to kill Iris first.

***

The interview with the Las Vegas cops went about as expected. First, he was correct in assuming getting drugged and robbed is more common than many think. Apparently, it's been happening all over the country, not just in Vegas. The LVMPD – Las Vegas Metropolitan Police Department – was, in fact, looking at close to a hundred and fifty cases in just this year alone so far. And they believed the numbers were higher because many victims are too embarrassed to come forward. Jim knew he'd be one of those – he'd never tell anyone if he didn't have to.

Also as expected, they wanted to know if there'd been any prior communication with the woman who robbed him.

"Did you meet her online? Any pictures of her? Did you exchange any emails or texts?"

No, he'd been at the bar having a drink when a total stranger he'd never seen or talked to before approached him and that's how it all started.

"What name did she give you?"

Jim had scrambled. For whatever reason, he'd not prepared an answer for this. "I think her name was Lisa."

"You think?"

"Sorry, it's kind of a blur now."

"What room did she take you to?"

"Oh god what was it …" He saw the numbers *312* in his mind. "Sorry, I just don't remember."

Jim had confidently offered up his phone to let them look through it. Earlier, as planned, he'd deleted his profile and all messages on Lù Chá before uninstalling the damned app. He then carefully perused his regular text messages to look for anything even vaguely scandalous but saw nothing. He then created a new Proton Mail account with some random username and a password no one could possibly figure out and forwarded the incriminating email with the pictures to that account. He then deleted the message off his regular mail. Then, to the best of his know-how, cleared all the browsing history and unused files on his phone. He didn't know what else to do.

The detective who interviewed him, a Lieutenant Justin Hesel, a man in his mid-fifties with thick white hair and a thin beard, had stared at Jim's phone for a moment and then waved it off. They didn't need to see it. The Lieutenant implied he was relieved not to spend any time doing that. Besides, people who were hiding things didn't so easily hand over their phones.

Part of it though was that Hesel seemed to be impressed by the line of work Mueller did. Jim showed the detective his HSPD-12 badge, and it looked very official. Hesel remarked that he'd not seen one of those before and asked what the "Q" meant. Jim gave him a good summary.

"What kind of assignment are you here on in Vegas?"

"It's actually north of Vegas, but I can't talk about it. It's classified."

Then came the scary part because the lies were starting to seriously add up. Hesel wanted a full description of this woman, everything Jim could remember about Lisa's appearance – tattoos, clothes, jewelry, mannerisms, any accent, et cetera.

Jim wanted to make sure Iris and her people knew he didn't give them up. He knew that like so many bad choices he'd made in recent years, lying could come back to bite him. But fear drove him forward. In the end he gave a vague description of a cute woman with sandy blonde hair in her late twenties or early thirties. After a moment, he realized he was describing of one the cocktail waitresses he saw that night.

"Where exactly were you, and during what time window did you talk to this woman?"

Jim actually told the truth here because his brain was getting tired and he was fearful of forgetting details. He said he'd been at the Cosmopolitan and even described the lounge. He did give a time that was much later though, saying it had been like close to 11:00 p.m. when he first ran into her.

"Why were you at the Cosmopolitan?"

A shrug. "It looked like a nice place to hang out."

Nervousness made him too uneasy to try to invent anything more. He may have to repeat this line of questioning at some point. In fact, he'd probably have to repeat it all to that Sergeant McClelland who'd call him from the lab.

Detective Hesel asked a few more questions trying to pinpoint times and locations. Then he stopped and paused. There was something that was bothering him. Jim had told the detective that the woman only stole a little cash out of his wallet, not even a hundred bucks. That's it? Even if they caught her, it'd be a misdemeanor at best. In the state of Nevada, theft and larceny were misdemeanors if the value of the goods or property stolen was less than $1,200. Such a conviction might get a person six months in the pen and a fine of 1,000 bucks.

"She didn't take your phone or credit cards?"

"Nope."

This really surprised Hesel. These thieves always took that stuff. They knew that within twelve to twenty-four hours, the victim would be reporting the theft, so they'd go on credit card buying sprees as fast as possible, draining bank accounts as well if they get hold of the victim's debit card PIN.

But all in all, the detective looked tired of dealing with these cases. There were just too many, and since Mueller wasn't physically hurt and the only financial crime was a misdemeanor, this one would definitely go to the lower half of the priority pile.

Slipping someone an illegal drug without their knowledge or consent was definitely a felony crime, but unless the victim did a blood toxicology test in a certified laboratory while it was still in his system, it couldn't be proven. Unless, of course, the perpetrator was caught and admitted it, but chances were, that wouldn't happen. Hesel didn't say any of this, but Jim felt it.

The interview abruptly ended.

We'll do what we can, Jim was assured. Give us a call if you think of anything else. Have a good rest of your stay and be careful.

Jim took Lieutenant Hesel's business card with the case number written on it.

When Jim got back to the hotel room, he powered up the laptop and decided he'd send that sergeant from the lab a mail instead of calling. He would also send a quick summary to his manager, Francis Lane. He just didn't feel like talking anymore about it. Besides, once he told them nothing sensitive or any equipment of theirs had been stolen, he assumed their reaction would be similar to Detective Hesel's – Mueller the idiot was suckered by some girl in Vegas.

He found Ronald McClelland's name in the lab's Outlook directory. In his email, Jim first assured McClelland that nothing of the lab's had been taken. Next, he provided the police report number he'd just filed. He then made assurances he was fine, no injuries, no trips to the hospital. Yes, he'd see the lab's medical about the drugs he thought he'd been given. If McClelland still wanted to talk, please call, otherwise Jim was coming back home shortly and they could meet in person. He then tossed Detective Hesel's business card in the trash.

Okay, that was done. Now see about the next flight home from this wretched city. He checked the website for Southwest and there was a flight back to Oakland at 7:00 p.m. this evening.

He looked at the little black flip phone on the desk. It sat there in silence, almost mocking him, a little timebomb ready to blow.

Chapter 18

Liang Huang proudly prepared another brief progress report for his superiors who resided in plush offices several hundred feet above ground. The only thing he envied about them was the exorbitant money they earned. Otherwise, they walked a much thinner political and tactical tightrope than he did. He was glad to be down in the ditch with the shovel rather than up there playing what amounted to career survival games.

Everything is going according to plan, he typed. *Contact has been made. Coercion and incentives have been delivered. Will be providing instructions to ops shortly.*

Huang sat back and smiled to himself. This was going to be the best "to kill two birds with one stone" assignment he'd ever worked on. And he would be rewarded handsomely.

The subject had booked a flight back to California. They would make the second contact and move quickly while fear still drove him and made him submissive.

A quick search and triangulation revealed that the mobile phone the subject had been given now travelled with his personal phone. He'd been wise to take it.

But there was one unknown that had to be clarified. Huang quickly dialed the MSS' Foreign Infiltration Office.

"Yes," the voice answered.

"I need a voice actor, age and gender unimportant."

"What agency to what agency?"

"US federal government employer to US police department. I'll provide a script shortly."

"One hour."

***

Lieutenant Justin Hesel was watching the clock, waiting for the last fifteen minutes of his shift to end so he could go home and recline on his La-Z-Boy with a good, strong drink. He would permit himself the adult beverage because he'd not be on call for a change.

He sighed deeply. He felt like hadn't gotten a good night's sleep in months. If he could, he'd retire now, today, but still had to ride out another two and a half years to make pension.

He used to be on a rotation where he was the detective on weekend call only once every five weeks. But as people quit or moved on, it became once every four, then every three, now it was sometimes every two. Mondays in particular had become especially tiring having to get into the office early. Crime scenes had to be looked at while they were fresh, so a.m. and p.m. didn't matter. Then when he got to the office, he was looking at two or three new cases before the work week had even started. Soon, he'd be free of the fetters of an erratic schedule that wasn't even really a schedule to begin with.

There were some perks. He didn't miss the uniform, especially in the dry Vegas heat. He also worked a lot in an air-conditioned office. The Ford Taurus unmarked car he drove back and forth to work wasn't the Dodge Charger highway patrol got, but at least it made him inconspicuous.

Today he'd returned seven calls, three of them from family members of a missing person case he'd been working on for the last two weeks. A sixteen-year-old kid had disappeared and his skateboard was found in a dumpster behind a grocery store about five miles from his part time job. At this point, the kid was considered a runaway and not endangered. They'd put out flyers around shopping centers and gas stations with the kid's picture and description, what he'd been wearing and so on, but so far, nothing.

Families of missing persons were always understandably desperate for answers, hoping you had solid leads, and terribly disappointed when you didn't. He'd done more reassuring than actual case solving in the last ten years, and it was starting to wear on him.

The rest of the job as detective was interviewing. Interviewing victims, interviewing witnesses, and interviewing suspects, many of whom had lawyers that did nothing but put roadblocks up and coach their clients what to say. Multiple witnesses to a crime meant contradicting statements, it was inevitable. Most suspect's answers were short and evasive and after twenty years you can see a liar a mile away, but you still need evidence before you can make the accusation.

During downtimes, he might call the lab and see about a piece of evidence from some case weeks or months back – blood on a carpet, a fingerprint on a window, footprint castings, photos of this or that. When the reports did come back, you *might* have enough to write up a search warrant for someone's car or house and then send a draft off to the district attorney's office for review. Then more waiting.

His desk phone rang. He pressed the speaker button. "Hesel."

"Good afternoon, Lieutenant Hesel," a firm and professional female voice said. "My name is Sandra Mercer from the Department of Energy Office of Human Resource. I'm calling from our headquarters on Independence Avenue in Washington, DC." Her voice was clear and held maybe a Midwestern accent.

Hesel frowned and grabbed a notepad and pen, anticipating having to write something down. "Uhm, yes? How can I help you?"

"I understand you filed a robbery report today for a Mr. James Mueller."

"Yes. Yes I did." *How the heck did they get wind of that already?*

The voice continued. "He's a Department of Energy employee who was on a special assignment when this incident occurred."

"Yes, he told me a little about his employment. But said he couldn't say much."

"That is correct, Lieutenant. His assignment was sensitive."

"I understand. It turned out to be not much of a case though. Not much was stolen. He couldn't provide much of anything for us to go on."

"We take these matters very seriously regardless of the circumstances. For our records, we would like a copy of your report. The Chief Human Capital Officer would like to see it A-SAP. We always conduct our own in-house investigations, as you may well understand."

"Oh, I do, yes," Hesel said, fighting off a yawn and writing a couple things down on the notepad.

"Let me provide you a secure fax number, and if you could send it to us as soon as possible we would be most grateful."

"Sure, no problem." He jotted down the fax number.

About twenty minutes later, Liang Huang, in his underground workspace in Beijing, had a copy of the Las Vegas police report the subject had filed earlier that day.

Huang scanned through it and smiled. "Lisa," he laughed.

Our boy was playing ball.

***

Jim had just sat down in his car in the long-term parking lot at Oakland International Airport when he felt the little black flip phone vibrate and sound off with that classic high-pitched digital ringtone phones of that era had. He'd stuck it in the breast pocket of his blazer and had been anticipating this moment with the apprehension of a convicted murderer awaiting sentencing.

He'd thought very carefully about his reaction once this call came and was actually grateful they'd given him a few hours to think about it. If they'd called while he was still in Vegas, he would have fumed and cursed and threatened and everything else, which may have gone bad for him. After all, they had him by the balls, literally; any move he made on the board could be calmly checkmated.

He looked around the parking lot as it rang but couldn't see much because it was already 8:30 p.m. On the phone's little screen, it said the call was from a "Restricted" number. After four rings, he hit the Send button, but said nothing.

"Jimmy?" came the sweet voice he'd been excited about just the other night.

Jim closed his eyes. He was still fuming. In fact, he was quickly becoming more angry than scared of these people. Part of it was the fact that he was trying hard not to care if they sent out those pictures. Of course, he did care and didn't want to see his life destroyed, but at the same time, he'd succumbed to fate that this was out of his control. He was already formulating Plan B to admit lying to the police and trying to convince everyone that none of this was his fault.

But no matter what he did, no matter how much he cooperated, they could and probably would hold this over him for the rest of his life. The thought brought on an irrational rage – a raw, visceral urge to kill that he'd not felt since he was in high school and wanted to murder a couple bullies.

"I know you're there, Jimmy," the voice drawled.

I'm not gonna ask what your real name is ...

Jim remained silent, perhaps because denying the woman he knew as "Iris" the satisfaction of making him beg for mercy was the only card he had to play at the moment. That's what people with power over others loved – control. Then again, these weren't the antagonizers of his youth, they were professionals with resources, and they wanted something from him. Play along for now, no choice.

"I know you're upset," the voice teased, with maybe a trace of actual compassion. "But please know this isn't anything personal."

Did she just say please? He took a deep breath. "What do you want?" he finally asked.

"An excellent question. We're glad you've carefully considered your situation." Now the voice had a smile to it, as if her next question might be, *did the pictures turn you on?*

Jim closed his eyes. "The only thing I've considered is what sick bastards you are. Is that welt on the girl's face real?"

"Yes. *Terrible* what you did to her."

Jim set the phone on his lap for a moment. "You bitch. You evil bitch," he said quietly, more to himself.

"I heard that, Jimmy," the voice came through the speaker.

He quickly brought the phone back up and snarled, "I asked you what you wanted."

"First off, you need to stay calm. You're distressed and feeling a lot of pressure right now, very understandable. But if you cooperate and not do anything stupid, you'll be able to get on with your life shortly."

"Bullshit."

"We appreciate that you didn't give the police a description of me. That was wise."

Jim rubbed the bridge of his nose with thumb and index finger. Just who were these people that they already knew what was in the Las Vegas police report? Perhaps he should be more frightened of what they were capable of.

He took another deep breath. "I don't have money. If that's what you're after, you've wasted your efforts," he said.

"We're aware you don't."

"Alright. I'm listening."

"Just keep this phone with you. I'll be in touch soon. And remember, nothing stupid."

The call ended.

Chapter 19

Joey Salvo had worked hard to get where he was. At eighteen he joined the Marine Corp and performed so well that just four years later, he was a Sergeant on the verge of promotion to Staff Sergeant. But he elected to opt out and was honorably discharged.

Upon returning, he enlisted in the Nevada state POST academy in Carson City and passed all medical, background, polygraph, and drug tests, with flying colors. Two and a half years later, after proving to be superior to most of his counterparts in discipline, firearms, written and verbal communication, investigative procedures and operations, and even basic field medical skills, he graduated a full-fledged police officer.

He then enrolled in a four-year Criminal Justice degree program at the University of Nevada, Reno. While doing that, he befriended a couple experienced old-school police detectives and learned everything he could from them. Of particular interest to Joey was how they tactfully delivered bad news to say, friends or family of a murder victim, and how they communicated with both firmness and empathy in heart-breaking but also time-sensitive investigations. These were skills acquired in the field, not in classrooms.

What was really fascinating though, was what experienced cops knew about reading body language and effectively interviewing witnesses and interrogating suspects. These are the two skills one needed to be successful, he was told more than once. And there's a difference. The former was about asking the right questions to gather information from people with different perspectives or who may not remember details well; the latter needed negotiation skills and a grasp of basic human psychology. Detectives who made the cut were part cop and part shrink, weeding through the facts versus the speculation or lies. You needed to get this right because if a suspect's lawyer convinces a judge that a person was coerced or entrapped, the evidence was tossed. To boot, what evidence you acquired better have been legally obtained, or else it was inadmissible – "fruit of the poisonous tree," as it was called.

Fast forward a few more years and Joey was now a fledgling detective and couldn't be more excited. He'd cut his teeth mostly in the mid-western portion of the state in Greater Reno and Carson City but was recently asked to go south and assist the boys in Vegas. Joey had jumped at the opportunity; a different venue and a different set of detectives meant more new things to learn.

Joey approached the desk of Lieutenant Justin Hesel. "Good morning. Lieutenant Hesel?"

Hesel rubbed his eyes and looked up at the tall, young man before him.

"Joey Salvo," he said stepping forward and extending his hand.

Hesel stared for a moment and then smiled, extending his. "Ah yes, I was told to expect you this week. You're early."

"We hear you've been a little swamped."

"That's putting it mildly," Hesel said, picking up a coffee cup. "I've heard good things about you. You've been climbing fast up there."

"I've been doing my best, Lieutenant," Joey said confidently, but not smugly.

Hesel waved it off. "Call me Justin. You and I are colleagues now. I've got an office right over here you can use."

As they walked, Salvo asked, "What are you mostly working on down here?"

"Probably the same stuff you are, although I hear the ten-thirty-twos and two-forty-fives have been steadily getting worse, particularly around Reno."

"Unfortunately, that's true."

"If you don't mind, I've got some low impact cases I just don't have a lot of time for. But I don't want to ignore them either."

"I'm here to work on anything you need me to."

"Good." Hesel paused at the office doorway. "I had one a couple days ago, typical drug 'n mug 'em case. But there's two things interesting about it. The victim, a James Mueller, is a Department of Energy guy with a top-secret clearance, whatever that entails, and was on a work assignment when it happened. Had a 'Q' on his ID badge."

Salvo nodded. "Probably like a military TS – top secret. Means he can look at classified information if he needs to know. Does he work where they did all the nuclear testing in the '50s?"

"Yeah, but he wouldn't tell me anything about his assignment, said was 'sensitive.'"

"What's the second interesting thing about the case?"

"The perpetrator, a blonde female in her thirties, according to Mueller, only took a little of his cash. Nothing else. Woke up with his phone, credit cards, everything still there. It doesn't add up. I've been a cop long enough to know when someone is keeping a few things in their back pocket. But I couldn't figure his motive. Anyway, might be nothing, but I'll give you the file. That and a couple of convenience store holdups."

"Sounds good. I'll get started right away."

***

The Reverend Jeremy Mueller, affectionately known to his flock as "Pastor J," smiled as the last of the Sunday's crowd exited. He gave a final wave goodbye, then shut and locked the main doors. The weather was sunny and beautiful, and people wanted to get back home to enjoy some leisure.

He turned and looked at the empty pews. Leading a small church was challenging work. The constant expectations were always high while the number of volunteers and resources were always low. But it wasn't just a job, it was who he was, as he'd discovered.

Recent years had seen some growth and with it a lot of excitement. He considered it the greatest privilege in the world to help someone get on or back to the straight and narrow path that led to salvation. This is what he wanted for his little brother Jimmy, to get him on that path that Jimmy had probably never been on in the first place.

Jeremy thought of something, pulled out his phone and looked up Jimmy's number. He typed a text message: *Hey Jimmy, how did your Vegas trip go? Also, R U going to be around next week?*

He sat on one of the pews and continued reflecting. At times, the responsibilities of leading a small congregation could feel overwhelming and exhausting – difficult people, juggling pastoral and leadership duties, always on call. You're the head of "everything," always having to do above and beyond more than you're called or trained for. When plumbers, painters and electricians can't be afforded or found in the congregation, you're it, or you try to be anyway.

People also disappoint and didn't follow through on commitments. Some were manipulators who try to take advantage of a pastor's generous heart. Plans fail, conflicts arise. Unlike a nine to five job, you didn't leave your duties once service was over, you took it all home. You were still a counselor, mentor, prayer partner and encourager twenty-four-seven. And your life was always in the spotlight.

But despite all this, it was also deeply satisfying. Jeremy had developed intimate relationships with wonderful people, and when vision and the right people came together, it was fulfilling in a way nothing else could be. He also had to be reminded by people he trusted that his personal worth wasn't about how "successful" his ministries were, it was about what he did day to day.

Pastors of large churches had executive and assistant pastors as well as lay ministers who could take over in a pinch, or if you were having a particularly stressful week and just needed a break. Occasionally, he wished he had these resources, especially back when he had to work Monday through Friday on top of his church duties.

But that had just changed in the last three months, and he couldn't be happier. The church was now bringing in enough money so he could be a full-time pastor. With that had come a refreshing abundance of free time during the week.

A beep indicated a text message. It was from Jimmy. *Yeah, I'm back in town and not going anywhere.*

Well, that was quick and to the point. Nothing said of the trip or his meeting with Iris. Interesting. Did something negative happen? Poor Jimmy was always digging holes then stumbling into them. Jeremy hit reply and typed: *Okay, just checking. I might be in your area soon.*

Awhile back, a friend of his had invited him to a pastor's conference held twice a year in the Silicon Valley area and it was coming up in just a few days. He'd not been able to make it before but would this time. While he was in the area, he'd pay a surprise visit to his kid brother. He'd enjoyed the last conversation with him and was hoping things were going well with his job. He was also curious what happened with Iris. He wished more that Jimmy and Vaneesa would work things out, but it didn't look like it was going to at this point.

People make their choices.

Chapter 20

The sun was just starting to glow above the horizon as Jim made his way along Highway 580 East. His thoughts swirled with what he was going to face when he got to work. His innards were feeling like simmering stew on a stove, and he fought fatigue. He felt like he wouldn't get good sleep for years at this point.

Had he really brought all this on himself, or was he once again the victim he'd so often felt like throughout his childhood?

He waited for that hideous little black phone to buzz and ring but it did not. It rested in his pocket, teasing and taunting. Normally he enjoyed driving in this early, but that was a feeling he may not ever have again, assuming he'd still have a job in the near future.

He exited and headed up the road to a gas station where he often bought a large coffee. Everything looked and felt different. Even the cool, morning air touched his skin differently.

As he turned up the small side street that only cars going into the laboratory take, his heart thudded a little stronger. He slowly drove past the "Please Dim Your Headlights" sign, which he normally ignored, but this time dutifully obeyed.

He watched as the guard in the gatehouse chatted with someone a couple cars ahead and wondered how he'd fare at such a job. The day would probably come when the main entrances were "manned" by robots. Despite the fact that top secret, classified work was done here, they still had not installed a double-check system, such as a machine verification post where someone had to swipe their badge after showing it to a guard.

Machines never got tired, never came to work hungover, never were distracted by financial, marital, or kid problems (not to mention never got blackmailed). And these machines would have a database of all seven thousand workers at the lab. One touch of the chip on the HSPD-12 card and they'd know everything about the person who carried it.

But for now, guards were fallible human beings. Humans get bored and used to certain "truisms." Jim wondered if guards ever let people in they knew well without checking their badge, like a colleague or a someone in a supervisor or managerial position, or just because they were wearing something around their neck. And how many of those got away with vouching for others, or claimed they forgot their badge at home or whatever the case?

Jim knew why he was thinking about such things. There were people who had him cornered who might be getting ready to ask him to do something here. They'd established it wasn't money they were after. What could it be?

He'd read somewhere that in August of 1945, a soviet spy in a laboratory in New Mexico smuggled some Manhattan Project secrets out in a tissue box. Diagrams of bomb designs and documents detailing how to deactivate locks on nuclear weapons, among other things. All those guns and gates and show-me-your-papers, and what worked? – a Kleenex box.

Would it be as easy today? Danny Weng had given him an earful on what they have to do to protect computer components and digital storage – things that weren't around back then.

Jim remembered when he'd first been hired. He went through several long training courses in preparation for his Q-Clearance. He was told he may be a target and in fact, should expect it. As a traveler for the United States government, he could be targeted by a foreign intelligence or security service anytime, anywhere. The fact of the matter was, many foreign governments and businesses still place a high priority on America's technology and information, even long after the end of the Cold War. And if one travelled overseas, the risk of becoming an intelligence target increased.

During one particularly interesting class, he saw a film of a former Soviet Union spy who surrendered himself and defected to the United States. In lieu of prison time, he consulted for the CIA. In the interview, he assured everyone that foreign agents will work any angle to get at people they could potentially recruit for espionage, no matter how long it took. The word he kept using was "patience." They'll be your acquaintance, your friend, your lover, whatever it took.

And it didn't matter if you were low on the totem pole and had no hands-on access to valuable assets. You may be a janitor or a secretary, but you might know someone, who knows someone, who knows someone. You might be approached while on business travel – a friendly stranger casually strikes up conversation while you're having a drink at the hotel bar or standing around outside the conference room.

Or anymore, hits you up on social media …

Jim remembered being told that usually, any intelligence gathering activities directed against a person will be conducted in an unobtrusive and non-threatening manner, although in some cases, they employ more aggressive tactics. If one found themselves being harassed, it was probably intentionally obvious and meant to intimidate or "test" a traveler's reactions. But most intelligence activities are conducted without the target's awareness.

Jim shook his head. He'd been suckered by all his own weaknesses. The booze and the women. Dammit. It had been too easy. He'd only had a handful of exchanges with Iris and then what, a two or three-hour conversation? Unbelievable.

And these people were clearly not patient. Whatever they wanted, they wanted it fast. Iris could have seduced him, become a fling for a while and tried to get him on her side incrementally. And sadly, he probably would have fallen for it hook, line and sinker. Not that she could have turned him into an actual spy, but everything else, oh yeah. He was hot for that lady. She, on the other hand, was no doubt relieved to not have been given that assignment. She would have hated it, like that poor kid they used.

Oh god ... don't even think about that little girl.

He drove forward to the guard, who said "Good morning," nodded, and took his badge.

Jim almost held his breath, waiting for the guard to say something along the lines of, *pull over there to the side and wait.* But nothing happened out of the ordinary. The badge was handed back, and Jim was waved through.

Well, there you have it. If he'd been a full-blown recruit for the People's Republic of China, here he was inside one of America's most esteemed research and weapons laboratories.

As he made his way around the curve of the northwest corner of the campus, he sped up to exactly twenty-five miles per hour, the speed limit when onsite. He was going to do nothing to draw attention. He was on a road that people got busted for speeding on all the time because it was long and straight and ran a good mile parallel to the perimeter fence.

He'd driven about 300 feet or so when in the dim light, his headlights picked up two or three individuals on the side of the road. One person donned what appeared to be a standard white lab coat, the other two were in a guard's camouflage uniform.

"What the –?" Jim said to himself.

Feeling like he recognized the guy in the coat, he slowed the car down to a crawl and peered at them. One of the guards gave a friendly wave.

"Jim!" the guy in the lab coat said. It was Peter Wright, a hardware engineer who had his hands in several Helios components.

"What are you guys doing out here so early?" Jim asked.

"Experimenting, of course. Taking advantage of the early morning traffic. Hey, this is good timing. Can you gimme a ride back? Save these guys the trouble," Peter said, gesturing at the two guards on either side.

"Sure, hop in," Jim said, grateful for the distraction.

Peter grabbed a thick plastic case and a laptop computer and lugged it toward Jim's car. He nodded at one of the guards who opened the rear door.

"Put this in here?" Peter asked.

"Is it a bomb?" Jim asked.

"Better. It finds bombs." Peter shoved the case and laptop in the back seat then hopped in the passenger side. "Thanks, gents!" he said to the guards who waved as they drove away.

Jim looked at Peter. "What new toy have you invented for Uncle Sam now?"

"It's a new and improved *meeram*," Peter said.

"Meer-am," Jim repeated.

"M, R, A, M. Means mobile radiation area monitor. They've actually been around since two-thousand-six, but they're better now."

"I love the acronyms around here. Enlighten me."

"Originally developed to stop dirty bombs. Try hauling radiological material over the border in a fast-moving truck, and 'meeram' will detect it. It can be a simple stand-alone radiation monitor or networked into a system of monitors to cover a big area. It can be used as a fixed detector to monitor slow-moving packages, luggage, or pedestrians, and as a portable detector. It's optimized to detect even small quantities of radioactive materials moving at highway speeds."

"That's what you were doing back there?"

"Correct. We were putting tiny amounts of radioactive material, not enough to hurt anyone, in the back of the security SUVs and then driving by at different speeds."

"How does it work, like the sniffers at airports?" Jim slowed as they approached the narrow entrances to the parking lot.

"No, no. Those sniffers look for trace residue of chemicals used to make bombs. Chemical reactions occur at the level of electrons. 'Meeram' looks for stuff based on fusion reactions, which are thermonuclear reactions, which means they occur at the level of the nucleus."

Jim just looked at Peter. "I believe you."

Peter continued, getting more excited. "It uses a thallium-doped sodium iodide crystal to detect even minute amounts of radiation in different s cenarios. T he crystal can be shielded on certain sides to 'point' the detector in a particular direction. The crystal detects full spectral data by dividing the spectrum into 1,024 energy bins, or channels. Unlike most detectors, which collect gross counts or divide the spectrum into only ten channels, 'meeram' counts single photons. The sensitivity can be adjusted as well. Its custom software gives results in near real time."

"I'm sorry I asked."

Peter laughed. "No, you're not. You know you love this stuff."

"Maybe." They pulled into the main parking lot in front of the area where the Helios lab was tucked away behind high fences and security portals.

Peter was on a roll and talking like a kid. "Monitoring for radiological material involves three steps: detection, localization, and identification. Each step used to require a different piece of equipment, depending on a system's design. In older systems, a large portal monitor might perform the initial detection phase of all vehicles. Suspect shipments would then be inspected using smaller handheld detectors to localize and identify the material. But 'meeram' combines detection and identification into a single step."

Jim was smiling and shaking his head. "I'll ask one more question even though curiosity has tried to kill *this* cat several times now. How, dare I ask, have you improved this?"

Peter beamed a proud smile. "So, for over a decade now, this technology has been everywhere. Floating inside buoys in our ocean ports around the country. Stationed at crossing borders. And in every major city, disguised as everything from telephone cable boxes to maintenance hole covers to decorative sidewalk and park barriers. But inside all that, 'meeram' is working around the clock, watching for anything radioactive that might float, walk, or drive by."

Jim nodded. "Okay. That *is* pretty interesting."

"Indeed. But now, it's half the size, half the weight, and nearly half the cost. Plus, it's even more sensitive."

"Thanks to you?"

"Well, me and my team," he said with pride.

Jim turned and looked at Peter as he pulled the car to a stop. He admired Peter the way he admired anyone who was so passionate about what they did.

"Help me carry the laptop in?" Peter asked.

"It's the least I can do for the service of my country."

Chapter 21

Detective Joey Salvo reread the robbery report for James Mueller. In some ways, the incident was typical, but like Justin Hesel said, in other ways it was kind of peculiar. Salvo's first thought was that classified material had been stolen and Mueller was afraid to talk about it. He'd seen that kind of thing happen in the military. Someone will make a mistake, even if just an honest and simple one, but afraid to come clean because of how it may affect their career.

Then there was the very vague description of the perp. "A cute blonde woman, maybe early 30s, hair in a ponytail, nice butt." After that Mueller couldn't remember anything. Really? Not even what she was wearing, nothing? If he was going to be that nebulous, why file a police report at all?

First off, no matter how much a person had to drink, they remembered more about the thief that swindled them. The reason was the anticipation of an intimate evening with that person. That typically meant a lot of flirting, staring at body parts, looking each other in the eye while making phony and shallow conversation. This bit of game playing typically went on anywhere from an hour to several.

Salvo sat back and thought. There was one way to find out what this woman looked like and how long she and Mr. Mueller had conversed. Casinos had cameras everywhere. As well, they may have more information on the perp if they'd documented her before. With private contractors and lots of resources, casinos had perfected the art of facial recognition, even before a lot of government agencies had. In fact, the FBI went to them years ago for consulting services on the technology. The nice thing was that casinos were always eager to cooperate with law enforcement when it came to busting thieves, who they hated, because it deterred customers.

Salvo looked up the Cosmopolitan's security console contact info and dialed their number.

"Cosmopolitan," a man's voice said.

"This is Detective Joey Salvo over here at Vegas PD. We're investigating a recent robbery at your establishment. Would you be able to get me surveillance footage of a certain area, during a certain timeframe, in one your bar-lounges?"

"Of course, detective. My name's Marty and I'll be happy to assist. Just give me the details."

***

"Hesel," he said as he picked up the phone.

"Good morning, my name is Sergeant Ronald McClelland. Is this Lieutenant Justin Hesel?"

"It is. How can I help you, sergeant?"

"I am in the security and crime investigation section that contracts for the Department of Energy laboratory that employs a Mr. James Mueller. I understand you filed a report for Mr. Mueller regarding a theft. I have the case number."

"Oh yes. Mr. Mueller. I remember."

"May I request a copy of the official report you filed, please? You may send it via fax if that would be easiest."

Hesel furrowed his eyebrows. "I already faxed the report to DOE headquarters, human resources I think."

"I see. By who's request?"

"By … uhm, ah, what's her name … the chief officer of human resources or something. Oh, I don't remember. Anyway, I faxed it off, but if you need another copy, I can provide it."

"I'm sorry, I'm a little confused," McClelland said. "The Office of Personnel Management was only just made aware of this incident, from me actually, and has requested more details. Can you give me the name and number of the person you sent the fax to?"

"Can you hold for a minute? I've got it written down." Hesel hit a button and walked over to Joey Salvo's office and saw Joey staring intently at his computer screen. "Knock, knock," he said.

Joey looked up. "Hey."

"You got the Mueller case there?"

"Right here," Joey said, putting a hand on a folder.

"Do I have a written note in there about faxing that report to someone at the Department of Energy human resources?"

Joey thumbed through the folder and found it toward the back. "Yeah, right here. A Sandra Mercer and a number."

"Lemme see that note," Hesel said. He walked back to his desk and picked up the phone. "Sergeant McClelland? I have it here."

McClelland called back in twenty minutes. "Lieutenant Hesel, we've got a problem. There is no one by the name of Sandra Mercer at the Office of the Chief Human Capital Officer. Do you have the resources to look into that fax number?"

"I do."

"In the interim, I have another fax number for you to send that report." He gave Hesel the number.

"Lemme make a call and I'll get back to you." Hesel shook his head. He knew he'd smelled something about this case. In his years of travels, he'd gotten to know many individuals who could be of help in a time of need, and one of them was Doug Thomas, the Special Agent in Charge of the FBI field office off West Lake Mead in Las Vegas. When it came to tracking and looking things up, those guys had all kinds of tricks up their sleeves. He dialed their number.

"Federal Bureau of Investigation," a woman's voice said.

"Good morning, this is Lieutenant Hesel over at LVMPD. May I speak to Mr. Thomas?"

"One moment, Lieutenant." There was a pause of about forty-five seconds.

"Good morning, Justin, Cynthia here," said Cynthia Arroyo, one of the assistants to Thomas. "Doug's out of the office right now. How can we help you?"

"Hi Cynthia. I have a mysterious fax number I'd like you guys to run for me, if you would. We're working on a dope 'n rob case at one of the casinos and things are looking weird."

"Sure. Whatcha got?"

He gave Cynthia the number and then waited. The call came back in about thirty minutes.

"Hi Justin. You're gonna love this," Cynthia said. "Although that number you gave us has a DC area code, it hops and hops and hops and you'll never guess where it ends up."

"You got me."

"Beijing, China. From there, the trace gets lost."

Hesel almost spilled his coffee. "Thanks, Cynthia. I owe you guys on top of everything else I owe on top of that."

"On top of all the other things. Don't mention it. Hey, is this something we're going to get involved with?"

"Maybe, I'll let you know."

Hesel hit a button for a new line and quickly dialed a number in California.

"Security and investigation," a voice said.

"Is Sergeant Ronald McClelland there, please."

***

The phone rang. "Salvo."

"Detective Salvo, Marty here at the Cosmopolitan."

"Hi Marty. What do you have?"

"Nothing. Zero. That matches your descriptions"

"Are you sure you got the right location?"

"Based on what you guys told me was in the original report, yes. Are you sure you got the right window of time?"

"Frankly, I'm not sure of anything right now."

"Wanna come over and take a look for yourself?"

"I'd love to. I want to bring the detective that actually interviewed the victim. That okay?"

"Sure, just lemme know when you wanna be here and I'll have someone waiting."

"Thanks, Marty. Call you back." He dialed Hesel's desk.

"Joey," Hesel said. "I was on my way over. I've got some info on the Mueller case. Something really strange."

"So do I. Let's take a trip to the Cosmopolitan. The security guys are gonna show us some video."

"Sounds good, I'll fill you in along the way."

Chapter 22

The phone call came the next morning as Jim was driving in at his usual early morning time. Although he'd been anticipating the call, the shrill digital beeping made him jump.

He flipped the little black phone open. "What," he said into it.

"Take the next exit, First Street. Go east and drive for two miles then wait."

Jim tossed the phone on the passenger seat, feeling once again the anger rising. He exited and looked at his odometer. His Honda CRV had 56,208 miles on it. At 56,210, he'd stop and find out what these scumbags wanted.

But first, he had a little stop to make.

Pulling into a gas station, he found a parking spot and turned off the engine. Reaching into the glovebox, he felt around until his fingers found the "shirt button" hidden camera that was no bigger or thicker than a common USB drive. He'd won the gadget at a raffle drawing about year ago at a technology expo in San Jose. He'd been shocked at the time because he never won anything. Afterwards, someone had offered to buy it from him, but he decided to keep it.

At the top of one end of the device was a round, plastic object that resembled a common button, but was actually a tiny camera lens. He found the little switch on the side and flipped it to the "On" position. It supposedly had a three-hour continuous recording capacity and the last time he'd only used it for a few minutes just to try it out.

Unbuttoning the top two buttons of his denim collar shirt, he slipped the camera button through the second buttonhole then buttoned up the top again. He then patted his chest. The little gizmo was virtually unnoticeable unless someone took a really close look. Videos were produced in .AVI format and recorded to a microSD card so any PC or Mac could play them back. The last time he tested it, he attached the card to a USB cord and transferred the files to his machine; he'd been surprised at how clear the sound and images were.

He pulled back onto the main road. Traffic was still relatively clear, just the way he liked it this time of day. Or used to like it, anyway. He passed a sandwich shop he'd visited a few times for lunch. He saw trucks with their various loads going somewhere to make deliveries. He gripped the steering wheel hard, his mind staving off a hundred thoughts of rage and regret.

Glancing at the odometer, he pulled over to the side of the road next to a small strip mall and put the car in park. The phone buzzed and rang.

"Turn your engine off. Walk toward the CJ's Café to your right. Don't hang up."

He exited the car and began walking through the parking lot, glancing around. The café was open and a handful of customers were inside.

He kept the phone to his ear. Just as he stepped onto the sidewalk, he heard, "Turn around."

A delivery vehicle, similar to a UPS truck but a little smaller and painted plain white, came to a stop. A side door opened, and a man motioned him to get in.

Well, if they're gonna kill me, they could have done that in Vegas ...

He stepped into the dark interior and was motioned to a seat against the side.

In nervousness, he was still holding the phone to his ear, and as soon as the door shut, he heard it beep. He looked at the screen and saw that it had lost signal. They were probably using one of those handheld cellphone jammers. The truck jerked a little and began to move. A dim interior light was turned on and he looked around.

Inside the small space, a man he'd never seen before sat in one corner looking hard at him. In his hand was a gun with a long, smooth, black silencer screwed onto the end. In the other corner was a woman in a leather jacket. On her head was a tan, canvas Mao cap, and she donned what looked like yellow lensed night driving glasses that partially obscured her eyes. But he instantly recognized her as Iris.

Jim looked around again and shrugged with his hands. No words were spoken as the truck rumbled and bounced along. He looked at the man with the gun. "Who hurt that little girl? Was it you, you sick bastard?"

The man smiled. "Maybe it was you." His accent was noticeably Chinese.

Jim glared at the man for a moment, then looked at the woman. "Okay, *Iris*, what now?"

"I told you to stay calm, Jimmy. That's the only way we're going to get through this."

"Oh, I'm perfectly calm. Wait'll I really get all stirred up about this." He shifted his body a little more to face her.

The woman raised her chin slightly and calmly stared back, unfazed by the threat.

The truck came to a stop and the engine was turned off.

"Now then," the woman said. "I thought we'd continue our conversation in Las Vegas."

"And what conversation was that?"

"About the security system you work on at the laboratory."

Jim put his face in his hands. *Here we go* … "Listen. I don't know anything. And I don't have anything."

"You might."

Jim genuinely laughed. "You've wasted your time."

"We'll decide that."

"If I gave you everything I had, I mean *everything*, you'd still never break into the place. Or any other place that system guards. And even if you did get past the front gate, where would you go? How would you get into the buildings and into the vaults? You think you're gonna get at the uranium and plutonium stashes? The nuclear warhead designs? Do you know how many layers of security that stuff is behind? I myself have never been anywhere near it. Whatever you're planning, it's not gonna work."

"We'll worry about *our* plans."

Jim put his hands out, palms forward. "Listen to me. I want to make sure the expectations are crystal clear here, so you don't think I'm holding out on anything. I don't have access to what you need, okay? I'm just a little writer and trainer. A tiny cog in the wheel. I could give you general information, that's it."

"Jimmy, hush."

"It's *Jim*, bitch."

She held out a thick, black-colored thumb drive that Jim immediately recognized as an Ironkey, the only encrypted portable drive the laboratory allowed. She tossed it at him and he caught it.

Jim turned it over a couple times in his hands. "What do you want me to do with this?"

"Plug it into a port in one of the application server computers of the security system."

"Why?"

"Just do as you're told."

"I can't do anything with this. There are long-ass passwords on all those machines. And even if I could login, I wouldn't know what files to copy."

"You don't have to do anything. It will do all the work. Those machines also access the laboratory's email system, is that correct?"

"Yeah. I think so. The Windows ones. So?"

"Leave it plugged in for a couple days, then retrieve it."

"Listen to me," Jim said again. "The only thing I get to see, and that's only occasionally, is a lab where they work on this system. But it's a *test environment* only. It's used to play with new software and hardware and simulate alarm scenarios. The real system, the one that actually guards the lab is behind four doors with special access I don't have. I've never even seen it."

"Jimmy, I need you to stay focused and do what we say."

"Oh my *god* …" Jim moaned.

"I also want you to get as much information as you can regarding those security booths you told me about."

Now he wanted to cry. Did he really open his big, drunken mouth and talk about that? *You fool. You stupid, stupid, fool.* He breathed deeply. "There gonna know it's me. I'll be charged with treason or something."

"No, you won't."

"There are cameras all over that place. I'll be recorded."

"You know how these things work. No one checks video surveillance unless a known incident occurs. And no one's going to know, right, Jimmy?"

"I'm gonna go to prison."

"The alternative is the same. Maybe we'll start with your wife, Vaneesa, right? She goes to her mailbox next week expecting the usual bills and junk mail. But wait, what's this envelope? What are these pictures? Imagine how her attorney's mind will react and what kind of firestorm she'll start. She'll ask herself, what kind of monster did I marry? Or maybe we just speed up the process and send to your HR department."

Jim clenched a fist and punched his own palm, but then slumped in defeat. Every cell in his body wanted to lash out, curse and scream. But it wouldn't help. If he suddenly leaped up and somehow subdued the man with the gun before he could fire, what would it accomplish? He felt a desperation he couldn't remember feeling before.

The man with the gun knocked three times against the side. The truck's engine rumbled to life and it jerked into movement again. Jim kept his head down and didn't even want to look at the woman. They rode in silence until it came to a stop, then the man stood, opened the side door, and motioned with his head to get out.

Jim saw that they'd pulled to a stop next to his car. He hopped out and watched as the truck drove away. Both his personal phone and the little black phone beeped as they found a network signal again from some nearby cell tower.

He patted his chest again and felt the camera. Maybe he had something, maybe not.

Chapter 23

Lieutenant Justin Hesel and Detective Joey Salvo pulled up in front of the huge white columns that graced the Cosmopolitan's main entrance. A valet parking attendant sharply dressed in black slacks, a black vest, and a starch white dress shirt with a bowtie, ran up to greet them.

Salvo flashed his badge and said they were here to see Marty from security. The attendant nodded and jogged back to the valet shack. Another gentleman, this one in a full suit and tie approached the window.

"Good afternoon detectives." He pointed forward. "Please follow the road around to the north side where it says, 'Employee Parking' and someone will be there to meet you."

Hesel and Salvo did as they were instructed and came to an entrance with a standard barrier gate arm. An attendant with a radio earpiece stepped out of his booth, around the gate and up to the window. Both detectives showed him their badges.

The attendant gave instructions to go forward and stay in the right lane and a little way up they'll see a ramp going down under the building. Someone will be there. He then raised the gate arm.

"Beijing, huh," Salvo said as he maneuvered the car along the garage wall. "What do you think?"

"At this point, I've no idea what to think," Hesel replied.

Another couple turns, and they saw the entrance. It had no sign and was secured with a thick steel barrier, the kind a car couldn't just ram through. They watched as a fully armed security guard approached.

"This place has security like an embassy," Hesel said quietly.

The guard asked to see their IDs. Both detectives showed him their credentials. The guard then stepped back and said something in his radio. The gate hummed and purred as it slid open.

When they'd driven down underneath the building, another guard pointed to their right and told them to pick any one of the dozen or so empty spaces next to some large elevator doors.

The guard waited patiently by the elevator until the two detectives approached. He then stuck a key into a slot next to the buttons and twisted it three times clockwise. When the elevator door opened, he stepped inside, inserted his key again by the number pad, and hit a number. He then stepped out and held the doors with an extended arm.

When the detectives entered the elevator, the guard told them that someone will be waiting. He then stepped back and watched to make sure the doors shut with the two men inside.

"You know those movies about robbing these places?" Hesel asked. "Forget it."

Salvo chuckled. "In all your time, haven't you been inside a casino's security before?"

"It's been twenty years. Back then it was a side office next to the main floor with a little keep out sign tacked to it. Times have changed."

When the doors opened, a man in a suit with an earpiece was standing there with a pleasant smile, but cold, suspicious eyes. "Welcome detectives," he said. "Please follow me."

They walked down a long hallway that appeared to be circular in shape until they came to a thick door. The man turned his back to block the view and entered a code into a number pad next to the door. There was a loud click and the door opened. He gestured with his arm for the detectives to enter.

Hesel and Salvo found themselves in a room that could be a small version of the NASA Space Station Flight Control room in Houston. There were six long tables covered in monitors, separated into two rows. At the back was another larger table for what appeared to be maybe a supervisor. On the huge wall in front of the tables were four rows of seventy-five-inch flat screen monitors, ten monitors per row. Running parallel to the tables on the far wall was a single row of monitors. The screens displayed all sorts of images from every angle in, out, and around the casino.

"Damn," Salvo said, looking around. "Imagine if we could monitor downtown like this."

"They're already doing that in the UK," Hesel said.

"Detective Salvo?" a voice said. They both turned to see a man approaching. He wasn't very tall, five-seven at the most, and young, barely thirty. He wore slacks and a rumpled short-sleeved dress shirt, no tie. A large belly bulged out over his belt. He donned a thick light brown moustache, presumably to look older and maybe tougher; it didn't work, he still looked more like a techie geek than a security guy.

"I'm Marty," he said, extending his hand.

After introductions, Marty said, "Let's go over to this table."

Marty gathered a couple chairs and positioned them on each side of a desk console, then took a seat in the middle.

"Okay, I took the description Detective Salvo gave me and we know it's the Galaxy Lounge. And southwest of the main bar, down the 'Route 66' road, is where we think your robbery victim was seated as he spoke to the perpetrator. Assuming he was telling the truth."

"In retrospect, I think that was the only part he was truthful about," Hesel said. "By then he was fidgety, wringing his hands and shifting in his seat. Lots of that involuntary stuff."

"Isn't that an indication he was lying?" Marty asked.

"No, he'd been looking me confidently in the eye and lying before that. By then he was worn out and worried I'd seen through him."

Marty shrugged then played with a joystick, a knob, and some buttons as the monitor, now divided into five smaller screens, showed different angles of a group of lounge chairs and loveseats. The screens were clear and in color, not like in the movies where they're always black and white and grainy.

"This is the area we're focusing on." Marty turned to Hesel. "You were the one who interviewed the victim?"

"That is correct."

"What's your best description of him?"

Hesel leaned back and looked up. "Well first, I checked his driver's license and he's forty-one years old. But he looked a little older, like he's had a lot of stress in his life. He's Caucasian, 'bout five-ten, average build though on the thinner side of average. His hair was thick and slightly longish, grey and dark brown, like a salt and pepper thing. He had a small goatee and wore black rimmed glasses. He looked pretty worn out from whatever the woman slipped him. Complained a couple times about a headache."

"Chloral hydrate?" Salvo asked.

"Or maybe Rohypnol," Hesel said.

Marty shook his head in disgust. "We hate those women," he said. "Bad for business."

"I asked him what he was wearing that evening," Hesel continued. "And he said a black blazer with tan pants."

"Should be easy to spot," Marty said. "Again, assuming he was being truthful." He pushed a couple buttons and bending the joystick, they watched as the images blurred by in fast motion, the people in the screens scurrying about like cockroaches. He stopped. "Here we are at ten PM," Marty said. "Detective Salvo said that's when the victim said he met the woman?"

"Yes," Salvo said. "Said the woman, a total stranger who he'd never seen before approached him between ten and eleven. Closer to eleven."

"Okay," Marty said quietly to himself as he scanned the screens and moved the joystick just a hair to make the images move slightly faster. After a couple more button pushes, the screens displayed what looked like the lounging area Mueller had described but at different angles, some further away than others. Marty sped the images up a little more. They sat for almost ten minutes watching over an hour's worth of time fly by on the screen. There was no sign of Mueller.

Marty stopped and looked at Salvo who looked at Hesel.

"Let's go backward in time," Hesel said after a moment.

"How far?" Marty asked.

"Oh, I don't know. Let's go back to like eight. Can you make the screen jump forward incrementally, like in five-minute chunks?"

"Can do," Marty said with a little pride. "I can even make it go backwards like that. Wanna start at ten PM again?"

"Sure."

After a few more button presses and knob turns, the images on the screen began jerking, pausing, and playing video footage backwards in four second intervals before skipping another five minutes back again.

After a few minutes, Salvo asked, "What time are we here?"

Marty peered at the timestamp. "We're past nine PM and moving toward eight-thirty."

"Come on, come on. Where are you Mueller?" Hesel asked quietly.

"Is that his name, Mueller?" Marty asked.

Hesel and Salvo didn't answer. All three stared at the screen intently for another few minutes. It was difficult not being distracted by the cocktail waitresses in their tight-fitting little outfits.

"There!" Salvo suddenly said, looking at the bottom center of one of the screens. In it was a man in a dark blazer with a woman across from him in a loveseat, separated by a drink table. Only the upper half of their bodies were visible over the bottom frame.

"Gotcha," Marty said, pausing the screens. "Hang on." He started rapidly pushing buttons, changing the cameras, and adjusting to the timestamp. One by one, the views switched to center on that section of seating at four different angles.

"That's him alright," Hesel said. "That's our boy."

"And that's no blonde woman," Salvo said.

"There you are, bitch," Marty sneered.

Salvo and Hesel exchanged glances.

"Why did you lie about the girl, James?" Hesel said thoughtfully.

"James Mueller? That's his name?" Marty asked.

Once again, he didn't get an answer.

All three watched the screens as the two talked for a few minutes. The woman was smiling as Mueller appeared to be telling her a story or something. Suddenly she stood, went around the table, and sat beside him. They talked for another minute until they both stood and walked out of the camera frame, Mueller half stumbling.

"He definitely looks like he's had a few too many," Salvo said.

"I can track them to see where they went," Marty said.

"Let's do that," Hesel said. "But first, let's go back to when they first met up. I wanna see how that played out."

Marty cranked the joystick and they watched the images blur by in quick reverse until suddenly they saw Mueller alone in the chair.

"What's the time there?" Salvo asked.

"Five fifty-five," Marty said.

Salvo looked at Hesel and they both nodded. Mueller had indeed lied about the time too. The question was why.

Marty reversed the images until they saw Mueller walk to the chair, look around and then then sit down as he studied his phone. The timestamp said 5:46 p.m.

"So now we know when he got there," Hesel said. "Let's see when this woman shows up."

As they watched, Mueller looked at his phone several more times and appeared nervous. He kept glancing around.

"He's definitely waiting for someone. This was prearranged," Salvo said.

Mueller was staring off in some direction when the woman finally appeared in the frame. She stood to his right for a moment watching him with a serious expression that was hard to interpret. Mueller suddenly turned and her countenance immediately transformed into a beaming smile. They exchanged a couple words and then Jim awkwardly stood up.

"Six-seventeen," Marty said.

"I'm thinking she's Chinese," Salvo said.

"Yeah, especially after the news about the fax number," Hesel replied.

"Fax number?" Marty asked.

"Never mind," Hesel said. "Can you put your facial software on her?"

"Yeah, as soon as she sits down."

They waited, and when the woman sat across from Mueller, Marty froze the screen and zoomed in on her face, making the image a bit more blurry.

"Can't get much closer," Marty said. He pressed play and let the footage skip forward a few minutes. "And she's keeping her face a little pointed down." After a moment, he froze it again when she looked up slightly. Marty hit some controls and dots suddenly appeared over the woman's face, above and below her eyes, then on her cheekbones, then around her mouth. Dots kept appearing until they got denser and started forming bending curves. Lines then appeared, connecting the dots, creating a geometric shaped grid over her face. Marty punched a button which grabbed the dots and lines data and started running it through a database.

The three watched the small screen in the upper-right as it quickly flashed through hundreds of facial images, pausing here and there, making comparisons.

"All the major casinos share this database now," Marty said. "We didn't used to, but it's one of the few areas in which we fully cooperate with the competition. The FBI taps into it all the time. We don't always have names to go with faces, but we categorize and flag the cheaters and hustlers, and their accomplices if any."

After about three minutes, the computer came back with zero matches.

"That just means she's not been inputted into the database yet. But she will be after today. I'll flag her as a drug 'em, mug 'em suspect."

"Alright, let's watch these two for a while, maybe make it skip forward in two-minute intervals," Hesel said.

They watched the encounter play out and saw them order at least seven drinks.

"I'd be on the floor if I drank that much," Salvo said, then added, "No way she's drinking all that too. Wait, go back a minute." Then he saw it. "There! Go back a little and watch her right hand."

Sure enough, they watched as the woman stealthily and quickly poured some of her drink into the potted plant next to her when Mueller was distracted.

"Clever girl. She got the plant drunk that night," Hesel mused.

Marty scoffed.

After another few minutes of watching, they got to the end again and watched as Mueller and the woman walked away.

"Okay, here we go," Marty said, punching buttons.

Another set of camera angles appeared, showing a section with a row of blackjack tables. They saw the couple make their way across, the woman giggling and rubbing Mueller's arm he lumbered along. When they walked out of that frame, Marty punched a few more buttons and this time, the cameras showed a section with a group of slot machines. As the couple walked by, the woman stopped Mueller and said something to him. She then pulled something out of her bag and hand it to Mueller. Mueller gave her his drink and turned toward one of the slot machines. As Mueller inserted the coins and cranked the handle, she turned her back to the camera, set the drinks down on another machine and appeared to hunch over the glasses.

"Is that where she's slipping in the drug?" Salvo asked.

"Could be, can't see from here," Hesel said.

"Sorry, no camera in front of her there," Marty said.

After a moment, Mueller turned around with a big grin and a shrug. She handed him his drink and they paused, both taking a big gulp from their tumblers, or at least the woman appeared to be drinking. They then moved away and out of the camera frames.

"She owns him at this point," Salvo said.

"Probably owned him an hour before," Hesel said.

Marty shook his head in disgust, then hit some buttons, and this time they saw a hallway entrance. Mueller and the woman walked into it, with Mueller swaying and stumbling even more.

Marty changed the cameras to inside the hallway where elevator doors were. He watched carefully as one opened and they stepped in.

"Elevator ... six-ten-B, northwest," he said, punching more buttons.

Suddenly a closeup image of Mueller and woman inside the elevator was on the screens. She was pretending to drink while Mueller was taking large gulps of his. She grinned and laughed at everything he was saying. The elevator opened and they exited.

"She's playing her part well," Salvo said.

"Third floor," Marty said, as he hit a couple buttons.

They watched as the couple made their way down the hall. As they passed a table, they saw the woman dump the rest of her drink into a flower vase. Marty breathed heavily in frustration.

The couple stopped at a door about thirty feet from the camera. She faced him again and Mueller drained the rest of his drink, almost falling backward as the woman unlocked the door.

"Can we get any closer?" Hesel asked.

"'Fraid not. Not here in this hallway. But it looks like room ... three-twelve," Marty said. "I'll confirm who that room was registered to."

"That would be helpful. I think we've seen enough. Can you get us printouts of the two of them in the lounge and a couple closeups of the woman? Maybe a couple of them walking to the elevator?"

"Sure," Marty said. "I'll include the timestamps. Gimme ten minutes."

Chapter 24

Jim sat in his office staring at his work email and felt an eerie quiet, like a calm before the storm. There was nothing from anyone. No mails from Gerard or Kay. No voice messages on his work phone. It was as if not a single thing had happened, when it felt like everything had happened. Then again, as far as anyone else was concerned, he'd been duped and robbed and that was it. Hopefully, they just felt sorry for him, besides thinking him a bonehead.

It was hard to believe the last time he sat here he was eagerly watching his phone for a note from Iris, and with that, a hope he'd found something good. It had provided some needed excitement for a change, something to look forward to. Now he once again felt the sting of letdown and disillusionment.

It reminded him of when he was young and naïve, maybe twenty-two, and fell for the old speaker scam that was popular in the '80s and '90s. He was walking across the parking lot outside his work when these two guys, nicely dressed but not in a uniform, pulled up in a delivery truck and showed him these fancy looking speakers. They said they deliver these for big retailers and named a couple of those places that were around at the time. But because of a cancelled order, they had these extras. They told him they were worth about $1,200 but were willing to let them go for half that. You could easily resell them, he was told. The thing that made it more believable was that they they'd pretended to have a little chat with each other in front of him, like they couldn't decide how much of a discount they could let the items go for. Probably a well-rehearsed routine. "We're losing big time here, but we'll do it for you," was the message. And Jim the sucker, fell for it. Went to his bank and took out the cash and licked his lips at the thought of doubling his money. When he found out he'd been taken and actually purchased cheap, Chinese-made junk, it embittered him. From then on, and to this day, if anyone approached him for a service he didn't ask for – didn't matter if they were selling Bibles or hot dogs – he told them to piss off. Not exactly a healthy response, but that's what his reaction had been.

And now, all these years later, here he sat at work feeling the same way – violated and defiled. Only this time it was far worse. Deep inside he knew no matter what happened, even if they never released those pictures, he'd never get over this. Even if he gave them whatever they wanted and never heard from them again, he knew he couldn't move beyond this. Ten years, twenty years from now, he'd still rage at just the thought of what they'd done.

He also knew that all this did nothing but reinforce how he'd felt about himself for years – the unwanted stepchild to

Jeremy. Jim had done everything wrong while big brother did everything right. His parents never said that outright, but he'd felt it. One of the many manifestations of these feelings were that it'd made him an insecure pushover all throughout grade and high school. Bullies saw this right way and took full advantage. These experiences shaped who he became. He knew his internal identity as a victim to one degree or another was so deeply ingrained, he wore it like a badge. It was almost as if resentment against others had become not only a form of entertainment, but a safe haven where he was in control.

His desk phone suddenly rang, breaking his thoughts.

"Jim here."

"Mr. Mueller, this is Sergeant Ronald McClelland over in investigations. You sent me a mail the other day."

"Yes, yes, I did."

"We see you're back on campus. I'd like to talk to you about your recent trip. Can you stop by building two-twenty-one?"

Jim glanced at his monitor and wondered if they were watching him through the USB camera resting on it. "Uh, sure. Yeah. What time?"

"How about in one hour? John Lewis conference room on the main floor."

An hour later Jim found himself in a spacious meeting room in the Security Division's main building. He looked around at the pictures and posters on the wall. He stared at one photo which depicted a guard receiving an award of some kind, a large bronze medallion-looking object in a picture frame with fancy writing. He looked at another sign that said, "Safety First!" and had a list of hazards to watch out for in the workspace.

"Mr. Mueller?" a voice said.

Jim turned and saw Sergeant McClelland walk purposefully in and seat himself on the other side of the table. No handshake. No introduction. All business.

McClelland was maybe in his mid-fifties with a big, round face that donned rimless eyeglasses. His forehead was wide and flat, and greying hair wrapped around the back of a mostly bald head. He also wore the standard thick moustache. He had a hard stare and a stern face that bore the milage of one who'd spent decades holding bad people with bad intentions accountable for their actions.

He paused and gave Jim an odd look up and down.

I'm great. Feeling fine. Thanks for asking, Jim thought.

McClelland adjusted his glasses, looked down at some papers he was holding and then said, "You spelled out your situation in pretty good detail in the note you sent, but I'd like to hear it in your own words again."

Jim shrugged a little. "I'm not sure what else to tell you. Did what's his name ... Detective Hesel, send you the police report?"

"Yes," McClelland said, patting the papers in front of him. "I have it right here."

"Okay. Well, I was in the main lounge there, or one of them anyway ..."

"At the Cosmopolitan?"

"Yes."

"Do you remember where in the Cosmopolitan?"

Jim paused and feigned confusion, when, in fact, he remembered perfectly well. "No. No, uhm, just one of the many places there."

"And what time was this?"

Jim paused again. *Be consistent.* "I'm not positive, but I'm guessing ten PM-ish, a little after. Closer to eleven maybe."

"I see. And then what?"

"Well, this woman came up to me, all smiles and friendly like and introduces herself. She asked if she could have a drink with me. What am I gonna do, say no?"

McClelland was watching closely. "What name did she give you?"

What did I say to Hesel? You didn't really forget? McClelland's staring was making Jim nervous. "Uh, Lisa," he finally said, shaking his head.

"Lisa," McClelland repeated, in a voice dripping with skepticism.

"Yeah, yeah, Lisa. Could have been a fake name."

"Could have. Your description of her is very vague here. There's nothing else you can remember?"

"No. Blonde, cute. Hair was in a ponytail I think."

"Accent?"

"Say again?"

"Did she speak with a noticeable accent of any kind, or was her English perfect?"

"Oh, uhm … no, no accent."

"Heavy makeup? Fancy jewelry?"

Jim shook his head. "None that I can remember, no."

McClelland looked incredulous. "How old do you think she was?"

"Early, mid-thirties."

"Thin, heavy, average?"

"Average. More thin."

"Height?"

Jim shrugged.

"You walked with her to her room. Was she shorter than you, taller?"

"A couple inches shorter."

"Hair and skin color?"

"Besides blonde, I really don't know. She was Caucasian."

McClelland's mouth almost formed a smirk. "Garden variety Caucasian, right. What was she wearing?"

"I don't know."

"Was she wearing a dress, pants, you don't know? Her shoes?"

An image of Iris in that black dress and those strap shoes flashed in his mind. He was thinking it was very sexy at the time. But why was McClelland so interested in all these non-Lab related details? This was unnerving.

"I'm having a hard time remembering. She was in a dress. A red dress." No wait, he'd told Hesel it was black. "I mean black. Black dress."

McClelland rubbed his nose. "Was it red or black?"

"Black."

"Did she wear glasses, have a hat on, any tattoos, piercings, scars?"

Jim's mind was in a tumult. How could he have been so stupid to not prepare for such questions. "I really don't recall."

"I see." After a long pause, McClelland asked, "How long did you two talk?"

"Not sure. An hour and a half, maybe two."

"Then at some point you think you were drugged?"

"Had to have been, yeah."

"What makes you think so?"

"I started to feel weird. Like in a way I've never felt before. It was then things got weirder. I remember her taking me by the hand and leading me to the elevator then up to her room. My head was swimming. I was just kinda following her."

"How many drinks did you have, Mr. Mueller?"

He needed to be careful. The DOE didn't take kindly to giving security clearances to people with drinking problems. "Just a couple."

"You sure about that?"

"No, not really. It's kind of fuzzy still."

"How did you pay for the drinks?"

"Uhm … cash, I guess. Yeah, cash."

"What room did she take you to?"

"I don't recall."

"Then what happened?"

"I've no idea. I woke up sometime the next day. It was like I'd blacked out and lost a chunk of time. She was long gone."

"What did this woman steal?"

How much did I tell Hesel? Don't remember. Oh god...
"I don't know, just the cash out of my wallet. It wasn't a lot. A hundred bucks maybe."

"She left your wallet there?"

"Yeah, just took the money." Saying this out loud again a couple days after the drug left his system made him realize how implausible that sounded now.

"Your credit cards, watch, cell phone, everything was still there?"

"Uhm, yeah. Looked like it."

McClelland watched for a long moment, then said, "Are you absolutely positive nothing that belongs to the laboratory was taken?"

"Positive. I didn't have anything with me. My lab phone and laptop were back in my own hotel room. Hampton Inn."

"Was your hotel key in your wallet or pocket?"

"Yeah. Still there." Jim felt his heart thudding.

McClelland set his papers down and folded his fingers together. He took a long, slow breath, letting his eyes wander up and down Jim for a moment. Finally, he said, "Is there anything else you want to tell me, Mr. Mueller?"

Jim stared back for a moment, unable to think. He'd thought this conversation was going to be easy, but it turned out to be more difficult than the one with the Las Vegas police.

"No," he said, shaking his head. "That's pretty much it."

McClelland glanced at his notes then looked back up. "I'll need you to report to medical, today. Tell them what happened. They'll give you a blood and urine test."

Jim knew the testing wasn't so much a concern for his health and wellbeing; it was to see if he'd smoked weed or snorted coke or something with this girl. It made him pause and wonder once again what Iris had given him. Whatever it was, would it still show on a blood test?

"I'll call them as soon as I get back."

"I'll be waiting for their report," McClelland said, standing. "Then I'll be in touch."

Chapter 25

Detective Joey Salvo picked up the phone. "Salvo."

"Detective Salvo, Marty over at the Cosmopolitan."

"Yes Marty. You got something on that room, what was it …?"

"Three-one-two, yes. It was registered to a Mary Jane Anderson. The front desk photocopied the driver's license as normal. The picture on the ID doesn't look like the woman we saw with the victim, maybe not even Asian, very generic. Could be a makeup job, a digital makeover, or anyone, really. The bill was paid with a credit card in the same name."

"Can you send us a photocopy of the ID and the credit card number? We'll have it checked."

"Sure, no problem. But there's more."

"I'm listening," Salvo said.

Marty took a deep breath. "So, I got curious and I watched the footage from that camera that showed, what was his name, Mueller?"

"Yes."

"Okay, so the footage of Mueller and the woman entering the room. I fast forwarded, and about an hour after they went in, three more people showed up."

Salvo sat up. "Go on."

"It was difficult to make out faces because of the distance, and those hallways are kind of dim. But it looked like two adult men and a young girl, twelve or thirteen maybe."

"Ho-lee-cow," Salvo said, grabbing a notepad.

Marty continued. "The girl and one of the men had baseball caps, the other was keeping his head down. One of the men had a small rolling suitcase. I fast forwarded some more and they were all in there for over two hours. Then all of them, including the woman Mueller had been with earlier, exited."

Salvo was scribbling notes. "Mueller stayed in the room after they left?"

"Looked like it, yeah."

"Were you able to get their faces?"

"No. They went the other way and took the stairs. I lost them after that because it looked like they went through the pool and spa area where we have less cameras. They could have separated and exited in a hundred different places."

"Wow ... wow ... when did Mueller finally leave the room?"

"Don't know, I've not looked that far."

"Can we come over again?"

"Our casa es su casa."

"Twenty minutes." Salvo hit a button on his phone. "Justin, we need to get back to the Cosmopolitan and see Marty again. Yes, *A-SAP*."

***

Jim saw the encrypted mail pop into the preview frame. He clicked it and entered his password. Opening it, he saw it was a note from the lab's health services department. A mail with a "You have a new test result" message bade him to login to where his personal medical records were stored.

The results were positive for trace amounts of a type of benzodiazepine in his bloodstream, but not enough to draw a firm conclusion. Results indicated it was probably Flunitrazepam, a drug that was banned from importation to the United States. There would be further investigation.

Great. He'd probably have to take a polygraph, which he'd no doubt fail.

Digging into a pocket, he produced the Ironkey thumb drive Iris had given him. It looked perfectly innocent, as there were a thousand of these around the lab. But it *felt* sinister, especially not knowing what it was going to do.

On one hand, he despised being forced into this position. On the other, he'd expected much more. He thought they were going to ask him to steal laptops or hard drives or something. How would he have done that? Perhaps stick one of those orange "Destruction" stickers on one, then follow it to where Danny Weng and his crew dismantled and destroyed them. No way he'd ever get away with that. If literally the only thing he had to do was stick a thumb drive into a machine, then give it back, he considered himself lucky. But then, would they really stop there? What other demands would they make down the road?

He stuck it back into his pocket.

Picking up the phone, he paused as he considered the last four digits of Shane Well's phone. His hand almost shook as he reluctantly dialed the numbers.

"Shane here," he heard the familiar voice say.

"Hey Shane, it's Jim."

"Jim!" Shane said loudly, then lowered his voice. "You okay? What happened, man?"

"Long, stupid story. Actually, it's not that long. I messed up, man." Jim rubbed the bridge of his nose. He was tired of rehashing details.

He heard what sounded like Shane moving the phone from one ear to the other. Then Shane said, "We heard you got drugged and robbed."

"Yeah, that's the gist of it."

"Dang. Who was she?"

"No idea. Never met her before. Hot blonde babe. Easy to fall for."

"What did she do, slip something in your drink?"

"I guess. Never saw it."

"Wow. That's crazy."

"I know. It's gonna be hard to trust anyone I meet at a pickup joint again. Or anywhere, really."

"So what happened, you just woke up in strange room and found your stuff missing?"

"Pretty much, yeah."

"But nothing from the lab was taken, was it?"

"Fortunately no, or I'd probably not be here right now."

"I'm so sorry, man. That's scary."

"Uh, yeah. You could say that. Not to mention I missed my chance to see area fifty-one. They'll never send me again."

"Area what?" Shane said, with a wink in his voice.

"Right. Listen, I'm calling to ask if you're gonna be in the Helios lab tomorrow morning."

"Wasn't planning on it. But could be. Why?"

"I wanna run some diagrams by you of the LTO backup system and a couple other things."

"You could just send 'em to me. Just be sure to encrypt the mail."

"Yeah, but I'd like to work out a couple things in real time, not go back and forth. It'll go faster that way. Thirty minutes max, I promise."

"Sure, I can be there at eight."

"Sounds good. Thanks, Shane." He hung up and looked at the timestamp on his machine. He'd be at the Helios lab around 7:30.

Was this really happening … was he now a classic insider threat? Jim paused and considered everything he knew about the access control and intrusion detection system he'd devoted the last couple years of his life to. U.S. taxpayers had shelled out millions to build it and paid millions each year to maintain it across the country. In many ways it was foolproof, and an outsider with little or no knowledge of the inner workings had a slim if any chance of getting anywhere near the high consequence assets the laboratory possessed.

But he was on the inside. He had access to places they did not.

Insider adversaries were on a whole different level. In his Silicon Valley days, he'd once been commissioned to help put together a workshop for high tech companies to self-assess and evaluate how easy it would be for an insider to steal propriety information or sabotage something. It was all very revealing. Companies had to carefully balance the act of not fully trusting anyone while at the same time not demoralizing workers with too much scrutiny and restrictions.

But in the world of top-secret military or nuclear research it was different. Screw your feelings, as far as the government was concerned. We don't trust you or anyone else and we're gonna remind you of that every day. This place constantly made sure everyone knew there was nothing private on the lab's network. Anything and everything could at any time be looked at. We could stop you on the sidewalk and search you. We could pull you over and rummage through your vehicle. We could randomly ask you to piss in a cup or blow into a breathalyzer. If you wanted to work for this place, that was the price you paid.

Jim sat back and thought about it like a trainer. What would he tell people who wanted to know about insider adversaries at a nuclear research laboratory or power plant?

Who were they? What drove them?

The first obvious motivation was money. That's why if you're going through bankruptcy or are otherwise in financial trouble, they are hesitant to grant you a clearance. He'd been told about several case studies. There was David Dale, a worker at a nuclear fuel plant in North Carolina in the late '70s who stole two five-gallon buckets of uranium oxide and tried to blackmail the company. As an insider, he knew how to gain unauthorized entry, knew how to prepare a crucial door that should always be locked to be unlocked and ready, knew when to take advantage of some construction going on that resulted in fences and barriers not being where they normally would. But this guy was a little mental and said he needed the money to take his girlfriend to dinner.

But there was also greed and ego. John Anthony Walker, the U.S. Navy warrant officer who helped the Soviets decipher more than a million encrypted naval messages for almost twenty years, late '60s through the mid '80s. He had a great, well-paying job, top secret clearance, and was even in the Personnel Reliability Program, the Navy's equivalent to the DOE's HRP.

Then there was ideology. Rodney Wilkinson, a protestor in South Africa in the early '80s, was a worker in a nuclear power plant and had access to the plant's blueprints. He was able to smuggle in four magnetic limpet mines, one at a time, and place them in strategic places to inflict the costliest damage and delay the opening of the reactors.

Insiders were also motivated by revenge or coercion. They could be unwitting and tricked into doing something. They could be passive, active, or violent in how they carry out their plans. All the security in the world won't help you if someone on the inside with enough access and knowledge decides to derail things.

What was Jim's motivation? Coercion via plain, unadulterated fear. They had his life in their hands; he was a puppet on their string. And it hurt even more to think of how that had happened – trickery and manipulation.

He knew people less selfish than him would be far more concerned about that poor girl they used. Many, perhaps, would have gone straight to the police for the kid's sake – consequences be damned. They'd take the fall. It'd be worth it to try to get these people caught and prosecuted.

So why wasn't he doing this? He knew the answer to that question.

No one would believe him.

Neither his family nor certain acquaintances knew the full, sordid extent of his history with booze and hookers, as well as party drugs in his youth. But he still had a reputation. He had done well keeping a lid on that sort of thing. But Vaneesa knew about some of the more recent activities – she'd throw him under the bus without thinking twice. His family had always considered him the black sheep. They may feel terrible for him, but deep down they'd believe he'd gone after children. And it would break their hearts. How could he ever face anyone again, especially Jeremy?

Was there anything worse a person could be accused of in this world than using children like that?

He sat back and looked at the time. Three more hours to go before he left for the day. Tomorrow morning, he was probably going to commit espionage and there'd be no turning back.

Chapter 26

Justin Hesel and Joey Salvo sat staring at video surveillance footage of the three individuals entering the hotel room where James Mueller and the mysterious woman had gone. This time they had gotten not just stills, but the actual video from Marty, as well as the driver's license and credit card number of the woman who had registered the room. They also had footage of Mueller finally stumbling out of the room around 2:30 in the afternoon the next day.

"He looks terrible. Barely able to walk," Hesel remarked.

"This is incredible!" Joey said. "This is the most intriguing case I've ever seen, not that I've been around that long. But still. I mean, look at this. You could make a career out of this case." He clapped his hands and rubbed them together in excitement.

Hesel looked at Salvo and had a moment of envy that Salvo was still so young and full of gumption. "Joey, I hate to burst your bubble, but this is gonna be out of our hands soon."

Salvo turned, wide-eyed. "Why?"

Hesel sighed. "Now that we know there's a minor involved, we gotta bring this to the Bureau. And besides, when we got back earlier, I had a message from Cynthia."

"Cynthia?"

"Cynthia Arroyo. She's an assistant to the agent in charge at the FBI field office here in Vegas. She was the one who ran that fax number we got."

"Okay."

"She wants to know what I sent to that number. I kinda brushed her off the other day, but they're not letting it go. I gotta do that soon, like today. She's gonna be peeved at me because we at least knew Mueller had a federal security clearance and didn't tell them. And you know what's gonna happen once they see the police report I kindly faxed over to China, right?"

"No, what?"

Hesel leaned back. "Think about it. They're gonna run this James Mueller guy and find out he's a Department of Energy employee. They'll be down at the Cosmo the same day getting the same video footage from Marty we're looking at now. They're gonna think it's mighty strange that a police report on Mueller, one that details him getting robbed *while on assignment* for the DOE, got faxed to a mysterious front number that ends up in Beijing. That alone is gonna raise eyebrows. And I'd bet my reputation that the ID for 'Ms. Anderson,' who registered that room, is gonna turn out fake. And now we got a kid involved? You know how fast this'll go to the top? I mean the top, like the secretary, to offices and pay grades you and I'll never see.

Well, you're a young and rising star, who knows where you'll end up. But not grizzled, old me who's getting ready to sunset."

Salvo sat back, the eager look in his eyes melting into despondence. "Will they let us help?"

"No, we're not federal. We're just the local boys. Out of our jurisdiction. They may not even bother to thank us for doing all this initial leg work."

"Damn," said Salvo.

"Hey, they're gonna know about you now anyway. Your name is on the paperwork. Might be a career booster."

Salvo sighed. "Let's hang on to it for a couple more days. See what else we can find out. Lemme interview Mueller."

Hesel shook his head. "No way. This could be a case involving child trafficking with foreign nationals on US soil. The Bureau is gonna find out we got this video and ask why we didn't say something. You don't want to jeopardize your career over this. I already told Mueller's employer about the fax number the other day, so who knows, maybe they've already moved this up the chain. If I say something now and come clean on everything, we're covered."

"You make it sound like *we're* the criminals."

"I don't play around with the feds. Not worth it."

Salvo shook his head sadly. He looked up at Hesel. "You don't think this Mueller guy is into kids, do you? You think he hired someone to hook him up for something like that?"

"It's possible, but my instincts say no. I've been around molesters before. Mueller may have issues with binging and chasing skirts, but I don't think he's into kids. And besides, he came to us and volunteered to file a report. Why would he do that and risk everything?"

"But he lied. He covered for that woman."

"True. But I still say I don't think so. Who knows, maybe he's being blackmailed or something."

"I'd love to pursue that angle."

"I'm sure you would. But don't count on it." Hesel stood up. "I gotta make that call to Cynthia."

Salvo looked at a pile of folders on his desk. "Gee, I can't wait to get back to the petty thefts and liquor store holdups."

Hesel smiled. "You'll get your chance, Joey. You still have a long way to go. No reason to stay in this hot, dusty state your whole life."

***

Jim's hand shook as he slid it into the HGU next to the door outside the Helios lab. In his other hand was his laptop. The door clicked and he opened it.

Stepping inside, he looked around and saw no one, as he'd hoped, because it was early.

He looked at the time – 7:33 a.m.

Walking quickly but not *too* quickly, he made his way through the software and hardware rooms and into the main room where the mock alarm console was. Save for the sounds of a dozen powerful desktop computer cooling fans, everything was empty and quiet.

Approaching the console, he set his laptop down and stared at the lineup of desktops that hooked everything together. Some were Windows machines, some were Oracle database servers, some were dedicated to one function like running the video playback controls.

As he looked around the console table, he saw a red plastic bowl on the end filled with several Ironkey thumb drives, just like the one in his pocket. He'd been here before with Shane or Dirk and had seen thumb drives stuck in the ports of some of these machines. If they found his, they'd probably just toss it into that bowl. He'd have to mark his somehow so he could find it again.

Glancing around, his eyes landed on a Sharpie pen. It was black though and wouldn't show on the dark colored surface of the drive. Removing the thumb drive from his pocket and quickly uncapping the pen, he darkened out the "R" and "K" letters on the side of the device displaying the brand name. That should do it. He slid the cap back on.

"James," a female voice said behind him. It startled him so badly he almost threw the thumb drive in the air. He turned around to see Kay Allison.

"Oh, hey," he stammered. "You startled me." He sat down in a chair next to him.

Kay looked at him for a moment, her eyes slightly narrowing, and asked, "Are you okay?"

Jim glanced around. "Uhm, no, I-I mean, yeah, I'm okay. Still feeling weird. Embarrassed really. I'm sorry."

"As long as you're alright. We've all heard stories about that kind of thing." Her expression and voice conveyed a touch of sympathy but was more laced with the kind of scorn a disapproving parent has for a grown but naïve child.

Jim twirled the drive with his thumb and index finger. "Yeah, so had I. But you know how it is, you never think it could happen to you."

Kay just nodded.

"The police told me it's going on all over the place," Jim added.

Kay nodded again, an odd look on her face.

"I feel pretty stupid," Jim went on. "I guess I make an easy target for that sort of thing. At least nothing of the lab's was taken. Sorry about not getting what you needed me to get at, well, you know, *that* place."

"It's okay, we'll work it out." Her expression turned more impersonal. "What brings you here at this hour?" she asked, glancing at the thumb drive in his hand.

Keeping his cool and very deliberately not following Kay's eyes to his hand, he said, "I'm just here to go over some stuff with Shane. The LTO backup. He should be here any minute." He made no attempt to hide the drive. He even twirled it again in his fingers.

Kay nodded, looked at him for another moment, and said, "I'm glad you're okay." Then turned to leave.

Jim closed his eyes and took several deep breaths.

Alright, where was I?

Several screens on the Helios test console were always on. There were three large monitors that showed different areas or buildings of the lab, depending on what the last thing was that was viewed. The three-dimensional details the AutoCAD layouts displayed always amazed him.

He wiggled the mouse and moved it around the map of one of the buildings and then looked under the desk. He was pretty sure which desktop he should use because he'd seen QA testers copy screen captures onto thumb drives from it.

He was also fully aware that between the three rooms that made up the Helios lab, at least eight cameras had recorded him come in here. Three were watching him right now and recording because there was movement in the room. And this Helios lab was different in that it was considered a vault-type room. That meant it was a designated alarm sector in and of itself and had a dedicated remote processor guarding just it. The moment he'd walked in at 7:33, sensors came alive and not only started recording, but flagged the logs.

But here's where the system had weaknesses. Motion and video were flagged all day here and the other many vault-type spaces around the site, so no one really paid attention. Iris had been correct in that he'd never heard of people looking at video surveillance just for the heck of it. Who had time for that? You looked if there was a specific incident to be investigated.

Still though, it would be on record for years, maybe indefinitely, so it *could* be looked at someday.

Iris ... I'd truly enjoy seeing you die about now.

Making an effort not to look around like a suspicious person would, he played with the drive in his hand while pretending to look at the screen. Then, in one smooth motion, reached down and inserted the drive into one of the ports. The tiny, capsule-shaped light at the end of the drive blinked a cool blue a couple times, indicating the machine recognized it.

Leave it a few days and then retrieve it, he was told. Sure, no problem.

A thought struck him, and it made his hands cold. The deed had been done. He was now guilty of … something.

You're staring too long. He sat back up.

"Hey Jim," he heard Shane Wells say. Jim almost gasped. Too many frights in too short a timeframe.

Shane strolled through the doorway. "Kay said you were already here."

Jim sometimes forgot that the developers and engineers had offices right here in the same building.

"Yeah, I was bored. How's it going?" he asked, reaching for his laptop.

"I'm fine. But you look a little pale. How are *you* doing?" Shane said, pulling up a chair.

"Great. Happy to still be here serving my country."

Chapter 27

The inevitable call came. Lieutenant Justin Hesel hit a button on his desk phone and picked it up. "Hesel."

"Justin, Doug Thomas here."

"Why Special Agent in Charge Thomas, what a surprise."

"I can hear the shock and awe in your voice."

"I could never possibly guess why I'm getting a call from you. Oh wait, perhaps I can. A certain Mr. James Mueller?"

"Good surmise."

"You guys have everything we have, or had," Hesel said with a shrug in his voice.

"We should, yes. So there's three reasons I'm calling. The first is to personally thank you for doing the groundwork on this. There are people in high places who are very interested in this case."

"That's what I figured. And thanks for saying that. Joey will appreciate it."

"Yes, Detective Salvo. Cynthia filled me in."

"He's young and eager. He's the one who initiated going after the video."

"He's got good instincts. Well, the second reason for the call is that the police report you filed on behalf of Mr. Mueller is very vague about what was stolen as well as the description of the perpetrator. We of course now know he was lying about her ethnicity and appearance, as well as when they met. The only real truth was where their encounter had taken place."

Hesel dropped his head. "No, I didn't document all that too well, and I apologize for that. We just talked about it a little. I could have probed further." He rubbed his eyes. "Look, it'd had been a long day and I was tired, and at that point I'm thinking it's just a petty robbery. You gotta cut me some slack on –"

"Justin, Justin, hold up. I'm glad you didn't. Have you spoken to anyone about the video surveillance?"

"No."

"Have you spoken to anyone else about any other details of your interview with Mr. Mueller?"

"Besides Joey, absolutely not. And security at the Cosmopolitan doesn't know about the fax number or anything else about Mueller. They just wanna get the woman."

"Excellent. Let's keep it that way. Whoever received that report in Beijing is hopefully thinking we're not aware of what the woman really looks like."

"Or that we've seen the video footage."

"Precisely. We may be able to use that to our advantage."

"We think Mueller might be getting blackmailed," Hesel offered.

"We're pursuing all angles right now."

"Of course."

"The third reason I called is I need to ask you, Justin. How long did hold on to this before you let us know?"

"Doug, on my mother's grave, I picked up the phone and told Cynthia the same day we saw the video of the kid going into the room."

"Okay. But you knew about the fax number a couple days before that. If you hadn't needed us to run it and acquired information yourself, would you have told us then?"

"Honestly, we were in sleuthing mode, doing what we detectives do – running with it. I would have told you soon enough. I did tell Mueller's employer the same day I found out. In fact, they were the ones who asked me to look into that fax number. I had no idea how big this was going to be."

"I understand. And yes, I've spoken to Sergeant McClelland over at the laboratory. Just making sure we're on the same page in case anything like this happens in the future."

"Scout's honor, Doug." Hesel wiped his forehead with a napkin.

"I need to ask that you and Detective Salvo don't mention this case or any of its details to anyone, whether it's on the report or not. Especially no faxing or emailing. Consider it need-to-know only. And anything else related you run into, I'll be expecting a call from you."

"Count on it."

"Have a great day, Justin. And thanks again. Oh, and tell Joey Salvo, excellent work."

***

Around 11:30, Jim found himself in line at the lab's cafeteria trying to decide if he felt like a chicken burrito or a tuna melt. His stomach was in knots so maybe he didn't want anything. He had to keep eating though to keep his energy up.

He felt a tap on his shoulder. He turned around to see Danny Weng who bore an uncharacteristically serious expression.

Jim managed a small smile. "Hi Danny."

Danny glanced around. "Are you okay?"

Jim feigned confusion. "Why?"

"I heard about what happened in Las Vegas."

"Wow, this is a small town."

Danny nodded. "Dale over in security told me. Said crimes and investigation was doing a robbery while on assignment case. I said who? When he mentioned your name, I couldn't believe it."

"Well believe it, it's true."

The line moved forward and Jim stepped up and ordered the tuna melt. "Wanna have lunch?" he asked.

Danny agreed, ordered a salad, and the two found a table in the back of the cafeteria.

Jim retold the story about meeting the woman at the bar, getting drugged, and waking up the next day with some cash missing. Basically, the same half-truths he'd been telling everyone. Danny listened intently and focused his questions mainly on what the woman asked and what their conversation was about.

"She was blonde, Caucasian?" Danny asked with curiosity.

"As white as me, yeah. I told her nothing about this job or even where I work. I was just another lonely sucker down there trying to have a good time."

"Well, that's good. I mean, not that you got robbed."

"I know what you mean."

"Did she get hold of your credit cards?"

"No. She just took the cash."

Danny frowned. "That's odd."

"Yeah, that's what everyone keeps telling me. Maybe I got lucky. Maybe she didn't want to be seen on video surveillance at the stores or ATM's or whatever."

"Maybe," Danny said thoughtfully, taking a quick glance at Jim's phone resting on the table.

Jim watched Danny eating his salad for a moment. Perhaps he could get some intel out of him. "Danny, how much damage could someone do with a thumb drive?"

Danny looked up. "Like what, if they stole one with sensitive information on it?"

"Well, that's one scenario."

"We use military grade encryption – FIPS one-forty-two level-three or higher. It'd be hard to bust into those."

"Yeah, I've heard. But what if someone had a program or something on a thumb drive and stuck it into one of our machines."

"Oh, now that's a different story. That can be highly dangerous. You know those links on phishing mails? They can install stuff, malware and whatnot. Do you know how many phishing attempts this lab gets per day?"

"Enlighten me."

"A hundred and fifty thousand. Plus, about fifty thousand spam emails."

Jim was genuinely surprised. "Every day? I had no idea."

"Yeah. There's a lot of parties interested in what we do here."

Tell me about it, Jim thought. He took a big bite of the tuna melt and immediately thought it wasn't that great.

Danny continued. "But back to your question about thumb drives. That's like opening the floodgates. Security deals with this stuff all the time. You know the badge office parking lot? Thumb drives get 'accidentally' left there with malware. They might have enticing labels on them like 'Payroll' or something that will get someone curious enough to go to their office and plug it in."

"That's pretty clever."

"As someone who does security related stuff every day, I'd never stick a thumb drive in a machine here that I'd found on the ground. But I can see why others may not know better. Personally, I would pre-scan anything I wasn't a hundred percent sure of, on a separate scanning node."

"That isn't part of our training." Jim took another bite and decided that'd be the last.

"Exactly," said Danny. "It should be. The moment you stick a thumb drive into a machine, you've crossed the airgap. All those precautions to stop hackers go out the window."

"What would or could be a scenario like that?"

Danny chewed his salad for a minute. "Well, the drive could contain a worm that will install itself and execute routines related to the attack. While it's doing that, it propagates and copies itself. Then a malware bundle known as a rootkit will do things like hide files processes, making it hard to detect. Sometimes it'll lay dormant in a system until it detects and zeros in on something it's specifically targeting."

"What does it do when it finds its target?"

"Whatever it's been programmed to – modify code, destroy data, even destroy certain kinds of hardware. Hackers can setup remote control systems that are not air gapped, send data wherever they like." Danny went back to his salad.

Jim looked at his soggy tuna melt for a minute and wished he'd gone for the burrito. "Copy data back on to the thumb drive?"

"If that's what it was programmed to do, yes."

"But say a worm gets on a tightly air gapped system. It can't go any further than that system, right? Hackers can't remote into that."

"Correct. That's the whole point of an airgap. But maybe you've got a test system where people are using it to plug hardware in and portable drives and whatever and then take these things back to other systems. Those systems could now be infected."

"Wow."

"There's a reason why it's called a virus." Danny thought while he chewed some more, then said, "Malware can be tricky with criminal and cybercrime laws. There's a lot of loopholes; hard to prosecute a user of it. Plus, in America you can't be busted just for possessing it, like in Europe."

Jim was pleasantly surprised. "Really?"

"Yeah. Say you're in America but victimized by malware from another country. Outside of legal jurisdiction. The perp will probably never be caught and convicted. Plus, the source of the virus or worm can be hard to trace."

Jim looked down in thought and smiled.

"It's still a federal crime to intentionally use it to harm or steal information without authorization though," said Danny.

"Oh." Jim's positive feelings vanished.

"There are ways to stop that stuff. In the group policy, you can restrict read and/or write access for removable storage."

"Why don't we?"

Danny shrugged. "In a few classified systems we do. But people still need to move large amounts of data around and we can't use the cloud. What's this system you're referring to?"

Jim shoved the tuna melt aside. "Just a hypothetical scenario, in case I ever need to train about the subject … What if this system had access to the lab's employee email?"

"Then it wouldn't be air gapped. It's connected somewhere to the employee network."

Jim felt his heart flutter. "I see."

Danny paused and looked at Jim. "Your building is general access, yellow network. Where else do you go around here that's sensitive?"

Jim shrugged. "Nowhere really, 'cept the Helios building now and then."

"Oh, now that place has some classified areas, red network. I don't cover that area, but we've destroyed end-of-life equipment from it."

"Like the Helios test lab?"

"Probably, yeah. You know you're in a classified area if those little lockers are outside where you need to leave your personal electronics before entering."

"Not sure I've seen those."

"Do the phones there have TSG devices?"

"TSG devices?"

"Telecommunications Security Group, the policy resource for all aspects of technical surveillance countermeasures. Little box like the size of one of those older external drives. Used for headsets, softphones, and web cameras. Has a physical disconnect and isolation measure that protects against transmitting on-hook audio from leaving the area unintentionally. *Voip*, or voice over internet protocol, digital soft phones that go through our computers, are especially vulnerable."

"I don't think I've seen TSG devices."

"Some phones have an inherent risk because while on hook, they pick up and transmit conversation occurring in its vicinity. The only way to ensure audio protection is to plug headsets into a TSG device."

Jim shook his head. "You're an encyclopedia on this stuff."

Danny shrugged. "That's what I do. Sounds like that Helios lab isn't classified. Why are you asking about all this?"

"Oh I dunno. I've been here awhile now and it seems I'm still learning something new all the time. I figure once my curiosity goes, I'm probably done living."

Danny nodded in agreement and went back to his salad.

***

The next few days were an agonizing waiting game – waiting for *something* to happen. Jim spent his time creating the software and hardware installation and configuration guides for the LTO tape drive backup system for Helios. But it was hard to concentrate.

With every email that came in there was dread and anticipation. With every set of footsteps he heard coming down the hall, he expected two security guards to walk in and order him to take his hands off the keyboard and come with them. With every phone call, he anticipated Sergeant McClelland or someone calling to tell him to come over for another round of interrogation.

But nothing happened. Not a peep from anyone.

The week flew by and he was grateful for the distraction of the LTO rollout project. He even had a couple good conversations with Shane to get some final details. Kay had approved it after only a couple minor corrections, which was unheard of.

Now, sitting here waiting, he almost felt physically sick from the suspense. He wanted badly to know what was happening with that Ironkey drive in the Helios lab. If cybersecurity were called in to investigate, he would never hear about it. Unless someone looked at the Helios lab's surveillance footage. Something had to happen soon or he was going to go bonkers.

But then something did. That little black flip phone buzzed and rang again.

Chapter 28

"Jimmy, we need the drive back," the calm but cold voice said. "Did you retrieve it?"

"No. But I'm working on it."

"You're not working hard enough. The more time passes, the more risk it will be discovered."

"I can't just go marching in there whenever I feel like it. I've already raised suspicions."

"Has anyone said anything to you?"

"No."

"Then what's the problem?"

"The *problem* is that I've violated my agreement with the United States government about secrecy."

"Perhaps you're not taking this as seriously as you should be."

"Believe me, I am."

"Check your mail."

The phone call ended.

Jim scrambled to his personal phone and waited, and a few seconds later, the New Mail icon flashed. He clicked it, noticing it was sent from a Proton Mail address with some random numbers for a username.

Attached to the mail was a picture – a closeup of the girl lying on his bare chest looking toward the camera. Her young, innocent eyes looked so sad and yet so angry. Within the picture frame was his face up to about the center of his forehead. He was turned slightly toward the camera as well, his eyes closed and his mouth in a pleasant smirk. The image showed no nudity, but it didn't have to.

What he noticed next made his guts go watery. The note had been cc-ed to his work mail. From day one of employment, he been warned that anything sent or received on his work machine as well as anything searched for in any browser, could not only be reviewed, but was kept indefinitely, in case something needed to be dug up at some point in the future as part an investigation.

He pounded his desk with a fist and cursed. He was right – they were going to screw him no matter what he did or didn't do.

As quickly as he could, he first blocked the sender on his work mail. He then deleted the message and permanently emptied the Deleted Items folder. He then performed a Disk Cleanup and emptied out his TEMP folder. At least if they barged into his office and searched his machine right now, it'd be gone. But like the footage of him in the Helios lab, it was now on record, somewhere.

He gritted his teeth. "I'm going to kill you, *Iris*," he hissed under his breath.

Jim checked the time again. It had been almost a week since he'd placed that thumb drive into the machine in the Helios lab. How was he going to get it back without causing suspicion? He needed to get in there when at least Kay wouldn't walk in on him. Dirk or someone like that, he could handle. Still though, he couldn't just wander in there without a reason.

In addition to anger, there was an uncomfortable feeling that was running through him that went above and beyond the dread he'd felt since Vegas. His mind was playing tricks as well. Every time his screen blinked, he thought someone from the IT department had secretly remoted into his computer and was watching and recording his screen. They had more than the capability to do that. Every time he heard an unfamiliar noise on the phone, he thought the line was tapped and someone was listening. He was becoming paranoid. It infuriated him that his life had been so disrupted.

Okay ... stay calm.

A new mail popped up on his work screen. Heart thudding, he warily opened it and read, *SAVE THE DATE: The Security Division is hosting a BBQ and Picnic this Thursday in the old pond area. Food and fun! Don't miss out...* blah, blah. The date was in four days.

Hey, this just might work. They'd all be at that gathering. Even Kay made brief appearances at these things.

Picking up his personal phone, he hit reply to the mail and typed, *I can get the drive in four days. That's the best I can do. And GO TO HELL for sending that to my work.*

He hit the Send button then leaned back heavily in his chair. Cursing at them would do no good. Nothing would. They were destroying him. And before they finished off his job, reputation, and freedom, they will have ruined him mentally. He was no more than a pawn in their game to be used, like that poor girl, whoever she was.

He'd already determined that *Iris* was going to pay dearly for this. She was almost a symbol now, a representation of everything that made him feel oppressed, rejected, used, or abused his whole life.

A thought suddenly struck him. Should he? He licked his lips.

***

Two days later, Jim was making his way across the Bay Bridge, the two-deck span of Interstate 80 that connects Oakland and San Francisco over one of the narrower sections of the famous tidal estuary. It had been months since he'd been to the city.

His mind was whirling, so he tried blaring his favorite classic rock station as a distraction but wasn't enjoying it. Instead, he opened his windows and let the cool, salty ocean air rush in over the sounds of other vehicles on the road.

The traffic was medium-heavy during this mid-morning hour and the weather was partially sunny. He'd never been to the address he was headed to and had no idea how his cousin Raimondo would react to seeing him, or if he'd even be there.

Just yesterday, not having a clue where this place was, he'd poked around online until he found a "Bellini's Delicatessen." He didn't know for sure that was it but had nowhere else to look. He'd toyed with the idea of calling the county health department to ask who owned the deli's food license, but decided he'd take a chance and just drive over, if anything but for the diversion.

Taking exit 2C, he merged onto Fremont Street. From there he worked his way to Pine, then Kearny, until he hit Columbus Avenue. At a stop light, he stared at the iconic tall, pointy Transamerica Pyramid. For years, it had been the tallest building in the city until the Salesforce Tower beat it in the mid-2010s. Even if this trip turned out to be a waste of time, he was already enjoying the cool air and the sights and sounds of downtown San Francisco.

A couple blocks later, he pulled up in front of a small shopping center with several businesses, including a dry cleaner, a printing and publishing shop, and a used clothing outlet. At the other end was the delicatessen.

Jim parked and looked at the shop. Two big display glass windows made up most of the deli's front with a door in the middle. Behind the glass was an array of items including wine bottles, cookbooks, some posters of old Italy, and crates of fresh fruit.

At a couple small tables outside, two men sat smoking cigarettes. As Jim approached and stood looking in the windows, the man closest to Jim, and the bigger of the two, turned and looked Jim up and down. He wore dark dress pants and shoes but had a white sleeveless muscle shirt on top. A creepy looking tattoo of the Trinacria, the three-legged woman with snakes in her hair like Medusa, prominently displayed on his upper shoulder area.

Jim returned the look. "Hi," he said.

The man just stared back without a blink or move.

"I'm looking for Raimondo," Jim said, now feeling awkward, shuffling his feet a little.

The big man's eyes wandered up and down Jim again, this time slower. He took a long pull on his cigarette while keeping his eyes locked on Jim's. Finally, he said, "*Mister* Bellini is kind of busy right now. And you are?"

"His cousin. Jimmy."

"Cousin Jimmy, huh" the man said softly. He looked at the other man across from him who shrugged. Sliding his chair back, he stood and strode into the shop, staring Jim down as he walked by.

Jim took note that the man was maybe six-two and pushing three bills. He turned and looked up and down the street, feeling the stare of the other man at the table. Finally, he heard a familiar voice boom out from inside the shop.

"Jimmy! What the hell?" An older and heavier Raimondo walked out of the store with his arms held open wide. He gave Jim a big hug and then stepped back. Raimondo wore immaculately clean striped suit pants, a white dress shirt with the sleeves rolled up to his elbows, and thick, red suspenders. His round cheeks and chin were shaved clean. He looked Jim up and down and said, "You're lookin' old and tired. What are you doin' here?"

Jim smiled weakly. "Hey, Raim. Long time."

"Come on in. You shoulda told me you were comin.'
You want somethin' to eat? We have the best Italian flavors
this side of North Beach."

"No, I'm good, thanks."

Jim followed Raimondo in and looked around the
interior. It wasn't very spacious inside. One main aisle with
a black and white checkered tile floor went from the front
door to the back where three or four display coolers filled
with soda, juice and beer were. The front counter to the
right was lined with refrigerated cases filled with various
deli meats, pasta salads, and cheese. On the left were steel
shelves stacked with canned and bottled goods, bags of
chips, various snacks and wrapped dry salami. The place
was a small, innocuous looking front for who knows what
behind the scenes.

"Grab a drink," Raimondo said. "Anything you want.
Or I got somethin' a bit more potent in the back. Then
we'll talk."

Jim looked at the assortment of beverages and thought,
oh why not? and grabbed a Blue Moon.

"You shoulda told me you were comin'," Raimondo
said again.

"I wasn't even sure this was the place."

"This way," Raimondo said turning to a small door on
the right.

Jim noticed Raimondo quickly peck something installed
on the wall next to the door, a shiny chrome framed number
pad with buttons that glowed a blueish color. It looked
modern and sophisticated next to the older door.

They entered another hallway and walked past three more doors. At the end, Raimondo ushered Jim into a clean and nicely furnished office. The atmosphere was dim and shadowed compared to the outside, lit only by a desk lamp and another small floor lamp in the corner. The carpet was a rich burgundy with unusual flowery and swirly patterns surrounding a big multi-pointed star in the middle.

Jim looked around and took note that they were now tucked away deep into the building – no windows, no way to see or hear anything from the outside. It was the kind of private space where private conversations and agreements were had away from prying eyes and ears.

"How's yer folks?" Raimondo asked, offering Jim a chair on the other side of a wide mahogany desk. He plopped himself down in a huge high-back leather executive chair. The air in the cushion hissed as his weight settled into it.

Jim's chair wasn't as fancy, but the brown leather lounge chair he seated himself into was comfortable.

"They're doing great, thanks." He glanced at the display cabinet on one wall filled with what looked like antique firearms and swords.

Raimondo regarded Jim. "And Jeremy, he still a preacher?"

"Still going strong. In fact, he was finally able to give up his day job and go full time in the ministry."

"Yeah? No kiddin' huh. I dunno what I'd do if I had preacher for a brother. 'Course, in my case, it'd be a priest I'd have to confess to." He laughed.

Jim tried to chuckle but couldn't. "How are things on your side?" he asked, putting a right ankle over his left knee.

Raimondo flipped the lid open on a glass cigarette holder on his desk. He turned it around and slid it a few inches in Jim's direction.

Jim held up a hand. "No. Thank you."

Raimondo took one for himself and lit it with a torch lighter. The lighter looked expensive, like the case was real silver, and Jim noticed the words *"Non mi va!"* engraved on the side.

"Auntie Alma died three years ago. Pancreatic cancer," Raimondo said, exhaling smoke. "Everyone else is doin' well."

"I'm sorry to hear."

Raimondo shrugged. "Life's short. You gotta live it up. You never know, ya know?"

"No, you don't. Life is a big swamp with a bunch of crocs. The one that gets you is the one you never saw coming."

"I didn't mean it quite that cynically. How's Vaneesa?"

"Mean as a snake. We're this close to calling it quits."

"Now *I'm* sorry to hear." Raimondo blew smoke.

Jim nodded at the door. "Your guy out there, he was suspicious of me."

Raimondo smiled. "That *goh-dee-ah* is suspicious of everyone. That's why I like 'im. But no worries, you don't look like outside muscle comin' round to cause any trouble. He was more amused by you. Said you looked scared."

Jim looked down, embarrassed.

Raimondo laughed. "Doh' worry about it. It ain't personal." He reached down and pulled a bottle of scotch from a drawer and popped it open.

Jim glanced around the room again. "You look like you're doing well."

"Fruits of my labor. I ensure all my friends have work, they in turn ensure I do well," he said as he poured a couple shots worth into a tumbler.

"Makes sense," Jim said, nodding. "I guess."

"In college they don't teach you how to use the system, how to bid your way to the top to get all the best jobs."

"I went to college to get the attention I *thought* I deserved." Jim said bitterly, shaking his head, then taking a long pull on his bottle.

Raimondo slapped the table. "That's what I'm talkin' about. Book smart versus street smart. Out here, you do the opposite – you *doh'n* draw attention to yourself." He raised his glass. "Salute!"

Jim clicked his beer bottle on Raimondo's glass and they both took a long drink.

"How do you not draw attention to yourself?" Jim asked.

Raimondo shrugged. "You keep a low profile. Doh'n do anything stupid. The guy next door with the laundromat needs some extra cash but he doh'n wanna to go to a bank. So he comes to you. You lend him a little, get it back with some interest. No paperwork. Just a handshake and an arrangement. Done. The cops don't care 'bout that kind of business."

"Or that you own a nice delicatessen."

"'Zactly. People have the wrong idea 'bout a guy like me," Raimondo said grinning, running his thumbs along his suspenders. "They see someone in nice clothes with some chains around his neck and think he's out there whackin' cops, pimpin' teenage girls, or dealin' drugs to kids. No way."

Jim used to laugh at talk like this from his cousin, but now all he could do was nod and look down sadly. He looked back up. "What happens if the laundromat guy doesn't pay back?"

Raimondo smiled a different kind of smile. "That doh'n happen often." He then looked hard at Jim. "How *you* doin' Jimmy?"

Jim feigned a casual shrug. "I'm okay."

"Jimmy, I seen my share of people with problems. And you look like a man with problems."

Jim sighed, set his beer on the desk, and put his hands on his lap. "I got trouble, Raim. A lot of trouble."

Raimondo tapped his cigarette in a decorative ashtray that looked like gold-colored ceramic with fire-breathing dragons carved around the edges. "Talk to me."

Jim glanced around once more. "We can say anything here, right?"

Raimondo spread his hands wide. "Anything you want."

Jim leaned closer and lowered his voice a little anyway. "I'm being blackmailed."

Raimondo's expression, which had been kind of a permanent smile, dropped to a scowl. "No shit. By who?"

Jim had prepared for all this and resolved to tell his cousin only what he needed to know, plus a little BS. He wasn't sure how the man would react to something big enough to have international implications. But the blackmail part needed to be emphasized so that his cousin would understand the seriousness of it.

Jim took a deep breath. "Some woman I met in Vegas. We hook up in a bar and start talking. I'm hot for her and all and at some point she slipped me something. I wake up the next day in a room I don't recognize."

Raimondo pulled on his cigarette, nodding and listening with fascination. "So she robbed you. I heard of that kind of thing goin' on there."

"It's not just Vegas, it's everywhere. There's a lot of weird stuff going on."

"You knew her before this?"

"No, total stranger."

"So you wake up, then what?"

"I wake up in a strange room and I'm naked on the bed. Don't remember a thing. I'm feeling all out of it like I'm still high. I look around and my clothes are there but everything else is gone – wallet, cell phone, watch." Jim hated lying to his cousin, but didn't want to mention much else, considering the request he was about to make.

"And? What'd she do, take your credit cards and go shoppin'?"

"Yeah, drained my account, everything. So long story short. I got a coworker to wire me some money and I used my work ID to get a Greyhound back."

"Yer work ID?"

"Yeah, I have this badge with my picture that fortunately I left back at my hotel room. When I get home there's an email waiting for me from this girl. She took pictures of me on the bed. Posed nude with me in some with one of those decorative Mardi Gras kind of eye masks on. Told me she'd send the pics to my wife and employer if I didn't start giving her regular money. She downloaded all my contacts from my phone – names, addresses, everything."

Raimondo folded his arms and narrowed his eyes. "I feel like I'm missin' somethin' here. You do stuff like this to politicians and rich people. And you're neither. I'm guessin' 'bout the rich part."

"You're correct. I'm not rich. But she's gonna take everything I have."

Raimondo gave a big shrug. "I can't believe I'm sayin' this but, go to the cops. You got pics of her. Blackmail is a crime. You were drugged, not your fault."

Jim held up a hand. "First off, Vaneesa is gonna go nuts. She's already caught me cheating. She'll divorce me and then I'll have two women taking money from me. She's an attorney, she'll know what to do to make it as painful as possible. But the worst part is my job. This woman posed smoking a joint with me. In one she had a little mirror lying on my chest with what looked like lines of coke on it."

"Still not your fault."

"I'm afraid my reputation precedes me. I'm gonna lose everything over this. They'll take away my security clearance and blacklist me from ever getting a job like this again. It's gonna ruin my life. This woman needs to be stopped." He paused, then added, "By *any* means necessary."

Raimondo stared for a moment then laughed and shook his head. "And I thought today was gonna be just another boring day."

"Raim, I'm being serious here."

"How do you know she didn't send copies of those pictures around to someone else?"

"I don't."

Raimondo put his arms on his desk. "Jimmy ... So if I'm readin' this right, you want me to step in with some old-fashioned street justice. Put a rocket in this broad's pocket. But I feel like I'm not seein' the whole picture here – no pun intended. Or you're not tellin' me."

"Like what?"

"I've been around, you know? I find it odd that someone would go to this length to blackmail someone, no offence, like *you*. And as far as what you're askin' me to do, this isn't New York in the '70s. Back then people got whacked for lookin' at someone wrong. Today it's different. It's a lot more risky."

"All know is that this bitch is gonna destroy me," Jim said, thudding the desk with a fist. "At the very least I'm her slave for life. She already sent one picture to my work mail. I deleted it before anyone saw it, I think. But it's still on record. She's got your name and number too. At least your old number."

Raimondo shook his head. "Jimmy, I ..."

"Remember when you told me you owed me for life?"

"'Course I do. You know your old man came to my old man years ago and asked us to keep you and your brother away from some of our side of the family's … dealings."

"Yes, I know. But look, I've never asked anything of you. Ever. Until now. I saved your life. You gotta save mine."

"This isn't to save your life though. She's not threatenin' to kill you."

"She may as well. My job, reputation, marriage, all my money? That's pretty much my life."

Raimondo retrieved another cigarette, his eyes shifting in thought. "The cops are gonna get hold of her phone. And email. Find those pics. Find out she's been talkin' to you. You'll be their first suspect."

"They'll know I didn't do it because I won't be there. And they'll never know we had this conversation. Besides, I'm trusting in your expertise to make it look like an accident or something."

Raimondo laughed. "Sometimes that works, sometimes it don't." He paused, taking a couple puffs from his smoke while thinking.

"You gotta do this for me, Raim," Jim said, trying not to sound whiny.

Raimondo stared back for a moment. "What's this girl look like?"

"Asian. Kinda pretty."

"Asian?"

"Chinese. Specifically."

Raimondo rubbed his chin. "Hot?"

"Sorta hot."

"What'd she call herself?"

"Iris."

"You fell for a sorta hot stranger named *Iris* in Vegas."

"Yeah … I'd had a few to drink."

"She musta had sum'm goin' for her. A helluva set of knockers or sum'm."

Jim sighed. "You know, other guys ask me, are you a leg man, a breast man? I tell them, I'm an ass man. I know this cuz my whole life people have been telling me, you're an *ass*, man."

Raimondo stared for a moment, his eyebrows furrowed, then burst out laughing. "That's good, Jimmy."

"Okay, I stole that from Rodney Dangerfield. But it's kind of true for me."

Raimondo shook his head. "You need therapy, man."

"Don't I know …"

Raimondo leaned back and turned serious, taking a long pull on his smoke. "You know Jimmy, once somethin' like this is set in motion, there's no turnin' back. No changin' yer mind. And sometimes there's repercussions."

"I understand."

"What's gonna happen after this? What if she gave the pics to someone else?"

"I don't know."

"You may fold under questioning, Jimmy. You'll be behind bars the resta yer life. Not worth it. And if you say anything about me …" He cocked his head and looked hard at Jim.

Jim put up his right hand. "Raim, my word as a man and as your family. I'd never do that. I just gotta do something."

Raimondo shook his head and sighed deeply. "I do this, we're square, right?"

"Absolutely."

"Okay, where do we find her? And I'll need a picture."

"I don't have much," Jim said pulling out his phone. "At least of her without a mask." He thumbed through some images then handed Raimondo his phone.

Raimondo inhaled a big lungful of smoke while looking at a grainy image of a black-haired woman in a dark corner of some kind. Her head was mostly covered with a cap and she donned yellow-lensed glasses that obscured her eyes. He frowned at the image. "This the best you got?"

"Unfortunately, yes. She's going to meet me on Tuesday. Probably near where I work."

Raimondo took a business card and jotted a phone number on the back, then slid it across the desk. "Call this numba, and only this numba when you get the details. But not on your own phone. Nothin' attached to you. And when you call, you don't discuss nothin' about this. And don't use my name or your full name. Just say, 'this is cousin Jimmy.'"

"No problem."

Raimondo retrieved a fresh cigarette from the glass holder. "Hey, next time you're feelin' lonely, I know some cute Italian girls that would go for a serious, sour face like yerself."

"Gee, thanks cuz."

Chapter 29

The nephew of Uncle Wong-fat sat in his usual place in the far corner at one of the small tables that made up the eatery at the Hung and Fat Mart.

He closed his eyes as he prepared his thoughts. Picking up a cup of tea, he blew into it and enjoyed the aroma that rose to his nose. He took a sip, set the cup down, and began typing.

The Chinese Communist Party continues to ensure history will always repeat itself.

There are now so many of the so-called "death vans" that run along the highway in the southern province of Yunnan, a person cannot drive to and from the courts anymore without passing one or two.

"It's progress," one official said proudly of the vehicles being dispatched all over China.

The CCP's idea of "progress" actually originated in World War II. Nazi engineers, being the clever people they were, wanted a more efficient and cost-saving way to exterminate condemned prisoners. So why not have them be dead and gone by the time they arrived at the disposal facilities for mass cremation or burial? To accomplish this, they created "gas wagons" equipped with an airtight enclosure that filled with carbon monoxide from the engine's exhaust as it drove. These wagons were first tested on Polish children to make sure they fine-tuned the design. The prisoners – mostly Jews, but also Christians, the handicapped, homosexuals and others – were robbed of all possessions and stripped, then locked in the death wagon where those on the outside could hear the muffled screams and pounding as the vehicle moved along. When the bodies arrived, gold fillings from teeth were removed with pliers or knives.

The condemned of the CCP have it a little better. They are restrained to a nice new bed in a clean, modern vehicle where a lethal cocktail of sodium thiopental (to induce unconsciousness), pancuronium bromide (to stop breathing), and potassium chloride (to stop the heart) are administered while a video camera records their murder.

We're assured it's quick and painless – which in no way justifies it – but since those who could testify never survive, no one knows.

Immediately upon passing, a dedicated team, assembled and trained specifically for the task, quickly removes the victim's corneas, pancreas, lungs, livers and kidneys, packages them in ice, and rushes them off to the black market. Their hearts would be taken as well, were they not contaminated by the drugs. Once parts are removed, the bodies are quickly cremated before family members get a chance to view them.

These death vans allow for a more efficient way to extract body parts, as opposed to the traditional bullet in the back of the head in a prison camp, which creates the inconvenience of having to rush to save the organs. One remaining silver lining to the bullet method is that the heart can still be used for profit.

Who gets this final ride in a death van? If you think only murderers or those accused of high treason, think again. Fraud and tax evasion may land you this fate, or just being a member of the Uighurs or other ethnic minorities in the Xinjiang region that the CCP is committing genocide against.

In a country where there are no moral reservations about the death penalty, why not profit while you're at it? And who is paying? – anyone with money. Body parts are quickly transported to hospitals and clinics in cities like Guangzhou, Shanghai, and Beijing, which then sell them to the wealthy as well as body part "tourists" from Japan, Singapore, South Korea, and Taiwan. And it's not just doctors profiting from others' demise. Investigations by human rights' groups show that the police as well as many members of China's judiciary system take a cut.

It was also revealed that Americans, through an organ broker in New York, are purchasing these parts for themselves or loved ones. Since then, we now know this is happening in every major city across the United States, Australia, the United Kingdom, and other parts of Europe. (See links below for contact information of these peddlers of murdered human parts and join us in alerting authorities.)

When customers of these stolen organs feel their heartbeat at night as they fall asleep, can they really enjoy nice dreams knowing their body is now kept alive by parts forcibly taken from a father, mother, or child, first dragged away from their home, locked up in a camp, tortured and raped, before having their lives taken?

Shame on all of you who participate in or turn a blind eye to these atrocities against humanity.

***

The reverend Jeremy Mueller checked into a modest motel on the border of Santa Clara and Milpitas. The average rating for the place was just three and a half stars, but he didn't need much. For the next couple days, he'd be attending a bi-annual pastor's conference he'd been wanting to go to for several years. How good it felt to finally have enough free time. After that, he hoped he would have some time with his little brother Jimmy before heading back up north.

Checking the nightstand drawer, he was pleased to find a Bible with the famous stamp in the lower left – the pitcher and torch in the circle – indicating it was placed by the Gideons International. But it didn't matter who placed it, what was important was that it was there for anyone who may need it.

His phone rang. "PJ here."

"PJ? As in Pastor Jeremy?" came a woman's voice.

"Pastor J, speaking, yes. And who might this be?"

"Hi Pastor. Sophia Diaz from *Who's in Your Cornerstone?* magazine."

"Oh, hello Ms. Diaz. I wasn't expecting your call until the end of the week."

"I did say I might be early. Is this not a good time?"

"I happen to be out of town on travel, but I have a few minutes, sure."

"Excellent. I'll try to be brief. As you know from our email exchange, we're doing a series of interviews on being a pastor and being single. I have a few questions for you."

Jeremy sat on the bed. "Well, being that I've been a single ordained minister for the last fourteen and half years, I just may have some answers."

"Excellent. I've seen your picture and some videos of you online. I hope you don't mind me saying, but you're an attractive man. What happens when women are interested in you?"

"Why Ms. Diaz …" Jeremy said tongue in cheek.

Diaz giggled. "You know what I mean, Pastor."

"Yes, yes, I'm joking. Well, thank you first off. But to your question. It isn't that there haven't been women who have piqued my interest, or women who suggested I've piqued theirs. There's also the occasional church member who tries to play matchmaker. The truth is, I'm not all that sure why I'm still unwed. I supposed God will lead me when the time is right."

"What do you think single pastors face that married pastors do not?"

"Well, being single is hard enough for many regular church attenders, but being a single *pastor* has many more challenges. Seminaries train pastors how to juggle ministry and family life, but what is often neglected is what to expect when there's no spouse or children. I think the biggest challenge is people just wondering why you're not married and making that an issue. And single women in ministry have even more challenges."

"Like what?"

"Well, they have to set more boundaries. That male church goer who gives her an uncomfortably long hug, or who's attracted to her and asks for private prayer."

"Don't women in the church ask male pastors for private prayer or counseling?"

"Oh, all the time. But it's more, how shall we say, normal and accepted for a male pastor to talk to a woman in the congregation one on one."

"Have you faced any discrimination for being single?"

"Well, when I was still in school earning my bachelor's in theology, I had been a faithful lay minister at a larger church in the Folsom area. When the couple who had pastored that church for many years – Pastor Greg Bailey and his wife Donna – began talking about retiring, I jumped at the opportunity to finish my degree, get ordained and take over. But Donna Bailey simply would not consider an unmarried pastor, and she convinced Pastor Greg to go along with that. That always bothered me."

"Why did it bother you?"

"Why was being a single pastor a disqualifying constraint? Wasn't this prejudicial? And it's interesting because in First Corinthians, the Apostle Paul actually sounded quite *anti*-marriage, saying that singles are able to care more for the work of the Lord, rather than the legally hitched who are distracted taking care of each other."

"So in your opinion, singles have more time for ministry."

"Oh yes."

"But many say that because a pastor's wife plays so many roles in the church, or tends to, the pastor is able to do more."

"I don't think that's true. Whatever extra time there may be needs to be devoted to their marriage. Paul basically recommended that singles just stay single unless you couldn't control yourself sexually. I can stand before God with a clean conscious on that issue."

"If I may ask, do you think single pastors struggle more with lust?"

Jeremy thought for a moment and decided to go all out and be transparent. "I think all men do, and a lot of women too, based on counseling I've done and from what I've been told. As for me, I have had my moments with attractive woman, even in church. And pornography is too prevalent not to tempt almost anyone. But I've stayed true." He thought of his brother Jimmy but would never say his name. "And I've known men who've brought heaps of trouble on themselves in this area."

"Tell me more about the discrimination you say you've felt being a single pastor."

"Well, I always think of Timothy in the Bible, who was both young and single, as well, not just a pastor, but a bishop over the churches in Ephesus. That meant he pastored other pastors. Would Mrs. Bailey have rejected him? It's true that in First Timothy it says that a person who aspires to be a pastor must be the husband of one wife. But isn't that just an exhortation against polygyny? It certainly isn't to say singles shouldn't be pastors. Oh, and a quick reminder – Jesus himself was single!"

Sophia laughed. "Very true Pastor J."

"But to your question about discrimination, churches often place marriage above all other types of relationships. Which often doesn't work out. I have family members for whom marriage caused more pain than anything else. I remind people that there's an equal amount of beauty and joy to be found in other relationships like friendships. But there remains a persistent presumption in the church that people aren't 'complete' until they marry and the primary reason you're there is to hunt for a spouse. But that isn't biblical. God created whole and complete people in his image, not wandering 'halves.' That kind of thing brings a certain shame to singleness."

"Do you struggle with shame, pastor?"

"The first several years, a little. But not anymore. I know I'm exactly where God wants me to be. And frankly, I enjoy the freedom singleness avails."

"So I gather your church is a good place for singles?"

"I sure hope so. I've always made an effort to welcome singles, especially those aspiring to get into ministry. That's been a big component in making my church grow. One of the beauties of church is that members are called to be a loving, supportive community for all people, single, married, or separated."

"I really appreciate your time and insight Pastor Jeremy."

"Thank you, Ms. Diaz. God bless."

Jeremy sat for a moment reflecting. He really was happy with who and where he was right now. He wished the same contentment and satisfaction for his little brother. He was even happy with his humble midnight blue Toyota Prius out in the parking lot, a car Jimmy had made fun of.

"Wow, cool Prius!" Jimmy said one day. "You know who says that?"

"Who?"

"No one."

Jeremy had laughed. What were little brothers for, after all?

Tomorrow after the first day of the conference, he'd give Jimmy a call and try to hook up, maybe have dinner somewhere. He was curious to know how the Vegas trip went. And although he disapproved, he was also curious what happened with Iris.

Chapter 30

Jim Mueller stared at the computer screen and tried to keep his hands from shaking. He'd just finished a big chapter for an update in a user manual on tailoring custom gateway software processes. The anxiety of the last several days was making it hard to focus.

The shaking wasn't so much from all the typing but rather the clock-watching and anticipation of what he was going to do shortly. He'd already broken trust with not only his employer, but the United States government, and the reality was hitting hard.

He wasn't sure what would happen if they found malware, assuming that's what was on that thumb drive. Danny Weng had told him that was hard to prosecute. He could always tell the truth and say he had no idea what was on it. Still though, he was the one who put it there knowing it could very well be malicious.

But the security booth schematics, that was another story. Once he removed that and gave it to them, that'd be it. It probably fell under the Espionage Act. He could hear the prosecutor now telling the judge and jury about the various charges – willfully disclosing classified information to a foreign entity and so on. But would that apply to UCNI information? The law didn't care if a person shared sensitive information with America's enemies or the press. Nor did it care why. The punishment was the same.

The login screen bade him to enter his credentials to access the secure portal where Helios developers and engineers stored their documentation. He was pretty sure nothing here was full-blown classified. If it was, the person who posted it had violated some rules.

All branches of the military as well as the White House used the Secure Internet Protocol Router Network, known as *SIPRNet,* to communicate around the world and share classified information. It was a system of computer networks air gapped and separate from the public, unprotected Internet.

But was this data storehouse in Kansas City air gapped the same way? Probably not since he could access it from anywhere as long as he used a lab-imaged machine with VPN.

It was kind of an elaborate login process. First, he had to login to the lab domain with his Department of Energy credentials. Then he had to insert his HSPD-12 badge into his laptop or an attached card reader and enter his PIN. Then an automated call was sent to his mobile phone with a numeric code he had to enter.

Why all the fuss? So they'd know exactly who was logged in, when, for how long, and what information was uploaded or downloaded. Jim wasn't sure they documented what was just viewed, but he may be finding out soon. Even if they did, were there people that really went through the reports? There was quite a bit of traffic on the site. It wasn't just the Helios group that used this data repository – all the DOE laboratories used it for various projects, or at least the ones involved in nuclear power or weapons research.

Jim refocused on his reason for being here – the security booth schematics he'd seen recently. Not remembering where they were though, he'd have to fish around. After spending about twenty minutes going through files of individuals he knew had worked on Helios hardware, he realized these directories weren't very well organized. People just sort of threw things in here. Up until now, he'd only looked at certain folders when directed by a developer or engineer to retrieve information on some new hardware or software update. But now he was shooting in the dark.

He went back to the main home directory for Helios. Scrolling down about two pages, he ran into a "New Projects" folder. Opening it, he found about a dozen more folders with cryptic names and numbers that gave no indication of what they were.

Starting at the top, he went through the folders one by one.

The first three were suggestions for an improved battery backup system design for the remote processors that managed Helios alarm sectors. The next folder described a modification to the CCTV function allowing sites with analog cameras to route the output to a solid-state recorder.

And then he ran into it – the security booth folder he'd seen before. There was a white paper, so he opened it and saw the letters "UCNI" boldly displayed in red on the top and bottom. The paper contained information he was mostly already aware of. A secure access point booth is a room with two doors which acts as a portal from a low to high side or vice versa. Most booths had pushbuttons for easy access from the low side. But getting out to the high side required an HSPD-12 badge with the right credentials, including biometrics if mandated. While you were in the booth, there could be any number of sensors scanning you. Cameras feeding images to CCTV and recording systems, as well as platforms with facial recognition functionality, a weight sensor built into the floor, radiation sniffers, even gun powder sensors.

He paused on the gun powder sensor. He'd wanted to read about this before. Apparently, the detectors had been around since 2017 and were now so sensitive, they could detect gunpowder in a bullet, in a gun, in a trunk, up to nine feet away. The sensor sniffs out the unique electric field that naturally occurs in materials such as smokeless gunpowder. These electric fields occur at very low frequencies and pass through clothing and other barriers used to conceal weapons. It can find loaded firearms and gunpowder bombs among a crowd, behind walls and doors, or anywhere inside a vehicle.

There was also a polarimetric radar that looked for concealed guns. People normally wore guns on their chest, hips, or tucked away near the groin, so that's where the sensors auto-target. They searched for things like a particular glare from a bulge, anomalies normally not seen, like what a hidden rigid or solid object might create. It worked via polarization, sending out waves and analyzing the signal that bounced back. An irregular object, like the protrusion of something hard plastic or metallic, can change the polarization of the signal, allowing for the detection of any concealed items, not just firearms.

Wow ...

Anyway, back to the booths. There were a couple of these booths being constructed and tested in both Jim's laboratory and one in Tennessee. After testing, they were going to be installed in two Category 1 sites in Nevada and New Mexico.

Jim opened the images files, which also had the "UCNI" header and footer. There were six blue and white schematic images, each one with a high-resolution detailed graphic that was 10,000 by 7,500 pixels. The images showed the booth in complete detail – from the steel and glass exterior, to the electrical and device laden innards, from all sides, including top and bottom points of view. The graphics went into every dimension and measurement, every type of material, where the circuit boards and sensors were installed, the wiring, voltage levels, power supply, and the regulated lines that went to and from Helios.

Jim rubbed his chin and thought. What could someone with this intel really do? Just to get anywhere close to this thing would mean getting by a handful of guards, a couple gates, and a dozen cameras. Even if you disabled certain sensors without triggering an alarm, Helios would not let you out of the booth. You'd have to break into the steel frame to the circuits, know which line to hack, then trick Helios by sending the correct voltage level that translated to "Okay" to disengage the lock. But would Helios still do it without also having the correct credentials that came from a person whose name was on the right access list?

This was crazy, and here he was risking everything for it.

He took a deep breath and looked up at his door, which was shut. He then glanced around his small, empty office space just to make himself feel better. After right-clicking the first image, he stopped and hovered his mouse arrow over the Save As menu option but didn't want to click it. The moment he did, there'd be a record somewhere of what data he'd downloaded.

Let's try another approach.

Using the ctrl and minus buttons, he reduced the size of the image to where it fully fit the browser window. The lines and words in the schematics now looked tiny and almost unreadable, but it would have to do.

Bringing up his favorite screen shot capture program, he drew a box around the image and hit Save. He now had a copy on his desktop. He saved it into a folder under an innocuous name.

In less than five minutes, all the images were copied over.

He then retrieved an extra Ironkey thumb drive he had lying around that had been wiped clean earlier, stuck it in a USB port, and moved the images to it.

Tucking the thumb drive in his pocket and closing his eyes, he thought, *what in God's good name are you doing …*

***

Sergeant Ronald McClelland slowly set the phone back down in the cradle. Although his group, the laboratory's Security and Crime Investigation Section, had indirectly provided the FBI with information in prior investigations, this was now the second time he'd spoken personally to anyone in the bureau, in this case, Doug Thomas, the Special Agent in Charge at the FBI field office in Las Vegas.

A week and a half ago or so, McClelland's associate director, Bob Branum, had been called first. But when it was found that McClelland had dealt personally with James Mueller, they wanted to speak with McClelland directly.

Branum was about ten years McClelland's junior and still had a younger man's energy. He had wanted to be there in McClelland's office and listen to the conversation on speaker phone. Unlike McClelland, who had a military police background, Branum had worked in corporate security for three decades. While they both had different approaches to preventing and solving crime, they worked together nicely.

McClelland looked up at Branum. "Thomas is being pretty tightlipped. How big you think this is?"

"Big," Branum said. "International."

"Really …"

"Yeah."

McClelland thumped his desk with a fist. "I say pull Mueller in now. Give him a polygraph. Scare 'im. See what he knows. I know he was holding out on me, so I drilled him on every detail. He was squirming."

Branum smiled. "I know, I know. But I wanna watch him first. See what his next move is."

"What do you want to do?"

Branum thought for a moment. "Who does Mueller work for?"

"His direct supervisor is a gal named Francis Lane. She's an operations training and writing manager at the institutional level, reports directly to the director's office. Her group round robins for different directorates."

Branum nodded. "Start with her. Find out what projects Mueller has been working on and who he reports to for those projects. Everything needs to be kept under the lid. Make that crystal clear."

McClelland nodded, then asked, "What else have you heard about this? Why international?"

Branum looked down in thought for a moment, then looked back up. "Ron, I have the deepest respect for you and your work here, but I gotta stick to the need-to-know on this one. When this thing blows, you'll hear all about it."

McClelland nodded. "I see."

***

Jim looked at his phone for the fifth time in the last five minutes. The security division's picnic social officially started about twenty minutes ago. He wanted to give everyone in the Helios building time to stop whatever they were doing and wander over there. He knew though that many of the engineers, especially the hardware folks, were on the odd side of social, some a little eccentric at times, and may not even be going to this thing. Lots of people skipped stuff like this. But he had to chance it – this was his only shot.

If he failed again, who knows what Iris and her people would do. Actually, he had a pretty good idea of what these evil scum might do.

Grabbing a napkin from a pile he kept on his desk, he wiped the sweat off his forehead and tried to remain calm. What could he say if someone caught him in the Helios lab? What possible excuse could he have to be there alone? Perhaps he could get away with, "I was looking for Shane so we could go to the picnic." But he could hear the reply now. "Shane's already down there, didn't he tell you? His office is right down the hall – why are you looking for him here?" Blah, blah.

He put his hand to his chest. He was tired of these adrenaline-fused panic attacks. He looked at his phone again. Okay, by the time he got there, the picnic will have been underway already for thirty minutes. This had to work.

He briskly walked to his car, hopped in, and made the eight-minute drive to the parking lot facing the Helios development building. He took a deep breath, then slapped the steering wheel in both fear and frustration.

Exiting the car, he walked calmly but purposefully to the booth that would let him into the Q-only area. After entering his badge and PIN, the high-side door unlocked. Picking up the pace and with his head down, he swung the heavy front doors to the Helios building open and made his way down the hallway.

Be casual. Look around. No sign of anyone. Save for that damned white noise maker on the ceiling, the building was quiet and sounded empty. Good. *You all enjoy your hotdog and soda while I break my vow and betray the trust bestowed upon me by the American people.*

With his fingers quivering, he accidentally entered the wrong PIN twice on the remote access terminal next to the door of the Helios lab. He paused and carefully tried once more. Three bad attempts and it would lock him out. Then he'd need to get his PIN reset and have to explain why he was trying to get into the Helios lab when this happened.

Less than a minute later, after putting his sweat-slick hand into the HGU, he was in.

He paused in the first room and looked around. Other than the usual hum of computer fans, there wasn't a sound. He almost glanced up at the three cameras mounted near the ceiling but stopped himself. May as well not look *that* suspicious.

Moving forward into the next room, he paused only for a second to see if he heard voices coming from the alarm console room. Hearing nothing, he continued forward a little slower and stopped in the doorway. The lab appeared to be empty.

Get moving.

Navigating around a couple desks and chairs, he went straight to the desktop computer under the main alarm screen and his heart jumped. As he'd half expected but hoped not, the USB ports were empty. Someone had taken the thumb drive out.

He sat up and scanned the tabletop. Nothing.

He looked for the red plastic bowl where it had sat before. It wasn't there.

Oh no …

Where? On a shelf? In a drawer?

There! Someone had moved the bowl to the other side of the console and put it on a small desk next to a whiteboard where developers sometimes had meetings to discuss software workflow.

Pulling the bowl close to him, he picked up each Ironkey thumb drive and quickly examined it. One of them appeared to have a small sticky note attached to it, facing the bottom of the bowl. The drive had to be his because the letters "R" and "K" were darkened out by a sharpie pen. He turned it over and saw that someone had written the words "What's this?" on the sticky note with a ballpoint pen.

He paused and considered. Someone had found the thumb drive and not knowing what it was, just put it aside with this note. There hadn't been enough curiosity or time to bother doing any investigating into it. He got lucky.

He stuffed the drive with the note into his pocket, consciously aware of the cameras recording his every move. He could only hope that whoever had found the drive would forget about it and not bother to follow up.

He looked around the room and the table to see if he forgot anything. All was clear.

Time to scram.

Then his heart almost stopped. He suddenly heard the distinct voice of Kay Allison talking to someone as she made her way through the two adjacent rooms toward the alarm console.

Think ... think!

A large, curved desk sat a few feet away from the console. It was spacious and pushed back against a low, portable partition wall.

I can't believe I'm doing this.

Stooping and ducking, he crawled under the desk just as he heard Kay walk in.

"We need to find out why the first login was timing out before the validator could login," Kay was saying.

"I know. I'm looking at the events log now," a voice replied with a Spanish accent. Ricardo Martinez.

"What about your theory this is only happening when one remote access terminal is accessing more than two alarm sectors?" Kay asked.

"Still a good theory," Ricardo answered.

Jim watched from under the desk and saw the legs of Kay and Ricardo move into his view directly in front of him. His heart thudded so loudly he was afraid they'd hear it.

"Look right here," Ricardo said.

They both stood in front of the main center monitor while Ricardo pecked at the keyboard and moved the mouse.

"These two alarm sectors are managed by this one access terminal," Ricardo said. "We're testing what happens when more than fifty percent of the regulated lines to the remote processor are sending signals when a two-person login rule is being employed."

"Okay," Kay replied. "Lemme know."

Jim watched as Kay's legs turned around and she appeared to pause, as if listening and looking around the room. He held his breath. To get caught hiding under a desk in a place like this would be akin to getting found in a car, pants down with a hooker on your lap, and cocaine residue on your upper lip.

"What is it?" he heard Ricardo say after a few seconds.

Kay remained silent, her knees just four feet in front of Jim's position on the floor. The seconds ticked by with appalling sluggishness.

"Nothing," she finally said, turning around.

He heard Ricardo say, "I'm *hambriento*. Let's get outta here, join the fiesta."

"There's nothing there I can eat," Kay replied.

Jim watched as their legs moved out of view and toward the exit.

"Just have a water then," he heard Ricardo say.

Jim listened to their voices fade and vowed not to move a muscle for at least two minutes. He heard the lab's door shut and then silence. Well, maybe he wouldn't have to wait quite that long.

He carefully eased out from under the desk, pausing every five seconds and listening for noise.

Again, moving briskly, he beelined for the door to the adjacent room, strolled quickly through and to the exit. Clutching the handle, he gently pushed the lever down until he heard the click. Through the open crack, he saw an empty hallway, no movement.

Slipping out, he began the agonizingly long walk down the hallway to the building's exit. As he passed the second to the last door where the Helios IT support guys worked, he glanced in and saw Kay's back a couple feet inside the doorway talking to one of the techs.

Shit ...

Continuing forward, he pushed the front door open hard and jogged down the steps. When he hit the pavement below, he couldn't help but to turn around and look through the rectangular windows on the doors. He saw Kay standing in the hallway outside the IT door staring curiously at him as he walked away.

He smiled, gave a small wave, and kept walking.

Chapter 31

The little black phone buzzed and rang.

Jim snatched it up and flipped it open. "What do you want."

"Do you have the drive?"

"Yes."

For whatever reason, he decided not to mention the security booth schematics. Let them ask.

"Put it in a plain white envelope and seal it. Leave your workplace now. Head toward the freeway and get on five-eighty east, then take the Greenville Road exit."

"Wait –" Jim started to say, but the call ended. "Damn these people," he said, grabbing his wallet and keys off his desk.

Ten minutes later, as he was taking the Greenville exit, the phone buzzed again. He flipped it open but said nothing.

"Follow the hotel signs to the La Quinta Inn. Next to it is a restaurant. Go in and sit at the counter. Take the envelope out and place it on your left."

Five minutes later, he was looking at the restaurant, a standard American diner kind of place. Looking in the windows, it appeared to be maybe half full of customers.

He paused and slowly looked around the parking lot. There was no sign of that delivery truck he'd taken a little ride in a few days ago. No suspicious characters watching, at least none he could see. He glanced at the glovebox. Oh, screw the shirt button camera this time.

Exiting the car, he made his way to the front door and entered.

A hostess was at the cash register writing something. She looked up. "Hi, one?"

Jim nodded. "I'll just go to the counter."

"Help yourself."

Again, he paused and looked around. No one was paying any attention to him. He chose the third stool from the end.

A busied and somewhat tired-looking waitress appeared. She had a name lapel pin on her uniform that said "Joanne" and looked to be in her mid-forties – a career server. "What can I get for you, hon?"

"Uhm, just coffee, please, while I decide."

He waited for Joanne to pour him a cup and then eased the envelope out of his pocket. Once more, he glanced around, and seeing no one, set the envelope down on a napkin to his left.

A small flat screen monitor was attached above the window to the kitchen where servers bustled back and forth with plates and glasses.

Two college football teams, the Texas Longhorns and Ohio State Buckeyes, were duking it out on the screen. In his younger years, Jim hated watching sports because it reminded him of how lousy he'd been at them in his youth. No one ever wanted him on their team. Now as he sat watching in a kind of daze, he realized he didn't care anymore. There were some advantages to getting older.

The little black phone buzzed in his pocket. He flipped it open and sighed into it.

"You sound tired, Jimmy."

Taking a sip of coffee, he didn't respond.

"Do you see that woman to your right?"

Jim turned. There were a couple families at tables; a young mother was wiping the mouth of a toddler in a highchair. Two men in construction outfits were at a small table by the window.

"No."

"More to the right, near the front window."

Jim turned more and scanned the tables along the sides and back. At one table, two middle-aged women sat talking, a couple glasses of white wine between them.

"Who am I looking for."

"The Chinese woman."

"I don't see any Chinese woman."

After a pause, "You're right. She's not there. Enjoy your coffee."

The phone call ended.

Jim quickly swiveled around and looked on the counter.

The envelope was gone.

He looked toward the entrance to the restaurant and saw no one leaving. Standing up, he headed hastily toward the restrooms, located on the other side of the main seating area.

A sign for the restrooms pointed toward a narrow hallway. He started down it and heard a door shut. Picking up his pace to a jog, he opened the last door in the hallway and saw he was in the rear corner of the kitchen. Two cooks with their backs to him were busy preparing something and paid no attention.

To the left was a door with a "Deliveries" sign above. Opening it quickly, he heard the sound of a car's engine and turned to see a white Nissan Maxima with a license plate frame advertising a car rental company driving away. He could see only the back of two dark-haired heads as he watched the car turn to go around the building and out to the main parking lot.

"Damn …" he muttered.

That same afternoon, the thumb drive was placed in a heavy-duty bubble mailer envelope and given to a Chinese-owned freight company that provided rapid international door to door shipping. About a day and a half later, it would be placed in an anonymous post office box in downtown Beijing, then picked up and transported to the mailroom at the MSS building. It would later be taken to Liang Huang in his underground cubby who would promptly begin analysis on the acquired data.

***

Kay Allison stared at her arugula, grapefruit and parmesan salad and wished it tasted a little better. It had in the beginning, and every effort was made to create a variety of meals throughout the week, but this particular one was getting old.

She sighed. Maybe she'd go to the cafeteria and get a little cheat meal. She'd been good. She deserved it.

Her phone rang. "Kay."

"Ms. Allison, my name is Sergeant Ronald McClelland and I'm with the laboratory's security and crime investigation section. I hope I'm not catching you at a bad time."

She set her fork down. "Not at all, sergeant. How can I help you?"

"Do you have time to go over something? It's high priority and time critical."

"I guess so. It's a little busy around here. But then it always is."

"It's a sensitive matter and I can't go into details on the phone. May I stop by your office?"

"Uhm, sure. Right now?"

"Yes, I will be there in about fifteen minutes."

Kay went to the kitchen and scraped the rest of the salad into the garbage can. Seventeen minutes later, Sergeant McClelland knocked on the doorframe of her office.

"Good morning."

Kay stood.

McClelland smiled. "At ease, Ms. Allison."

Kay sat back down. "You made me a little nervous with your 'sensitive' talk."

McClelland turned to the door. "May I?" he asked, closing it, not waiting for permission. He then sat on the other side of Kay's desk.

McClelland put his palms together and rubbed them a couple times. "We have a delicate situation here at the laboratory. I need to ask that you keep this conversation confidential."

Kay just nodded and stared back. In her position, she'd long become accustomed to the bureaucracy that went hand-in-hand with the nature of the lab's hush-hush work. While most people only saw the "official use only" aspects of Helios, she oversaw the classified stuff when vulnerabilities were discovered or when something broke.

McClelland folded his fingers together on her desk. "I'm here because of a certain James Mueller. Most know him as Jim. I understand he works on Helios."

"I'm very familiar with James Mueller. I don't see him often, but I've seen all his work over the last couple years. He oversees training and documentation for Helios."

McClelland nodded. "I see."

"But he doesn't work directly for me. I'm not his immediate supervisor. His directorate is the writing and training group."

"Yes, I know. I've already spoken to his group's associate director, Francis Lane. She wasn't able to tell me much because Mr. Mueller has been busy doing work for your group. That's why I am here."

"I don't understand. Is James in trouble?"

McClelland looked down in thought, then looked back up. "Has Mr. Mueller exhibited any behavior lately that you might consider suspicious?"

"Suspicious?"

"Anything at all that might raise a red flag."

Kay shook her head. "No, none that I can think of."

"Something subtle perhaps. An anomaly that gave you pause."

Kay stared at her desk in thought.

McClelland gave her a moment, then said, "I know you said you don't see him often, but when you have, particularly recently, is there anything at all you can think of?"

"Recently, as in …"

"The last two or three weeks."

Kay raised her eyebrows. "Does this have to do with him getting robbed in Las Vegas?"

"I'm afraid I can't go into detail about any of that right now."

"Okay. Well …" She drummed her fingers on the table in thought. "Actually, there is something now that you mention it."

"Yes?"

"Last Thursday, I saw him leaving the building when no one else was around."

"This building?"

"Yes."

"Was it particularly early or late in the day?"

"No. It was lunch time. There was no one around because the group was having a picnic."

"I see. Do you know more precisely what time that was?"

"Yes, in fact. Because the picnic started at eleven-thirty. I was there talking to Ricardo, and we were discussing a problem. Ricardo Martinez. We were in the lab right before that."

"The lab?"

"Sorry. The Helios lab. That's where we test fly new software and hardware releases for Helios. I exited the lab and went down to talk to our IT guys before I headed over to the picnic. By then it was maybe twelve-fifteen."

"What happened next?"

"I heard the main door open and was wondering who it was. Maybe I could join them on the way to the picnic. So I stepped out into the hallway and saw James walking quickly away. I remember thinking that was odd."

"Why was that odd?"

"Because he normally isn't in the Helios building unless he's there to see one of our engineers to talk about a training or documentation project."

"I see. Is he not supposed to be there otherwise?"

"Not necessarily. It's just that, everyone was gone to the picnic so there wasn't really a reason for him to be there."

"Is this Helios lab a classified area?"

"No, but it's restricted. A vault-type room. The access list for it is limited only to those who work with Helios."

"Is Mr. Mueller on this access list?"

"Yes."

"So he can come and go as he pleases?"

"Yes. But again, I normally don't see him there, unless there's a specific reason. His office is in some building on the other side of the campus."

"That is correct."

"The thing is, a few days before this, I ran into him there, in the lab, and he was by himself. I asked him what he was doing and he said he was meeting with Shane."

"Shane?"

"Shane Wells. He's one of my senior engineers."

"I see. And this was how long before the day of the picnic?"

"Not sure. A week, maybe more. I remember James was acting a little weird."

"How do you mean?"

"Like he was nervous. Like I'd startled him. The anomaly you mentioned. I took note because normally he just looks at me with dull indifference. I remember thinking he might still be shaken up from what happened in Las Vegas. He told me he was embarrassed about the whole thing."

"What is the connection between that incident and you seeing him leave the building on the day of the group picnic?"

Kay shrugged. "None. That I know of. I just thought of it because you asked."

"And was Mr. Mueller in the Helios lab the day of the picnic? Before you saw him leave the building."

"I don't know."

"Do you have cameras in the Helios lab?"

"Oh yes. Nine total between the three adjoining areas."

"And they're always recording?"

"When there's motion in the room, yes."

McClelland pursed his lips. "Would it be too difficult to see footage inside the Helios lab on the day of the group picnic? This way we'll know for sure if Mr. Mueller was in that area."

"Yes. But I can't access those video clips here. With the video playback function in the lab we could."

"I'm sorry to take your time for this, Ms. Allison. But may I ask if we could do this now?"

"Sure. Follow me."

Five minutes later, Kay and McClelland were seated in front of the Helios mock alarm console looking at a particular flatscreen that had been turned sideways so that it displayed vertically. On it were a dozen thumbnails of various video clips with dates and timestamps.

Kay went to a keyboard and brought up the video gateway application and punched in the date for the prior Thursday. A few seconds later, thirty-two video events came up in a list. The last one was at 3:32 p.m. Kay played it and she and McClelland watched as two individuals strolled through the rooms into the alarm console area.

"That's Shane Wells and Dirk Reynolds," Kay said. "This was after the picnic was over."

She skipped the events that occurred after the picnic ended and zeroed in on several that were in a timeframe shortly after the picnic had started. They watched as a clip of her and Ricardo Martinez walked through the software area and toward the alarm console room. She skipped a couple more events back. They watched the three angles of her and Ricardo standing in front of the center monitor for a few seconds and then Kay turning and looking around. Then they both walked away.

"Looks like you two were alone," McClelland said.

"I remember thinking I thought I'd heard something, but I didn't see anyone."

McClelland was rubbing his chin. "Play the one right before this, please."

When she hit the link, she almost gasped as they saw two angles of Jim Mueller rummaging through a plastic bowl.

"Wow," Kay said.

"What's in that bowl?"

"Thumb drives the developers use. In fact, there it is right there," she said, pointing to the bowl at the end of the console desk. She looked at McClelland but he was staring at the screen. She reached for the keyboard.

McClelland put up a hand. "Hold on. Let's see what happens here."

They stared, mouths agape as they saw Mueller suddenly turn, look around like he was frightened, then quickly crawl under the desk across from the console. A moment later, Kay and Ricardo walked into the frame.

"Oh my god," Kay said.

McClelland looked at Kay. "I'm going to need copies of all this footage, from the time Mueller entered and exited.

The day of the picnic as well as the other events a few days prior. I am also going to need the DOE property numbers of the desktops in that lab."

Kay was still staring at the screen in disbelief.

"And Ms. Allison." He waited for her to turn and look at him. "Not one word of this to anyone."

Chapter 32

Deep below the Ministry of State Security's building in Beijing, Liang Huang studied the standard form number 86, known simply as the "SF-86," of their primary target. Although it had taken a few days, it had almost been too easy.

The customized worm their coerced insider had installed for them now worked its way through several security layers. This worm was special in that it was capable of capturing screen images and eavesdropping using the cameras and microphones built into laptops and monitors. But those functions created unneeded risk and hadn't been utilized.

In a very short amount of time, they now had the most personal information of employees of the famed American laboratory: full names, birth dates, addresses, age, gender, race, social security number, military records, job and pay history, insurance, even pension information. They also had fingerprints collected during the security clearance background checks.

To get this far, the first thing Huang had been able to do was exfiltrate several of the laboratory's IT architecture systems. From that information, it found credentials used by a contractor that assisted with compiling information during background checks. This contractor had access to many systems and databases, but the standard two-factor authentication had been a challenge.

To mitigate this, a series of phishing mails were sent to the contractor, a busy office with personnel trying hard to please their customers so they could get funding again next year when the contract was renewed.

After acquiring four names of investigative assistants, a phishing text was sent that perfectly copied their authenticating page, indicating that someone attempted to access the user's account. A few minutes later, the users received an email masquerading as a database login attempt notification. To complete the deception, the e-mail was populated with the user's unique details such as login name, e-mail address, even a profile picture. The message instructed users to change their password. One of the four individuals fell for it and was redirected to a second phishing page where keystrokes were recorded.

With Huang closely monitoring the phishing page, the user changed their password, allowing Huang to login to the user's account with the new password. This triggered a genuine text message to the user, which contained an authentication code, which the user entered into the same phishing site. The code had just thirty seconds before it expired, but that was enough time for Huang to fully login, change the password again, and seize control. He now commanded a machine that had the laboratory's network and VPN settings and was already logged into the restricted network, one layer above the common access network. He was still separated from the classified network, but it wasn't necessary to go there.

From here, he had to move quicky; once the employee realized something was wrong, he or she would probably go to their IT department which may trigger an investigation.

First, he went to employee records and stole the login names of several more individuals who worked for the contracting company, including one that was a root user on one of the databases. Armed with this, an active directory privilege escalation technique was utilized to obtain full root access. He now had the information needed to create a machine that mimicked one that was bound into the laboratory's active directory domain.

He then loaded keyloggers onto database administrators' workstations, which would effectively begin stealing consecutive keystrokes users entered on their keyboards. Huang could now help himself to the laboratory's personnel records.

From here, exfiltrating the background investigation data had been child's play. In addition to commanding the administrative server that was used to login to other servers, with root access, he installed more malware, including a remote access tool to navigate around systems where he could compress and smuggle data out. An automated process was established to gather small amounts of innocuous looking information, nothing big enough to raise alarms, at random intervals during the busiest times of the day, between 10:00 a.m. and 3:00 p.m., Pacific Standard Time.

Once this information was gathered, it secretly moved the data to a hijacked server in Lisbon, Portugal by hiding it in triple-encrypted data packets sent over a clandestine channel using a covert file transfer protocol, one that Huang engineered specifically for this job. This protocol circumvented the laboratory's firewalls that limit the outgoing traffic to a few allowed application protocols. But not only was this slow moving, the little digital highway wouldn't work during maintenance or certain upgrades, plus, the connection to Portugal could be severed any time, so data was also duplicated and migrated to hidden folders on the thumb drive their subject had put in place.

Concealing messages within another message or a physical object requires content as cover, such as a computer file, message, image, or video. This is a practice known as steganography that Huang had used many times, but even when encrypted, network administrators can still see the communication patterns and traffic flow. He didn't want to underestimate the brains that worked at this laboratory. So he utilized a covert protocol technique based on the record route option of the IP header and Internet Control Message Protocol, or ICMP. It transmitted information in the IPv6 destination headers and this header carried optional information for the packet's destination node. If the option type is set so that the receiver ignores the option, covert information can be directly encoded as option data. Huang's protocol hid data masked as IP addresses in the IP record route option where information can be encoded in frame or packet padding. If the protocol standard didn't enforce specific values for the padding bytes, which many networks did not, any data can be used. This allowed secret data to be sent by embedding it in extended standard headers, thus establishing an effective backdoor.

With everything preplanned and premade, it took Huang less than fifteen minutes to plant all the seeds. He then logged out of the highjacked machine and deliberately entered bad passwords until the account locked up. Hopefully, the employee would think they did something wrong during the password change and ask for a reset.

Business as usual.

For the last couple days, Huang had sat back and waited as his well-oiled machine went to work. To avoid the risk of detection, he only utilized the remote access tool once just to ensure things were running smoothly. While it ran in the background, the program constantly sniffed for certain attributes associated with malware analysis and if it believes it's been detected, will immediately take action by deleting certain key directories as a distraction. While doing that, it inundates file directories with random characters over the original code, making it impossible to know what it was.

When the thumb drive was delivered and in Huang's hands, he had all the information he needed. But the icing on the cake was a work email recently sent by the subject.

Amusingly, the message was about the old slang term *lù chá biǎo* – someone was teaching him Chinese. The mail mentioned an alias name they'd been suspecting for a while now, and with that, Huang made the final needed connection between that and a name they had from prior exchanges to a Hong Kong protest leader. They now knew who their primary target was, and Huang was looking at the SF-86 form for that person now.

The jigsaw puzzle was complete. It was time.

"We've got you," Huang said to the screen.

***

Three days later, two men deboarded a Boeing 787 Dreamliner at the San Francisco International Airport and made their way through the terminal. The flight had been pleasant enough, but they were glad it was over and eager to complete the mission they were on. They each carried their only luggage, a small shoulder bag which they'd stowed under their seats. This was going to be a short trip.

The older of the two wore a wig of thick dark hair over his naturally bald scalp. He bore a passport with the name, "Dennis Yang," and was thinking this was probably the last time he'd ever land in the bustling SFO. It didn't sadden him; he'd made the trip a dozen times over the years and was ready to quit and relax. For decades, men in his position were expected to follow the old party slogan by, "working for the revolution with their last breath and last drop of blood." But fortunately, that mentality started going away in the early 2000s. His last assignment, to train and mentor the young man he was with was so far going fine, but they were on a critical mission that could not fail.

The other man was twenty-five years younger and had a passport with the name, "Andrew Lim." He couldn't be more excited to be on his first international assignment as well as see the famous American city for the first time. He still had a thick head of real black hair and sharp, eager eyes. He looked around with wonder, especially at the more exotic American and European women.

Both men wore stylish prop eyeglasses, the older, a vintage silver round frame style, the younger, more modern rectangular frames with a flat top. The purpose was so that if by small chance, for any reason, video from inside the airport would later be reviewed, they'd not be recognized as easily.

Each spoke fluent English and addressed each other by their assigned names. The older man did have a noticeable accent, but they wouldn't be talking much to anyone anyway.

At the Customs Clearance office, they smiled broadly and nodded with stereotypical exaggerated mannerisms as they were asked various questions.

"What is the purpose of your trip?"

"Just visiting some family."

"How long do you intend to stay?"

"Just a couple days."

"Where will you be staying?"

They both provided the names and addresses of real San Francisco Chinese households who were prepared to back their story in full detail.

"What is your occupation?"

Dennis Yang was a line manager at a factory for Hon Hai Precision Industry and was only a couple years from retiring. Looking forward to having more time to see loved ones!

Andrew Lim was an IT desktop support engineer for Beijing Friendship Hospital and was always happy to be part of the infrastructure that helped foreign visitors when in need!

They both provided names and numbers to call to verify employment if needed.

"Do you have anything to declare?"

"Just some delicious homemade custard buns and egg tarts!"

It was all believable and worked fine. Little did the customs agents know, but behind the toothy grins and pleasant mannerisms, were two highly trained cold-blooded killers who could end another's life without a blink of an eye.

They continued on their way. Unlike the bait and switch team, which had to make contact with others, they could travel together with relative safety. Dressed casually, they looked, perhaps, like a benign father and son team in town to visit relatives.

During the flight, Dennis had thought about what he was going to do when this was over. A few years ago, it was common in China to retire between age fifty and sixty and then draw from pensions and savings. But anymore, China had the same problem America was facing – people were healthier and living longer, resulting not only in the need for more healthcare, but the age for getting at retirement money was being pushed further back. It was more common now to see older people working as janitors or store clerks because they needed the income. Dennis would not be doing that. He'd made good money working for the MSS and ensured he'd saved plenty.

It didn't help that the Chinese were actually above the global average when it came to how many years they would spend in retirement. More than three-quarters of China's huge population were expected to live past age eighty. It made sense. In China, people stay busy and stick to solid routines of exercise and eating lots of fruits and vegetables. Unlike lazy Americans who want to sit around consuming alcohol and comfort food, many elderlies in China stay active in retirement and love to dance or partake in calisthenics and tai chi. Instead of red meat and dairy or sugary desserts, the Chinese opted for more poultry and fish, fruits, and nuts. Lactose intolerance among a large portion of the population took care of the dairy part. And it was good that junk food still wasn't all that popular in China.

Although Dennis had enjoyed the vigor of his youth, he did not envy Andrew, his younger counterpart. Stress about finances and the future among China's youth was doing nothing but increasing. To not be forced to work until their "last breath and last drop of blood," out of necessity, not loyalty to a cause, forced them to start planning early. And this had led to other unwanted results. Many youths of China today were turning soft, acting more like Westerners, and not wanting to contribute to the ancestral country as much as previous generations. People of Dennis' generation thought that was selfish.

Andrew had other plans. He was going to climb the career ladder as enthusiastically as he could. Unlike many of his peers, he was going to perform with excellence and be rewarded for it. In recent years, China had become a land of opportunity for those with courage and willing to hustle. China's youth now drove the economy and growth of the country. So far, his older mentor had given glowing reports about his performance to those who mattered. It was a bright future.

One thing Andrew did have in common with peers though, was that he had no desire to marry. He loved the company of women, but only for fun and pleasure, not long-term commitment. There was no time for marriage.

As he strolled through the busy airport with Dennis, he resolved to stay focused, despite all the distractions around. Dennis had made it clear how important their visit here was.

After renting a comfortable mid-sized SUV, the two men drove into the city to Chinatown where they parked and entered SF Noodletown, a popular eatery for locals. But they weren't there to eat. They would later enjoy a nice American steakhouse for dinner.

Approaching the counter, Dennis asked to see "Uncle Ren," the owner. There was no Uncle Ren, but someone in the back knew what he meant. They were ushered into a backroom office where a steel briefcase was produced from a large safe. It was set before them and unlocked. Inside the case were four nine-millimeter semi-automatic pistols with extra magazines. The men made their selections and were given an additional 200 extra rounds of ammunition.

Dennis was handed a description of their assignment.

"Where are we going?" Andrew asked.

"Brentwood, in the East Bay," Dennis said, shrugging. "Never been there."

Chapter 33

About a mile and a half from the Port de Saint-Tropez, between the town and beaches, in the region of Provence-Alpes-Côte d'Azur, Southern France, one of the local and most extravagant mansions was hosting a party.

The Aston Martin, Lamborghini, and Ferrari vehicles that packed the massive driveway and lined the street in front of Vincent Tremblay's mega estate made it clear what class of individuals had converged here.

Tremblay was somewhat of a shadowy figure to anyone outside the microcosm of high society and the superrich, but powerful politicians, celebrities, and business acquaintances from all over the globe knew him well and happily descended upon his manor as often as they could.

The two large beautifully carved and stained alder doors that made the front entrance were held open by servants while men strolled through donning luxury tailored suits, arm in arm with women in fantastically sexy evening gowns and diamond-studded stilettos and pumps.

The girls that surrounded these men were an important accessory, not merely for sex or companionship, but because they acted as capital, and made a person stand out. These prized assets were tall and thin, at least five foot nine inches without heals, and almost exclusively Caucasian. Occasionally, one with darker skin was added for a little splash of exotic variety.

Surrounded by beautiful females, ranging in age from sixteen to twenty-five, allowed entry to clubs, invitations to yachts, and hobnobbing events such as this one. In fact, Vincent Tremblay had almost twenty girls who lived full time on the premises which assured a steady stream of summons to the most exclusive of parties in the highest of echelons. This, in turn, meant the ability to network with those one could make business deals and other mutually beneficial arrangements.

But if you were one of Vincent's special VIP's, you might be there for a different reason. A large balcony and walkway surrounded the main floor where guests could sip champaign and pretend to gaze dreamily upon fine art while discussing activities the governments they represented would never hear of. In the center of this balcony, within a small doorway and guarded by a large man in a suit with an earpiece and radio, were elevator doors. This elevator, which required a passcode, transported guests below the house where a series of rooms and offices were, including a special one simply referred to as, "The Showroom."

The Showroom was a round raised stage surrounded by several private viewing booths. Professionally designed, the ceiling within the stage area was encircled by multicolored lighting, enhancing any makeup, hair, or costumes.

Each viewing room had a large window with one-way film, giving a clear view of the stage from inside, but appearing as large mirrors from the other side.

Mustafa Ahmad was one of the Showroom guests who sat in a comfortable leather chair next to a small table bearing an ashtray and tumbler filled with bourbon. He'd been there for over thirty minutes and wasn't terribly impressed by what he'd seen tonight. He pulled on a $750 Gurkha His Majesty's Reserve cigar, then tapped it in a gold ashtray. He was actually there representing a guest, the real buyer. At twenty-nine, tall, young, and handsome, Ahmad was in his prime and loving his job working for a wealthy Saudi Arabian businessman named Alwaleed Al-Amoudi.

For all outward appearances, Mr. Al-Amoudi was seen as a benevolent man and philanthropist who gave generously to multiple charities each year. He always wore the most opulent of Western suits and had nominal doctorate degrees from a couple esteemed universities. He owned three private aircraft and had a collection of at least twelve automobiles, each one with a price tag of anywhere from one point three to eight million U.S. dollars. The owner of many companies, ranging from construction to agriculture to energy, he'd also helped build major hospitals and industrial complexes.

Mustafa Ahmad himself was impeccably dressed in a Giorgio Armani wool and silk suit, his feet adorned with Gucci loafers. He watched with anticipation as the next subject was ushered to the Showroom's platform. Items for auction were always covered head to toe by a decorative, body length veil. The subject who just entered was short and slender, clearly very young.

When the veil was removed, Mustafa's heart raced with excitement. Before them stood the youngest girl he'd seen in the last four years he'd represented his buyer here. Dressed in yellow bikini style swimwear and heeled shoes that looked too "adult" for her small feet, was a girl who appeared no older than thirteen. Her long thick hair had been stylishly parted in the middle and hung beautifully on each side in long, rolling waves.

"Gentlemen," a soothing female voice said through speakers in each viewing room. "A young selection from Mongolia. Doctor certified, a virgin. Bidding will start at one hundred and fifty thousand US dollars."

Mustafa immediately hit his button, upping the price to $170,000. As other buyers cast their bids, the girl looked around at the surrounding mirrors with fear and confusion. Her handler took her by the shoulders and slowly turned her around, giving everyone a look at her smooth and adorable adolescent legs and bottom.

A virgin no less? What a find. Mr. Al-Amoudi normally went for light-skinned beauties with hair no darker than maybe medium brown – "Mocha brown, like chocolate I can sip from," he would say. His favorites were Eastern Europeans. But this girl, though her hair was a bit dark for his taste, had skin that was a light olive complexion, and it would drive him crazy. She'd be good for months, maybe longer.

Two more hit their buttons, then Mustafa hit his again. The price was now a quarter million dollars. So far, his boss hadn't given him a spending limit and he didn't want to acquire one now, but he had to have this girl.

Someone else clicked. Mustafa clicked again. The price was now $290,000 – mere pocket change for Mr. Al-Amoudi. It was worth it.

"Are there no other bids?" came the voice after a few moments.

Silence.

"Sold to the gentleman for two hundred and ninety thousand dollars. That concludes the bidding for tonight. Thank you for attending."

The girl was turned and ushered off the Showroom's stage.

Mustafa stood, swallowed the last of his bourbon, then straightened out his suit jacket. Mr. Al-Amoudi will be pleased. He turned and opened the door to his viewing cubby to see the two gentlemen who collected payments for Vincent Tremblay. Payments were in cash, U.S. dollars, and all merchandise taken as is, non-negotiable, non-refundable, non-tradable.

Mustafa handed them a briefcase that contained $340,000, which covered the purchase of the Mongolian girl plus an additional $50,000 for an older blonde woman he'd bid on earlier who was perhaps Polish, and already maybe twenty-four. She'd be good for a couple weeks, after which she'd be disposed of for $10,000 to $15,000 to the Armenian pimps who ran cheap brothels and managed street hookers in the north along the Belgium border towns.

Behind the big mansion, Chimeg was ushered into a large SUV which drove her down to the piers where a 400-million-dollar, 558-foot super yacht waited. The craft boasted a pool with three Havana bars, two helipads, fifteen water jets, a full screen theater, a library, and a 4,500 square foot master suite.

Two female employees took Chimeg to a large bathroom where she was stripped, bathed, and given a spa and beauty treatment for more than thirty minutes.

Alwaleed Al-Amoudi, dressed in nothing but a bathrobe, obese and with grey hairs curling off his double-chin, lay on his nine-by-nine-foot Alaskan king bed mattress in the master suite waiting in anticipation. He'd been assured tonight would be special.

When Chimeg was brought to him, he smiled as Mustafa gave the girl a small push toward the bed. She paused and pulled back, scoffing in disgust. Mustafa took her by the nape and led her forward to where Mr. Al-Amoudi could reach out and take her arm. This one was feisty and needed to be taught proper submission. He nodded at Mustafa who went to a closet and produced a small leather belt which he handed to Mr. Al-Amoudi.

The doors to the master suite were closed. The muffled screams of the young girl barely went beyond the walls of the bedroom and from there were deadened by the noise of the yacht's engines as it made its way south toward Barcelona.

Chimeg and her mother would never see each other again.

Chapter 34

The young nephew of Uncle Wong-fat finished up his latest article. He felt this was one his best, which actually made it one of the "worst." In fact, he had wiped away tears as he wrote it.

The title of the article was, "The continuing human rights abuses of the CCP against ethnic Kazakhs, Uighurs, and members of other minority groups in Xinjiang." It was filled with links to irrefutable evidence, like drone footage of people rounded up like cattle and put onto trains headed for detention camps, reminiscent of the last rides many had to Auschwitz in the early through mid '40s.

And now survivors of these camps who suffered beatings, electrocution, and waterboarding, are openly talking about the slave labor, torture, rape, and mass killing. For young women there's been forced birth control and sterilization, and those who had the misfortune of being pregnant in these places, forced abortions. All this is an attempt to quell natality among certain populations.

The article ended with a plea to join the millions of Chinese people around the globe who were leaving and disavowing the Chinese Communist Party.

The nephew finished his tea and shut down his laptop. During these moments, he again questioned his motivation to continue taking the risk he was. Clearly, he thought it was worth it or he wouldn't be here today. He'd taken every precaution humanly possible, but at the end of the day, one just couldn't be certain. There was always that unknown factor.

The only way to really be safe was to go completely off the grid which meant not being able to contribute anymore to what he believed in. He thought many times about what it would take to truly disappear from modern society.

First, you'd need to drive an older car that didn't have built-in GPS. In 2013, federal law was enacted that required manufacturers to have logging features in all new cars sold in the U.S., ostensibly as a theft deterrent. But realistically, to be sure there were no tracking devices hidden in your vehicle, you'd need one manufactured before 1990. And driving an older vehicle like that required mechanical skills when repairs were needed. He often wished he had more expertise in that area, but his forte was high-tech.

Next, being off the grid meant no regular cell phone. A burner phone with no ties to your real identity may work, but you could never say or text anything on it that could be flagged for a follow up investigation. Your friends and family could never call you on it. Communication with anyone would have to be done far from your homestead with what few public phones remained in hotels, railway stations, airports, and some pedestrian areas in cities.

And speaking of a homestead, you'd need to build a custom place of residence or buy one in a very rural area that didn't have the usual hookups to the local city's power supply or communications services like cable or internet. Power to your home would need to be solar panels along with generators and maybe a domestic wind turbine to supplement when there wasn't enough sunlight to keep the battery systems charged.

As for water, you couldn't depend on the local population's supply, so you'd need to have a river or well nearby, then have the skills to filter and disinfect the water for consumption. Additionally, you'd need to conserve and recycle whenever possible with maybe a greywater system. This way, water from washing dishes, the laundry, as well as showers or baths could be reused for gardening.

For sewage, you'd need a septic tank. But that would require cleaning out the solid waste with a vacuum truck which meant services coming to your place – that could be risky. A better alternative would be a method to regularly incinerate waste safely.

Finally, food. To truly live off the grid, you couldn't depend on your local grocery stores, even if there were any close enough. So you'd need gardening, farming, and hunting skills. Fishing abilities as well if you lived near a lake or stream where there were fish. If you ate only what you grew, you'd need more than 3,500 square feet of growing space per year just for one person. Additionally, you'd need refrigerators and freezers to keep food throughout the year, which, of course, require additional power.

And before making this switch, you'd need to ensure you had the proper clothing, depending on the location. If it gets cold and snows during the winter, the right clothing would be essential to survival. And in that case, other skills like being able to make a fire without depending on matches, butane lighters or fuel would be essential as well.

Although it seemed unlikely to ever convince anyone else to join in making such preparations, it was something on people's minds more and more as the world became less stable. The research had been done. If and when "the shit hits the fan" via an economic collapse, EMP attack, natural disaster, pestilence or foreign invasion, one simply couldn't stay in the city or suburb areas. It wouldn't be long before marauding gangs going house to house in search of food, weapons, or water will kick in your door. A single family, much less a single person, would not be able to defend everything around the clock in such circumstances. The only way to survive would be to have a place ready to go where a group of like-minded people with different skills in farming, medicine, mechanics, gunsmithing, and more could work together maintaining the compound and taking turns guarding.

Hopefully, things would never truly come to that.

Picking up his computer bag, he walked to the counter out front near the entrance where the cash register was.

Uncle Wong-fat was going through some receipts. He looked up. "Finished for today?"

"Yes, Uncle. I will see you again next week."

"Here, take this," Uncle Wong-fat said, producing a box from under the counter. It was shaped like a candy box, except it had a bright red cover with floral and tree designs.

The nephew looked at it for a moment.

"Open it!" Uncle Wong-fat said.

Inside the box were two beautifully designed and painted authentic bamboo Chinese chopsticks. At the top of each stick on the wider end was a carved golden dragon.

"I had them shipped from a friend I used to sell food next to on Wangfujing Street. These are the real deal!" he said proudly.

"They are exceptionally beautiful, Uncle. I shall never have a Chinese meal without them."

"We're all very proud of your achievements. See you next week!" Uncle Wong-fat smiled.

The nephew exited the Mart and made his way down the sidewalk toward his car. He looked up at the clouds and enjoyed the cooler weather they brought. It was going to be a pleasant day.

As he walked, he heard two car doors shut behind him, but otherwise paid no attention. There were several other businesses here and there was always activity and foot traffic.

A few moments later though, he went on alert as the sounds of footsteps began to get closer. He was parked in front of a closed shop so there was no reason for whoever it was to be walking up to him.

With his heart beating a little faster, he considered the loaded .38 snub-nosed revolver he kept in the trunk under the covering where the car's jack and tire iron were stored. Would there be enough time? For a while he always carried the weapon on his person, but he'd become lax, and now it was going to cost him.

The footsteps were close now. Too late.

What he heard next made his skin turn clammy.

"Good afternoon, Mr. Danny Weng."

He slowly turned around. Before him stood two Chinese men with dark sunglasses, one older and one younger. They wore slacks; the older man had a nylon coach jacket, the other casual leather.

"That is not my name, sorry," Danny said, turning to walk around to the driver's side.

As the two men followed, he heard the unmistakable sound of a semi-automatic pistol's slide being racked to chamber a round.

"I'm sorry," one of the men said. "I meant, Jin Chou."

Danny's heart sank as he turned around again to see a large handgun with a silencer attached to the end pointed directly at his face. How had they found him? What had he missed?

"You were hard to catch, but the rabbit has finally been snared," the armed man said, grinning.

"Go to hell, gòngfěi," Danny said. Then he thought, *I am sorry, Uncle. Forgive me for what I have done ...*

The last thing Danny Weng saw was the pistol jerking and a spray of sparks before feeling the odd sensation of his face partially caving in. It didn't hurt and lasted only a moment before darkness swept over his vision and he felt his body relax.

***

"Lotus flower," the voice said through the radio.

Li Ming Tan picked up her radio. "Yes."

The one-way radios they were using encrypted the voice payload over the carrier signal with a software-set dynamic key. Only listeners with the same radios and the same key could understand the transmission, everyone else heard unintelligible garble. Despite the precaution, they still spoke in code.

"Target acquired and uprooted. No complications."

Well, that had been easy. "Excellent. And the equipment used?"

"A laptop and thumb drive were recovered."

"Good. Take to rendezvous at six PM local time."

"How about the location where target performed the work?"

"What is it?"

"A place of business. Small market. Groceries. Food. Possible family connection."

She thought for a moment. "Is it clear?"

"No. There are multiple cameras."

"Not worth it. We need to move quickly now and draw operation to conclusion before discovery."

"Okay. Will await further instructions for time and location."

***

Beijing received the update within thirty minutes. It was done. As well, the mysterious computer that had kept changing MAC addresses was confiscated. The entire effort had been a great success.

Throughout the decades, MSS agents had infiltrated both of America's prized information organizations: the Central Intelligence Agency and the Federal Bureau of Investigation. Some agents had been caught, but most had not. And now here Liang Huang was, deep below the ground in China pulling sensitive data from one of America's most famous and esteemed nuclear research laboratories.

He stood and gave out a victory yell, something he never did. Didn't matter, no one heard him. He was already anticipating his rewards. How big would probably surprise even him. For starters, he would spend the next three months on paid vacation. Smiling, he knew exactly where he was going to go.

He started jotting down notes of the debriefing he was going to give his superiors. While he wrote, he also mentally made plans for his vacation in the Czech Republic. And while he was there, he just might happen to meet up with a young *krasivaya devushka* named Polina.

Just the thought excited him.

Chapter 35

Li Ming Tan and Rong Chiang met for what was supposed to be the last time in Rong's room at another four-star hotel on the east side of Pleasanton, California.

"It felt good to get out of that city built for the sole purpose of gluttony and excess," Li Ming said.

"I concur," Rong replied.

In secret, Rong loved Las Vegas. During one of the downtime nights, he'd snuck away and drove an hour down NV-160 West to the Chicken Ranch brothel. From there, he'd chosen two girls, both American, one a pretty Hispanic with light brown hair, the other a stark blonde. It had been wonderful, better than what he'd been fantasizing about since a week before the trip when he'd been given the assignment.

Back in China, the CCP had a long history of trying to eradicate prostitution, but starting in the '80s, "the oldest profession" made a huge comeback and had since become a considerable component of China's economy. While it has remained officially illegal, it is practiced openly at certain hotels, nightclubs, boxing clubs, massage parlors, and so on.

The reason it's allowed is the same reason for everything – money. Anyone who didn't cooperate with the system and pay the bribes and protection money was made an example of. Each year, police arrested a certain number of individuals just to make sure everyone knew who's really in control.

Because of this, Rong rarely indulged in rented pleasure back home anymore. First, since he did sensitive work for the MSS, there was risk. It would not look good for his employers if he got caught doing such a thing, and he'd never work an assignment like this again. In the past, when he'd felt the urge, he would have to jump through hoops with disguises, phony identification and sneaking around. It was a tiring game he had played fairly easily in his younger years, but one he now found strenuous. He mused at the double-meaning of the old phrase: "The juice isn't worth the squeeze."

But the biggest reason why he didn't enjoy hired pleasure as much back home was that everywhere he went, it was the same dark-haired Chinese women. And most of them were average. The really attractive ones were too expensive and frankly, too well-used. But here in America there was so much more variety. Any fantasy could be fulfilled, especially in a city like Las Vegas. He would dream of his next visit.

Li Ming had entirely different reflections. She thought about how China had changed in recent years as it became more Westernized. In fact, China now led most of the world in the mentality that one's success and value rested in what one owned. Even though America's capitalism had encouraged this, Chinese citizens generally have a low opinion of the United States. But then Americans don't like China either, blaming it for everything from spreading diseases to manipulating the world's economy to tainting children's toys with lead-contaminated paint.

She was tired and ready to get back to her structured life in Beijing. She hoped she would never have to return to the glitter and glamor of Las Vegas, the very epitome of American hedonism.

Although this assignment had been relatively easy, it had also been mentally taxing, at least for Li Ming. The mission had been a success, but she continued to fight feelings she had for Chimeg, the young Mongolian girl they had used.

Li Ming herself had not been abused but had been emotionally neglected by parental figures who put achievement and loyalty to the Chinese Communist Party above all else. From them, she'd been taught to live with ambition, living and breathing higher education as well as grand goals and dreams. This, she'd done. But another part of her often wondered how life would have been different if she'd been born elsewhere.

Li Ming never had a problem behaving with the aggression of her male counterparts, and she came to understand why. A memory of when she was three or four had surfaced where she recalled her mother saying her father had wished she was a boy. This was typical in Chinese culture – everyone wanted boys to inherit the family name and care for them financially as they grew older. But she refused to apologize for not being male or reject her femininity to try to win her parents' approval. This toughened her and prepared her for a life of problem solving without relying on a man's help as many females did. The more others underestimated her, the more she worked hard to prove them all wrong. It had made her successful.

Why then, did a part of her care for Chimeg, this anonymous girl from a country Li Ming cared nothing for? Because when she looked into that child's eyes, she saw the same fighting spirit she had seen in the mirror growing up. That meant Chimeg could have had a life as a leader and achiever. Just like herself. Who knows, Chimeg may have become a mover and shaker in the world. But Li Ming had played a part in taking that future away and utterly destroying it. Would Li Ming someday shed tears over this? Perhaps, but not now. Never in front of her colleagues.

All that mattered was the future of the communist party, not the future of one person. Not even herself.

"Are we ready?" Rong asked.

"Yes," Li Ming said. "Let's finish this and go home."

***

The phone call from the usual restricted number finally came as Jim was sitting in his office trying in vain to enjoy a cup of coffee. He'd intended to get some comfort food, something deep fried and full of fat and grease, but just didn't have the appetite. He was still too livid, and it was time to take action. The plan he'd devised and set into motion was the one and only source of pleasant and even emboldening feelings he had.

He flipped the phone open and with as much sarcasm as he could muster, said, "Why hello, *Iris*, so good to hear from you."

"Jimmy –"

"Oh, by the way. This phone is starting to run low on battery. I'm going to need a charger."

"You may dispose of the phone after we're finished. Don't bother doing anything stupid like giving it to the police."

"Right. Oh, I have something for you that you forgot."

"And what is that?"

"The plans for the security booths. Detailed printouts. Everything you could possibly want to know about them. Got 'em on another thumb drive."

The phone remained silent for a moment as if the woman on the other end was considering. This raised a red flag in Jim's gut. How could they forget something they'd asked him to smuggle out of the laboratory? Had they even wanted it in the first place?

"I got detailed plans," Jim continued. "The full schematics." He paused and decided to wait for a response.

"We will tell you where to go and when. Tomorrow about ten in the morning," she finally said.

"Alright. I'm going to be having breakfast at that CJ's Café where we first met on First Street at ten. See you then." He quickly hung up.

Yes! For the first time since all this started, he felt like he had some semblance of control over that phone call. It felt good even though no real victory of any sort had been achieved, not yet. All he could do was hope it worked.

The little black phone began to buzz and ring again. He ignored it. Retrieving his own phone, he pulled the little card Raimondo had given him out of his wallet. He started to dial and then remembered what his cousin had told him.

Shutting his office door, he went down the hall to where the small kitchen and breakroom was for the students taking training classes. In there, a phone rested on one of the shelves. He picked it up, hit the eight for an outside line, then dialed slowly, as if trying to delay a decision he'd already made. The sound of ringing on the other end made him anxious.

"Yes?" a voice answered after three rings. It didn't sound like Raimondo.

"Uh, yes, can I speak to, uhm, Mr. B."

"There's no one here by that name. How can I help you?" The accent sounded New York-ish.

"This is his cousin, Jim, uh, Jimmy. I was told to –"

"Lemme stop you right there. Do you have a pencil and paper?"

"Uh, yes. Yeah." He turned and found a sticky notepad and pen on the small table in front of the chairs. "Okay, yeah."

"Write down this address."

Jim wrote it down. The address was on Columbus Street in the city and probably not far from the deli he'd visited a few days ago.

"When can you be there?"

Jim looked at the time. "An hour?"

"Okay, someone will meet you there."

The call ended.

Wow, this was it. Maybe. Hopefully.

About fifty minutes later, Jim found himself pulling over to the side of the road in front of a renovated warehouse with a big sign that said, "Darrel's Appliances." Jim got out, looked around, then paid for thirty minutes at the parking meter.

After waiting outside about ten minutes, pretending to look at his phone but taking regular glances up and down the sidewalk, he went in and looked around. The place sold the usual washers, dryers, stoves, and refrigerators. On one end of the showroom was a row of bar stools set up next to a kitchen counter display. He casually walked over and sat down at one of the stools. Pulling out his phone, he looked to see if there were any messages.

About two minutes later he sensed the presence of someone walking up to him and turned to see large, beefy man approaching. The man's eyes were mostly covered by rectangular sunglasses that reminded him of the Gargoyles Arnold Schwarzenegger had worn as *The Terminator*. The man's hair was cropped short, dark on top and greying on the sides. He wore a black designer dress shirt with the top three buttons undone revealing a large gold medallion of some kind hanging from a gold chain.

He casually stepped around the kitchen display and faced Jim across the counter, leaning forward a little and resting his elbows.

Jim fought the urge to look around before saying anything. Instead, he just nodded.

"Same girl you showed Mr. Bellini?" the man asked quietly. It was definitely the same voice who'd answered the phone earlier.

Jim nodded again. This time he glanced around. No one was paying the slightest bit of attention to the two of them.

"Where and when?" the man asked.

"Tomorrow. Around ten AM. On First Street, in the East Bay." He gave the man the address for CJ's Café on a sticky note.

"This is where she's gonna be?" the man asked.

"She should be, yes." Jim knew he didn't sound confident when he said that. "I don't know where exactly though. She might stop somewhere in or around the parking lot."

The man raised his face and stared hard at Jim through the sunglasses. "Mr. Bellini says you may not be fully committed to this."

Jim took a deep breath. "I am. That woman needs to go."

The man continued to stare for a moment then shrugged with his mouth.

It occurred to Jim that he was talking to an enforcer, a killer, a man who'd probably ended dozens of lives with no more feeling than that little shrug he just saw.

"She respond to the name Iris?" the man asked.

"Not her real name, but she probably will, yes."

The man leaned in. "Once I leave here, the deal is done," he said. "It's a go. No more phone calls. No changin' your mind. You understand?"

"I do."

"And if any of this in any way, shape or form points back to our mutual acquaintance, you understand there will be consequences."

"I understand."

"Alright then." The man turned and strolled out toward the front door of the store, leaving Jim by himself wondering what in the hell he was doing.

Chapter 36

The little black phone rang at 9:00 a.m. Jim had been expecting this and resolved not to answer. It rang and buzzed four times then stopped.

Moving quickly, and cursing himself for not doing it sooner, he opened his work email and went to the Automatic Replies function. Clicking the "Send automatic replies" radio button, he entered today's date as both the start and end time. In the text box below, he typed, *Hi, I am away from my desk most of today. I'll get back to you as soon as I can. – Jim*

Now, if they sent a threatening note to his work mail, they'd get the autoreply and not know if he was there or not. If they sent a message to his personal mail, he'd ignore it. If they called his personal or work phone, he'd let it go to voicemail. He had to get that woman to CJ's Café at 10:00 a.m. If this didn't work, he'd probably not be on good terms with his cousin again. And he certainly didn't want The Terminator mad at him.

Just the thought of Iris and her people sending more pictures to his work mail made him fume and grind his teeth.

But after this, he was going to have to prepare for the reality of having those pictures released. At that point, he'd have to come clean with everyone and hope for mercy. He'd claim he did nothing. He'd never mention putting that thumb drive in the machine in the Helios lab. He'd never talk about the security booth designs. He'd just say they'd tried to get him to steal some hard drives or something, but he'd refused. If that didn't work, well, we'll see. At least after all the dust cleared, they wouldn't own him anymore.

"You're mine now, *Iris*," he muttered.

***

Vaneesa Loveless-Mueller slowly made her way down the hall with a diet soda in her hand, listening to the dull quietness around. She wondered for the hundredth time about her career and wished her useless husband would make more money so she could just divorce the pig and retire.

Her job had been mentally stimulating a few years ago, especially when she was learning new things, but it just wasn't anymore. Clients never gave her anything exciting to do, never asked her to travel for them with a promise to pay all expenses.

Jim, on the other hand, had travelled several times for his job, so much so that he was now sick of it. Really? Sick of getting paid to see and experience new things?

No, for her it was just, *review this eighty-page agreement and tell me what you think.*

"What's up, V?" asked the friendly voice of Nora, the only other female lawyer in the group.

Vaneesa had been staring at the floor. "Oh, just basking in the reverie of my recent thirty-day tropical cruise. How about you?"

Nora laughed, the dark eyeliner surrounding her eyes narrowing with her grinning countenance.

Vaneesa watched her for a moment. Nora had several advantages that Vaneesa had to make a daily effort not to be jealous of. Nora was a few years younger and her slim Puerto Rican figure fit nicely into just about anything she wore. And unlike Vaneesa, she enjoyed flirting with the men. She seemed to take everything in stride. But the pretty lady was so amicable and genuine it was hard to hold anything against her.

"I'm feeling wonderful," Nora said. "You look tired."

"I am. And this suit is feeling tighter than usual today."

Nora smiled and looked around for a moment allowing Vaneesa to let her eyes rove up and down the woman. A female lawyer, or any female white-collar professional for that matter, had to dress in a way that others could take in at a glance and not gawk at because it was too revealing. That meant skirts that weren't too short, and tops that covered up cleavage. It was true that women had more options than men, they could expose shoulders, arms, or upper chest areas. They could also wear open shoes like sandals. But such choices could compromise a career. Somehow, Nora balanced all that sort of thing perfectly.

Vaneesa lowered her voice. "At least we live in a day in age where a professional woman can wear pants. The only drawback is that we have to draw more attention to our work, achievements and brain power than our bodies."

"You overthink things, Vaneesa," Nora said. "You're beautiful. Be proud to look your best."

Sweet Nora. It was true that she and Nora didn't have to come in looking flawless and dressed in a Burberry suit like their male counterparts, but there were other pressures. That fine line between looking attractive but not sexy the way a female would do who desired attention more than respect.

"What are you up to today?" Nora asked.

"The usual – quietly concentrating and reviewing documents. Reading each and every word a dozen times over to look for the unpardonable sin of typos, grammar or spelling errors. You remember how bookstores back in the day were nice and quiet? I loved relaxing in those. But now I have to work in it all day. Other than that, my exhilarating bucket list for the week includes the usual filing documents to the court, plea drafting, a deposition on Thursday which will probably last five hours, and then a trip to the court to request evidence, for which I'll have to pull from my hard sell and browbeating skills."

Nora laughed again. "If I had my way, we'd be playing salsa and I'd be teaching some of these over-serious men how to dance."

Vaneesa sighed. Law firms never had music playing and no one ever watched anything entertaining. It was always like a church, and as such, you could hear what few conversations there were going around you. Occasionally these conversations could be interesting when they escalated into threatening or manipulating. It didn't require a skill in eavesdropping, it just required ears.

"Gotta go. Hasta la vista!" Nora said with a grin and started down the hall.

As Vaneesa made her way back to her office, she stopped at a space near the kitchen entrance where someone had suggested to at least install a fish tank, like those nice reef tanks you sometimes saw in seafood restaurants. The bubbling and gurgling might make nice white noise. But the numbers were run and when the cost of setting up and maintaining such a thing was reviewed, it was instantly dismissed. So now, the only excitement in the office was when a computer blew up or a new printer or copier machine was installed.

As she entered her office, she thought of Jim. When was the last time she actually wanted to be alone with him? When was the last time just the thought of intimacy roused her emotions? Lately, she genuinely felt more like herself when he *wasn't* around. She looked forward to getting away from him and felt nothing positive when thinking or talking about him. The fact was, their marriage was on its last death throes and there was no use pretending otherwise. She couldn't even remember the last time she initiated a conversation with him that didn't have something to do with criticizing his latest behavior. If she had to write down three things they still had in common anymore, she probably couldn't.

Perhaps it was time to do what he'd done to her – pursue another relationship. Life is so short, why not? He'd leapt into the beds of other women pretty easily, and probably would have never confessed if he hadn't been caught. It made her wonder how many times that had happened that she wasn't aware of.

She took another sip of the diet soda and decided it would be the last – the chemically sweetened stuff was starting to taste bad. Her phone beeped indicating a new message had been sent to her personal email. Not recognizing the strange Proton Mail address, she assumed it was spam and was about to delete it when she saw the subject line which read, *JM on vacation*.

JM? Jim?

She opened it and saw one picture attached with no other message. She gasped loudly and slapped a hand over her mouth.

***

The Reverend Jeremy Mueller made his way toward the famous laboratory where his brother had landed a job several years ago. Since today was Jeremy's last day in the area, and since it was kind of on the way back up north, why not? A few minutes ago, he'd tried for the second time to call Jim, but it went to voicemail again. He wanted to surprise his little brother and go to lunch with him, but this time he left a message.

"Hey little brother, it's me. I happen to be in town. Thought I'd swing by and we could grab something to eat.

Give me a jingle back if you're not too busy. Praying for you. Love you. Hope to hear from you soon."

He'd try calling once more when he got there and if there was still no answer, oh well, he'd just start heading home. Maybe he'd stop somewhere around the area to get some food for the road. Try something new.

The way Jim talked about the laboratory, or rather what was implied in conversation, was that it was more or less just another job, but with a lot more restrictions. It did pay well and had good benefits though. But to someone on the outside, it was a very mysterious place.

The official press releases about the lab were that it was a federally funded research and development complex for various types of classified projects related to national security and threats to the United States' energy production. More recently, it and other Department of Energy laboratories had been involved in making sure the nuclear weapons stockpile from the Cold War era was still viable after sitting around all these years. "Stockpile Stewardship," as they called it. That had been all over the news.

What everyone knew though, Jim had said one day, but was only hinted at from time to time, was that the lab's main purpose was for designing newer, smaller, better nuclear warheads and dealt with a lot of research involving uranium and plutonium on the premises. And that was at least eighty percent of its multi-billion dollar a year budget. Sold as "Nuclear Deterrence," the real reason was a military term called *mutual assured destruction* ... the most effective form of discouraging attack there was.

Humanity was a sorry bunch, indeed. That's why we all needed God.

"I don't have anything to do with the weapons of mass destruction stuff," Jim had said one day. Who knows, maybe he was just following protocol and keeping his mouth shut. And that was okay; we all had duties to our employers.

"What about all the wild conspiracy theories?" Jeremy asked. Over the years, people had talked about everything from an invisible bigfoot-like creature that occupied one of the research buildings in the '60s and '70s, to reverse engineering alien technology, to time travel and interdimensional portals. Jeremy was aware Jim held a fascination with some of that stuff, particularly the items of alien persuasion.

"Oh, who knows?" Jim had replied.

"I don't give much credence to any of it," Jeremy had said. "And not just because the Judeo-Christian Bible doesn't mention any of that. The fact is, humans are terrible at keeping secrets and if such things went on, there'd be a lot more whistleblowers."

"There's lots of secrets being kept!" Jim said.

"Yes, but it doesn't take a PhD in psychology or the experience of a counseling pastor to know how draining it is to the human mind to keep and maintain secrets. You know what the most common secrets are, right? Thinking about or actually cheating on an intimate relationship, as well as hiding sexual fantasies or behaviors."

"Gee, what a shocker," Jim had smirked.

"I knew that one would floor you."

"What's that supposed to mean?" Jim asked.

"Come on, Jimmy. But really, keeping secrets, particularly big ones, raises a person's stress hormones and can even cause health problems. But once we tell someone, the related health issues magically disappear."

Human psychology was a fascinating topic. Our brains are made up of many competing areas. That's why people experience "mixed feelings" about things they've done or events they've heard about or witnessed. This is why we can get angry at ourselves. One side of a person may love the thrill and dopamine release from viewing pornography, while another part of that same person feels guilty and condemns the behavior as immoral. Pastors hear about this stuff all the time.

"Is this another lesson on morality?" Jim asked. "You know that's just evolution and self and group survival. All creatures do two things, seek pleasure and avoid pain."

"Jimmy, science will never explain away a 'guilty consciousness.' There's still not a shred of explanation for why humans inherently know the difference between right and wrong, or more precisely, what we ought and ought not to do. For me it's simple, we're made in the image of a personal God who instilled these values in us. That's why objective morality goes across all cultures and people groups."

And this is where we came to conspiracy theories. Some of the biggest scandals in history were revealed because one of just a couple people couldn't keep their mouths shut. It bothered them. They knew it was wrong to keep the secret, even though there were consequences for talking. Examples included political parties spying on each other, abuse at military prisons, companies deliberately selling dangerous and harmful products, and big pharma lying about research to sell drugs and hype.

In light of this, how could, say, dozens know about an invisible bigfoot or alien spacecraft and not say anything? Over the years, when one or two have said something, they were discredited and dismissed, in some cases killed. So fear of consequences was a factor. Still though, the more that know, the more are going to talk. It was human nature.

Jeremy checked his maps app again. From the southern direction he'd come from, it was quicker to head north up First Street and then head west down Portola Avenue. It was a pleasant day to drive someplace new and a pleasure to not feel some kind of time pressure.

Chapter 37

Jim looked at the time on the dashboard. 9:35 a.m. Good. He wanted to be there a little early, ahead of them. This had to work. Feeling his chest, he verified the shirt button camera was in place like before.

He fought several conflicting feelings. The first was fear about what he was doing. He was messing with people who had the resources to wreak havoc in his life. They could easily kill him if they wanted to. They'd already demonstrated the lengths to which they'd go. He still couldn't believe they'd done all this to him. Even Raimondo had questioned their motives. There was so much unexplained.

Speaking of Raim, there was also the fear of bringing his cousin into this. For the rest of his life, he'd have to live with the fact that he'd arranged a murder. That could put him in the pen till he died. But perhaps it was worth it for that young girl's sake. The world didn't need people like Iris running around destroying lives for whatever motive.

If they ended up releasing those evil pictures anyway and no one believed him, he was already considering suicide as a quick and easy way out. The problem was that while, if asked, he'd probably say he was an atheist, at heart he feared where death might take him. Jeremy had told him years ago with perfect peace that he didn't fear death at all and knew exactly where he was going. Jim envied that. No one had ever died and came back to tell about it though, so how could one be at peace about it?

Fear led to the next feeling – rage. How dare they victimize him like this. If this woman could so easily dupe him, how many other schmucks had gotten caught in her web of deceit? Or worse, how many other children had been used by these people to get what they wanted? That girl was the biggest victim here, not Jim, despite all his self-focused feelings. Her life was no doubt ruined, and perhaps he was the only one who could at least somewhat avenge her. He slammed the steering wheel and cursed Iris and her people to the lowest circles of Hell.

He slowed the car down as he recognized the area where CJ's Café was.

***

Pastor Jeremy Mueller cruised casually down First Street watching the map. Never having been here in this area before, he drove a tad under the speed limit to get a look around. This caused annoyed drivers to race past him, many of them throwing dirty stares on the way by. Jeremy said a quick prayer for each one, asking that God would reveal himself to them and show them the way of peace and salvation.

His thoughts drifted as he drove. For years, he felt like he'd been going a hundred miles per hour nonstop, then suddenly got a break this week. And it felt good. It was a time of reflection, a time to slow down and think. And he'd thought about some changes he was going to make when he returned.

One of those changes was to find other leaders in the church he could delegate authority to. So far, he'd managed to run the whole show, be the Pastor Jack of all Trades. But at his age, mid-forties now, he knew he couldn't keep that up forever. That mentality had to stop.

He had an idea for creating a calendar for individuals or small teams to work together in planning and executing worship services. He'd give them guidelines and provide training, and let different leaders take a service and run with it. He already had a couple individuals in mind. He'd let them be creative, pick the worship songs, make the announcements, everything. He'd step back and watch from the last row.

He was looking forward to this. In the book of Exodus, Chapter 18, Moses was running himself ragged doing all the work, judging every dispute that came up in a population many scholars think was close to two and a half million people. His father-in-law, Jethro, gave him advice to delegate authority and let other people carry the load. Moses took this advice and chose competent individuals from all of Israel and appointed them leaders over thousands, hundreds, fifties, and tens. Jeremy felt the Lord was asking him to do the same in his little church up in Redding, although the population he was working with wasn't even a hundred. Not yet, anyway.

As he neared an intersection, just past a small strip mall, he was almost tempted to stop and gas up the car. Nah, he'd wait a few more miles.

Wait, is that Jimmy?

Jeremy watched as Jim barreled past him in his Honda CRV, looking anxious and distracted. Watching the rearview mirror, he saw Jimmy turn into the strip mall parking lot.

Wow, what timing. As usual, his brother looked like he needed prayer. Jeremy took a right turn and began heading around the block. He'd pull into the place and give his brother a *hopefully* pleasant surprise.

***

Jim came to a quick stop near the gas station at the north end of the parking lot so he could look down the length of it. Glancing from row to row, car to car, he saw nothing out of the ordinary. He looked in particular at the cars in front of CJ's Café, which was a bit pointless; they weren't going to park there.

Of course, he was also looking for his stone-faced friend he'd met in the appliance store. He never got the guy's name and was glad he didn't. The less he knew, the better. What kind of car does someone like that drive? A big, black Beemer, a Mercedes SUV? Probably not. He was sure people like that drove unremarkable cars and dressed in unremarkable clothing when on an assignment. The man was probably in some older sedan with tinted windows and was the most inconspicuous person here.

Jim's personal phone suddenly gave the indication a new mail had come in. He tried to ignore it, but curiosity caused him to pick up the phone. It was from Vaneesa.

Now what?

The subject of the forwarded mail read, *What the fuck is this?*

Oh boy ...

He glanced around the parking lot, then clicked open the mail. He immediately recognized one of the photos of him lying on the bed. The little girl was resting on top of him looking toward the camera. But his face had been obscured with a black rectangular shape over his eyes. In fact, it obscured his identity enough so that he really wasn't that recognizable.

Except to his wife.

His face flushed with a visceral wrath he could not remember feeling before.

The little black phone suddenly rang and buzzed, making Jim jump. He stared at it for a moment. Had they seen him pull in? He couldn't let them talk him into leaving to go to another location. He let it ring and go to a voicemail he'd never set up. Ignore them; it was his show now.

Tapping his shirt one last time and feeling the camera, he stepped out and started hiking up the sidewalk. He wore sunglasses and kept his head down. Entering CJ's Café, he looked for a counter, but didn't see one, so he waited until a waitress came by. One did, a portly woman in her late thirties with a lapel pin that said "Sheila" made from one of those old embossing label makers.

Jim tried to smile. "Table for one. Can I be over there at the end near the window?" It looked like a good place to keep an eye on most of the parking lot.

Sheila shrugged. "Sure. Follow me," she said, grabbing a one-sheet laminated menu.

Jim followed her while keeping an eye on things outside. The place smelled of artery-clogging lard. He glanced at his phone. It was now 9:48 a.m.

"Coffee?" Sheila asked as he sat down.

"Uh, yes. Thanks." He breathed deep. This was it.

Come on ... come on.

***

Two men in a midsized SUV were cruising northeast on First Street approaching the parking lot where the café was. As they slowed, the driver of a blue Toyota Prius made a right turn ahead of them from a side street. The driver looked at them to make sure he was clear and then moved in front.

Andrew Lim snatched up a radio. "The subject just turned in front of us."

"Are you sure it's him?" came the reply.

"Positive. He looked right at us. Looks like he's turning into the parking lot."

"If you have an opening, take it."

Andrew set the radio down, then reached into a shoulder holster and retrieved a CF-98 semiautomatic pistol with a threaded barrel. From a coat pocket, he pulled out a long, dimpled cylinder-shaped silencer and began screwing it on to the end of the barrel. Quickly racking the pistol slide, he loaded one of the nine-millimeter hollow point bullets from the magazine into the chamber.

"When I say it's clear," Dennis Yang said.

They slowly followed the Prius into the parking lot and parked several rows down from it.

***

Jim was pretending to read through the menu but every few seconds, glanced out the window. So far everything looked normal, but there was a rising tension in the air, the unmistakable feeling that something was about to go down.

"Have you decided?" a voice said next to him, making him turn quickly. Sheila, the waitress.

"Oh, uhm, some sourdough toast would be good."

"That's all?"

"For now, yes. Thanks."

Jim watched the waitress move down the aisle and start talking to another table, then returned his eyes to the window. The events of the last several days tore through his mind. How had things come to this? When all this was over, what would the consequences be?

Wait ... what was that? Something caught his eye.

He leaned forward and peered around the edge of the window to the far right of the parking lot. He recognized the blue Prius.

Is that Jeremy? Can't be. Looks like him though.

***

Li Ming Tan pulled her car to a stop across the street from the strip mall parking lot. She wore large dark sunglasses that completely covered her eyes.

She looked around for Rong Chiang but didn't see him. Just like when they were in Vegas, they were never seen together in public. His job as the photographer and video person had really been completed the other night, but he was told to remain and assist her in any way needed. It wasn't necessary since the kill team was here and had easily accomplished their main objective the other day. Today they were just tying up a loose end.

Still though, she was not comfortable with what was happening. Jim Mueller had forced their hand into meeting him here for some reason while doing a poor job of pretending not to. She smelled a setup, and she and Rong had to be extra careful.

Would Mueller be stupid enough to have the police here? Surely he would know that there were others ready and waiting to send out those photos. But as much as she'd wanted to wait, her superiors in Beijing wanted things wrapped up quickly. Now that the primary mission was taken care of, they wanted everyone out of the country before authorities started investigating.

As punishment for not answering his phone, Jim's wife Vaneesa had been sent a photo. If they succeeded in doing what they came here to do, it wouldn't matter for Jim. But it would cause authorities to focus on the wrong things. With Jim out of the way, he would not be able to confess what he'd done for them at the laboratory, and everyone would think it was a simple case of a pervert and financial extortion. If they did not succeed, the best way to get him out of the way was to send the rest of the uncensored photos to both his wife and employer.

The radio chirped. "We have an opening," the voice said. "No one near, no visible cameras."

"Go ahead and take it," Li Ming said. "Try to recover the phone. As well, there is a thumb drive that may be in his pocket or glove box. But that's not crucial if it cannot be found."

Li Ming sighed and set the radio down. Had Mueller really believed they wanted those security booth plans? That information was already known and useless. And that's what bothered her about everything this morning. While Mueller had weaknesses that had been easily exploited, he wasn't stupid.

She glanced at the time. She had a flight leaving from SFO back to Beijing tonight at 6:00 p.m. Three days from now she was going to fly to Berlin to be with her secret boy toy, Luca, who was currently on assignment as a business development manager for Commerzbank. He was almost ten years younger than her and hornier than a racehorse in heat. She squirmed a little at the thought of being naked for a week straight, holed up in his apartment with little else to do.

***

Jim continued leaning over, staring out the window. It was definitely Jeremy.

What the hell was he doing here?

Oh my gosh … Jeremy had sent a text that he might be in town. Jim had totally forgotten. He leaned back and tried to remain steady. Should he go out there and talk to him? No way, not with all that was going on.

What to do … what to do …

He leaned forward again and his breathing came to a stop as he saw two men walking purposefully toward Jeremy's car. It wasn't just how they looked and how they moved, it was the fact that even from here and behind sunglasses, they appeared Asian, probably Chinese.

Oh my god – they think it's me!

Grabbing his phone, he dialed Jeremy's number as quickly as he could. As the phone started ringing, he saw Jeremy look down and smile, then start to answer. But just as he did, one of the men tapped on the driver's window and Jeremy turned. In a flash a gun was out and even at that distance and through the glass of the restaurant's window, he heard the *thwack* of the silencer, like a single hit from a jackhammer on a sidewalk. He watched in horror as Jeremy's head snapped back and his body slump sideways.

"NOOOOO!" Jim screamed, leaping to his feet.

The two men quickly looked around while one went to the passenger side. They both opened the car doors and leaned in.

No one in the café seemed to notice what had just happened in the parking lot, and all eyes turned to Jim as he fell to his knees and began sobbing.

***

"No sign of the phone," the voice said through the radio. "And no thumb drive."

"Twenty more seconds, then leave," Li Ming replied. No problem. Authorities would never be able to trace that phone back to anyone involved.

The temperature was warming up, so she rolled her window down to let some breeze in. All at once, a man's voice she didn't recognize from behind on the sidewalk caused a cold jolt to run through her body.

"Iris?" he asked.

She slowly turned to see a large, serious face staring down at her. He was Caucasian, middle-aged with short, cropped hair. His eyes were icy cold and empty. Her mouth went dry. In the last several years, she'd been around enough killers to know why this man was here.

"Jimmy sends his regards," he said.

Li Ming's right hand snapped down to the console where she kept a Beretta M9_22LR pistol. But no sooner had her fingers touched the handle, when she heard the boom and felt a bullet pass through her jaw, shattering teeth and blowing out the right side of her face. The impact instantly caused a numbing shock, her hearing dampened, and she felt her muscles start to relax. She turned her head slightly to see the man raise the end of a silencer a little higher and fire again.

Li Ming briefly saw the windshield turn sideways as she lost control of her body, and then there was blackness.

***

Pauli "The Polar Bear" Avellino, the foot soldier Raimondo Bellini had sent to do the job, looked up at the sound of squealing tires across the street. He froze as a van rushed up to a car in the adjacent parking lot with two men leaning into it. A heavily armed team leaped out and quickly surrounded the car, grabbing the men and throwing them to the ground.

Is that the letters "FBI" on the jackets?

"Holy shit," he muttered, as he put the gun away under his coat. He glanced both ways up and down the street and saw no one coming his way. Taking one more quick look in the car to make sure the girl was dead, he turned and made his way up the sidewalk while looking away from the parking lot.

Just who was this Cousin Jimmy?

***

Rong Chiang tried to suppress a panic as he watched the scene unfold from the south end of the parking lot. He didn't see Li Ming, didn't know where she was. He'd been listening to the radio communication all this time and everything sounded as if it was going according to plan.

But now, everything that could have possibly gone wrong was happening.

He picked up the radio. "Lotus flower," he said. There was no response. "Lotus, can you hear me?" With a sinking heart, he knew something dreadful had happened.

There were at least three teams of the American FBI now in and around the small café. They were going to start combing the parking lot soon. He had to go.

Starting the engine, he reversed as far back as he could, then turned and slowly made his way out the closest exit to the street and eased into traffic. Studying his rearview mirror, it looked as though no one had noticed or was following.

When he was at a safe distance, he would stop and send a quick report to Beijing. They were not going to be happy.

***

More rage overtook Jim, more than he'd been feeling for the last week. He scrambled to his feet and was determined to go out and confront his brother's killers. He didn't have a weapon and they would shoot him, but he didn't care at this point. Who knows, maybe the camera in his shirt could at least help catch them down the road.

But as soon as he stood, he saw three men and a woman running toward the restaurant's door. One of the men and the woman wore the classic dark blue nylon jackets with the big yellow "FBI" letters on the left breast. The two other men wore what looked like bullet proof vests with the same letters.

As quickly as he could, Jim reached into his pocket and dug out the thumb drive with the security booth schematics. Without looking at it, he threw it to the side with a flick of his wrist under an unoccupied table to his left. He was grateful that before he left work, he'd destroyed the business card with the number Raimondo had given him in one of Danny Weng's P-7 shredders.

The four agents burst through the door, guns drawn.

"FBI! Hands in the air!" one of the men yelled.

Several patrons screamed as Jim raised his hands. He looked out the window and saw another four or five agents around Jeremy's car. They had the two men on the ground as they frisked and handcuffed them.

More tears welled up in Jim's eyes. Jeremy was really gone.

"On the ground!"

Jim slowly got to his knees, then lay down face-first. A heavy knee came down on his back as his wrists were wrenched behind and his glasses mashed into his face. He then felt the cold of steel as handcuffs were snapped on.

It was over.

It was finally over.

Chapter 38

Liang Huang waited patiently at the Beijing Capital International Airport listening for announcements regarding his Hainan Airlines flight to the Václav Havel Airport Prague. He'd been waiting months for this moment.

The shortest flight he could find would be over fourteen hours, but that included an almost three-hour layover in Brussels. During the flight he was going to rehearse everything he was going to say in pure Russian. He was going to dazzle Polina – she had no idea he was that fluent.

Looking at his phone, he thumbed through recent pictures she'd sent. One in particular, which made his heart race with excitement, was her in a bikini and on a boat making its way along the Vltava River with the Bohemian Forest in the background. Every time he looked at her, she was more beautiful.

She'd responded well to photos he'd sent. The first time he'd sent one of himself resting an arm on his new, shiny brick-red Mercedes Benz E-Class, she replied with a simple, *you are kind of cute*.

"Kind of cute." Well, that's being honest. He loved honest. With this girl, anyway.

As he sent more photos, the compliments became better, but never over the top with statements like, *you're the hottest man I've ever seen*. He knew he wasn't that. She was far more attractive as a female than he was as a male. And yet, she'd kept up the communication and was now curious enough to meet him in person. He could live with "cute" for now, and then impress her more with his brains and achievements.

The phone he was using was a burner phone, unconnected to his real identity. He'd taken every precaution and had no worries.

A new message suddenly popped up from Polina. *Hi Liang, I have a surprise for you.*

He scrambled to reply. *Really? What's that?*

I decided to come here first! I'm in Beijing!

Huang paused, then wrote, *What! Are you joking?* Then he frowned. Polina didn't have the money to travel, at least from what she'd told him. Plus, it just seemed out of character. She would have said something sooner. Something wasn't right.

Where are you? he wrote.

A moment later, a rough male voice said, "Behind you."

Huang dropped his head and shook it sadly. He then turned and faced two men while a third walked around and stood behind him. He recognized the pudgy, middle-aged man who had spoken as Chih-Cheng Wu, one of the Ministry of State Security investigators.

"No doubt you think I am sexier in person," Wu said with a smiling mouth, but indignant eyes.

Despite himself, Huang took one last look at the picture of the beauty he thought he'd been covertly corresponding with for the last several months. One last glimpse of the fantasy that would never be.

"Her name is Rubina Sarafyan," Wu said. "A random Armenian girl with dreams of becoming an actress." He held out his hand. "The phone."

Huang handed Wu the phone and dropped his head again.

"Were you not warned against unauthorized relationships with foreign nationals?" Wu asked.

Huang nodded. He knew what he now faced. His career was over. All that he had worked for, all his achievements, now meant nothing. He would probably work as a waiter in a restaurant if they didn't send him off to live out his life in a slave labor prison camp.

Wu was looking at the phone with a sad smirk. He looked up at Huang. "If I were a young man like you …" He nodded at his men who took Huang by the arms and led him away with Wu falling behind.

Within the hour, every security clearance Huang had possessed was permanently revoked. His workspace deep below the ground at the MSS was swept clean and all electronics were confiscated.

Liang Huang would never step foot into the MSS building again.

***

Jim Mueller sat in a large conference room before a group of seven individuals, five men and two women, at the FBI field office on Golden Gate Avenue in San Francisco. Everyone wore nice but not extravagant suits, all dark in color, to convey the image of professional and serious. The women wore pants suits. He recognized Kimberly Hampton, the laboratory's deputy director. He also recognized Dr. Gregory, who had introduced himself as a forensic psychologist and had briefly talked to Jim in his jail cell yesterday morning after his arrest.

One of the men who was older and greyer than most and carried an air of authority began. "Mr. Mueller, my name is Sam Struthers and I am the Special Agent in Charge here in San Francisco." He gestured to the man next to him. "This is Doug Thomas, Special Agent in Charge at the Las Vegas FBI field office." He went down the row of seats. "You're familiar with Dr. Gregory, and you probably recognize Kimberly Hampton. This here is Special Agent Tammy Adame, that is Special Agent Stephen Anderson, and over there, Special Agent Don Triventi."

Wow, they were all special. Anderson and Triventi were the two youngest, probably the greenhorns and there to learn.

"We're recording this, is that okay with you?" Struthers asked.

Jim nodded and glanced up at a microphone hanging from the ceiling over the center of the table.

"I need you to verbally say yes if you agree."

"*Yes.*"

"Would you state your full name, please."

"James Mueller."

"Middle name as well, please."

"James. Wayne. Mueller."

Struthers smiled like a used car salesman. "We here to ask some general questions as part of the investigation. You have the right to remain silent and you have the right to legal representation." He paused. "But we'd rather not leave you in that cell at County and delay this anymore. You understand, I'm sure."

Jim almost laughed. "I'm fine with that."

A large flatscreen monitor on the wall at the front of the room was turned on and showed the clear images taken by two ceiling mounted cameras of Jim crawling out from under the table in the Helios lab. They then watched as Jim fished a thumb drive out of the plastic bowl, study it for a moment, then pocket it.

"Is this the area known as the 'Helios lab' at the laboratory?" Struthers asked.

"Yes."

"What were you doing under the table?"

Jim rubbed the bridge of his nose. He'd spent the last three days in isolated custody at the San Francisco County Jail and for most of that time, he'd cried over Jeremy. He'd never get over the guilt. Now, sitting here, the bright orange jumpsuit he donned felt damp and dirty, as if several prisoners before him had worn it and it never got washed. At least they'd been kind enough to remove the handcuffs, but his ankles were still secured with a short chain between them.

Jim shrugged. "Looks like I was hiding."

"From who?"

Jim shrugged again.

"From Kay Allison, who was walking in with another individual?"

Jim sighed. "That is correct. Her and Ricardo. Martinez. Mainly her."

"Why?"

"Because she was never quite comfortable with me, and I didn't want her seeing me in there alone."

"What makes you think she wasn't comfortable with you?" Kimberly Hampton asked.

"I dunno, just a feeling."

"What were you doing there in the Helios lab?" Agent Anderson asked.

Jim leaned back. "I was looking for a thumb drive I had accidentally left the last time I was there with Shane Wells. He's one of the engineers. I found it."

"If you weren't doing anything wrong, then why hide from Ms. Allison?" Doug Thomas asked.

"I don't know. Like I said, she never really liked me. I didn't want her dirty looks and questions."

The group glanced at Dr. Gregory who shook his head.

"How old are you Mr. Mueller?" Struthers asked.

"I think you know that."

"A forty-one-year-old man is hiding under a desk to avoid dirty looks and questions from someone he's not comfortable around?"

Jim smiled and shrugged.

The group stared at Jim waiting for him to say more, but he remained quiet.

"What was on the thumb drive?" Thomas asked.

Jim had prepared, at least he thought, for these questions. "Just some generic training stuff about a tape backup system. Nothing sensitive."

One of the agents clicked a button which caused a second set of video footage that showed him entering the Helios lab a few days prior. They watched as Jim slid his arm under the alarm console desk.

"This was one week prior. What were you doing there this time?" Struthers asked.

"I was getting ready to copy some AutoCAD images from the main screen for some training I was doing. I accidently left the drive there."

"Is this the same drive you were looking for in that plastic bowl a week later?"

"I don't remember. Might have been. A lot of stuff gets copied on those all the time."

"Mr. Mueller," Agent Triventi said. "You have a number of serious charges that are being leveled at you. Including giving classified information to an unauthorized person. Do you understand the implications of this?"

Jim nodded, then said, "I never touched anything classified and you all know it." He thought it sounded weak, but it was all he had. Armed with information he'd gotten from Danny Weng, he added, "And that system there isn't tied to the lab's classified network. It's a sandbox and test setup. Kay can confirm that. So can Ms. Hampton. I don't even have access to classified systems."

The agents cast a glance at Kimberly Hampton who nodded.

"Mr. Mueller, it's time for you to come clean and tell us everything," Thomas said. "The more you cooperate now, the better it will go for you."

Jim smirked bitterly. That's what Iris had told him. Besides, he knew that one of the lies cops were legally allowed to tell people was that they'll "get off easy" if they cooperate. Other things cops lied to people all the time about were, we can get a search warrant in minutes, your fingerprints are all over the crime scene, and we have a witness. But none of those others pertained here.

Agent Tammy Adame, whose salt and pepper hair was pulled back tightly and held in place by hair braids, chimed in. "Who was the woman at the Cosmopolitan hotel? You told Detective Hesel at the Las Vegas PD the woman was blonde and Caucasian. That's not what we saw."

Jim looked up startled.

"We have the hotel's surveillance video, Mr. Mueller," Adame continued. "Why did you lie about the woman's appearance and ethnicity?"

Jim just shook his head and shrugged. He should have figured this was coming. He and Iris had even talked about the casino's security.

"Were you soliciting this woman to arrange for sex with minors?" Adame asked.

"No!" Jim said loudly.

Thomas produced an envelope. "We received these from Sergeant McClelland at your place of employment. The head of human recourses received these from an anonymous email address, who then passed them to your crimes and investigation group."

Photographs were pulled out and laid on the table. Jim glanced at them in horror and embarrassment even though he'd expected this. He leaned forward and put his face in his hands. "I was drugged. I don't even remember them doing that to me. You gotta believe me. I don't go after children."

"Mr. Mueller," Struthers said. "You've lied about a number of things already. You lied to the Las Vegas police about the woman you met, as well as when you met her. And just a minute ago, you tried to lie about what you were doing in the Helios lab at your place of employment. And now you ask us to believe you?"

Jim remained silent.

"How did you and the woman meet?" Adame asked.

"Random. I'm there and she walked up and we start talking."

"The meeting wasn't prearranged?"

"No."

"We saw the footage from the hidden camera in your shirt," Triventi said. "We saw the woman give you what looked like a thumb drive."

"Oh yeah … forgot about that."

"Are you taking this seriously, Mr. Mueller?" Thomas said. "I'm gonna be straight up with you. We don't believe you. We think your meeting with the woman was planned. And we particularly don't believe you about that thumb drive."

Mueller threw his hands up in resignation. He was feeling spent from lying. But he still had to hold tight to certain things to try to save himself. Finally, he said, "I was blackmailed, okay?"

"Blackmailed to do what?" Struthers asked.

Jim sighed. "To stick that thumb drive into one of the computers."

The agents cast a glance at Kimberly Hampton.

"If I didn't cooperate, they were going to send out those pictures."

Jim saw Hampton shake her head, then she asked, "What was on that thumb drive?"

"I have *no idea*. And that's the truth. Danny told me it could have been malware, like a worm. But I'm no programmer. I don't know about that stuff."

The agents exchanged glances.

"Are you talking about a Mr. Danny Weng?" Struthers asked.

"Yeah." Jim paused. He should not have invoked Danny's name and instantly regretted it. He noticed Kimberly Hampton drop her head and didn't like the way Struthers had asked that question. "I mean, Danny didn't know what I was doing. I was talking to him a few days after that, asking about stuff like malware because he's a security expert. I figured he'd know. But he didn't know about anything I was doing. He had nothing to do with any of this."

The room remained silent for a few long seconds.

"What did the woman say her name was?" Triventi asked.

"Iris." Jim said flatly and sighed again. He hated to even say the name.

"Not Lisa?"

Holy crap, he'd forgotten that was the name he'd told Detective Hesel, and Sergeant McClelland. He shook his head and chuckled bitterly. "No."

"That's what you told the Las Vegas police," Thomas said.

Jim put his hands up. "I know … I know. I was scared out of my mind. So I covered for the woman."

"And you didn't have any contact with this woman before this?"

Jim looked up at the ceiling. He was starting to give up. "Okay … We met on a phone app called 'loo-cha.' It's kind of a dating slash flirting app. She didn't post her picture. We only had a few exchanges."

"She reached out to you first on this app?" Anderson asked.

"Yes."

"How do you spell the name of that app?"

"L, u … C, h, a. I deleted it off my phone. All our back and forth. The entire app. You can look at my phone."

"We already have, Mr. Mueller," Anderson said as he scribbled notes.

There were a couple minutes of silence as three of the agents quietly went over some papers in front of them.

"What was her profile name on this loo-cha app?" Anderson asked.

"I don't know. I just saw the name Iris. Most users don't list full names."

"And you say she had no photo of herself?"

"No, just a cartoon avatar." Jim snorted. "Lǜ chá biǎo ..."

"Excuse me?" Struthers asked.

"Green tea *bitch*. That's what *Lǜ chá biǎo* means. That's what Iris is – one serious green tea bitch."

The agents exchanged glances; two of them shrugged. Anderson was jotting the phrase down on his notepad.

Struthers spoke up. "Her name was Li Ming Tan. She was an operative for the Chinese Communist Party's Ministry of State Security."

Jim actually laughed. "Gee, that's a shocker. And why do you say she *was*? Did she defect or something?"

There was a pause, then, "Ms. Tan was assassinated, Mr. Mueller," Struthers said in a matter-of-fact way.

"What?" Jim tried to convey genuine surprise. In fact, he was relieved to know Raim's man had done the job.

"Same day you were arrested, in the vicinity of the same location. We were wondering what you knew about that."

Jim looked at the ground. Everyone in the room stared hard at him, especially Dr. Gregory, gauging his response. Jim knew he was no trained actor but had to feign astonishment. He shook his head and mumbled, "This is unbelievable."

"Is it?" Thomas asked.

Jim shrugged.

"You don't look too surprised, Mr. Mueller," Anderson said.

Jim looked straight back at Anderson, feeling some of that familiar anger. "I'm not, and I'm glad she's dead."

The agents exchanged glances again. Dr. Gregory was taking notes.

"Who do you think would want to kill this woman?" Tammy Adame asked.

"How should I know? You just told me she's a communist agent. Probably had lots of enemies."

The image of Jeremy getting shot played again in Jim's mind and despite himself, felt tears forming in his eyes.

"You must have been pretty upset at her for deceiving you the way she did," Triventi said.

"Screw you, man," Jim snarled.

Struthers threw Triventi a disapproving glance, then raised the volume of his voice just a hair. "Take it easy, Mr. Mueller."

"Whatever."

"Are you sure you had nothing to do with what happened to Ms. Tan?" Adame asked.

"Nope. Wish I did though."

"Let's go back to these photos, Mr. Mueller," Thomas said.

Jim groaned. "Let's not …"

"You and Ms. Tan entered room three-twelve at the Cosmopolitan and then a short time later, three more individuals entered the same room. Two adult males and the young girl in these photographs."

Jim slumped forward. "I remember absolutely nothing. I don't remember the girl there or anyone else. All I recall was being in the room with Iris, or Ling-a-ming-ding, what's her name, and then nothing. I wake up the next day alone feeling like I got hit by a truck."

"And that's when you found this phone?" Thomas asked, holding up the little black flip phone.

"Correct, along with my stuff."

"Nothing was stolen?"

"Not that I saw, no."

"Not even your cash?"

Dammit. "No …"

"They contacted you with this phone?"

"I think you know that."

"How many times did they call you on it?" Anderson asked.

"I dunno. Four or five times."

"To give you instructions?"

"Yes."

"And what were those instructions?"

"Like I said, to put the thumb drive in the computer. Leave it there for a few days then retrieve it and give it back."

"There were no other instructions?" Thomas asked.

"No."

"They needed to call four or five times just for that?"

"Well, first I had to meet them to get the drive. That's when I had that little shirt button camera on me. Then meet them again to return it and so on."

"What was the meeting about the morning you were arrested?" Struthers asked.

"I don't know."

"The meeting had to be about something. Were you there to give them something else?"

"No, yes, I don't know. Final instructions or something. I think they wanted to kill me." Jim slumped forward again and felt like crying. He took his glasses off and rubbed the bridge of his nose. "That's why they killed Jeremy."

There was silence in the room for a few seconds while they let Jim have a moment.

"James," Struthers said softly. He waited for Jim to look up at him. "What was your brother doing there?"

Jim shook his head. "I have no idea. We didn't plan it. Actually no, he'd texted me. He was in the area and maybe going to visit. I'd forgotten with all that was going on."

"Mr. Mueller," Thomas said.

Jim looked at him.

"Danny Weng was also assassinated."

Everyone paused and looked hard again at Jim who could only stare back, wide-eyed, and utterly dumbfounded. Dr. Gregory looked at the other agents and nodded. They believed Jim's response this time had been genuine.

It occurred to Jim they were deliberately bouncing back and forth between topics to throw him off guard to evaluate the authenticity of his reactions.

"We don't suppose you know anything about that, do you?" Adame asked.

Jim looked down. "No ..." he said softly. He looked back up. "Does this have anything to do with me getting blackmailed?"

"We were hoping you could shed some light on that, Mr. Mueller," Adame said.

"Well ... I can't."

"Did you know Mr. Weng by any other name?" Thomas asked.

Jim looked up, genuinely surprised, then said, "No ..." He didn't bother asking why.

"Mr. Mueller," Thomas said. "One last chance to help yourself here. Did you do anything else at all for these people besides put the thumb drive in the computer, then retrieve it and give it back?"

Jim considered his options and knew he'd have to answer quickly. If they were aware of the other thumb drive with the security booth schematics, this was a test. If he failed the test, they would add additional charges relating to obstruction of justice and false statements. He decided to go all in.

Looking up and using the real sadness he felt for his brother, said with as much confidence and seriousness as he could muster, "No, nothing else. I want a lawyer now."

Chapter 39

Will Stanley had been a janitor his whole life. Over the years, he'd cleaned office buildings, private residences, sports stadiums, and was now cleaning restaurants. A high school drop-out with no real ambition or drive, he figured it was more or less his destiny to do little else. But he was grateful he'd always enjoyed good health, and at age fifty-two, could still be on his feet all day with no problems.

Over the years, he not only vacuumed thousands of floors and wiped thousands of desks, chairs, and windows, he'd often served as security as well. For most of his office jobs, he worked at night after regular employees left and had been asked to make sure certain doors were locked and no one was roaming around who shouldn't be there. He'd also become familiar with alarm systems and other things a lot of employees didn't know about. Because of this, he'd been paid more than most would probably assume, and it afforded him a decent truck he proudly called his own.

But now that he was older, he opted for daytime hours and a simpler set of responsibilities. He liked CJ's Café, not because it was an easier hustle than any other place he worked. In fact, it was a popular grease hole and a lot of people stopped by for a quick and easy breakfast or lunch. Kids especially made messes here all the time that had to be cleaned up. And that was okay. He didn't worry about anyone wondering what they were paying him for.

What he really liked though was that he got along well with his coworkers and manager, and the place was like a small family. They, like him, led uncomplicated lives and appeared to be fine with that. Peace and contentment were rare commodities in this world.

Really though, all his managers over the years had liked him because he was reliable. He was capable of doing the exact same thing every day, over and over, with meticulousness and without complaint.

Will was normally a happy fellow and whistled jaunty tunes as he went about his duties. But today he was little shaken up after Sheila, one of the long-time servers there, told him about the incident the other day.

"You should have seen it," she had said. "A bunch of people came barging in with guns yelling at this guy I'd just taken an order from. Then we heard someone got shot right out there in the parking lot. Craziest thing I've ever heard of."

Will was glad he'd not been there. It would have scared him something awful. He'd never even touched a gun much less been around one being fired. He'd seen death before though. One afternoon a few years ago at an office building in Oakland, a manager he knew pretty well, an older guy getting ready to retire, dropped dead of a heart attack in front of him. That had been bad enough. But just the thought of someone getting *murdered* right out there gave him the shivers.

Stooping down under the last table in the row next to the main windows, he ran his broom under and around the center metal post that held the table in place. The broom's bristles dragged a small plastic looking object out that Will scraped toward him. He picked it up and was surprised it felt solid and heavy, like it was made from smooth, machined metal.

He walked over to the server station by the kitchen counter. "Sheila, what's this?" he said, holding it up.

Shelia turned and looked at it. "I don't know. Lemme see."

Will handed her the object and she turned it over a few times. "Ironkey, hmm … Oh, wait, I know," she said, pulling the end cap off. "It's a USB thumb drive. Looks like a fancy one though." She handed it back.

Brad, the cook and a lifelong hippy, who was nearby scraping a countertop griddle, looked over with a grin. "Hey Will, maybe there's some *dirty* pictures on it."

"You're terrible, Brad," Sheila said.

Will looked witlessly at the device. "How do you get dirty pictures onto *this*?"

Brad laughed.

"It's probably nothing, Will," Sheila said, picking up a tray full of empty coffee cups and walking away.

Will shrugged and put in his pocket.

That evening, at a mobile home park, the drive was tossed into the back of a junk drawer, promptly forgotten, and never looked at again.

***

In a U.S. District Court courtroom for the Northern District of California, Jim Mueller stood before a federal judge and was feeling mighty relieved not to be wearing one of those orange getups. His lawyer, Martin Manzer, stood next to him.

Today, Jim had on slacks, a dress shirt, and a very decent blazer. In Counselor Manzer's main suite was an office filled with "court clothes" they lent to people they represented when appearing before a judge or jury. It was from this stash Jim had been supplied. These items were provided to the courtroom bailiff who took Jim to a nearby changing room and allowed him to dress up before appearing.

It was common practice to ask the client's family for suitable clothes, but Vaneesa Loveless-Mueller had refused to even visit. When she saw the toxicity report, however, she began to believe Jim had indeed been drugged and was the victim, not the perpetrator. Given Jim's propensity for hitting the sauce and chasing women, it wasn't difficult to believe he'd gotten himself into such a situation. Jim had talked about smoking a little pot in high school and college, but besides booze, he was no druggy. She'd had enough compassion to contact a colleague of hers, Martin Manzer, who worked criminal defense, rather than see Jim represented by some state appointed attorney who may not care or even be on Jim's side. As much as she disliked the man she was planning to divorce, having the false accusation of pedophilia wasn't something even he deserved. But she also had a selfish reason to help – with Jim in jail, he wouldn't be able to work and send money after the divorce.

At first Jim said he didn't care how he was dressed, but Manzer had convinced him that seeing the jail jumpsuit can lead to an inference of guilt, as well, it was actually his right *not* to be seen by jurors in custody clothing until a verdict is reached. So he went ahead and got dressed. He also found out later he could have asked for the clothes he'd been wearing when arrested, but they were just black jeans and an old denim dress shirt.

Federal trials almost always had juries, but several things in succession had happened that changed that.

Martin Manzer had a private conversation with the federal prosecutors, and they tried hard to convince him that keeping this whole thing under wraps was the best way out.

"We don't really need a jury for this," they had said.

"That depends," Manzer had replied.

First, Manzer had actually dared them to try going after Mueller on the charge of unlawful sexual conduct with a minor. Manzer assured them that would result in the biggest and most public lawsuit they'd ever seen. They briefly toyed with the idea, but when their own forensic psychologist, Dr. Gregory, said that in his professional opinion, Mueller was not a pedophile, they declined to pursue that angle.

Next, in a grandiose scheme to scare Jim into pleading guilty, and believing he'd confess as more evidence was uncovered, they threatened to charge him with three felonies: giving classified information to an unauthorized party, stealing government property, and disclosing intelligence information. These charges alone could land a person thirty-five years in the slammer. As icing on the cake, they also hinted at other charges like illegal use of a controlled substance and conspiring to commit murder. But they had to actually charge him with something, so they opted to start with conspiring to introduce malware.

But they were empty threats, and one by one, went by the wayside.

Laboratory authorities confirmed that while the Helios lab equipment was connected to the internal, unclassified general support system, it was indeed separate from the classified network. Additionally, Mueller had no access to any classified systems at all anyway, nor could it be shown that he'd ever attempted access to anything classified. Furthermore, he never accessed anything he hadn't before as part of his job duties. There went that charge.

Next, it could not be proven he stole anything. All his network activities were scrutinized and there was no evidence he'd downloaded or moved a single file or byte of the laboratory's property either by email or to a portable storage device. It couldn't even be argued he stole a $250 Ironkey thumb drive since it was given to him by his blackmailers. So much for that charge.

This led Martin Mazer to keep asking the next obvious question: what intelligence information was disclosed? Show us the records. The records could not be shown. The charge wasn't filed.

Finally, it could not be proven the thumb drive he put in the computer that day in the Helios lab contained any malware. The lab's IT and cybersecurity departments went over everything with a fine-tooth comb and were unable to come up with anything definitive.

The judge had asked, why put the drive into a machine in the Helios lab, why not just use Jim's work laptop, since it accessed the restricted network via VPN? A cybersecurity expert from the lab told investigators that due to increased vulnerability, end user machines were scrutinized more than machines in a vault-type room. Using the Helios lab was a good way for any malware or a worm to "soak" and go undetected for a longer period of time, assuming that's what it was. Investigators did find a bunch of useless digital mumbo jumbo that could have been a worm program at some point that had appeared in several places around the same timeframe, but it could not be proven it came from the drive Mueller had inserted that day. They also suspected that a large amount of encrypted traffic had left certain personnel file databases, but it was unclear what was copied or moved as there were only bits and pieces of highly encrypted trails left behind. There was simply no connection between the thumb drive they saw Mueller insert that day and anything they'd managed to find. So the one charge they had filed to get Mueller into a courtroom in the first place was dropped.

It *was* proven that Mueller had trace amounts of possibly Flunitrazepam in his bloodstream, based on a sample taken by the laboratory's medical staff. This drug, considered a narcotic, is available as a prescription-only medication in some European countries, but banned in the United States. The video surveillance footage from the Cosmopolitan didn't conclusively show Li Ming Tan giving him the drug, although that seemed to be the only plausible explanation. But the amount found in his bloodstream wasn't enough to draw firm conclusions. Additionally, Mueller had passed all prior drug tests leading to his security clearance with flying colors. No illegal use of a controlled substance charge was filed.

One more thing they'd played with was the possibility of any connection between Mueller and the murder of Li Ming Tan. Instinct told them there was, but there was no way to connect the dots. Mueller had been in the café when Li Ming was shot. He certainly had the motivation, but he didn't have the means. Mueller had no history of violent behavior, nor did he own any firearms except for an older 270 Winchester hunting rifle he'd inherited from his father that hadn't been used in years. Dr. Gregory wasn't fully convinced Mueller had been truthful when questioned about this, but in the end, like everything else, nothing could be proven.

One thing did come together – ballistics showed that the same 9mm Chinese made pistol that killed Jeremy Mueller had also killed Jin Chou, aka Danny Weng. Now they were certain the people who had blackmailed Mueller had really been after Weng the whole time and Mueller had merely been used to acquire information. Now it was a matter of how much information they could get out of the two men they had arrested in front of CJ's Café.

But the weapon that killed Li Ming Tan was different, and nowhere to be found. As well, the .45 ACP bullet casings left behind had no fingerprints. Ballistics on the two bullets recovered, one embedded in the passenger side door and one still in her skull, did not raise any flags in the database of known firearms used in crimes.

Feeling completely confident, Mazer convinced Mueller to waive a jury trial in writing. The federal prosecutors got what they wanted, and the court approved. Thus, it became a bench trial with a single judge making the decisions and Mueller never having to stand before a jury and watch their reaction to him ducking and hiding under a desk in a restricted area in a national nuclear research laboratory. In return, the Department of Energy didn't have to run a public relations damage control campaign and agreed to walk away.

The one crime left that Mueller had committed, by virtue of his own testimony, was altering or misrepresenting factual information or evidence to the Las Vegas Metropolitan Police Department. It was a given he'd be charged with this, but it wasn't going to be done by the federal prosecutors. In most states, this was a felony, and in California, it carried a penalty of one to three years in jail or state prison. But he'd committed this crime in Nevada, so he spent another three nights in San Francisco County waiting for a ride.

Before he left California, a representative from the U.S. Office of Personnel Management paid a visit and informed Jim that his security clearance was indefinitely revoked and that going forward, he was not to bother applying for any federal jobs.

"Good luck, Mr. Mueller."

Because Jim was considered a low security risk, he got to ride to Nevada by himself in a spacious van. And it wasn't even one of those with a hard bench in a cage, it was a regular seat, but he did have to remain accessorized with cuffs on his wrists and ankles for the three-and-a-half-hour ride.

Upon arrival, he was taken to a cell at the Reno Jail where he had to sit for another week and await his appearance at the U.S. District Court, District of Nevada while the local prosecutor prepared her case. During that week, Martin Manzer visited and said he'd spoken to the Honorable Judge Franklin Nelson and Christine Lee, the local prosecutor, and things were going to be okay. Detective Justin Hesel wouldn't even have to testify.

In the state of Nevada, the punishment for altering or misrepresenting factual information or evidence carried a one to four year stay in Nevada State Prison. But after considering the circumstances Mueller had been in as well as the fact that he'd not been in any kind of trouble like this before, Judge Nelson showed mercy and Lee had no objections.

"You have no priors, not even any misdemeanors. This is your saving grace," he was told.

In the end, Mueller was sentenced to two years felony probation, during which time his parole officer could order random drug tests performed as well have his Internet and phone activity reviewed. Since his permanent residency was in California, any travel outside the golden state had to be detailed in advance and approved. Jim shrugged it off – he was used to the drug tests and didn't have any plans for travel anyway.

Because Jim had been a federal employee with a top-secret clearance and an assassination attempt had been made, Manzer suggested Jim disappear into the witness protection program. Jim had thought, why not? Start over and get away from Vaneesa. Ultimately, the request was denied, and the judge explained why. Under Title 18, United States Code, Section 1961 for organized crime and racketeering, the witness protection program was for drug traffickers, felony convicts who provide testimony in court which may result in violent retaliation, and some civil cases in which a testimony may put the witness in clear and present danger. Since Jim hadn't testified against anyone, at least no one still alive, and since the assassins who targeted him were in custody, he didn't fit the bill. China "most likely" won't bother sending more operatives, the feds said. The main objective had been Danny Weng; going after Mueller again wouldn't be worth the effort or risk.

Martin Manzer later took Jim aside and said the real reason they didn't want to bother spending the time and money on witness protection was that they wouldn't lose any sleep if Jim did get assassinated. "They neither need nor want you anymore for anything and are sore you're not going to prison," Manzer said. "It'd be good riddance if you got whacked, as far as they're concerned."

When the dust finally settled and Jim was back in California, he marveled at how everything turned out spectacularly better than he'd thought it would. It weighed pretty heavily on him though that for the rest of his life, he would be a convicted felon. But it weighed a lot more knowing that the information they got through him had gotten Danny Weng killed, and they never told him why.

The biggest and darkest place in his heart though was where Jeremy would forever be.

Chapter 40

One Year Later …

Jim Mueller sat in his home office and watched his two bubble eye goldfish, "Jack" and "Jill," as they clumsily swam-wiggled about their ten-gallon environment. Having never been into fish keeping before, he'd been reluctant to take the tank from a neighbor who had to make an emergency move across state. In twenty minutes, he'd gotten a crash course on daily, weekly, and bi-weekly maintenance: feed only small amounts they can finish in just a couple minutes, remove and replace ten to fifteen percent of the water every two weeks with the gravel siphon, add water conditioner and chlorine remover to the tap water you put back in, clean the sponges in the filter, et cetera.

He figured he'd have given the tank away by now, but realized he'd become addicted to the hypnotic sound of the bubbling water and taking breaks watching the two creatures that appeared perfectly gratified to exist in their limited environment. They made him wish he could be happy with a simpler life.

He shook his head. Was he envious of two goldfish now?

He picked up his cell phone and dialed voicemail. After entering his password, he listened once again to the last message his late brother Jeremy had left him on that fateful day.

"Hey little brother, it's me. I happen to be in town. Thought I'd swing by and we could grab something to eat. Give me a jingle back if you're not too busy. Praying for you. Love you. Hope to hear from you soon."

For the first couple weeks, Jim had not been able to get through the message without hanging up and crying. Pastor J would still be alive and well, leading his little church were it not for the stupid actions of his younger brother.

His parents had wrapped things up quickly. They had Jeremy cremated and laid to rest in Petaluma before Jim was back in California. Their father had started the first Ace Hardware franchise there shortly before Jeremy was born and the two brothers had been raised in that area. Jim had only visited his brother's plot once at the Cypress Hill Memorial Park Cemetery. He'd spent the whole time crying and apologizing. He'd have to visit again soon.

After listening to the message, he hit the nine on the dial pad to tell the system to once again save and archive the message. This time he found himself smiling. Time wouldn't really heal all this so much as make the thoughts and feelings bearable to exist with.

He also thought about that young girl in the photos from time to time. What was her name? Where did she come from? What happened to her?

Glancing at his laptop, he saw that two more students had turned in their homework. He'd been lucky. About two months after starting his parole, he'd applied for several jobs in the education field. Everyone seemed to use a third-party automated background checker for job applicants anymore and he was surprised at its completeness which included a social security number trace, a county and federal court search, a Department of Justice sex offender search, as well as a peek to see if there were any extended global sanctions on him. Everything was online. Thank God he was never convicted for going after underaged children. As expected though, his conviction of altering or misrepresenting factual information or evidence in the state of Nevada showed up.

After finding out he had a criminal record, they all turned him down except for one, a technical trade college based in the state of Washington who was desperate for qualified online teachers. Between his master's in education and experience at a famous research laboratory, they wanted him. Someone in their human resources department hurried the paperwork through and Jim was promptly hired to teach students how to write technical user manuals and on-the-job training references.

He'd officially started class and begun communicating with students when he got a call from the school's dean, Dr. Harry Cannon.

"I'm going to be honest with you, Mr. Mueller, we normally wouldn't hire someone with a felony conviction, but with your qualifications and the fact that you've no other prior issues, perhaps there's a way to make this work," Dr. Cannon had said.

The phone call lasted over an hour and Jim came clean about what happened. Well, he didn't divulge details of the young girl, nor did he talk about what he'd done at the laboratory while being blackmailed. He did admit lying to the police about the thief because he'd been scared and that's what ultimately got him into trouble. Dr. Cannon listened and appeared sympathetic with Jim's situation and said he'd talk to the board. A week later the decision came through that they would keep Jim but as a probationary part-time employee, to see how things worked out. This meant, among other things, they could fire him on the fly with no explanation. Jim thought this was amusing – he was now a double parolee. So far so good though; he was now on his second semester with the school and doing fine.

Vaneesa hadn't yet followed through with the divorce. Jim knew she was biding her time to see if his new career took off and he'd start making more than the roughly forty-five an hour, part-time, he was now. It didn't really matter since they lived separately now, her in the original house and him in a small apartment. He'd heard she was dating someone and that her new beau was occasionally spending the night. And that was okay; she was entitled. Jeremy wouldn't approve.

To his surprise, when Jim invited Vaneesa out to dinner on the week of her birthday a couple months ago, she accepted, probably just to see if he was drinking himself into oblivion about all the recent events. But she'd seemed pleasantly surprised when she saw him, and twice said, "you look good, Jim." This didn't mean they were going to reconcile, but it did, maybe mean, they could part on decent terms and she wouldn't ream him as bad with the money.

"What made you decide I was innocent?" he had asked Vanessa.

"Because when I saw those terrible pictures, I could see by the look on your face, even with your eyes closed, you had no idea what was going on."

Truth be told, he'd actually done well in the last year. He not only quit drinking, but this had led to no searching online for dangerous, scandalous, and illicit activity. And he felt so much freer for it. This, Jeremy would approve of. He still wasn't ready to take the spiritual deep-dive his brother had, but the possibility seemed a lot more plausible now. The way he'd been living before just hadn't worked.

If he did dive into faith, he'd have to find a God that was willing to forgive him for asking his cousin to setup a murder. Jeremy once told Jim about King David from the Bible. The renowned king not only committed adultery with another man's wife but arranged to have her husband killed. Although this caused a lot of turmoil in the king's life and family, in the end, David repented, and God forgave. After David's death, it was even said that the king had served God's purpose in his own generation. Guess there was hope.

The last thing Jim wondered about from time to time was just how much damage had been done by him sticking that thumb drive into the machine in the Helios lab. He'd never know. Whatever it was, it had been so expertly devised that even the lab's cybersecurity group couldn't see exactly what had happened. What secrets were stolen? At least nothing classified, hopefully. But it had to have something to do with Danny Weng. What that meant was that his actions not only led to the demise of his brother, but also a friend and coworker. This was another mystery he'd never know – why did the Chinese government want Danny? Jeremy was wrong, there were plenty of secrets being kept all over the world. The thoughts came with an intense urge to drink until his mind was obliterated of all feelings, but he would try to resist that learned response.

A direct message from one of the students popped into view. He clicked it and saw it was from a "Suzy Kwan." The small avatar showed a cute Asian face with a broad smile. He clicked it to see her profile. For obvious reasons, student profiles didn't say anything about age, ethnicity, marital status, or any of that, but she looked to be late twenties and damn cute with long, flowing hair. From her appearance and name, she was definitely Chinese.

Hi Professor Mueller, can I call you that? LOL. I'm really looking forward to going through this class. Being a knowledge transfer professional is my dream. I'd love to hear more about your experiences at the research laboratory. How exciting! Talk to you soon. – Suzy

Oh boy …

www.ingramcontent.com/pod-product-compliance
Lightning Source LLC
Chambersburg PA
CBHW021125260626
47169CB00005B/1449